THE TEMPLAR ENIGMA

AN EDEN BLACK THRILLER

LUKE RICHARDSON

1

Paris, France. March 18^{th,} 1314.

BROTHER THOMAS SHOVED his way through the crowds lining Rue de Seine. The tension that had gripped the city for the last few days was now reaching a fever pitch. Thomas elbowed his way between the throngs of people, heading in the direction of the River Seine.

He tugged the hood of his robes down low across his face, both to shield him from the biting cold, but also to keep prying eyes from recognizing him. It wouldn't be wise for anyone to recognize him now, not when he had such an important task to complete.

He wound his way through the narrow, cobbled lane. The stone walls of houses lined both sides of the street. Behind shuttered windows, Thomas thought he heard voices. The inhabitants locked themselves away, perhaps in fear of what might happen on this macabre day.

Thomas walked on, the air growing thick with the taste of smoke from torches and open fires. Following the flow of the crowd, he emerged from the labyrinthine streets and out on the banks of the Seine. The river, a mercury-colored band glinting with the reflection of a thousand torches, slipped onwards with its usual indifference.

Thomas peered to the left and spied the formidable silhouette of Notre Dame's twin towers. The mountains of stone rose into the darkening sky. Although the cathedral was yet to be finished—the construction had only inched forward during Thomas' life—it was already an imposing structure, the Gothic architecture dwarfing the rest of the city.

Thomas turned and pushed his way through down Rue de Marché Palu. On any other day, the market would be vibrant, with traders selling fabrics, spices, and provisions, but not today. No one was working today.

Thomas elbowed his way through a crowd, his chin down and shoulders hunched against shouts of protest. Voices swirled around him like gusts of winter wind. These people, like half of Paris, had been drawn from their houses not just for the spectacle of death, but to see the ultimate fall from grace. They were here to witness the final act of an order that had once spanned Europe and eclipsed kings. An order which was soon to be no more.

Thomas crossed the Seine and onto the Île aux Juifs. The island, normally a barren sliver of land amid the Seine, was now overrun with spectators.

Thomas pushed on, jostling his way through the crowd. He elbowed his way past a group of noblemen dressed in shimmering robes and saw the pyre for the first time. His heart rate doubled in time and bile rose in his stomach. The mound had been constructed from carefully arranged kindling, straw, and logs. Thomas had no doubt that it would soon turn into a merciless inferno. The pyre had been arranged in the center of the island, where the ground rose ever so slightly, improving the view for the spectators. In the center of the pyre, Thomas saw, with a feeling like a punch to the stomach, a thick wooden stake driven into the earth.

Excitement moved through the crowd and the jostling increased. Voices raised and heads whipped from side to side. The crowd pressed closer, everyone eager to witness the grim spectacle.

Thomas used his strength to force his way forward, then wished he hadn't. Thirty feet away, he saw the Grand Master, Jacques de Molay. After seven years of imprisonment, Molay was a shadow of the man who had led the order with a fiery passion. Molay's body was now gaunt and pale, his bones jutting through his skin.

Two burly executioners dragged the Grand Master to the pyre. Molay's disfigured feet, curved inwards like rotten fruit, bumped uselessly across the ground.

A wave of repulsion surged within Thomas, threatening to overwhelm him. He grasped the hilt of his sword, fighting the temptation to slay the executioners where they stood. He drew a fortifying gulp of air. Right now, he was just one man, and he had an important job to do. A cold revenge, striking the heart of the country, would come soon. But not yet.

The executioners reached the pyre. They wrapped chains around his wrists, waist, and ankles, securing him in place. One executioner stood beside the pyre, while the other fetched a flaming torch. Orange flames flickered across Molay's haggard cheeks as the executioner approached.

Thomas gazed at the Grand Master and observed the same relentless determination as when he had entrusted Thomas to the task all those years ago. Despite the countless hours of pain, Molay clearly retained the same spark of fervor that had once inspired thousands of knights. Thomas supposed that right now, that look of rebellion was all Molay had. That and the knowledge Thomas was nearby and ready to carry out his final orders.

The executioner strode toward the pyre, the torch flaring.

Thomas' throat tightened, his senses finely tuned.

The executioner took another step.

The crowd stood motionless, waiting.

Receiving the signal he required, the executioner lunged, shoving the torch into the base of the fire. The kindling caught. The gentle hiss and pop of the fire sounded incongruous as it started its devilish work. The flames licked at the edges of the wood, climbing hungrily toward Molay's crumpled body.

The silence of a séance fell across the crowd. Hundreds, maybe thousands of people watched, stunned and motionless.

The fire grew in intensity, its orange tongues licking at Molay's feet and legs. The heat became so intense that those in the front rows of the crowd cowered away or covered their faces.

In the center of the rising flames, Molay straightened up, resolute against the inferno. His features settled into a look of peaceful resignation, reflecting the calm resolve of one willing to sacrifice everything for his cause. The serenity etched upon his countenance was the embodiment of both a martyr and a man who knows the war is not yet over.

The flames licked past Molay's feet, growing in ferocity and hunger with every passing moment.

Thomas watched the searing heat engulfing the Grand Master's legs and imagined the pain which would now consume his body. Despite the agony that had to be coursing through him, Molay remained steadfast, his gaze fixed upon the heavens above.

The crackling of the flames filled the air, punctuated by the occasional pop and hiss. Smoke billowed upwards, carrying with it an acrid scent.

The crowd watched in a mixture of horror and fascination, their stony faces illuminated by the glow of the pyre.

As the flames reached Molay's waist, a voice rose across the crowd. It took Thomas a moment to realize the voice was Molay's. The Grand Master's voice, weakened by the years of torture, was not the booming baritone it had once been, but his words remained distinguishable.

Thomas elbowed his way closer, desperate to hear more clearly. Understanding the Grand Master's final words was paramount.

"I make my peace before God," Molay said, his voice surprisingly steady considering the agonizing pain that had to be engulfing his body. "For God is the only one who can judge me. I tell you this: soon a calamity will occur to those who have condemned us to death. You have abused the word of faith for your greed, and for that, you will pay. Pope Clement and King Philip, you will be summoned to the tribunal of Heaven before the year is out!"

Molay sunk into silence, his gaze rising to the heavens, as though waiting for his deliverance into the next life. The flames roared higher, carrying Molay's words with them.

Seeing the gesture, Thomas knew Molay had spoken his last. It was now time for Thomas to get to work. While the flames consumed what was left of the Grand Master, Thomas turned and weaved his way back through the crowd. He had a long journey ahead of him and not a moment to waste.

2

─────────

The City of London, England. Present day.

Eden Black leaned on the railing of the Millennium Bridge and peered suspiciously down at the stone-colored waters of the River Thames. Although the surrounding scene was one of peace and tranquility, with tourists wandering from the nearby Tate Modern and St Paul's Cathedral, her mind was clouded with much darker thoughts. Eden's memory replayed the event —standing on top of a barge a few hundred feet down river, fighting a man who was stronger than her in almost every way.

"I can't stop eating these, they're so good," Athena said, joining Eden at the railing. Athena passed over a cup of roasted nuts.

Eden popped a few of the nuts into her mouth and crunched. "You're not wrong," she said, swallowing and stuffing her face with half a dozen more.

"Is it strange for you to be back here?" Athena said, leaning over the side of the bridge and looking down at the water. "You know, after what happened?"

Eden glanced at her friend, once again surprised at Athena's uncanny ability to read her mind. "Am I that predictable?" she said through a mouthful of nuts.

"It's lucky that you are, as I've no idea what you're saying with your mouth full."

Eden laughed, almost choking, then swallowed. "That was gross, sorry."

"I wouldn't say predictable, but I know I'd be the same. We lead stressful lives, and those stressful memories end up being linked to places like this." Athena swept a hand through the air, indicating London's skyline.

"That's true," Eden said, chomping again. "I'm glad we've stayed around here a bit longer. I've always enjoyed this city."

"Except for the weather." Athena mock shivered.

"It's nice today." Eden glanced up at the sky, which for once was not shrouded by clouds.

"I don't trust it. Give me a warm climate any day."

The pair dropped into silence as a party boat slipped beneath the bridge, loud music booming.

"Okay, it's a cool city," Athena said. "But let's be fair. We're not here to soak in the vibe. We're here because your dad has that council meeting. If it wasn't for that, he'd have us back on the *Balonia* already."

"Let's make the most of it. In a week or so, we will be surrounded by a thousand miles of open water again." Eden whipped around and eyed her friend. "I've got a challenge for us."

Athena rolled her eyes. "Why does everything you do have to be a challenge? Can't we just have an unchallenging, pleasant time?"

Eden scrunched up her eyebrows, genuinely puzzled.

"Okay, forget it." Athena threw up her arms. "What's the challenge?"

"I know this will be difficult, especially for you," Eden quipped. "Let's try to visit a historic site with no one trying to kill us."

Athena barked out a laugh. "That's a challenge I can accept." She finished the last of the nuts and dropped the cup in the trash. "In fact, I've got an idea. There's a great historical place nearby which I think you're going to love."

"Okay..." Eden said, now sounding less sure.

"Better than that, I can almost guarantee that no one will try and kill us. Follow me." Athena set off walking briskly, winding her way around the groups of tourists posing for photographs against the skyline.

Eden ate the last of the nuts and gave chase. "Not being in mortal danger, probably means we don't need to run!" she shouted, although Athena was already too far away to hear.

Ten minutes later, the women stood in a narrow-cobbled lane, looking up at a nondescript, old brick building.

"And what is this place?" Eden said, peering in through one of the gloomy windows.

Athena swung her arm around Eden's shoulders. "This is Ye Old Cheshire Cheese, one of London's most historic pubs."

"That's not quite what I meant when I suggested we went somewhere historic."

"You won't get much more historic than this," Athena said, placing her hands on her hips. "You know, there's been a pub in this location since the sixteenth century. The original building was destroyed in the Great Fire of London, and this one was built as a replacement."

"How do you know all this?" Eden said, throwing her friend a glance.

"Come on, you know a lot about various things. Growing up in England, you just didn't take an interest in the history here."

Although Athena's words stung, Eden knew her friend was right. She had been surrounded by all this English history her whole life but had always been more interested in what went on overseas. "Okay, I'll give you that," Eden said. "But the problem is the place isn't even—"

The clanging of the bells from the nearby St Paul's Cathedral interrupted Eden in the middle of her sentence. The bells were joined by the sound of someone drawing back a lock on the inside of the pub's door. The heavy wooden door swung open, sending a cloud of warm, beer-smelling air out into the street.

"I think you'll find it is now open," Athena said, striding inside and ducking through the low doorway. "Just as it has been for the last four hundred years."

"Fine," Eden said, a grin spreading across her face. She ducked and followed her friend inside.

Five minutes later, Eden was ensconced in a booth at the back of the pub while Athena fetched their drinks. Eden's eyes roamed across the low beamed ceiling and walls covered with black and white photographs. Eden's pulse quickened with the familiar thrill of ancient temples and far-off lands.

"Two pints of their finest brown ale," Athena said, placing two large glasses on the table. Athena shot Eden a penetrating look. "Don't tell me you're going to make a fuss about having a historic drink, too?"

"Absolutely not," Eden said, picking up the glass and taking a swig. While ale wasn't her usual drink of choice, she was now enjoying this as a cultural experience in a familiar city. The ale was sweet, hoppy and, Eden had to admit, delicious.

"That's Charles Dickens' seat you're in," Athena said, pointing at a plaque on the back of the bench. "He was one of the locals here. As was Arthur Conan Doyle, of Sherlock Holmes' fame."

"Alright, I get it, I'm enjoying myself," Eden said, taking another sip of the beer.

"Good, because you need to relax and put what happened back there behind you." Athena pointed in the general direction of the river.

"Have I been moody?" Eden said, the alcohol already loosening her inhibitions.

"Let's just say, it's been like living with a teenager."

"That bad?" Eden made a hissing sound through her teeth.

"Yeah. You need to snap out of it before we're trapped back on the *Balonia* with you, otherwise, the bets are on as to who will drop you in the ocean first."

"I'd like to see you try," Eden muttered. Suddenly, a thought occurred to her. "My dad, or Baxter?" she said, her gaze drilling into Athena.

"What?" Athena said.

"Who put you up to this? This whole, take Eden out and mollycoddle her for a bit. It's got to be one of them."

Athena kept a straight face, although her eyes panned from side to side, proving to Eden that she was on to the truth.

"Don't answer that," Eden said, pointing a finger at her friend. "You're all in on it together!"

Athena sighed. "Okay," she said, placing her hands flat

on the table. "We were in on it together, but only because we—"

"Don't give me that," Eden barked, trying as hard as she could to sound stern, rather than being touched by her friend's consideration. A grin escaped her lips. To hide it, Eden picked up the glass and took a big gulp. "Alright," she said after she'd drunk half the beer. "Let's do this. Although here are my rules—"

"Go for it," Athena said.

"There's only one, and it's simple."

"I'm listening..."

"You're paying for the drinks."

"That, I can do," Athena said, raising her glass. The two women clinked glasses and then shared a long glance.

3

Templar Commandery near Lisbon, Portugal. April 19th, 1314.

BROTHER THOMAS dismounted from his horse and took a moment to steady himself. The journey from Paris had been long and arduous. With every hour of daylight spent in the saddle, and only stopping to rest and switch horses with people still loyal to the order, he had made the journey in record time.

Thomas led his horse into the stable, patting its neck as the animal panted, and tied it beside a feeding box.

Following that, he set off on the uphill climb toward the commandery building, which was located further up the steep slope.

Thomas paused for a second to assess a castle on the brow of the hill some distance away. Built by the Moors, the castle had since fallen into disrepair, but was still an imposing structure.

He turned his gaze to the commandery building.

Constructed from heavy stone and a slate roof, the building was practical, yet nondescript. It could have been mistaken for a farm building, like the hundreds Thomas had seen on his journey. The steep hillside was split into terraces and used to grow crops of all varieties. The garden surrounding the commandery provided much of the food for the stationed men. Thomas could see two men working on one of the top terraces, tiny shapes against the sky at this distance.

As Thomas ascended the path, he eyed the commandery's worn façade. There, etched into the brick, was the symbol that had marked his life's path—the Templar Cross. The cross sat prominently within a round window at the gable's peak, its arms spreading equally in all four directions. To Thomas and his brothers, this was not merely a decorative element, it was a perpetual reminder of the oath they had taken—poverty, chastity, obedience.

Thomas approached the heavy wooden door and knocked. Before the echoes died out, the door swung open. Thomas had clearly been expected.

A large man filled the doorway. Although he wore the clothes of a farmworker, the size of his muscles and the scars that traced lines on his face and forearms told of a life never far from violence.

"Beau Sire, Brother Duval," Thomas said, customarily bowing his head. It had been several years since Thomas had seen the other man, but he didn't look any different.

"It is done?" Duval replied, getting immediately to the point. The knight's voice was a gruff baritone.

The memory of Molay chained to the stake flashed again through Thomas' mind, as it had every time he'd let his mind wander in the last three weeks. Thomas didn't think the image would ever leave him.

"It is done," Thomas said, hands placed across his chest. "I am here to relay his final commandments."

"We must get to work." Duval turned around and led Thomas into the building.

Thomas swung the door shut and followed Duval into a hall that occupied the center of the building.

At the end of the room was a large table flanked by benches.

Two men worked in the room, one cutting vegetables, and the other preparing the fire for dinner.

Thomas peered up at a large tapestry hanging on the wall, which was a scene from the Holy Land.

Duval led Thomas to the chapel, positioned at the far end of the building. Four simple wooden pews faced an altar. Behind the altar, light streamed through a window shaped like a Templar Cross. The window was positioned to project the shape of the cross onto the floor in perfect clarity.

"Help me with this," Duval said, pulling the pews to one side. The two men cleared the room quickly, then rolled aside a faded woven rug.

"At sunrise on the equinox, that light will show you the way," Duval said, pointing at the projection of the Templar Cross on the floor.

"But... the equinox isn't until... ," Thomas said, instantly worried that they would have to wait.

Duval raised his hand. "Fortunately, I already know where to go, so we need not waste a moment."

Duval crossed the stone floor, counting the slabs as he went. He reached the slab he required and knelt. He removed a knife from beneath his robe and worked it beneath the stone. He pried the stone out of position and used his bare hands to pull it upright.

Thomas scooted across the floor to help Duval remove the stone from its position and place it against the wall. Both men peered down into the void which the removed slab had exposed.

Duval padded across to the altar and took two large candles, handing one to Thomas. Duval stepped down and disappeared completely into the subterranean passage.

Thomas followed one step behind. The passageway was roughly hewn from the rock on which the commandery was built. The flickering light from their candles cast eerie shapes on the walls as the men picked their way deeper into the labyrinth. After forty feet the passage widened, exposing a spiral staircase leading down into the earth. But, unlike the spiral staircases Thomas had seen in castles and other large buildings, this one was wide, curving around the outside of a shaft like a corkscrew.

"This place is amazing," Thomas said, his voice reverberating from the walls. "How long has it been here?"

"We've been working on this for almost one hundred years. When Acre fell, some of our relics were brought here."

The two men took the stairs slowly, the light only strong enough to illuminate a few feet in either direction. The air grew colder as they descended. The musty scent of the earth mingled with the burning candle wax.

With each spiral descent of the staircase, Thomas sensed a distancing from the world above, and a drawing nearer to something altogether different—something other-worldly. It was as though they were winding their way down into the coils of history.

"An eight-pointed star," Thomas said, the base of the shaft finally emerging from the gloom.

"Yes, the star points the way," Duval said, his voice a whisper.

"The star of Solomon?" Thomas said.

"Each of the star's points represents the qualities one needs to enter the Kingdom of Heaven."

"Truth, faith, repentance of sins, humility, justice, mercy, sincerity and persecution," Thomas said, repeating the eight obligations of the knighthood.

Duval paused at the base of the staircase. As far as Thomas could see, there was only one option here, a tunnel which led off into the darkness.

"Normally a seeker would have to do this alone, and without light," Duval said, the candle dancing under his breath.

For a moment, worry gnawed at Thomas' stomach at the thought of being down here alone in the dark. There was no knowing how far these passages extended beneath the hillside, or if he would ever find his way up. He chided himself —a knight who wore the red cross should have no such worries.

"'Tis but natural to feel the grip of fear," Duval said, holding the candle aloft. The small flame seemed to fight an ever-losing battle with the pressing gloom. "We tread now upon sacred earth. These tunnels are wrought to render us, the humblest of God's creatures, feeble and full of dread."

"To feel dread is the nature of man, yet to stand resolute in its shadow is the mark of valor true," Thomas said.

"Our dear Grand Master's words," Duval said, his tone tinged with sadness. "As time is short, and you have already been chosen by our Grand Master, I will show you the way." Without another word, Duval strode down the passage with Thomas in pursuit.

After five minutes they reached a junction, offering two

ways. One was broad and straight, the other narrow and twisted. Without a pause, Duval chose the small branch of the tunnel. As the walls closed in around them, Thomas thought about all the sacred rituals that had taken place down here, and how these stone walls would safeguard their secrets long after he and Duval were gone. The tunnel narrowed and the roof level dropped, forcing the pair to proceed hunched over. The roof sunk lower, forcing the pair to shuffle on hands and knees. Thomas struggled forward, holding the candle with one hand, and crawling with the other.

The air became humid and Thomas heard water running over stone.

"Follow the streams of arcane lore, coursing unseen through the earth's ancient floor," Duval said, glancing over his shoulder, the candlelight illuminating his face. Neither man had spoken in so long that the reverberating voice took Thomas by surprise.

After a few minutes of shuffling, the tunnel expanded, allowing the men to stand. Thomas swept his candle around, the flame reflecting against glimmering mineral stalactites, some thicker than a man.

Duval led them to another fork in the tunnel. Again, he took the narrower of the two branches, this time on the left. Once again, the tunnel narrowed, forcing both men to shuffle on. With each awkward step, the sound of the water and the taste of the moisture in the air increased. When they could stand again, the water didn't just burble like it had before; it roared.

Duval led them to the left, around a sharp corner, and into a small chamber. A stream of water thundered from a crack in the roof, down the rear wall, forming a pool on the floor.

"Behold the stream of arcane lore," Duval said, pointing at the waterfall.

Sidling up beside the bigger man, Thomas saw he wasn't pointing at the waterfall, but through it. Thomas saw that the other man was pointing at two horizontal wiggly lines etched into the stone.

"Aquarius," Thomas said, instantly recognizing the symbol.

"The very same." Duval cupped a hand the size of a bear's paw around his candle to protect it and set off, splashing through the water.

Thomas watched Duval as he walked to the side of the waterfall and then, right in front of Thomas' eyes, disappeared.

Thomas blinked hard, trying to understand what he had seen. He splashed through the pool, searching frantically for the other man.

For several seconds he saw nothing until he noticed a second flame glimmering. In a moment, the trick revealed itself. A reflective surface had been worked into the wall of the tunnel, mirroring the appearance of the rock back from the other side. To all but the most persistent observer, it would look as though the tunnel ended right there.

Thomas ducked around the mirror, an archaic piece of polished metal set within the walls of the passage, and quickened his pace to keep up with Duval. On the other side, the passage was completely dry. After a few paces, the passage widened and descended steeply. Steps were carved into the floor, making the descent easier.

Thomas reached the bottom of the staircase and stepped into a chamber. The air was still, allowing the flame of the candles to grow, bathing the room with light. Thomas studied the walls, hewn from the natural rock, and smoothed by the hands of masons long passed.

"What is this place?" Thomas asked, his voice trembling.

"We have always understood the fleeting nature of our mortal endeavors," Duval said. "This sacred chamber, and others like it across the globe, will guard our most hallowed relics for centuries to come. Only the righteous shall reach this far. For the undeserving, perils tenfold lie in wait. Come." Duval pointed at an altar standing in the center of the chamber.

Duval crossed to the altar and met Thomas' gaze.

"Judge's silent vigil. Scales that weigh the skies," Duval said, pointing to an incredibly intricate mosaic lining the floor. "Stand on Libra over there."

Thomas scanned the mosaic and saw the scales of Libra, about a foot from the altar. He paced across the mosaic, feeling guilty for treading on something so beautiful.

A violent shudder shook the chamber, vibrating the walls and floor. Dust streamed from the roof and chunks of rock skittered down the stairs.

Thomas dropped into a crouch and prepared to bolt up the stairs.

"Do not move!" Duval shouted over the noise. "You must stay right where you are!"

The rumble vibrated through the stone underfoot. The air filled with the sound of stone grating on stone. The trembling grew more intense, threatening to tear the room apart and bury them under thousands of tons of rock.

The candle flames danced to a frantic rhythm but refused to go out.

With a resonant crack that echoed like thunder, the stone altar room split in two. The two halves fell away to reveal a hidden cavity within.

Thomas' eyes locked on what was revealed within the divided altar. A velvet-lined box lay between the two stones, and within it lay a ring.

"The Seal of Solomon," Thomas said, gasping. "In all my life, I didn't think..."

"The very same," Duval said, pointing at the relic sitting in its hidden chamber. "Originally discovered by our founding brothers beneath the Temple Mount in Jerusalem, this is so much more than just a ring. It's the very talisman of power that Solomon himself used to build the temple, master the weather, and command demons to protect his kingdom."

Duval eyed the other man. "It is said that he who holds the seal holds the key to untold knowledge and the very secrets of creation. The Templars have guarded it through the centuries, its true purpose known only to the Grand Masters ... until now."

"Why has this been shown to me?" Thomas said, suddenly not understanding why they were there.

"Because you have been given an order from Grand Master De Molay. Come, you must place the ring on your finger."

Thomas stepped forward, his movements slow, and picked the seal from its hidden compartment. The ring was crafted from gold, patterned, and inscribed with what Thomas knew to be Ancient Hebrew. In the center of the ring, a large obsidian stone glinted like the eye of a snake, and carved into the stone was a symbol that Thomas knew well, a hexagram. With shaking hands, Thomas placed the ring on the index finger of his right hand. He cupped the other hand beneath the object.

"Be sure to replace the ring before you leave this chamber," Duval said. "Or you'll bring the whole thing crashing down on top of us."

Thomas nodded, nervously.

"Now, you must issue the words that you heard Grand Master de Molay say."

Thomas nodded once, and word for word repeated what he had heard.

"For God is the only one who can judge me...," Thomas began, repeating the promise Jacques De Molay had made as the flames engulfed him. Reaching the end of the monologue, Thomas was certain he could feel the flames searing his skin. His voice rose as he reached the final words. "Pope Clement and King Philip, you will be summoned to the tribunal of Heaven before the year is out!"

4

London, England. Present day.

"It's crazy isn't it?" Eden said, two hours later. They were still in the Cheshire Cheese and had made their way through a good number of the drinks on offer.

"What is?" Athena asked.

"A year ago, just one year ago, I didn't know you, or Baxter, and I thought my dad was dead."

"Yeah, I've got to admit, that isn't normal." Athena's tone turned serious. "I felt really sorry for you." Athena looked across the table and the two women held each other's gaze for a long moment.

"You didn't even know me. I might have been an idiot," Eden quipped.

Athena laughed. "I knew your dad, remember? I think that's a pretty good indication that you weren't going to be totally awful."

The two women sat in silence and sipped their drinks. The bar had grown busier over the last two hours, with various groups of people drawn by the place's famous former patrons and the promise of a cold drink.

"What was he like when you were growing up?" Athena asked, breaking the silence.

"What, my dad? It's hard to say, he's the only dad I've ever had."

"Sorry, silly question."

"No, it's not at all," Eden said, becoming thoughtful. "I idolized him, totally. I remember wanting nothing more than to stay with him, wherever he was going. When I got to, I loved it. We had the best time. We traveled the world, and investigated interesting historical sites, both famous ones and those that were still being excavated. I loved that life." Eden paused for a sip. "Then, when I was thirteen, he decided that I needed some formal education and sent me to a boarding school. That was the worst."

"Did you have to follow *rules*?" Athena pronounced the word as though it was disgusting.

Eden nodded. "So many rules, and all of them pointless. Needless to say, that didn't last long. I now understand why he sent me there. That's when he became the chairman of the Council of Selene."

"Ah, the great Helios!"

"Yeah. Secret societies and teenagers clearly don't go well together!"

"Can you imagine, a teenager stuck in the middle of all that weird stuff? You wouldn't know what to do. I think you were probably better in your awful school breaking all the rules."

Something in what Athena said suddenly caught Eden's attention. She eyed Athena and hid her intrigue with a sip of beer.

"Let me get these refilled," Eden said. She paced back to the bar. Since learning of her dad's position in the Council of Selene, Eden had been dying to know what exactly he did, and what happened at the meetings. The fact she knew nothing about either made her even more curious. Despite how much she asked, no one would tell her a single thing.

Eden ran through what Athena had said once again: *all that weird stuff.* Eden reached the bar and peered back at her friend. Athena sat by the window facing the other way. *All that weird stuff they do* could mean only one thing: Athena had attended at least one of her father's council meetings.

"I figured it was time for gin and tonic," Eden said, returning to the table.

Athena grinned and they clinked their glasses.

Twenty minutes later, Eden returned to the topic of conversation that interested her so much. Eden leaned across the table, and Athena instinctively copied the gesture.

"I know you shouldn't tell me," Eden whispered, "and I don't want to get you in any trouble, but exactly what weird stuff happens at these council meetings?"

Athena grinned wolfishly and sipped her drink. "Each council member is allowed to bring an assistant, so I've been to a couple of the meetings in that capacity. It's very strange. They hire out this giant building, usually a hotel."

"They hire the whole place?" Eden said, wanting to keep the exchange feeling like a conversation rather than an interrogation.

"Yeah! Sometimes for several weeks. There's a security team that goes in before to check it over. I think they're looking for recording devices, but probably all sorts of other things too."

"What happens when the council is there?"

"You'd hate it. There are so many rules!" Athena giggled.

"Each council member is only allowed in specific areas at specific times. You must come in that door and use that staircase at that time, for example. It's a challenge to remember it all."

"Why are there so many rules?" Eden asked.

"That wasn't even clear to me at the start, but your dad told me. I'm not sure if he was supposed to."

Eden shifted another inch in anticipation.

"All of the council members are anonymous to each other. No one, not even your father, knows the true identity of the other people. You can imagine how difficult that is..." As Athena continued talking about the logistics of the place, including the allotted times for this and exit routes for that, Eden thought through what she'd learned.

"Hold on a second," Eden said, poking at the table. "How does that work? Surely all the council members are in the same room together having this meeting?"

"The council chamber, they call it, is kept completely dark. Each member has a seat which they find using a rope or something like that. There's a tiny light on their desk so they can take notes, but it's so dim that they can't see the other members. It's a big room."

"How weird," Eden said, shaking her head.

"Tell me about it. The first time I went I didn't have a clue what was going on. I had to wait in this room all day, then your dad would come out and ask me to read this, or research that, or contact this person. No technology is allowed near the chamber you see, so I had to go to another part of the building to do it."

"I bet the security is tight."

Athena nodded. "Although most of it is kept out of sight. They don't have armed guards on the door or anything. But you certainly wouldn't be able to walk in off the street."

Eden shook her head slowly. "Do you have any idea the sort of things they talk about?"

"Not really, as I never even got close to the chamber," Athena said. "I know they address a variety of issues, ranging from the development of new technologies and medicines to the selection of movies and TV shows to produce."

"Why would they be interested in film and TV?" Eden asked.

"From what I understand, the council members them-selves are not involved in the writing or commissioning of films or anything like that but select them based on their agenda. For instance, if the leaders of a particular country go against the council's decisions, they may try to destabilize that country." Eden nodded, hanging on every one of Athena's words. "Then they make sure that country's seen in the media as an enemy. That way, whenever the name of that country is mentioned in the news or wherever, the public thinks they're bad. In reality, though, it's just a handful of people in that country's government who aren't following the council's rules."

"That's insane," Eden said, folding her arms, "and makes total sense. That's why every film villain during the Cold War era was Russian."

"Our beloved council at work," Athena said, shrugging. "And then after the millennium all the villains became Arab-looking. That was the council's way of preparing us for the war over there…"

"They did what?"

"At the very least they knew a war in the Middle East was coming, so they prepared citizens by putting them on a diet of stories that showed war in those countries."

"Then when it actually happened, no one was

surprised," Eden said, slumping back in the seat, her mind spinning.

"Anyway, that's all I know. They're very good at keeping things under wraps."

"I can understand why," Eden said.

5

Fontainebleau, France. Early November, 1314.

THE LATE FALL LEAVES, a tapestry of gold, rust and crimson, crunched beneath the hooves of King Philip's steed as he navigated through the dense forest. The ancient oaks and maples towered above him; their branches reaching out like gnarled fingers, casting dappled shadows across the forest floor. Philip relished these moments of escape, where he could leave the weight of his crown behind and immerse himself in the thrill of the hunt. He inhaled the crisp, cool air. The musty scent of the forest filled his lungs.

His keen eyes scanned the surrounding trees, searching for the telltale signs of a deer—a flash of movement, a glimpse of antlers, or the rustling of undergrowth. The king's senses were heightened, attuned to the slightest sounds and movements in the otherwise tranquil woodland.

Since the death of Pope Clement, one month after what was now being termed The Curse of the Last Templar, an all-consuming anxiety had befallen Philip. The eerie coincidence of Clement's death, so closely following Jacques de

Molay's ominous curse, had planted a seed of fear in Philip's mind.

In the weeks that followed, the king had become increasingly paranoid, seeing shadows and conspiracies at every turn. He had doubled the number of men on his personal guard, handpicking only the most loyal and trustworthy soldiers. He had also reduced his public appearances, choosing to remain in his castle when possible.

Whilst Philip had never considered himself a superstitious man, the weight of recent events had eroded his sense of rationality. He couldn't help but wonder if there was some truth to the Templar's Curse, and if he might be its next victim. The thought of members of the order still lurking in the shadows, plotting their revenge, gnawed at his mind, robbing him of sleep and peace.

As the days turned into weeks, Philip's once unshakable confidence had been replaced by a pervasive sense of unease, a feeling that his fate was no longer entirely in his own hands.

Fed up with the constant state of suspicion and paranoia, and afraid that cowering in his castle would make him appear weak in the eyes of his subjects, Philip had arranged today's hunt to demonstrate his strength and resilience. He needed to show that he still had what it took to lead the country.

Something in the undergrowth caught Philip's eye. He shook the reins, urging his steed on. The horse responded instantly, turning, and pacing toward the spot which had captured the king's attention.

Philip leaned to the side, focusing on a small sapling which lay crushed on the ground. The color of the sapling, and the sap oozing from the broken trunk, told Philip all he needed to know. Something had come through here recently. Something big.

"This way Sire, deer have been sighted near the ridge," another of the hunting party shouted from the group behind him.

"I'll catch you up," Philip replied, waving away the other man.

He would catch whatever creature had passed between these bushes, and with that prove that he still had the instinct and the spirit to wear the crown.

"As you wish," the man replied, kicking his horse into action and galloping away.

Philip turned his attention back to the sapling. With a gentle squeeze of his legs, he urged his horse to move. The steed responded with a smooth, steady trot between the trees. As they ventured deeper into the forest, the towering trees blocked out more and more sunlight. The air grew cooler, and the sounds of the forest became muted.

Further indications of whatever beast had walked through the forest revealed themselves. A bush, once lush and full, now stood shredded of its leaves. A series of snapped and broken branches littered the ground.

The king scanned for any movement. He strained to pick up the faintest sounds. A sudden noise caught Philip's attention—the distinct snapping of leaves underfoot. He pulled back on the reins, bringing his horse to a stop. The steed, sensing its master's tension, stood motionless. The animal's ears pricked up, its muscles quivering with anticipation.

Philip searched the trees ahead, his gaze darting from one shadow to the next. For several long seconds, both man and steed remained frozen in place, scarcely daring to breathe.

As though materializing from the air, a magnificent stag strolled between the trees.

Philip held his breath. He willed his steed to stay silent, too.

Although still some distance away, Philip saw the stag in all its glory. The animal's glossy coat rippled with muscles. The crown of antlers on its head rose with the majestic grandeur of an ancient oak tree.

Philip's heart raced. This was, without a doubt, one of the most impressive stags he had ever encountered in all his years of hunting. To bring this back to the castle was exactly what he had in mind to restore his honor.

The king reached for his bow, his fingers closing around the weapon. With practiced ease, he positioned an arrow and drew back on the string. His eyes narrowed, focusing on the deer with hawk-like intensity. He pulled a steady breath. His whole body tensed in preparation to loose the arrow and claim his prize.

A cloud moved across the sun, plunging the forest into deeper shadow than before. The air, which a moment ago had been still, now whipped through the trees with a sudden ferocity. The wind howled, shaking the branches.

Breaking his focus, Philip peered upwards. The sky which had previously been clear, was now an ominous shade of gray. A flash of lightning danced across the heavens, followed by thunder, which shook with a deep rumbling crescendo.

Philip looked back at the stag to see it bolt away, revealing something else, horrifying and disturbing. In swirling shadows, caused by the wind through the trees and storm clouds shrouding the sun, Philip saw something that sent a spear through his heart.

King Philip's attention remained on the shadows as they

shifted and morphed. A shiver ran down his spine. He let go of the bow and the arrow zipped off amid the trees. The shadows twisted once more into a horrifying figure. Philip recognized the ghostly visage of Jacques de Molay.

Lightning cracked again across the sky, and thunder boomed.

The apparition's eyes burned with an otherworldly intensity, fixing the king with a haunting stare.

Philip's horse, sensing the unnatural presence, reared up in terror, its hooves flailing wildly. The king, caught off guard, was thrown from the saddle, landing hard on the forest floor. As he lay there, his body convulsed violently, gripped by an inexplicable seizure. The world around him blurred, and the image of Jacques de Molay loomed closer, a spectral hand reaching for the helpless monarch.

"Sire, Sire!" cries came through the forest as the thunder was replaced with the pounding of hooves nearing the king's position.

King Philip blinked, his vision blurry and his body unable to move. He tried to speak, but the words wouldn't come.

Men jumped down from their horses and surrounded the king. Carefully, they picked up King Philip and returned him to the castle for urgent medical attention. The care of the best doctors in the land made no difference. Three weeks later, King Philip was dead.

6

London, England. Present day

End of Days Countdown: 6 days remaining

Alexander Winslow, called Helios by the members of the Council of Selene, stepped into the council chamber, and quickly found his seat. He sat without speaking for three minutes as the other members shuffled to their allotted places. In total darkness, the members couldn't see each other, allowing each to maintain their anonymity. This had been decided many centuries ago, as it allowed each member to speak freely without fear of retribution outside.

Each council member sat before a small desk which was illuminated by a tiny light, allowing the members to read or take notes. No technology was permitted inside the chamber, for the fear that it could be hacked into or misused in some other way.

When the shuffling had abated, Winslow cleared his throat. He was the chairman of The Council—had been for nearly twenty years—so he was tasked with leading the proceedings.

"Thank you all for joining," Winslow began. Speaking into the microphone, his voice was distorted by the speaker system. "We have one item on the agenda for the meeting today. As you all know, with five days remaining, the End of Days is fast approaching. As the date nears, all the work we have done on this matter will be tested, so we must remain focused. First on the agenda today, Uriel has a report to deliver."

Someone shuffled on the other side of the room. A council member coughed.

Winslow settled back into his seat.

"Thank you, Helios," Uriel began, his digitally masked voice booming across the chamber. "As you all know, we've been working on a study about how humans react to a change in their environment. Using data from the past two decades, we developed a sophisticated computer model to predict what might happen as we approach the End of Days. This model helped us understand potential responses from societies worldwide."

"I can't see what the point of this is when we don't know what the End of Days actually is," a female voice interrupted. "That's what we need to know."

"No interruptions at this time please," Winslow said. "You are right that the prophecy is frustratingly unclear about what the End of Days will involve."

"If we don't know, how is any of this useful?" Hera continued, her tone nasal and grating. "I understand this council was established thousands of years ago, and through some ancient wisdom, a date has been picked on which the End of Days could happen, but that really isn't much to go on. It could be anything from an earthquake to nuclear hellfire—"

"Or nothing at all," another voice chimed in.

"You are, of course, correct," Winslow said, raising his voice over the interruption. "But these prophecies have been accurate in the past, and we would be foolish to ignore them. 1914 was marked a great conflict that would engulf the world. Again in 1939, the prophecy warned of an event which would once again plunge the world into peril. We all know the unimaginable horrors of the World Wars." Winslow paused for a moment allowing the importance of his words to sink in. "Time and time again, these prophecies have proven themselves. We may not understand the full meaning until the events come to pass, but we cannot afford to dismiss them. The End of Days is coming, and it is our duty to prepare for it, whatever form it may take."

"We've stepped up environmental and governmental monitoring. If something changes, we will know about it," Apollo said.

"Thank you," Helios said. "Now are we able to continue? The clock is quite literally ticking."

Several council members grumbled their agreement.

"Continue Uriel," Winslow said. "Please forgive the interruption."

"Using the computational model, we have established a four-stage process, which the majority of the population— around 85% by our calculations—will move through. There will, of course, be outliers, that is to be expected." Uriel paused and shuffled some papers on his desk.

"The first phase is Cognitive Dissonance."

"What do you mean by Cognitive Dissonance?" a member interrupted.

"My apologies," Uriel said. "Cognitive Dissonance is a

psychological construct, which suggests a conflict between known reality and new information. It will lead to a series of defense mechanisms including denial, minimization, and rationalization."

"You're saying that people will deny anything is happening and carry on as normal?" the interrupter said again.

"That's exactly right. It's a defense mechanism designed to protect people from the harmful truth. Thanks to our increase of negative and hyperbolic media output in the last twenty years, this has now become something of a social norm."

"What's the second phase?" Winslow said, steering them back on course.

"Phase two is Information Contagion. Our predictions show a spike in collective anxiety. This is expected to lead to widespread information-seeking behaviors, where people will seek both accurate information and speculative stories."

Uriel paused clearly expecting someone to interrupt him. When no one did, he continued.

"Phase three is Behavioral Disruption and Group Polarization. We expect major changes in how people behave. We think people will split into different groups—some will form survival-based communities, while others will attempt to escape from reality. This division will grow stronger because people often only interact with others who share their views, both online and in person."

"This is good," another voice interrupted. "We seek to divide people as much as possible. They're easier to control that way."

"And the final phase?" Winslow said.

"The last phase, which depends on how the earlier phases go, is about adapting and building resilience. Being mentally resilient will be key to how people cope, whether that's together as a community or on their own."

"Again, we have been training the public to be more resilient for decades now."

"Yes, that's certainly helped. Of course, our findings suggest a range of human responses, influenced by various factors."

"This is bigger though, far bigger," came a voice that had not spoken yet. "How certain can you be that people will react in these typical patterns?"

"We have run several experiments," Uriel said, calmly fielding the question. "The data collected is certainly statistically relevant."

"I understand that," the voice came again. "But what we're dealing with here, is something different entirely."

7

London, England. Present day.

"I'VE GOT TO RUN," Robert Schiffman said, rushing through the kitchen and kissing his girlfriend, Dee, on the lips.

"Wait a second," Dee said, catching him by the shoulders. "Let's not make it obvious that you left in a hurry." Dee took his tie in her hands, loosened the knot, and did it up once again. She placed a hand against his chest and rose on to her toes to plant her lips against his.

"Thanks," Robert said, patting the tie and flashing a smile at the woman who, in the last few months, had quite literally changed his life. Robert grabbed his car keys and strode out of the house.

Robert's life had undergone a complete transformation in the six months since Dee had first stepped into his office. Gone were the days when he would dedicate every waking hour to his work at the legal firm. The evenings he once spent networking with men he believed to be as lonely as himself or socializing with his fellow members at the Order of the All-Seeing Eye, had also become a thing of the past. Meeting Dee had turned his world upside down.

Robert slid into his Porsche and gazed back up at the Georgian townhouse which, before Dee arrived, he had occupied alone for almost twenty years. The townhouse stood regally amidst the bustle of modern London. Over the past six months, vibrant plants and blooming flowers breathed new life into the once-empty windows.

The Order of the All-Seeing Eye had changed in that time, too. They had recently appointed a frustratingly old-fashioned man called William Wolff to the position of Grand Master. Under the old Grand Master, the order was a place to network, do business, and cultivate influential alliances. All Wolff did was preach about how sinful the world had become and how the order planned to right the wrongs of the world at large.

Hopefully, Robert thought as he reached the end of the road and swung the Porsche into a gap in the traffic, William Wolff wouldn't be Grand Master for much longer. In fact, a few brothers and he had discussed strategies for removing the Grand Master from his position. They needed a vote from fifty brothers to take the motion and, after that, the support of at least half the order. Any of them would make a much better leader, and profits would once again flow.

Sure, Robert understood that humanity had its flaws, but he wasn't about to renounce capitalism and worldly pleasures just because the Grand Master said so. Robert had, like the other men in the order, taken the oath of initiation. The oath remained as it had for hundreds of years—poverty, chastity, and obedience. But that was more a nod to the knights of old, than an actual reason to stay away from women—or so Robert thought.

Robert was meeting with three other brothers after

today's assembly, hoping to add their names to his growing list of those dissatisfied with Grand Master Wolff's leadership.

The founding partner of one of London's top law firms, Robert had been approached by the Order of the All-Seeing Eye ten years ago. On joining the brotherhood, doors throughout the city's upper echelons opened for him, giving him opportunities that he could only have dreamed of in the past. He quickly learned that poverty was no longer part of the order's principles as his business increased tenfold and tenfold again since he'd been in the brotherhood's warm embrace.

The perks weren't limited to the clients who came knocking at his door, though. The order had members within the city's various police forces who made paperwork disappear or re-appear when it suited Robert's interests. Several members stalked the halls of government, pushing causes up the agendas of policymakers, or hiding them completely. Robert had also made use of the private security force that came with being part of the brotherhood when a group of thieves had thought it prudent to target his office and steal some potentially embarrassing documents. Robert knew that the guilty people now rested somewhere at the bottom of the North Sea; all thanks to the shadier side of the Order of the All-Seeing Eye.

Robert hit the gas, and the Porsche roared around a bus, earning a flash from a taxi coming the other way.

As far as Robert understood it, the Order of the All-Seeing Eye had various types of members. Some, like Robert, were men in influential positions, who continued their normal jobs on joining the order.

Being in the order made little difference to men like

Robert on a day-to-day basis, except that life's minor frustrations, things like laws and taxes, no longer applied.

Members like Robert paid for their membership by donating a percentage of their personal wealth to the order, leaving the order their entire estate upon death, and helping in other ways when required.

There were other men who lived and worked within the order, much like the typical warrior monks of old. These men kept the order secure, funded, and made sure the constant prying eyes of the internet age sought entertainment elsewhere.

Half an hour later, Robert slid the Porsche into a parking space outside the chapel in the City of London. He climbed out and glanced around the parking lot. Hidden between the area's historical buildings, the parking lot was almost always empty. Today, however, countless top of the range cars filled the spaces.

Robert peered at his watch and groaned. He was late.

Robert leaped out of the Porsche and ran into the chapel.

"Brother Schiffman, your presence honors us." A man adorned in the order's ceremonial cloak approached, extending a garment draped over his arm. All members of the order wore the same gown whilst the order was in session. The thick black fabric covered each man from crown to toe.

"Please, don your robes, brother," the man said.

"Thank you, brother," Robert said, accepting the garment and slipping it on over his suit. He flipped the hood up and positioned it so that it almost covered his eyes. Then Robert pulled open the door and shuffled into the crypt.

8

The Order of the All-Seeing Eye Headquarters, London.

End of Days Countdown: 6 days remaining.

The Grand Master of the Order of the All-Seeing Eye, William Wolff, stepped up to the stone podium at one end of the crypt. Nestled beneath London's bustling streets, under the very foundation that once supported the headquarters of the Templar Knights, the subterranean chamber resonated with the whispers of ancient times.

Standing on the podium, Wolff took a deep breath of the musty air and waited for the men to shuffle into position. Wolff stepped up to the lectern, thinking about all the times he had trodden this path, and all the men who had done so before him. Reaching the lectern, Wolff placed down his notes and eyed the assembled ranks of men before him.

Each man stood rigid, aligned in precise rows. The black gowns they wore billowed slightly; the fabric whispering across the floor. The symbol of the Order of the All-Seeing

Eye, a triangle with an eye in the center, was embroidered across each man's chest.

The gown was more than a uniform; it was a reminder to each man that they were bound to the cause, until death. Unfortunately, Wolff remembered, for one man standing before him right now, that death was coming more quickly than most.

Wolff cleared his throat and cast a glance around the space. Illuminated only by candlelight—as it had been for centuries—the brothers at the back were almost invisible to Wolff. The men at the front, though, his high-ranking officers, were cast in a dancing orange glow.

Although Wolff had known each of the men for countless years, he knew little about them. Conversation within the order, unless it was functional, or tactical, was banned. Where men came from, or even something as trivial as their given names, was an unnecessary detail within these walls. These men were soldiers, and with their eyes cast at the floor and their hands locked in front of them, they looked the part.

Wolff cleared his throat and used the sleeve of his gown to wipe a slick of sweat from his brow. Although it wasn't warm in the crypt, an angry fire burned in Wolff's stomach.

"Brothers," he began, his voice resonating through the crypt, "we are bound by a sacred duty. We are heirs to a legacy that dates to the valiant knights of old. Your dedication is the bedrock upon which our Order stands." Wolff swung his arms wide, signaling that his proclamations extended to everyone in the room. "Together, there is no adversity we cannot overcome, no secret we cannot unearth. For the eye and the earth!"

In Wolff's mind, the words ran out like a war cry, steeling the hearts of the men before him. In reality, the weak and nasal tone of his voice made the cry sound more like a tele-phone operator's request for a caller to stay on the line.

"For the eye and the earth!" the brothers shouted in reply, their united voices filling the crypt far more than their leader's sniveling tones.

Wolff wiped away another sliver of sweat, this time from his cheek. "We stand on the cusp of reclaiming what is rightfully ours," Wolff declared, his voice reverberating with all the intensity he could muster. He clenched his fists and bashed them against the lectern. "For centuries, our order has been confined to the shadows while society has descended further and further into the gutter. The modern world has stripped the honor of humankind. People now live in squalor, with sin in their hearts. They idolize the ignorant and revere the disgusting." Wolff balled one fist and placed it in the palm of his other hand. "This needs to change. We will create this change."

A few of the men shuffled from foot to foot, clearly growing impatient at their leader's postulations.

"Members of this order have shared with me their honest thoughts," Wolff continued. They have claimed: "Grand Master, but we are merely one hundred men. How can we create such a change in the world? And I ask you this, how did our fore-brothers protect pilgrims journeying to Jerusalem, out-manned as they were by adversaries? How did they conquer and hold the Holy Land against such odds? How did they amass so much wealth which extended across the whole of—"

"Permission to speak, Grand Master." A voice from beside the podium cut Wolff off in mid-flow.

"What is it, Brother Jenkins?" Wolff said.

"Manifestation," Jenkins said, his eyes wild. "I bet they did it through manifestation. If you want something hard enough, and picture it in your mind." Brother Jenkins placed his fingers against his temples. "Then it just sort of, appears. Like magic!"

"No, it was not through manifestation!" Wolff roared, a vein in his forehead visibly throbbing. "This is not some new-age nonsense. This is the work of our fore-brothers. These men built an empire, and we serve in their honor."

"It sounds like it to—"

"Stop!" Wolff yelled, pointing a finger at Jenkins.

Brother Jenkins made the slapstick gesture of zipping his mouth shut.

"Brothers, you are right to be skeptical. What I am talking about is not an ordinary military undertaking." Wolff turned and paced across the podium as though he were delivering a lecture.

"It is manifestation!" Jenkins hissed.

"This is far more powerful!" Wolff shouted, his voice reaching a pitch that was usually only heard by dogs. He spoke quickly now, afraid of losing the brothers' attention altogether. "On March 18th, 1314, while being burned at the stake in Paris, the Grand Master of the Knights Templar, Jacques de Molay issued these words: Pope Clement and King Philip, you will be summoned to the tribunal of Heaven before the year is out. Just eight months later, both Pope Clement and King Philip were dead!"

"The power of the mind!" Jenkins hissed.

"Not the power of the mind!" Wolff roared. "What we're dealing with here is far more powerful than the human mind. This was the Curse of the Last Templar!"

"The Curse of the Last Templar!" the entire brotherhood repeated back.

"Grand Master, can I ask a question, please?" Jenkins said, raising his hand as though he were in school.

"What?" Wolff turned to face the other man.

"How do you plan to use the Templar Curse to our advantage?"

Wolff blinked three times, stunned that Jenkins had asked a relevant question. Although a loyal brother and good soldier, Jenkins had an annoying habit of interrupting almost constantly.

"In order to bring the Templar Curse to life, the Templars used one of their many relics... the Seal of Solomon."

"The Seal of Solomon," the brothers chanted in reply.

Wolff held a finger up in the air, his voice now ear-splitting enough to shatter glass. "Together we will find the Seal of Solomon and re-instate the order as a guiding light for humankind. We will use the power of the seal to teach the values which first allowed our race to crawl out of the jungles, and once again make civilization shine."

Wolff halted, his gaze sweeping over his brethren. Each member was captivated, hanging on to the leader's words. Sensing his power over the brothers, Wolff crossed to the podium.

"We will dispel the shadows that have crept into the hearts and minds of people across the globe," he continued. "We will cleanse the sin that has taken root in the soul of humanity."

"Soul of humanity," the brothers chanted, leaning in shared excitement.

"Grand Master?" Jenkins said. "Isn't the Seal of Solomon supposed to control bad juju or something like that?"

"No, it allows the wearer to talk to animals," another brother offered.

A murmur of intrigue rippled through the assembled men.

Brother Jenkins was the one who eventually voiced the question that the men had in mind.

"How is talking to animals going to help us drive the sin from humankind?"

Wolff went into a full rage, whirling around and shouting at the men. His lips quivered and spittle flew from his mouth. "The seal's power does not just allow the wearer to rule over spirits and demons! The seal gives the wearer many powers, including power over the weather."

"Over the weather!" Jenkins snorted. "Take an umbrella, then you're covered for both rain and shine."

"No, you fool!" Wolff shouted, his eyes blazing with a fervor that bordered on madness. He paced to the wall and grasped the edge of a heavy curtain. Yanking the curtain aside, Wolff revealed a vast world map, meticulously detailed in vivid colors and intricate lines.

"We will combine the power we will get from the seal with the upcoming End of Days."

"The End of Days," the brothers chanted.

"We will use the people's superstitions against them, united with the power of the seal, to plunge entire regions of the world into chaos and despair," Wolff declared, his voice rising with each word. "We will unleash the fury of the elements upon the unsuspecting masses. In some places crops will wither and die, their harvests reduced to dust. In other places, rivers will swell and surge beyond their banks, swallowing entire towns."

Wolff faced his brothers, his eyes gleaming with a zealous light. "And who will be there to help? Who will extend a hand to lift humanity from the depths of their misery?" Afraid that Brother Jenkins might start talking about yoga or some other new-age fad, Wolff answered his own question. "We will be there to help! We will emerge from the shadows like saviors, offering hope and salvation to the struggling nations of the world. When they witness the miracles we can perform, when they see that our way of piety has the power to restore nature's balance and bring an end to their suffering, they will flock to our door."

"Flock to our door!" the brothers chanted, a few raising fists in excitement.

"One by one, the nations will embrace our teachings, our way of life, until the entire world is united." Wolff stepped away from the map, his chest heaving.

"And talk to animals?" Jenkins asked again.

"No! There will be no talking to animals!" Wolff roared, raising his hands to the heavens. "We, the Order of the All-Seeing Eye, have been chosen to shepherd this transformation. To bear the seal is to bear the responsibility for the future of all. We will not falter. We will not fail. When we have the seal, the power of the world will be in my hands." Wolff said, holding his hands high.

"Who's hands?" Jenkins said.

"I mean *our* hands. The power of the world will be in *our* hands!"

9

The Order of the All-Seeing Eye Headquarters, London.

A HUSH FELL at Wolff's pause; the air heavy with anticipation.

Wolff drew a slow and meditative breath. Around him, a hundred men stood motionless, every one of them waiting for him to continue.

"But, right now, finding the seal is an impossibility for us," Wolff said, his tone hardening.

The members murmured in confusion.

"No talking to animals," Jenkins said, glancing up at Wolff.

"That's right," Wolff said, pointing a finger out at the assembled men. "The Seal of Solomon will not reveal itself to us due to the actions of one man in the room."

The brothers murmured louder than before. Several men cast accusatory glances at their neighbor.

"One of our brothers, one man in this room, has broken the cardinal rule," Wolff continued. "They have engaged in relations outside of this order." Wolff's pig-like eyes swept across the crowd. "Intimate relations," he pronounced the words slowly, giving each of them more syllables than they would normally have.

The men recoiled; their eyes wide with shock.

"Hell hath no place for a man like that!" Jenkins wailed.

"I hope you understand the severity of this," Wolff continued, his voice dropping into a murmur. "Because of this man, the Seal of Solomon will not reveal itself to us. His mortal weaknesses have tainted our order."

"Oh, the pain! Oh, the disappointment!" Jenkins added, a hand covering his eyes. "Make it stop!"

"We cannot lead this charge into the light if there is corruption in our core," Wolff shouted, spittle flying.

Another moan of disquiet stirred. The men eyed each other, clearly trying to work out who the traitor might be.

"Don't look at me," Jenkins huffed at the man beside him, folding his arms. "Why am I always getting the blame?"

"Fortunately, I, as Grand Master of the order, am one step ahead. When I learned of this subterfuge, I did some research of my own. Brother Pyne, step forward, please."

A giant of a man, nearly seven feet tall, stepped to the front of the crypt. With the hood down over his eyes, all Wolff could see was the man's cleanly shaven chin. As Pyne turned, the brothers settled into silence. Jealousy panged Wolff's stomach that he held none of this man's gravitas.

"Thank you, Grand Master," Brother Pyne began, his voice deep and steady. "As you requested, I initiated an inquiry into a member within our ranks having relations outside the order, with a female."

Another gasp arose from the brothers.

"Not a female!" Jenkins moaned, fanning himself with his fingers.

"I remind all brothers of the oath of chastity we all took on entering the order," Wolff interjected.

"I now have evidence to back up this claim," Brother Pyne said, pulling a manilla envelope from beneath his cloak. He stepped up to the lectern, every bit the leader of men. One hundred pairs of eyes followed Pyne's every move, as though under the power of a spell.

Wolff rushed across the podium and elbowed his way in front of Pyne. He shoved Pyne away from the lectern, snatched up the envelope and slid out the contents. Several photographs fell into his hands. He flicked through them slowly, disgust lining his mouth. The images showed a man and a woman in various settings—walking through the city, eating dinner, and the most incriminating of all, kissing on the front steps of a large house. Bile rose in Wolff's throat as the level of the deceit became truly apparent.

The men murmured with impatience. Those at the front craned their necks, trying to see what had made the Grand Master even paler than usual.

Wolff slammed the photographs down. "I'm afraid that this is much more serious than I expected," he said through clenched teeth. "This is not a simple case of unchecked lust, but an ongoing relationship."

The brothers gasped in unison, causing the candles to dance in a wild, frenetic display.

"What is the name of this brother?" Wolff growled, tapping at the photographs.

Brother Pyne cleared his throat, the sound cutting through the silence like a knife. When he finally spoke, his voice was deep and ominous. "The man who has betrayed us, Grand Master, is Brother Schiffman."

HEARING HIS NAME, Robert Schiffman froze. A cold bead of sweat trickled down his spine. His heart pounded as though trying to escape the confines of his ribcage. He broke his downcast meditative stare and peered up at the Grand Master, who was now eyeing the brothers.

With every fiber of his being screaming to take flight, Robert scanned the room behind him. Having arrived late, he was twenty feet from the staircase which led back up to the car park. He thought of his Porsche, sitting in the parking lot fifty feet from the door. Within a minute, he could be back up there and driving away.

"Where is Brother Schiffman?" Wolff shouted, gesticulating at the assembled men. "Find him and bring him here!"

The brothers spun from side to side, looking for Schiffman amid the sea of cloaks.

Robert dipped his head to obscure his face. He used the movement of the other men to hide a shuffle toward the door. As the movement of the men became more frantic, Robert darted around a pair of brothers locked in a joint accusative stare.

"Stop wasting time!" Wolff pounded his fists against the lectern, knocking the photographs to the floor. "Remove your hoods and expose this traitor."

"The humiliation!" Jenkins howled.

The brothers froze, gazing at the Grand Master as though the order was a trick. Wearing the correct robes during meetings of the brotherhood was entrenched in protocol. Since Wolff had taken power, something as insignificant as not wearing the cloak correctly was punishable by a hefty fine or even suspension from the order.

"Stop messing around!" Wolff roared, his cheeks turning the color of beetroot. "Lower your hoods, now!"

As though controlled by a single mind, the brothers flipped down their hoods. The men whipped one way and then the next, searching for Brother Schiffman.

Realizing his freedom was to be short-lived, Robert spun on his heel and sprinted for the stairs.

"There he is!" one brother shouted. "The traitor is running!"

"Running like a rat!" Brother Jenkins' voice cut through the noise.

"Catch him! Catch him!" Wolff roared, his voice almost lost in the clamor.

As Schiffman made for the stairs, a man sprang out, blocking his path. The assailant swung his arms wide, trying to catch Schiffman in something of a bear hug. Fortunately for Schiffman, this guy was not one of the order's soldiers, but an accountant from Hounslow.

Schiffman ducked to the left, causing the other man to change position. Schiffman leaped to the right, circling the other man in two nimble steps. When he was behind the other man, Schiffman shoved him hard on the back, sending the accountant careening into two other pursuers. The three men fell into a heap on the floor.

Schiffman spun around and reached the staircase in two big steps. He bolted up the stairs three at a time. Half way up, his foot slipped, and his knees slammed against the stone. Ignoring the pain, Schiffman staggered up again and continued to climb.

The sound of running feet reverberated behind him up the narrow staircase.

Schiffman reached the ground floor and sprinted out of the staircase. Standing in the passageway which led toward the car park, he paused. Spinning around, Schiffman noticed a thick wooden door, which, when closed, would seal the crypt. Schiffman swung the door closed. In another incredible stroke of luck, he noticed a heavy iron bolt. Schiffman pushed the bolt home as the first pair of feet reached the top step on the other side. The pursuer banged against the door, doing little more than rattling the antique fixture.

Schiffman rushed down the passage, running frantically to the car park. He stepped out into the foyer and was momentarily dazzled by bright light streaming through several high windows. Without a delay, Schiffman yanked on the heavy wooden door. The door didn't move. A wave of panic surged through him. He tugged at the door with increased desperation, throwing his entire weight into each yank. The door didn't move.

"I'm afraid that's locked," came a voice from behind him.

Schiffman turned around to see the same older gentleman who had given him the robe a few minutes before. The man sat on a chair in the corner of the room. Schiffman knew that this gentleman, Brother Lennox, was an auxiliary member—responsible for the administration of the order. His hope returning, Schiffman realized that meant Lennox hadn't been in the meeting and as yet didn't yet know about his transgressions.

"I've got the key right here," Lennox said, pacing to the door. "Has the meeting finished already?"

"Yes... I mean no," Schiffman stuttered, trying, but failing to sound calm. "There's an emergency that I must see to... on behalf of the Grand Master."

"I see. Let me get this open for you," Lennox said, pacing

across to the door. He slid a bony hand inside his cloak and rooted around for the key. "I have the key somewhere."

Schiffman stole a look over his shoulder as the banging reverberated with increased fervor from the crypt door.

"There it is!" Lennox said, his face lighting with a smile. He pulled out an oversize key which Schiffman didn't think it would be possible to lose in a forest, let alone a pocket.

Painstakingly slowly, Lennox slid the key in the lock. The mechanism clunked and groaned.

Schiffman drew his car keys from his pocket and prepared himself to bolt as soon as the door was open.

"These old locks," Lennox said, shaking his head. He twisted his wrist the other way. The mechanism clunked again and then, not a moment too soon, the lock released.

Schiffman tore the door open, almost knocking the old man over. Without looking, he charged through, relief welling through him as the outside air tingled his face.

The next moment Schiffman collided with something hard, and fell, sprawling backward across the flagstones. Bewildered, Schiffman peered up to see three of the order's most fearsome knights standing over him.

"You think that's the only way out of the crypt?" Brother Pyne said, seizing Schiffman by the cloak and hauling him back up to his feet. The knights dragged Schiffman into the back of a waiting van.

10

"HE NO LONGER DESERVES TO WEAR THE garments of our order. Disrobe him now," Wolff commanded, striding around Schiffman who was slumped on a chair in the middle of the room. Although Schiffman wasn't tied in place, two of the knights who had bundled him in the back of the van and driven him halfway across London, stood either side of him.

The men crouched, lifted Schiffman from the chair, and tore away his robes.

Wolff stopped pacing and eyed Schiffman closely for the first time. Schiffman was an athletic man in his middle years and wore a suit that would not have been out of place in the city's boardrooms. Although this man was not a warrior, he clearly took care of himself.

"You have betrayed the trust bestowed upon you by this sacred order," Wolff said, his lips twisting together in disgust.

Schiffman assessed their new location for the first time. His head having been forcibly covered by the hood on the way here, he didn't know where they were. The room was starkly lit with a large steel machine at one end. It smelled of medical disinfectant, with white tiles lining the walls and floor. Catching sight of a stainless-steel gurney near the door, Schiffman's complexion grew even more ashen. Four knights and the Grand Master stood around him.

"Where are we?" Schiffman said, swallowing hard.

"That is none of your concern," Wolff roared, jowls shuddering. "You have deceived us, and for that, you must pay."

"I'm sorry about that," Schiffman said, his hands spread in a gesture of surrender. "I wanted to talk to you, actually, Grand Master. I think being part of this order is no longer for me."

For a moment, no one spoke. Wolff tilted his head back and emitted a laugh that sounded like a bird of prey expelling the bones of its last victim. The humorless cackle reverberated around the sterile room. Copying their leader, the knights laughed too.

"You remember that oath you swore to?" Wolff said, suddenly serious. "You vowed to uphold the sanctity of our order, to safeguard our secrets with your life. You pledged loyalty not only to the cause but to your brothers beside you. And above all, you pledged poverty, chastity, and obedience."

"And after all that, you had relations with a woman!" Jenkins added, shock still lacing his voice. "A woman!" he repeated, louder than before.

"Yes, I am afraid that is true," Schiffman said, adopting the calm and affable tone usually reserved for judges and clients. "I must confess, though, I thought that was one of those oaths people made because they were traditional, rather than with any intention of remaining alone for the rest of my life."

Wolff's eyes became so wide that a band of white was visible around the pupil. "The sanctity of our brotherhood lives and dies by the oaths you have made! Not only have you broken one of our most sacred rules, but now you offend the order!"

The men murmured their disgust.

"Okay, look, I'm sorry," Schiffman said, trying to placate the Grand Master. "I'm afraid this has all rather caught me by surprise. I never intended to feel this way." Schiffman's face morphed into a soft smile. "Seriously, though, what is this place?" Schiffman eyed the gurney and his smile disappeared. "It really is quite creepy."

"It's..." Brother Jenkins began answering but was silenced by the Grand Master's elbow to his ribs.

"You are in no position to apologize," Wolff said. "What you have done cannot be undone. It's shocking ..."

"It came as a total surprise to me, too. If you'd told me a year ago that I would be in such a beautiful relationship..." Schiffman continued, smiling warmly.

Watching the expression light Schiffman's face, Wolff felt a physical sickness broil within him. This was what happened when weak people fraternized with those outside of the order.

"We don't want to hear about the inner workings of your sinful life," Wolff snapped.

"You speak for yourself," Jenkins said, hands on his hips. "How did you first meet?"

"She walked into my office one day looking for someone to represent her," Schiffman said, his voice taking on the tone of a romantic poet in the throes of passion. "Our eyes met across the room and—"

"Enough!" Wolff roared, shaking his arms like a petulant child. The flesh around his neck and face quivered, shaking beads of sweat off into the air. "You have already fouled our order. Do not fill our minds with temptation, too."

"That's why I think it's better that we get this over and done with. We all have lives to get on with," Schiffman said, trying to stand. One of the knights forced him back into the chair with a hand that was almost as big as a tennis racket. "I realize you have protocol to go through," Schiffman said, clearly shaken by the force but trying not to show it. "If we can speed this up, I'll get out of here and you'll never hear from me again."

"Yesssss," Wolff said. "We certainly will speed this up." Wolff snapped his fingers. One knight strode through a set of double doors at the back of the room.

"I'm glad you agree," Schiffman said. "We can put this down to a big misunderstanding. I'm questioning your methods, but why do we need to do this here? What is this place?" Schiffman cast another glance around the room.

"It's Broo—" Jenkins started but was again silenced by the Grand Master. Jenkins clamped a hand across his mouth as though providing a physical barrier against the words.

"In this place we right the wrongs of the sinner. Even the most troubled souls can be purged," Wolff said, his arms spread wide.

Brother Jenkins pushed his hand harder against his face, his skin turning an unnatural shade.

"Within these walls, we take the offender and deliver him to a life of peace for eternity," Wolff continued.

The brother returned to the room, dragging something in through the door. The doors banged, emitting a hollow thud, as the object moved between them.

"It's here that we snub out the effects of sin and—"

"It's Brookfield Crematorium!" Jenkins shouted, pulling in a deep breath as though he were suffocating.

Registering the words, and the object that had been dragged into his eyeline, Schiffman kicked out and forced himself to stand. The knights behind him lunged out, trying to grab his shoulders, but Schiffman had moved too quickly.

His feet slipping across the tiled floor, Schiffman bolted for the door.

"Stop him!" Wolff bellowed.

Schiffman made it three steps before two more knights stepped in through the door, seized him by the shoulders and dragged him back to the chair. Schiffman twisted and fought against the knights but got nowhere.

"You said you wanted out of this order," Wolff said, gesturing at the ominous object before them. "In the Order of the All-Seeing Eye, departure comes at an ultimate cost."

With panicked eyes, Schiffman watched a knight maneuver a coffin, strapped on top of a gurney, into the center of the room. The wheels squeaked and rattled as he positioned the coffin and removed the lid.

"You can't be serious?" Schiffman said, kicking out at the knights, but getting nowhere.

"Consider this your final lesson," Wolff continued, his voice reverberating around the room. "Throughout the ages, fire has claimed countless members of our order. It is a rite of passage that dates back to our founding."

"No! You're crazy! You can't do this!" Schiffman shouted. He thrashed wildly with renewed energy, struggling desperately against the iron grip which held him in place.

"I am far from crazy," Wolff said, holding Schiffman's gaze. "It is you who is crazy. I have not been tainted by the whims of modern life. Once you have been purged from our order, we will return the world to riotousness."

"Don't you mean righteousness?" Jenkins offered.

"That's what I said," Wolff roared, his hands vibrating as though conducting electricity. "Start the furnace!"

"Grand Master, are you sure this is necessary?" Brother Pyne said, stepping forward. "I think Brother Schiffman has learned his lesson."

Wolff whirled around to face the knight. The Grand Master rose onto his tiptoes, attempting to meet the knight's eyeline, although he was still at least three feet too short.

"How dare you question my orders!" Wolff howled, his eyes burning with rage. "You will do as you are told, or you will share the fate of this disgusting specimen!" Wolff pointed at one of the other men. "Start the furnace, now! We have no time to waste!"

Another of the knights strode across to a control panel on the wall beside the large metal contraption at the back of the room. He flipped a switch, and the machine hummed. He turned a dial, and the furnace roared to life.

The sound sent Schiffman into a frenzy. His arms flailed, seeking leverage. He struck one knight with an elbow and tried to kick the other. The knights responded by further tightening their grip, their muscles like hydraulic pistons.

"Over seven hundred years ago, our leader was burned at the stake," Wolff said, his voice now a sinister whisper. "Today, that is not possible, not in a city, at least. So, we will provide you with the next best thing. Whilst it is an honor you do not deserve, we are merciful in our judgments."

"Merciful in our judgments," the knights echoed in reply.

11

London, England. Present day.

EDEN LED Athena through the low doorway, exiting into the street from The Cheshire Cheese. She turned right, heading for the Underground station.

Although Eden's mind still spun with the revelations Athena had shared, Eden forced them away for now. At some point she would discuss it all with her father, but that wouldn't happen today.

"Thanks for that," Eden said. "It was great to get out and just be normal for once."

"My pleasure," Athena said. "I told you we could do history without the risk of death."

"For once, you were right," Eden said. They rounded a corner and strode toward an intersection.

"I would suggest we do that more often," Athena said. "If we weren't stuck in the middle of the ocean most of the time."

"I like it there too," Eden laughed. "I generally like wherever I am."

"Yeah, I forget you lived on a converted bus in the woods," Athena teased.

"My truck is not a bus!" Eden said, wheeling around and pointing at Athena. "My truck is a DAF T244 conversion. And it's the best night's sleep I've ever had."

"I'm just going on what Beaumont told me." Athena shrugged. "He said it was a bus, and that you fed him instant noodles."

Eden frowned in mock anger. "I'm going to have some serious words with Beaumont when he finally stops flitting around the globe."

"Do you think you'll ever go back?" Athena asked.

"Back to the truck? Yeah, absolutely, I'd love to. That thing is my pride and joy. It's in storage right now—a friend of mine is making sure it stays in tiptop condition."

"You'd miss us, though, right? Me and Baxter?" Athena emphasized Baxter's name, giving the question an undertone that Eden didn't like one bit. She kept her eyes locked on the road ahead, working hard to avoid Athena's stare.

"I'd miss you both, that's for sure," Eden said, when it became clear Athena would not change the subject for her. "I'd miss you both equally, because you're both my friends," she added, to avoid any misinterpretation.

They reached the intersection and wandered to a crosswalk.

"How are you finding life with us?" Athena asked as they waited for the green light. "There isn't that much privacy on board the *Balonia*. Although I suppose it's better than living on a bus."

Eden shot her friend a look. "It is fun, I like it—"

The sound of a powerful engine, a guttural, menacing growl, cut Eden off in mid-sentence.

Eden and Athena whipped around to face the noise. A

black van screamed around the corner and sped up. The van cut around two parked taxis and closed in on them.

"Are we expecting company?" Eden said, assessing their position. On the side of a road, there was little chance of outrunning a vehicle. Adrenaline jolted through her system as the threat registered.

"Nope, but people do love to ruin our fun," Athena replied.

The van covered the distance in a matter of seconds and then the driver hit the brake, sending the van into a skid.

Eden and Athena shared a worried look, took a step backward, and inched together. Both adopted their fighting stances, their feet shoulder-width apart and knees slightly bent. The relaxation of their drinks and conversation in the pub was now a thing of the past. In less than a second, the pair was ready for anything.

The van's side door slid open even before the van had completely stopped and two masked men sprang out. Two more men followed from the front passenger door.

"I told you it wasn't possible," Eden said, angling herself to face their attackers.

"What's that?" Athena replied.

"There was no way we could visit a historic place without someone trying to kill us."

The men fanned out, surrounding Eden and Athena. Fortunately, the sidewalk was wide, giving Eden a moment to assess the incoming threat. Each man wore identical black fatigues; their faces concealed behind ski masks. The men moved as one; their synchronized actions leaving no doubt that they were a professional unit.

"You looking for a fancy dress party?" Eden said as the first man closed in.

Without a word, the man lunged, his arms outstretched.

The move told Eden that this was an abduction rather than a hit. Although that wasn't great, it was preferable to a fight to the death.

Eden darted to the side, avoiding the grab by a hair's breadth. She swung around and used the man's momentum against him. She caught his arm and twisted it behind his back in one fluid motion. The man grunted in pain as Eden applied pressure, forcing him to his knees. Eden swung a kick into his ribs, sending the man sprawling across the sidewalk.

"Maybe they're lost," Athena said, side-stepping an attack. The man doubled back and swung a fist, hitting nothing but air.

Undoubtedly seeing his friend underestimate their target, another thug lunged at Athena from the side. Athena pivoted on her heel, narrowly avoiding the second man's grasp. As he stumbled past her, Athena delivered a swift elbow strike to his back, sending him sprawling to the ground.

"London can be confusing for idiots," Eden responded, bobbing out of the path of a brute charging at her with the grace of an elephant. Eden swung her leg out and delivered a powerful kick to the man's thigh as he passed. The man stumbled and slid, collapsing with flailing limbs.

"Happy to give you some directions, gents," Athena said, sidestepping another blow. "But we are going to have to stop this dance competition." She bobbed to the right again, saving herself from another strike, then turned her attention to the man she'd previously knocked to the ground. With a grunt of effort, he dragged himself up. He stepped toward Athena, his fists raised.

"I wish people like you would give up after round one," Athena groaned, ducking as a fist swung through the air above her head. Athena launched a quick one-two combination into the man's abdomen. She followed with a brutal elbow strike up and underneath the man's ski mask. The sound of splintering plastic joined the crunch of breaking teeth.

"These guys are really hands on," Eden said, darting out of the way as another man recovered and charged for her again. She hopped to the side and delivered a kick to the back of the guy's knee. His leg buckled beneath him, and the man stumbled. Eden grabbed the back of his shirt and shoved him face-first into the nearby wall.

"Guys like this are just after one thing," Athena said. "I hate it."

Eden swung around as another assailant approached. She landed a solid punch to his ribs. The man grunted, wheezed, and stepped aside for the wall-kisser to have another go.

Although there were only four men, they seemed to recover at such speed that Eden was struggling to keep up. Before she knew what was happening, the wall-kisser had parried her punch, and grabbed her arm like a vice. The other man appeared at Eden's other side and took hold, too.

"Now look at you, wanting to hold hands," Eden groaned, her voice restricted by the grip. She struggled, kicking out with her feet and knees, but her captors remained strong. The men hauled Eden to the van. As they approached the side of the vehicle, Eden shoved one man to the side, smashing him into the van's door with a clang that reverberated throughout the vehicle. Although the strike was good, his grip remained. Eden positioned her feet on the van's step and pushed, smashing the other thug's head into the roof.

The men who had been in combat with Athena,

retreated toward the waiting van. Athena went on the offensive, lashing out with a flurry of fists and feet. The men parried her blows and backed away toward the vehicle and Eden.

One man spun around and shoved Eden into the waiting van. The impact caught Eden off guard. She flew through the door and slumped against the seats. She spun around and lashed out. The thug weathered the strikes while two others scrambled inside the van and held her still.

With the three assailants and Eden now inside the vehicle, the fourth man slid the door closed and jumped into the front.

The van's engine roared, and the vehicle lurched.

Athena darted forward and made a grab for the vehicle. Her hands swept through the air but caught nothing. She bent, breathing heavily, as the van accelerated away.

12

ATHENA'S HEART pounded furiously as she watched the van careen down the street. Adrenaline surging through her veins, she sprinted after the vehicle, her boots pounding against the cobblestones.

Athena's muscles burned as she closed the distance. Her mind raced, assessing her surroundings with lightning speed. Her eyes darted left and right, scanning the street for anything that could aid in her pursuit. Athena realized she could use the crisscrossing ancient streets and the London traffic to her advantage. While a large vehicle was good on the open road, here they would struggle to reach high speed.

The van swerved recklessly ahead; its brake lights flashing as it wound around a corner. Athena gritted her teeth, determination etched on her face as she pushed herself even harder. She swung around the corner, almost knocking a pair of office workers off their feet. The men, one of them wearing a ridiculous pink shirt with a white collar, shouted as Athena sprinted on. If she didn't need to catch this van, Athena would have taken enjoyment in knocking the arrogant fools to the ground for fun.

The van disappeared beneath the arches of a railway bridge. Athena muttered under her breath and doubled her efforts. Her well-trained body responded to the commands and she raced on. Her breathing dropped into line and her heart picked up its pace. Less than a minute later, she reached the arch and ran through.

Athena reached the junction on the other side of the bridge, her heart pounding and her breath coming in ragged gasps. She skidded to a halt, her eyes frantically scanning the surroundings for any sign of the van. Her stomach dropped when she registered the van was nowhere to be seen.

She spun from side to side, searching for the vehicle. The road curved out of sight in both directions, disappearing behind towering structures.

Ignoring the traffic, Athena stepped out into the middle of the road. A dump truck screamed to a stop; the driver leaning on the horn.

"You think you're having a bad day," Athena muttered, doing another three-sixty from the center of the road where she could see further in each direction.

Then she saw it. The van swung from the main road and disappeared down a side street.

"Too far to run," Athena muttered. The van was over four hundred feet away, and with each passing second, getting further away. Desperation clawed at her chest as she swung around, her eyes frantically searching for a solution. Amidst the vehicles, Athena noticed a delivery driver on a motorbike cutting his way through the traffic.

Athena's mind raced, calculations and possibilities whirring through her head at breakneck speed. Although the bike wasn't the most powerful ride, it was perfect for London's narrow streets.

Athena dashed to the bike; her legs pumping. As she closed the distance, she caught the delivery driver's attention.

"I need your bike!" she shouted. Before the guy could reply, Athena grabbed the driver. In a blur of motion, she pulled the rider from the bike and dropped him on the sidewalk. Before the man could react, Athena leaped across the saddle, pulled back on the throttle, and sped away.

Athena threaded the bike between the vehicles. She swung into the street the van had disappeared down thirty seconds ago.

With just enough space for vehicles to go in one direction, the street was designed for a time before London's streets were filled with cars and trucks. Fortunately for Athena, the street was empty, and she made quick progress. The narrow street hit a curve to the right as it wound around the back of a skyscraper.

Athena leaned into the curve. The road opened up ahead and joined another larger road.

"Got ya," Athena shouted, noticing the van waiting in a line of traffic. Based on the van's position she figured that they planned to turn left. That would take them toward the river on one of the major roads.

Athena was so focused on the van ahead, that she didn't see a delivery truck pull out of a loading bay ahead. Athena's reflexes took over. She twisted the handlebars, her body low. The motorcycle's tires shrieked against the curb as Athena rode up and thundered down the cobblestone walkway.

A pair of pedestrians leaped aside; their shouts and curses lost in the noise. Athena barely even noticed; her focus locked on the van which inched to the junction.

The truck driver hit the brake, leaving a gap between the truck's grill and the rear wall of the building. Athena swept the bike in closer to the wall. The bricks whipped past an inch from her handlebars.

With a surge of acceleration, she shot past the truck and bumped back down onto the road.

Up ahead, the van pulled out into the traffic and swung left. The van sped up, quickly catching a bus, and then disappearing out of sight.

Athena tore the throttle to max. Right now, the traffic was working in her favor, but if the van hit an area of light traffic, they would be gone. Athena blazed down the road, weaving between two cars and sending pedestrians diving as she bolted across a crosswalk.

She reached the junction and didn't even slow. She weaved past three vehicles waiting to turn and shot straight out into the road, causing another taxi to hit the brake.

She squinted ahead, searching for her quarry. As she'd feared, the road here was straight, and the traffic was light enough for the van to have increased their lead. She pulled around a bus and accelerated hard.

Athena revved the engine, and the bike accelerated with a roar as she wove through the heavy traffic. Car horns blared and tires screeched as startled drivers swerved to avoid a collision.

Ahead, the van picked up speed. They'd clearly seen Athena on their tail and abandoned all attempts at subtlety. The van roared through a red light and across an intersection. A double-decker bus shuddered to a stop and three people on the crosswalk scattered in panic.

Athena gritted her teeth and weaved her way through the traffic. She reached the intersection and powered through, narrowly avoiding traffic coming the other way.

The road bore to the left and the imposing dome of St. Paul's Cathedral loomed ahead.

The speeding van headed toward the cathedral and mounted the curb with a violent jolt, two of its wheels lifting from the road. With a sudden motion, the van entered the square in front of St Paul's Cathedral and quickly gained speed. Tourists and worshippers scrambled for safety.

The van circled the central fountain and disappeared around the back of the ancient building.

Athena bumped up to the curb and gave chase. She powered across the square, swerving carefully around the terrified onlookers. Already out of sight, around the other side of the vast building, Athena was losing time. She gazed up at the vast stone staircase and made a split-second decision.

She swung the bike up the steps and pulled back on the handlebars. Reaching the top, she roared beneath the portico entrance. She leaned on the horn, scattering people lining up to enter the cathedral.

Reaching the other side of the building, she swung around and saw the van nose back into traffic. The van pulled out and powered past a delivery driver. Her shortcut through the cathedral's entrance had bought her some precious seconds.

Athena pulled back on the throttle, bumping the bike back down the stairs. She reached the bottom of the stairs as a patrol car sped into the square, sirens blaring.

Before the police could react, Athena hit the gas and gave chase, weaving out into the traffic in hot pursuit.

Ahead, the van swerved recklessly through the busy streets, weaving in and out of lanes. With a determined set in her jaw, Athena powered the motorcycle through a maze of cars and buses, reclaiming every inch of ground.

The van careened around a corner, narrowly missing a double-decker bus that had just pulled away from a stop. Athena leaned into the turn.

The van swerved to avoid a delivery truck. Its tires mounted the curb, sending pedestrians scattering like billiard balls. Athena seized the opportunity, accelerating through the narrow gap between the truck and a parked car. The motorcycle's mirrors barely cleared the tight space, but Athena didn't flinch.

Athena checked her rearview mirror. The patrol car, sirens wailing, was gaining on them both. If Athena were an optimist, she would assume that the police were here to help her liberate her kidnapped friend, but experience had taught her something different. The police officers' first instinct would be to drag her down to the station and ask her so many questions that by the time they believed her story, if they ever did, Eden would be long gone.

Noticing a gap in the traffic ahead, Athena yanked back on the throttle and closed the distance further.

The van made a sharp right turn and barreled down a narrow side street. Athena reacted instantly, leaning hard into the turn, and following the van into the alleyway. The motorcycle's engine roared, echoing from the walls of the buildings on either side.

The van sped past a dumpster, losing a wing mirror, and knocking trash all over the ground.

Athena navigated the obstacles with skilled precision. The motorcycle's suspension absorbed the bumps and jolts of the uneven terrain.

The van swerved onto a main road. Athena's heart raced as she noticed the road ahead curving onto London Bridge. In that split second, a realization struck her. The river marked the edge of the historic City of London. Established around the middle of the first century AD as the Roman settlement of Londinium, the City of London was a county in its own right and separate from the vast metropolis of Greater London. Operating with autonomy, the City of London even had its own police force. If Athena could get across the river, she would be out of reach of the police on her tail.

Athena throttled the bike over London Bridge, pushing the engine to its peak. The Thames swept past underneath, with the Southbank skyline unfurling before her. Athena eyed the mirror as the City of London Police cruisers closed in behind her. She tried to speed up, but the throttle was already maxed out.

Athena saw the trap into which she'd fallen. Ahead, parked in the center of the bridge, marking the boundary of their jurisdiction, two more police cruisers waited.

Clearly learning of Athena's approach, the cruisers moved into position, blocking the traffic, and cutting off her path. Athena's heart raced. She eyed the mirror again. The cruisers behind her fanned out to block the road. She had no way back and no way through.

Athena brought the bike to a skidding halt, banging the bumper of the car ahead. She dropped the bike and took to her feet. A police cruiser roared up behind her and four officers on foot approached from the front. They surrounded Athena quickly. Although, like most police in the UK, they weren't armed, Athena was outnumbered.

Athena turned to watch the van reach the other side of the bridge and disappear amid the south London traffic.

13

INSIDE THE VAN, Eden remembered something her father had once told her: *save your energy and wait for your chance.* Right now, locked in the van, outnumbered and overpowered, the best thing she could do was heed that advice. She begrudgingly settled into the seat as the van sped away.

When the van had settled into a forward motion, one of the men searched Eden. As his hands moved across her, Eden resisted the temptation to snap the guy's wrist.

The thug yanked Eden's smart phone from her pocket. He opened the door, the noise of the traffic flooding in, and threw the device out onto the street.

"Of course, you don't want anyone to interrupt our special time," Eden said. She intended to keep up her monologue, both to stop the men thinking she was scared and, hopefully, to annoy them.

The brute slid the door shut and the traffic noise sunk again.

"I've gotta say, you're going about this all the wrong way, though. I don't think we're going to be friends."

They bumped around another corner and Eden did a

quick assessment of the van's interior. A small light mounted on the ceiling washed the space in a dim glow. Thick metal lined the inside of the vehicle, which was clearly designed to make the vehicle even more secure— possibly even bulletproof. There was no window through to the cab and the back doors had been blocked up, turning the van into a cell. Hooks and anchor points studded the walls, allowing goods or even people to be fixed in place. A bench ran down either side of the van. Eden sat on one with a man on either side. The third man settled into the seat opposite.

The van gathered speed and swung to the left. Eden slid into the shoulder of the man beside her. She tried to picture their location in her mind's eye, but they had been bumping around so much she couldn't figure it out.

As the van straightened up, the men sitting on either side of Eden held her in place while the brute sitting opposite pulled out a black cloth bag and yanked it over Eden's head, plunging her into darkness.

"That's made me loads more comfortable, thanks guys," Eden groaned, pressing back against the wall. Her breathing echoed in her ears at a volume that would make Darth Vader proud. Over the growling engine, she heard the thugs moving around and probably removing their ski masks.

The van bumped over something. One thug bounced to the floor, grunting.

"I hope we didn't run someone over."

Eden found a little bit of solace knowing that Athena's actions were causing the van to drive erratically.

It was clear these men weren't getting away as easily as they had hoped they might.

"You guys know how far we've got to go?" Eden said. "This is not exactly first-class travel."

Without warning, the driver hit the brakes, and the van slammed around a corner. Eden sprawled against one of the men.

"Earth to meat-head number one," Eden said in a robotic voice. No reply. "Earth to meat-head number two." Still no reply.

For what felt like hours the van accelerated and then slowed, then turned aggressively. A few times, Eden heard sirens drawing near and wondered whether their crazy driving had alerted the police. When the noise of the sirens drifted away, Eden realized that, as usual, law enforcement would not come to the rescue.

To Eden, unable to see and with no idea where they were, the journey felt like a washing machine on a spin cycle. She suspected that if they had traveled in one direction, they would reach the suburbs now, but the traffic noise and the start and stop progress suggested they remained in central London. That meant they'd been driving in circles—either to confuse Eden or shake off the tail.

After a few turns, the van pulled to a stop. The driver thumped on the wall which separated the cab from the back. The men climbed to their feet and lifted Eden from the bench. Eden heard the van's door slide open and the men lifted her out.

Eden quieted her breathing and listened to their surroundings. Despite the distant hum of traffic, their immediate surroundings were silent. Cool air tingling the exposed skin of her forearms indicated to Eden they were outside. That suggested they weren't anywhere public, as moving someone with a bag over their head would definitely attract unwanted attention.

Holding an arm each, and clearly taking care to make sure she didn't fall, the men walked Eden across uneven cobbles and into a building. Even through the bag, Eden could tell that the place smelled musty and old. The men guided her through a passageway and down a set of narrow spiral steps.

As they descended, the smell of damp rose in Eden's nostrils. After thirty-five stairs, which Eden calculated to equal around two stories, the men led Eden across a jagged stone floor.

Eden once again counted out the steps, trying to calculate the distance. After they'd traveled around thirty feet, the men pushed her down into a chair. Eden took a deep breath and identified another scent in the air. She inhaled again and recognized it as the aroma of burning candles.

The cloth bag was torn from Eden's face. Light flooded into her eyes, making her blink. As her vision adapted to the dim light, she took a few moments to glance around. Vaulted ceilings curved overhead, and tombs lined the edges of the chamber, topped with sculpted figures.

"Nice place, although in future I'd prefer the Ritz," Eden said. From what she could tell they were in a crypt. She noticed the place was entirely lit by candlelight. Countless candles flickered all around her, their warm, ethereal light dancing shadows across the chamber.

"Thank you for coming to see me," came a voice from somewhere behind her. The voice was nasal and piercing; its echo briefly throwing Eden off balance. Eden spun around, trying to see the speaker but saw nothing.

"I hope you didn't find the journey too uncomfortable," the voice came again. Although Eden thought the voice was probably male, it was unusually high-pitched. "It is most regrettable that we should meet in such a dramatic way, but I'm afraid we don't have a lot of time."

A figure moved in the gloomy recesses of the crypt. The

man took a step, now a silhouette against a distant flickering flame. Eden assessed her host. He was wide and squat and wore a long black cloak which swept the floor as he walked.

"What is life, though, without a bit of flair?" The man strode further into the crypt and raised a hand. His stubby fingers unfurled and tightened again.

"If I wanted a show, I'd go to the theater," Eden said, leaning back in the chair and folding her arms. She executed a look she had spent over half her life honing—the unimpressed teenager. Although, in all honesty, intrigue now tickled her senses, she wasn't about to let this joker know it.

"I had heard that you were a funny one, Miss Black." The man barked a laugh that reverberated around the crypt. He took another step, the candles illuminating his face and allowing Eden to see him properly for the first time.

Her host was a ball of a man—probably as wide as he was tall. Despite the cool air in the crypt, a sheen of sweat covered his hairless head. As he turned, Eden noticed an embroidered emblem glimmering from his chest. She recognized the symbol, and her intrigue sparked up a notch.

"The Order of the All-Seeing Eye," Eden said. "I thought you guys were a myth."

The man laughed again, sending the jowls that hung from his chin and neck into a fit of wobbles. "Yes, that's the way we like to keep it. We work hard to keep our order a secret, even from people like you."

"What do you mean, people like me?" Eden said, tightening her arms across her chest.

"We like to keep our existence a secret, even from people inside the Council of Selene."

Eden's gaze hardened on the little man as his words sent a shockwave through her. He was the first person she'd ever met outside of the organization who even knew the council existed.

"I knew that would get your attention." The man let out a giggle that resembled the sound of a deflating tire. "It pays for us to know things like this, you see."

"What's going to be hilarious, is when I knock your head against the wall and leave you to play this game on your own," Eden said in return.

Footsteps shuffled from the stairs behind her. She whirled around to see the two guards who had been standing on either side of the door take a step. Both wore similar cloaks to their leader, with hoods shading their faces.

The leader raised a hand, and the guards settled down. "That won't happen. It took four of my men to separate you from your friend and bring you here. I can keep you here as long as I wish."

Eden saw a hint of amusement in the man's eyes, followed by a flicker of something else that she couldn't quite place.

"Plus, I think you'll be interested in the reason I have brought you here." The man's voice echoed throughout the crypt.

"Say that's true, Mr. Whoever-You-Are. I'm still confident I could do some damage to that pretty face of yours before your guard dogs get here."

The men beside the door shuffled, clearly itching to drag Eden away.

"Even if they are well trained," Eden added. She unfolded her hands and eyed her fingernails casually. "You've got ten seconds to get to the point."

It was Eden's host's turn to fold his arms, which was no mean feat considering the width of his chest. "I'll concede to you that time is of the essence. First, my apologies for not introducing myself. I am William Wolff, the Grand Master of the Order of the All-Seeing Eye." Wolff placed a hand across the emblem on his chest.

"Hello Mr. Wolff," Eden said, in the manner of a school child addressing a teacher.

Wolff took a step nearer to Eden, his cloak trailing out behind him like a shadow. He extended a finger and leveled it at Eden. "Miss Black, you are here, honestly, because I, in fact, we all, need your help."

Eden rolled her eyes. "Not this again. Surely, it's someone else's go for once."

"Miss Black, the world stands on the precipice of a new epoch." Wolff spread his arms wide, his chins flapping like washing on a line. "What we're heading into is a period marked by both destruction and rebirth, chaos and order, darkness and light."

"Is there a point anywhere nearby?" Eden spun right to left. "If so, please get to it as right now I'm drowning in an ocean of vague statements."

"Our order has long held the belief that this era would come, and we have been preparing, safeguarding knowledge, and protecting artifacts, to ensure the future of humanity."

"Mr. Wolff, if I didn't know better, I'd say you were after an Oscar with this performance."

"The signs have become too frequent, too clear to ignore. Natural calamities, societal unrest, and the erosion of moral compasses worldwide. These are not mere coincidences but the harbingers of what is coming."

"And what exactly is that?" Eden said, speaking quickly to get her question in. "A Netflix series in which you play the lead?"

"This has been prophesied for centuries," Wolff responded, his voice steady as if reciting a passage from an ancient text. "The ancients predicted a time when the very fabric of society would fray, where discord would sow its seeds across nations, and the earth itself would rebel against mankind's transgressions."

"Point. Now!" Eden said, cupping her hands around her mouth and bellowing at the man.

Wolff tilted his head, his tiny dark eyes locking on Eden's. "Miss Black, I am talking about the End of Days."

14

EDEN MET WOLFF'S GAZE, her jaw clenched. A heavy silence hung between them for long and breathless seconds.

"I thought that would get your attention," Wolff said, the corner of his mouth twitching. His eyes remained locked on Eden's with an intensity that brought a sickening feeling to her stomach.

Eden shook herself into focus. "You don't seriously expect me to believe that, do you?" She climbed to her feet. The guards behind her might be watching her every move, but Eden didn't care. "You're right, people have been talking about the End of Days for centuries, but these people are lunatics. Stop wasting my time!"

Eden marched toward Wolff; her fists balled. Boots pounded across the flagstones behind her as though a stampede of wild horses were coming her way. Before Eden could reach the Grand Master, four powerful arms gripped her shoulders. The guards pulled Eden back, slamming her into the chair.

Grand Master Wolff regarded Eden with a condescending smile, his eyes glinting with amusement. He steepled his fingers and leaned on to his heels.

The pose provided him with a height advantage, which he clearly enjoyed, while Eden was forced to remain seated.

"Temper, temper, my dear Eden," Wolff drawled, his voice dripping with false concern. "Such displays are unbecoming. We must play nice. Without collaboration, we are nothing but mere animals."

Eden glared at Wolff, straining against the iron grip of her captors.

Wolff chuckled, a low, sinister sound that echoed through the crypt. "One way or another, Miss Black, you will help me. You have a role to play, and from that, there is no escape."

Another few seconds of silence drifted between the pair. Eden groaned and settled into her seat.

"Fine," she said, accepting that her options were limited. "Get these stinky brutes away from me and I'll listen."

Wolff flicked his wrist, and the guards stalked back to the door.

"I know you guys love the ways of old, but deodorant should be encouraged." Eden brushed one shoulder and then the other as though removing the residue from the place the guards had touched her. When she was finished, she turned to face the Grand Master. "Go on then, tell me about the End of Days. Are you talking about an apocalypse or Armageddon? You know, the Earth exploding in a great big fireball." She watched Wolff closely but saw nothing that indicated he wasn't totally serious.

"Not quite," Wolff said, pacing across the crypt. "The End of Days is not necessarily the world disintegrating in nuclear hellfire, war, plague, or famine."

"Let me guess," Eden sighed, her gaze locked on the Grand Master. "You don't know what you're talking about?"

"We don't know *exactly* what the result will be, but what we're talking about here is the disintegration of the fabric of society. Governments will cease to function, the monetary system will crumble, and institutions will fail. It won't take long before every person in the world is fighting for their lives."

Eden's mind raced as she processed Wolff's words. Sure, she'd heard stories about this sort of thing for as long as she could remember, but never considered them anything more than fairy tales.

"But there is a glimmer of hope." Wolff snatched a candle and held it close to his face. The flame flickered with the movement but refused to go out. "The prophecy states that we have one chance to reverse the seemingly inevitable course of these events." With the candle held so close, Wolff appeared almost ghostly. "There is said to be one chance to turn the tide of this cataclysm." He stopped pacing and turned to face Eden; the candlelight making his features even more gargoyle-like.

Eden blinked, the implications of Wolff's revelation dawning on her. She gazed hard into the Grand Master's eyes but didn't see a hint of doubt.

"Oh man, I know what's coming next," Eden groaned.

"Yes, I think you do," Wolff said, pulling the candle away from his face and eyeing the flame. "You are part of a larger design; one that transcends your understanding." Wolff held his arms out wide, the movement sending the candle into a trembling frenzy.

"Once again, please get to the point," Eden said. "I've got some paint I'd like to watch drying."

"We have but one chance to prevent this." Wolff brought

the candle in close to his face again. "One chance, or it's..." he blew the candle, and the flame went out.

Eden let the drama of the moment pass and then raised a hand as though she were in a classroom. "I have a question. We've never met before—"

"That is correct, but unimportant—"

"Just listen," Eden said, talking over the man. "What makes you think I am the person to do this?"

"That's a good question indeed," Wolff replied, pointing at Eden. "In this area, the prophecy is quite specific. The prophecy states it is the child of the one leading us toward the End of Days who is the sole bearer of redemption. It is a cruel twist of fate, I grant you. Or maybe it's the perfect irony..."

"In English, please?" Eden said.

Wolff stared at Eden for several seconds. His gaze was so hard that a shiver moved its way from Eden's feet to her crown. When Wolff spoke, his voice held more gravity than before.

"It is your father who will set us on this path. Yet in you, there is the chance for another outcome."

"Whoa there, Wolfman," Eden said, holding out her hands as though trying to placate a raging animal. "It's one thing to stand here and tell me we're heading for the end of the world—"

"The End of Days. Not necessarily the end of the world, there is a difference—"

"Whatever." Eden shrugged. "It is one thing to tell me about that, but it is quite another to tell me that my father is involved."

"Not just involved," Wolff said, pointing a finger at Eden. "He, as the man in charge of the Council of Selene, will be the orchestrator of this change. It has been prophesied for hundreds of years. That is how it will happen."

"You can't expect me to believe that? My father is one of the kindest, most—"

"It doesn't matter," Wolff shouted. The Grand Master gazed down at his fingernails. "We are all part of this system. We play the roles we are destined to—"

"Stop now," Eden snapped, pointing at Wolff. She shook her head. "I can't believe I'm even listening to this—"

"Yet, here you are," Wolff interrupted, turning his gaze on Eden. Looking back at the deep-set eyes, Eden got the impression that she was looking into the barrels of a shotgun.

"You know, deep inside, that there is something about the Council of Selene that makes you uncomfortable. All that secrecy. All those lies."

Remembering her conversation with Athena, Eden snapped her mouth shut.

"Tell me, do you know what your father does for the Council of Selene?" Wolff looked down his nose at Eden, his eyes boring deeper into hers.

Eden furrowed her brow and swallowed.

Wolff hoisted one of his sleeves and looked at his watch. "Your father is in a meeting with the council right now, not too far from here. Do you know what they will discuss?"

Eden remained silent, her teeth grinding.

"Of course, you don't know what they discuss inside the council chamber, because their meetings are secret," Wolff said. "The Council of Selene has been pulling the strings for over two thousand years. I ask you this, how many wars could they have prevented? How many deaths lie on the conscience of that group of people?"

Eden said nothing as Wolff's barbed words hit home. Her mind whirred.

"The End of Days is the work of The Council of Selene. They have been orchestrating it, working on it since their establishment. It will be your father's duty to carry it out unless—"

"I know," Eden said, drawing a deep breath. "Unless I stop it."

15

WOLFF AND EDEN stared at each other for a long time.

"Okay, Wolfman, you've got my attention," Eden said. "Let's say for a moment that I want to help you. The Council of Selene is a vast and powerful organization. How do you propose we stop this?"

Wolff grinned, then leveled his finger at Eden. "That is the question I hoped you would ask." Wolff swung his finger to the side of the crypt and pointed at a large stone casket. The lid of the casket was adorned with the effigy of a Templar Knight, his hands folded in eternal prayer over the hilt of a sword.

"That is the Tomb of William Marshall," Wolff said, nodding at the sarcophagus. "Marshall was a man of war and peace, pivotal in founding the Magna Carta and a guardian of England in times of upheaval."

Wolff spread his hands wide, as though he were giving a guided tour. He strode across to the sarcophagus and then beckoned to the guards. The men paced across the crypt.

"Don't get any ideas," Wolff said, looking from the

unguarded door to Eden. "A dozen more men are waiting at the top of those stairs in case you decide to run."

The guards reached the foot of the sarcophagus. Without instruction, they placed their hands against the stone and shoved it. Their feet slipped across the floor.

"Looks like you need some stronger guards," Eden quipped.

The guards repositioned themselves, bracing their shoulders against the stone. With a synchronized heave, they pushed again, muscles straining. As though mocking their efforts, the sarcophagus remained unmoved.

"You can't get the staff these days."

Wolff scowled at Eden and then at the men, as though he couldn't decide who he was more frustrated with.

The guards straightened up, their faces red with exertion. Like the men in the van, they were tall and heavily built.

"Don't just stand there, get on with it!" Wolff roared, pointing at the casket.

The guards crouched down again, placed their backs against the casket and heaved. This time, a grinding noise vibrated through the crypt. The floor beneath Eden's feet shook.

The guards grunted and groaned; their boots slipping across the floor. The casket shuddered and shook as it moved.

Intrigue overtaking annoyance, Eden got to her feet and stepped up close. In the candlelight, she saw a gap appear at one end of the casket. She couldn't yet see anything inside the void, but Wolff's excitement suggested it was important.

"In death, Marshall requested to be enshrined here, away from prying eyes." Wolff gestured to the crypt. The guards changed position and pushed again. The casket moved more easily now, the gap widening from six inches to three feet in one shove.

"A lifetime of conflict made Marshall a very mistrusting man, you see," Wolff said, pointing at the void. The gap became four feet across, revealing a narrow staircase hidden beneath the casket.

"Nifty stuff," Eden said. "Although it's not a new idea. I've seen this before."

"Yes, of course, Horsam Rassam's mausoleum in Brighton," Wolff said, grinning at Eden. "That was an impressive find."

Eden didn't reply, silently rebuking herself for not realizing Wolff knew about that too. The casket ground across the stone a little further and then stopped.

Wolff grabbed a pair of candles from a nearby stand and passed one to Eden. "Follow me," he said, stepping down to the staircase. Miraculously, his wide frame slipped into the void and he disappeared beneath the casket.

Protecting the candle's flame with a cupped hand, Eden followed the Grand Master down into the passage. The narrow stairs descended quickly and then widened beneath the floor of the crypt. Dust-laden cobwebs as thick as ropes hung across the passageway, proving that no one had been down here recently.

"Our fore-brothers were excellent at building tunnels," Wolff said, his movements sending clouds of dust into the air. "They built some of the finest tunnels in all the world." Wolff reached the end of a passageway and yanked open an iron door. The rusted hinges ground and shrieked after centuries without use.

Eden ducked through the door and into a small chamber. She held the candle out before her and did a three-sixty of the space. The chamber was an octagonal shape, with various reliefs carved into each of the walls. She stepped up to one of the walls, her candle held aloft to illuminate the intricate carvings.

She gently brushed aside some of the grime with her fingertips, revealing a scene that depicted a man bound to a stake, flames licking at his feet. His face was contorted in a mixture of pain and defiance, staring directly at Eden through the stone.

"Jacques de Molay, the last Grand Master of the Knights Templar," Wolff said, sidling up beside Eden, the light from his candle joining hers. "Over here you see King Philip IV of France, the monarch who ordered the persecution and destruction of the order." Wolff's finger traced a line across the wall to the next relief. "Here is where it gets really interesting."

Eden studied the skeletal figure, draped in a hooded robe. Its bony hand was outstretched, pointing an accusing finger at King Philip.

"On that fateful day, Jacques de Molay issued a curse," Wolff explained. "He vowed that both King Philip and Pope Clement would meet him before the throne of God that year. They were both dead within eight months. It is that same power we will harness to stop the End of Days." Wolff turned and bustled up to a stone altar on the other side of the chamber. He placed his candle down and picked up a leather pouch which sat in the center of the altar.

"As you know, our predecessors, the Poor Fellow-Soldiers of Christ and of the Temple of Solomon, were a very powerful order," Wolff said. He carefully undid the pouch and removed a roll of parchment. "Over centuries, the knights obtained many relics from all over the world. These aren't the trinkets you see in museums. These are objects which, when wielded correctly, have profound and supernatural power."

"You can't expect me to believe that?" Eden snapped. "You really think that a few words sentenced two men to death? Next, you'll claim that you can conjure up a plague of locusts or something."

"You're right to be skeptical," Wolff said, sweeping the dust away from the altar with the sleeve of his cloak. "Time has produced many charlatans who have obscured the genuine miracles." Wolff spun around and eyed Eden. The candlelight danced over his face. "Answer me this: how did the Knights Templar, a non-governmental organization, become one of the most influential groups in Europe during that era, and continue to have a lasting impact on the world today?"

"Growth mindset?" Eden shrugged.

Wolff emitted a hissing laugh, which sounded like a train letting off steam. "This is not some new-age nonsense. The true magic lies in the power emanating from the ancient relics they stumbled upon. I'm afraid, Eden, that this will be something of a rabbit hole, which I hope you're ready to dive into."

"Do I have a choice?"

"When the order was disbanded," Wolff continued, ignoring Eden's question, "my fore-brothers hid the relics around the world, leaving only clues to their whereabouts. It was their intention that, should any one of these powerful objects be needed in the future, a seeker would unpick the clues."

Wolff stopped and fixed Eden with a steady gaze. "This is what we've been waiting for. Our time is now."

"Okay," Eden said. "What sort of relic are we talking

about here? Marilyn Monroe's lipstick? Or maybe the skin of an alien?"

"Not quite," Wolff crowed. "There is one relic which has more power than all others. That is the key to our salvation." Wolff's arms again spread wide, sending the reek of body odor throughout the chamber. "I am talking about the Seal of Solomon."

"The Seal of Solomon?" Eden asked, failing to stop the intrigue from lacing her voice.

"Yes. The Seal of Solomon is a ring which was once worn by King Solomon himself. Endowed with the wisdom of the king, the ring is said to give the wearer the ability to command spirits, the weather, and to bend reality to their will." He pointed at the intricate relief on the other side of the chamber which showed several knights on horseback. "The brothers used the Seal of Solomon to deliver revenge to Pope Clement and King Philip, and it is this relic we will call upon now to save humankind."

Wolff placed a piece of parchment on the altar beside the candle.

Eden crossed the chamber and leaned in to see what was written on the parchment. The document was evidently centuries old; its edges ragged and its surface marred. Eden focused on the writing. Each letter was painstakingly crafted, with the flowing curves and sharp angles that spoke of a time when writing was a thing of great importance.

"Where the oracle's shadow in the desert lies deep, turn your gaze where the horizon's secrets keep, follow the falcon when the sky is split in twain. There, a sentinel of stone marks the hidden domain." Eden slowly read the riddle out loud, struggling in places to make out the ornate text. "Do you have any idea what that means?" she said, glancing at the Grand Master.

The place where Wolff had been standing was now empty. Eden whipped around and saw Wolff standing in the chamber's doorway.

"That is why I have brought you here," Wolff hissed. "You will work out what the riddle means, and where we need to go. When you have my answer, bang on this door. Until then, make yourself comfortable."

Realizing what Wolff was about to do, Eden launched herself across the chamber. The thick iron door slammed back into position when she was still halfway across. A heavy bolt clanged into position on the other side, sealing the door in place.

16

City of London Police Headquarters. Present Day.

ATHENA SLUMPED against the wall of the holding cell. Her back and legs were already aching from several hours on the thin rubber mattress. Although her situation was annoying, she was more worried about Eden, kidnapped and dragged to an unknown location by a bunch of thugs.

Since her arrest, Athena had done nothing but run their attack and the subsequent chase through her thoughts. She had memorized the van's license plate, although suspected that would lead them nowhere—the kidnappers were far too professional to use a traceable vehicle. It had been a slick operation, with Eden as the target.

Athena thought again about their targeting Eden. She knew from experience that it would have been easier for them, and less dangerous, to have kidnapped them both. Taking one target and leaving another, allowed for risks like them being pursued, the alarm being raised immediately, and someone searching for them straight away.

However, if both of them were taken, it could take hours

for their absence to be noticed and even longer for a thorough search to be organized.

That meant the men had strict instructions to kidnap Eden. The question, of course, was why. Then there was the way the men had moved, under a clear chain of command. They were slick, professional, and efficient. Although that meant they completed the job quickly, it was also a clue. There were only a few organizations in the world who employed people like that—and Athena and Eden worked for one of them.

Through the iron door, Athena heard footsteps pound down the corridor. Having heard the same footsteps going back and forth several times, she thought nothing of it. For a small section of London, the City Police HQ was busy.

This time, though, the footsteps slowed outside the door to Athena's cell. She heard the jangle of keys followed by the locking mechanism releasing. Athena sat up straight and turned to face the door. The door swung open to reveal the stern custody sergeant. Behind the sergeant stood a man Athena knew—Baxter, a friend whose knack for showing up when required was uncanny. Relief rushed through her as she realized what his presence meant.

Baxter's eyes locked on Athena's, and he placed a finger against his lips. His message was clear: stay quiet and let me do the talking.

Athena nodded almost imperceptibly and rose to her feet.

The sergeant, oblivious to the silent exchange between the two friends, stepped aside, allowing Baxter into the cell.

"Your lawyer's here," the sergeant grumbled.

Baxter stepped into the doorway; his body language oozing self-importance. Although Baxter had never passed the bar, he certainly was doing a great job of faking it.

"Jonathan Hale, from Pearson and Smythe," Baxter said, his voice oozing confidence. In one slick move, he produced a business card and passed it to Athena.

"I've no idea how you even knew she was here. She didn't even give us her name," the custody sergeant said, nodding at Athena.

"As I told your superior, it's her employer's policy to not divulge any information to law enforcement anywhere around the world," Baxter said. "Before we waste any more time, you've seen that the paperwork is all in order. I need you to release this prisoner now."

"Hold on one minute," the sergeant said. "I've got all these forms to do and I still don't know who she is."

Baxter wheeled around and eyed the man. "That is none of your concern. Waste my time with further unnecessary questions, and I'll have you up in front of the judge."

The officer muttered something unintelligible; a vein throbbing in his temple.

"Let's go," Baxter said, indicating that Athena should follow him.

"Thanks for the hospitality," Athena said, strolling casually out of the cell.

Two minutes later, Athena and Baxter stepped out into the afternoon sunlight.

"That's a nice suit," Athena said, looking her friend up and down. "Don't you scrub up nice. It's a shame Eden's not here to see it."

Athena and Baxter cut quickly through the traffic and, thirty minutes later, slid into the underground parking lot at One Hyde Park. Baxter lowered the window and presented a key card to the security guard. The guard took the card, scanned it, and opened the gate. Although the whole set up appeared to be low key, Athena knew that was a front. One

Hyde Park was one of London's most exclusive and secure residences. If the guard had any doubt the people entering weren't supposed to be there, he could call a dozen more men at the click of a button, and armed police at the press of another.

The team had taken up residence in an apartment on the top floor of the development a few weeks ago. They had ended up in London following a relic which was supposed to have been sunk along with the *Titanic*. With a council meeting coming up in London's Dorchester Hotel, Winslow had decided it was a good idea for them all to stay on in London for a few more weeks. The team had spent several months without a break on board the *Balonia*, so allowing them some time on land was welcome. Although Athena had agreed in principle, she would have preferred to stay somewhere warm.

Once upstairs, Baxter pulled off his tie and dropped into a seat behind his computer. Hyde Park looked bright and verdant through the apartment's floor-to-ceiling windows.

Baxter's fingers flashed over the keys, loading a large map on the screen.

"Where exactly did the ambush take place?" Baxter said, pointing at the map.

Athena studied the map. She traced their route from The Cheshire Cheese pub, counting off the junctions they crossed and crosschecking with the buildings nearby.

"Right there," she said, pointing at a junction. "The van came from that direction. It stopped there and then, once they'd bundled Eden inside, they went that way. You think you can get security camera footage?"

"I expect so," Baxter said, tapping frantically at the keys once again. "There are three cameras overlooking the location where the attack took place." Baxter tapped several more keys. "Oh, that's strange."

The tone of Baxter's voice told Athena that this wouldn't be good news. "What is?"

"All of those cameras were out of action at the time of the ambush." Baxter glanced up from the screen.

"How is that even possible?" Athena said.

"I've no idea. It just says here that the feed was cut."

"How long for?" Athena said, her tone hardening.

Baxter chose one of the cameras and zoomed back through the recording. An image of the street where the attack took place filled the screen. "It was working an hour before." He played the video at twenty times its normal speed. Traffic whizzed past and people zipped down the road. Everything appeared normal until the screen went black.

"That's really suspicious," Athena said. She checked the timestamp in the screen's corner. "That was a few minutes before the attack."

The image re-appeared a second later. Athena checked the time stamp and saw that as she'd suspected, this image was from after the attack took place.

"Let's see if we can get a visual on the van. What route did it take?" Baxter asked.

Athena studied the map again and described the route to Baxter, who noted down the cameras they passed. Baxter checked the cameras one by one, only to see that the same thing happened to them all.

"That's a dead end," Athena said dejectedly. "They've clearly got someone powerful covering their tracks." She brightened up with an idea and swung to face Baxter. "What about the call to the police? It's no coincidence they trapped me on the bridge. They knew which way we were going, even before I did."

"Good idea," Baxter said, already loading up another program which they could use to access the call recording logs for the emergency services. He scrolled through the logs for nearly five minutes without speaking. "That's strange too," he said, finally.

"What?" Athena strode beside Baxter and leaned in toward the screen.

"There isn't a call. No one reported the attack, or the pursuit."

"What does that mean?" Athena said, standing up and placing her hands on her hips.

"Right now, I don't know. I suppose you could have driven past a waiting squad car."

"True, but then they wouldn't have known to block off the bridge. It was like an ambush. Can we listen to a recording of the police communications? They must record them."

"Yes, they do," Baxter said, his fingers still working at warp-speed. "And yes, we can get access to them." Within two minutes, Baxter loaded the audio file. He hit play and the voice of a police officer filled the room.

Control to all units, we have a visual on female, driving a motorbike at high speeds through central London. Over.

Static hissed down the radio.

"I wasn't going that fast," Athena muttered. "It was only a little bike."

Unit One to Control, received. Can you confirm the last known location and direction of travel? Over.

Listening to the conversation, something occurred to Athena.

Affirmative, Unit One. Last spotted heading southbound in

the direction of London Bridge, excessive speed, weaving through traffic. Exercise caution. Over.

As the recording continued to buzz with radio updates, Athena's mind whirred.

Unit Two responding. We're in position on the bridge.

"Those must be guys who got you," Baxter pointed out, unhelpfully.

This is Unit Three. We have eyes on the motorbike. Requesting permission to engage in pursuit. Over.

All units, this is Control. Authorization granted to engage. Keep the radio clear for updates. Control out.

"Wait a second," Athena shouted, realization occurring. She slammed her fists down on the table. "The first call came from Control, right?"

Baxter zoomed back through the recording and hit play again. "That's correct," he said, giving the exact time of the message.

"That means I can't have been spotted by a squad car."

"Good point, but what does that mean?" Baxter asked, looking away from the screen for the first time in several minutes.

"It means that someone inside the police already knew this was going to happen."

17

"I CAN'T BELIEVE he tricked me," Eden groaned, looking at the door. The iron was blistered and rusted. She placed her hands against the surface and pushed. The door didn't even move, held firm by the bolt on the other side.

Eden turned her shoulder to the door and shoved against it. The door rattled in the jamb but remained in position. Getting out of there was going to be a challenge.

Eden huffed to herself and paced across the chamber. Both candles sat on an altar beside the parchment. She gazed at the candles and figured that she had about an hour of light before they went out. To extend the period of light, she extinguished the candle Wolff had brought, intending to light that when the other was nearing its end.

"What am I supposed to make of this?" she groaned, staring back at the parchment. "It could mean anything." In her frustration, Eden thought about throwing the parchment across the room. She took a deep breath, trying to calm her nerves and focus on the matter at hand.

Her mind roamed with the things Wolff had accused her father of. Conflict roared in Eden's stomach. Part of her was beyond certain that he would never be behind something that was bad for humanity, but the other part just didn't know. Her relationship with her father had been so fraught with secrets and lies, culminating in his admission a few weeks ago that she wasn't even his daughter by birth, that she didn't know what to think.

"Now you're being ridiculous," Eden hissed, remembering how worried he had been about the admission. Eden had seen in his eyes that night, on the roof terrace overlooking London, how much she meant to him. She realized he was trying to be more honest with her, but old habits did die hard. She thought about the Council of Selene and how uncomfortable she had been about the whole situation since she had first learned of it. Winslow had promised change was coming, although for Eden it wasn't coming quickly enough.

The candle's dancing flame brought Eden back to her present situation. She watched the flame for several seconds, as it flickered from right to left.

A realization shook her. "If this chamber is sealed, then why is the flame moving like that?" she said out loud. She watched the flame for several seconds.

"There's got to be a draft, and if there's a draft, there's a way out."

Eden picked up the candle and moved to the wall on her left. She held the flame out in front of her, watching it carefully. By this wall, the flame burned motionless. She moved on to the next wall. Again, she held the candle still. The flame burned without a flicker. She groaned. Maybe a trick of the light, or her imagination running in overdrive.

She moved on to the next wall, which contained the relief depicting Jacques de Molay's execution. As she neared the carvings, the flame danced and flickered.

"Of course it would be this wall," Eden said, her eyes moving from the haunting image of the Templar Grand Master to the candle. "Jacques de Molay is showing me the way."

She traced the candle around the outside of the relief and found that the flame flickered more at the sides. She placed the candle down carefully and ran her fingers over the stone. A cool breeze emanated from behind the relief. She searched for irregularities in the stone, anything which could hint at a hidden mechanism. Her fingers caught on a small protrusion in the stone. Eden pressed against it, and to her surprise, the entire section of the wall bearing the carved scene shifted slightly.

"There's always more than one way," she whispered to herself, putting her shoulder against the stone and pushing with all her strength. At first, the wall didn't budge; the ancient mechanism resisting her efforts. Eden gritted her teeth, bracing her feet against the floor and throwing all her weight into the push.

The stone scraped against the floor, echoing through the chamber and down into the passage beyond. Eden hoped Wolff, or his guards, weren't waiting right outside the door. The noise would certainly give the game away. When no one charged into the chamber to see what was going on, Eden was confident they weren't close enough to hear.

Eden's muscles strained; her shoulders aching from the exertion. The rough stone surface dug into her skin. The wall felt immovable; a solid mass of stone that had stood for centuries. Eden repositioned herself, finding a better angle, and pushed again, grunting with the effort. Colored blobs flashed in her vision at the exertion.

Slowly, with a heavy grinding sound, inch by hard-fought inch, the wall moved. The grinding sound intensified. Dust and small debris rained down from the edges of the hidden door. Eden's breath came in short, hard gasps as she poured all her strength into the task.

"This could really do with some oil," Eden said, the wall section swinging inward. Eden stumbled forward with the sudden movement, catching her balance on the door jamb. She stood for a moment, breathing heavily, her body trembling from the exertion. The dark passageway loomed before her.

Eden crossed the chamber, carefully rolled the parchment, and slid it inside the bag. Taking a deep breath, Eden stepped through the opening, the candle held high before her. The passage ahead was narrow and low-ceilinged. She strode on, shielding the candle close to her body. She brushed aside more ropes of cobwebs with her free hand, revealing the tunnel stretching ahead.

After thirty feet, the passage opened out into a narrow staircase. Eden picked her way up the staircase before reaching a stone slab placed on top of the staircase.

Eden placed her back against the slab and pushed with her legs. Already physically exhausted, Eden hoped this slab wouldn't take too much work. On the first push the slab moved, letting a beam of dazzling daylight into the passage.

It took Eden three more minutes to shuffle the heavy slab to the side, exposing a square of uncharacteristically blue sky.

Although Eden didn't know where she'd been taken, she figured they couldn't be more than an hour's drive from central London. Clambering out, she saw where she was and almost laughed out loud.

London's Temple Church, the Templars' home in London. The round nave, a distinctive feature of Templar churches, was adorned with intricate stone carvings and topped by a conical roof that seemed to reach for the heavens. She gazed up at the spires which towered over the church, their slender, intricately carved forms reaching up into the sky, and berated herself for not figuring it out sooner.

Temple Church was less than half a mile from where Wolff's men had bundled her into the van. Their deception of driving her around London for an hour had clearly proved successful.

Two black vans sat at the front of the building, suggesting that Wolff and his men were clearly still inside.

Eden shoved the slab back in place and scampered in close to the church. She hid behind one of the buttresses and watched the vans for three minutes to make sure they were empty. When she was certain no one was inside, she sprinted to the van nearest the gate and heaved open the driver's door. Clearly confident that no one would bother them, the Knights had left the vehicle unlocked.

Eden yanked off the ignition cover and made quick work of hot-wiring the van. Within minutes, the engine roared to life. With another swift glance to ensure the coast was clear, Eden shifted into gear, and powered off into the busy streets of London.

WOLFF PACED across the crypt and threw aside the curtain that obscured the world map. Picking up a candle, he drew the flame in close to the map.

"As soon as the seal is in our possession, then we will make our move. First, we will strike Europe and North America. We will blister them with hot weather they have never seen the like of before. Their crops will turn to dust. Hungry people will turn to their governments demanding answers. Prices will soar as governments bid against each other for what remains."

"Grand Master, I understand your desire to reinstate what we hold dear across the globe, but this will cause much suffering and death." A voice came from the assembled brothers.

Wolff whipped around and saw Brother Pyne step forward from the group. The man, a natural leader in his stature, approached the Grand Master.

"I believe, Grand Master, there must be a way we can achieve this without the widespread—"

"How dare you question me!" Wolff roared, jowls wobbling. He poked hard at a map. His finger jabbed through the paper. "This is the way it must go. Fire and famine are the only judgements. The weak and impure will perish, and we will reign supreme." Wolff raised his hands as though pulling energy from the air. "As soon as we have the seal, we will begin."

"Grand Master, Grand Master!" came another voice, followed by footsteps on the stairs.

Wolff whipped around to see Brother Jenkins appear from the secret passage. Jenkins ran across the crypt, pushing men out of the way as he proceeded.

"What is it, Jenkins?" Wolff growled. "This had better be good."

"Oh yes, sir. It certainly is, I think. I suppose that depends on your definition of good. I mean, good to one person can be bad to another."

"Get to the point, Jenkins!" Wolff roared.

"I was watching at the peep hole like you asked," Jenkins said, still panting. "The prisoner, Miss Black, she studied the parchment for a while and then moved around the room with the candle. I'm not sure what she was looking for, really. I mean, there are some quite special carvings in there—"

"The point, Jenkins!" Wolff howled, a vein pulsing in his temple.

"She found the secret passageway behind the relief and has gone!" Jenkins said, his tone trill.

The brothers inhaled in unison. A tense moment hung between them.

"Excellent," Wolff said, finally, a grin lighting his face. He checked his watch and raised an eyebrow. "In less time than I expected, too. The vans were left unlocked as requested?"

"Yes, sir," another brother replied.

"Then I expect she'll have taken one of them." Wolff wheeled around and stared hard at Brother Pyne.

"You are to follow her," Wolff said, addressing Pyne directly. "She won't have gone far. Do not let her out of your sight. Soon she will know the truth of this matter, and she will do the hard work for us. All we must do is stay one step behind."

Without a word, Pyne turned and rushed up the stairs.

Watching Pyne go, Wolff decided there was no time to punish the brother's insubordination now. When this was over, should Pyne survive, he would be dealt with.

Wolff gazed back at the map. "Soon the seal will be ours... and the world will too," he muttered, a maniacal grin lighting his face.

18

Eden drove the truck away from central London, turning frequently and watching the mirrors to make sure no one was following. Driving the large vehicle reminded her of the truck in which she used to live, before she had experienced anything of the Council of Selene and the work her father did. At the thought of her father, a pang of betrayal knotted in Eden's stomach. Her mind buzzed with thoughts as relentless as a swarm of locusts. Her stomach roiled in the grip of indecision.

Eden noticed a young woman with a stroller walking down the sidewalk. The woman's face, lit by the bright afternoon sun, held an expression of pure, uncomplicated joy as she gazed down at her child. The sight made Eden long to return to her father, to Baxter and Athena, and forget all about the strange meeting with Grand Master Wolff. The familiarity and comfort of her old life beckoned. It would be so easy to dump the van, head back to the safety of everything she knew and leave the Order of the All-Seeing Eye and their secrets behind. But the other part of her, the larger, more dominant part, sought the truth.

Eden gripped the steering wheel tighter. She couldn't go back and pretend that nothing had changed. If there was any truth in what Wolff had told her, then Eden had a responsibility to get to the bottom of it. The fate of countless people rested on the decisions she made.

She once again thought about her father. Alexander Winslow had always been a secretive man. Although the habit of a lifetime, Eden had frequently explained to him that he was not working on his own any more. He had promised many times to be more open with his daughter, and Eden had started to believe him. The meeting with Wolff had turned that on its head.

Besides that, despite being involved in the Council of Selene, and living aboard their floating HQ—*The Balonia*—Eden had no idea how the organization operated or what they really did. To her, it was shady, and she didn't like it.

She slowed the van and swung it around a roundabout. There was one thing Eden now knew for sure. This genie was not going back in the bottle—she needed answers and was going to get them, one way or another.

Eden pulled the van into a supermarket parking lot in Hounslow. She parked across two spaces in the far corner of the lot and climbed out. There was a good chance the van would be tagged, meaning it was only a matter of time before someone tracked it down.

Eden searched the van for anything she may find useful. Without a phone or money, she was running on instinct alone. She stuffed a few items into a large kit bag, including a tablet computer, binoculars and a few other bits and bobs. She scoured the cab and found some cash tucked away behind the sun visor. Swinging the bag to her back, Eden marched toward the train station.

Making a long circuitous journey back into central

London, Eden decided on her course of action. Running a few internet searches in a small café in Soho, she decided how it was going to play out, too.

Just before 7pm, Eden approached the Hyde Park Regency hotel. The hotel, in its final stages of construction, promised to be one of London's grandest, boasting luxurious rooms and scenic views of Hyde Park.

Set over an entire city block, the concrete shell of the building was vast. Eden wandered around the back until she found what she was looking for—an area of the rear wall that was not overlooked.

She removed a length of rope from her bag which she had taken from the truck earlier. She created a loop at one end, resembling a lasso. She swung the lasso over one of the security cameras and yanked it, pointing the camera down at the sidewalk. Then, she threw the lasso up and into the scaffolds which surrounded the building. The rope snagged on the second try, and Eden used it to scale the fence and gain access to the enclosed area. She found the stairs quickly and sprinted to the roof.

Once on the roof, Eden crawled to the edge of the building. She peered into the gloom several stories below and watched a security guard pace around the building, flashlight swinging from side to side. The guy appeared to be going about his usual patrols. That was a good sign, as it meant no one was aware of her entrance.

She pulled the binoculars out of her kit bag and aimed them at the apartment complex across the street; the same one she had called home for the past several weeks.

Eden saw Athena first, studying something on the table in the center of the living room. Although worry clouded Athena's face like a shroud, it was clear that she hadn't been injured in the brawl.

Baxter joined Athena three minutes later. He looked even more serious than usual, which Eden was surprised was even possible. The pair scrolled through something on the screen. Eden watched them for several minutes; a sense of loss rising in her stomach. She longed to go over there and hug the people she saw as the closet friends she'd probably ever had.

When Eden had been watching for over an hour, the person she really wanted to see stepped into the living room. With a welling sadness, Eden saw worry lining her father's face. His normally buoyant, warm, and engaging demeanor had been stripped away and now he walked like a condemned man.

Winslow crossed the room and placed a hand on Athena's shoulder. Winslow turned to Baxter and nodded solemnly.

Once again, Eden felt the urge to run across there and tell them she was fine, but instinct prevented her from doing so. She needed the truth, and until she was certain that she knew it, she was better as an outsider looking in.

Half an hour later, Winslow climbed the stairs to the roof terrace. Eden refocused the binoculars on her father as he stepped to the railing and gazed over Hyde Park.

Grief welled in Eden's stomach as she relived the countless conversations they had in that very position. Silently, she cursed Wolff and his allegations.

Winslow drew a packet of chamomile cigarettes from his pocket, placed one between his lips, and lit it.

"I knew you hadn't given up," Eden whispered to herself. Although she knew the chamomile cigarettes were nicotine-free, Winslow had promised to stop many times. The fact he hadn't was another thing he had failed to tell her.

At that moment, a plan occurred to her. There was one

way she could find out the truth and put an end to this once
and for all.

ALEXANDER WINSLOW STOOD at the railing, the chamomile
cigarette dangling from his fingers as he gazed out over the
city. The smoke curling lazily into the night air brought him
no respite from the worry and guilt that gnawed at his
insides.

His thoughts were consumed by Eden, his beloved
daughter, out there somewhere in the vast expanse of
London. Despite his unwavering faith in Eden's ability to
take care of herself, a skill she had demonstrated time and
time again, Winslow couldn't help but worry.

The problem was, Winslow supposed, he had always
tried to protect his daughter. To shield her from the life and
death decisions he had to make on a daily basis, for years he
didn't tell her about the Council of Selene. As far as she was
concerned, he was working on an archaeological investiga-
tion somewhere in the world and would return when the
job was done. Now, however, this desire to protect her had
created a web of lies and half-truths in which he had finally
become ensnared.

Winslow took another lungful of the smoke. Over the
past few months, he had started to let Eden in. She was
skillful and inquisitive and often figured things out on her
own. But it had to be done slowly. To reveal everything all at
once was not the way to do it. The problem was, now, yet
again, Winslow suspected that his dishonesty had put her in
danger.

Winslow took another drag of the cigarette; the smoke

burning his lungs. He pulled the half-smoked cigarette from his lips and eyed it closely. Even this, this small vice, was another lie and another promise broken. Winslow dropped the cigarette, as though the object itself was to blame for all this deception and crushed it out beneath his heel.

He gazed out at the twinkling lights of the city and felt the strange sensation that Eden was close by. Without knowing why, Winslow turned and eyed the construction site on the block beside them. The building's concrete skeleton jutted up into the sky.

At that moment, Winslow decided that once and for all the lies had to stop and the secrets had to end. If he ever hoped to have his daughter back, to repair the trust that had been broken, he needed to be the father she deserved.

When Eden came back, he thought, forcing himself to be positive, he would let her into the Council of Selene in a way that only he could.

19

EDEN PACKED her stuff quickly and retraced her steps back through the building site and across the perimeter fence. Once outside, she walked to the Dorchester Hotel on Park Lane. The hotel stood grandly amidst the lush greenery. Warm lights glowed from the cream-colored stone façade. For once, the hotel was quiet. Currently hosting the Council of Selene's sessions all week, it was closed to the public under the ruse of ongoing maintenance work.

Eden walked around the building twice, searching for points through which she could enter unseen. As Athena had told her a few hours ago—although it seemed like a lifetime—security was subtle, although tight.

Eden crossed Park Lane and back into Hyde Park. When she was one hundred feet away, she ducked in behind a tree and dug out her binoculars. There were two guards stationed at the hotel's front door. The only thing suggesting they weren't the usual doormen were the small communication devices mounted in their ears. Eden also suspected they concealed weapons beneath their long black coats. This meant that getting access from street level was out of the question. Of course, if she could charge in guns blazing, that might be a different matter, but she needed to get in and out again with no one ever knowing she was there.

She lowered the binoculars from her eyes and gazed up at the grand hotel building. For several seconds she analyzed the windows and balconies of the elegant structure. She leaned back on her heels and was struck by the solution like a physical blow.

"It's not a great plan, but it's the best we've got," Eden whispered to herself. And, in terms of the sort of stuff she came up with, it wasn't that crazy at all. Eden remembered the time she and Baxter had forced Lulu King's helicopter into high-voltage power lines using only the rising sun. Maybe that was the craziest of her plans, although the competition was stiff.

Her mind made up; Eden stalked into streets of nearby Mayfair. She found a bar, which was lively enough for no one to pay her any attention and slid into a booth at the back.

She dug the tablet computer from the kit bag and connected to the internet. There were a few things she needed for the next stage of her plan. First, she contacted an old friend, sending a list of the equipment she needed, including an untraceable phone with a top of the range smart watch. Then she accessed the booking system for the Hilton Hyde Park and reserved a room.

The response to her request for the equipment came quickly.

Great to hear from you. I thought you were retired, or dead.

Eden smiled and typed a response.

I will be one or the other by the time I've finished this job.

Two hours later, Eden walked to the Hilton Hyde Park. She paused on the sidewalk and gazed up at the building, stretching over three hundred feet into London's starless sky. One of the tallest buildings in the area, the hotel not only contrasted its surroundings in size but in style, too. Built in the 1960s, the four-hundred-room hotel was an angular and jarring tower of concrete and glass.

Eden hustled up the front steps and checked in using the fake registration she had made earlier. The night shift receptionist quickly issued Eden with a keycard and pointed her in the direction of the elevators. Once inside the elevator, Eden ignored the button for the floor on which her room was located, instead navigating to the top floor.

Once on the top floor, she paced past the closed-up restaurant—the last diners had left hours ago—and searched for a door marked with the telltale *do not enter* sign. Eden found the door at the end of a corridor and pulled out her set of lock picks.

"It beats me why people put *do not enter* on the door," Eden murmured to herself, as she slid her lock picks into the simple pin and tumbler mechanism. "When I'm told not to do something, that makes me want to do it even more."

The lock disengaged and Eden swung open the door.

"This looks like the place," she said, glancing up at the utilitarian stairwell of concrete and steel. She shoved the door closed behind her, sinking the stairwell into pitch darkness. Not risking the ceiling light, Eden slipped out her newly acquired flashlight and clicked it on. Eden climbed the stairs and reached a steel door. Yet again, she picked the lock in the time it might take a regular person to find the key and stepped out onto the roof.

She gently closed the door behind her and eyed London's skyline, which stretched out in every direction. Most windows of the surrounding buildings were dark now, although in a few, lights still glowed, reminding Eden that despite the late hour, a city like London never truly slept.

She peered up at the sky; the stars obscured by the ever-present glow of the city lights. The moon, however, was visible—a waning crescent that cast a faint, silvery light over the rooftop.

Eden picked her way across the rooftop, scrambling over various air ducts and wiring looms, then crawled to the precipice. Three hundred feet beneath her, Park Lane's evening traffic continued to flow. Somewhere unseen, a siren wailed.

The air up on the rooftop was cooler than at street level. The breeze tugged at her hair. With a deep breath, Eden refocused her attention on the task at hand.

She slung off her pack and placed it on the roof beside her. She dug out the binoculars and turned her attention to the Dorchester Hotel, the venue for the Council's meeting, about six hundred feet away. At eight stories, the Dorchester appeared modest next to the towering twenty-eight floors of the Hilton Hyde Park.

Eden examined the Dorchester's roof space carefully. Other than the usual network of vents and cables, it was empty. To Eden's relief, it didn't look as though security had been placed there. Clearly working on the assumption that anyone looking to gain access to the hotel couldn't fly, the security team had concentrated their efforts on the ground floor.

"Human assumption is the weakness in any system," Eden muttered, placing the binoculars on the roof beside her. She stood up and pulled a large bundle from her back-pack. Unrolling it, she revealed a compact paraglider system. The request she made to her contact had been a long shot, particularly at this late notice. But the man had come through for her.

Eden felt the paraglider between finger and thumb. It was a good quality system; the fabric a dark, mottled gray, perfect for blending into the night sky.

She strapped herself into the harness and checked each buckle and strap, ensuring that everything was secure and in place.

Once the harness was on, she attached the glider itself. The fabric rustled softly in the breeze as she spread it out behind her. She gave the lines a quick once-over, checking for any tangles or frays. Satisfied that everything was in order, she gathered the lines in her hands.

Eden stepped to the very edge of the rooftop; her toes jutting out over the precipice. Over three hundred feet below, a double-decker bus hissed to a stop and disgorged several people onto the sidewalk. A gust of wind ran up the side of the hotel, buffeting Eden's hair against her face. She fastened her hair and looked once more out into the night sky.

She took a deep breath, the adrenaline now coursing through her veins. Then, she counted down from three and jumped.

20

Eden hung in midair like a frame from a Roadrunner cartoon. The paraglider billowed above her, twisting in the wind. She pulled at the control lines and angled the glider toward Hyde Park's dark expanse.

For what felt like a long time, she swung, powerless from side to side. The paraglider finally caught the thermal currents rising from the city below. Her descent stabilized, and she wheeled out across the treetops.

Eden glanced behind her and, noticing she was now a safe distance from the building, decided it was time to refamiliarize herself with the workings of the glider.

"Right, let's do this," Eden said, taking the controls. "This one goes..." she pulled the cord, and the paraglider banked wide, climbing again, almost to the height she had been when she'd leaped from the roof. She scanned the park below her and saw several people walking along the illuminated pathways.

"No one looking this way," she said, reassured that she'd attracted no attention, circling silently overhead. With the black fabric of the paraglider matching her fatigues, she hoped to be as good as invisible against the night sky.

"Now this one." She pulled the other control line and banked into a circle in the opposite direction. The city's nocturnal sounds, the murmur of cars and music from a distant bar, drifted up to her, muffled and faint.

"That's enough messing around," she said after she'd completed several circles and bolstered her confidence. She swung around and set the Dorchester Hotel, standing proud of the treetops two hundred feet away, in her sights. Although the hotel rooftop was close, paragliders were notoriously difficult to control, meaning it could take a long time to travel a short distance if the air currents weren't playing ball. As though on cue, a sudden gust of wind dragged the glider to the left.

"No, you don't," Eden groaned, pulling on the cord to twist herself back the other way.

She glanced up at the sky, growing lighter with the coming dawn. A pang of anxiety spawned in Eden's stomach. Once the sky became light, she would attract the attention of everyone within hundreds of feet—including the security guards stationed around the Dorchester.

Eden tugged on the cable and sent the paraglider to the right. Her best chance of landing on the roof, she thought, was to approach with the wind behind her. The problem then, however, was the danger of being swept straight over the rooftop and into the unknown hazards beyond. She needed to balance her approach with precision, using the wind for momentum while controlling her descent carefully to avoid overshooting her target.

She gritted her teeth and carefully pulled the paraglider into a turn above the trees, which lined the edge of Hyde Park, and over Park Lane. In contrast to its quaint-sounding name, Park Lane was a multi-lane road that was still alive with traffic, even at this time of night.

"Does this place ever get quiet?" Eden said, glancing down at the cars which were moving too fast for anyone to notice her, thankfully. "Give me a truck in the woods, any day."

Nearing the Dorchester, Eden checked her bearings and aligned herself with the hotel's roof. She adjusted the cables minutely, angling her body against the airflow.

"Just a little more," she said, feeling the resistance, and making a micro adjustment to guide the paraglider toward her target. The rooftop loomed closer, allowing her a better view of the maintenance equipment, air conditioners, and a tangle of exhaust vents, alongside satellite dishes and a weathered water tank.

Eden steadied her breathing and tried to move as smoothly and precisely as possible, despite the pressure. Twenty feet from the edge of the roof, she pulled down on both cables, slowing the paraglider and forcing a descent.

She readied herself for landing, bending her knees to absorb the fall. A gust of wind buffeted up the buildings, sending her soaring upwards. She rose thirty feet in a few seconds; the paraglider wrenching her away from her intended target.

"Don't do this to me," Eden groaned, angling the paraglider into another circle. She took a few moments to calm herself, shake the tension from her muscles, and swung back towards the rooftop.

Now aware of the updraft, no doubt a result of the building itself, Eden aimed lower. She made minor adjustments to the paraglider, approaching at an angle that appeared as though she would hit the top of the building, rather than land on the roof. With the hotel empty of guests, she thought it unlikely that anyone would notice her approach from their window.

"Come on, come on," Eden said, slipping close to the rooftop once again. Ten feet away from the building's edge, she pulled down gently. The paraglider moved through the updraft, but this time she was ready for it. As the paraglider steadied, heading for a textbook landing, Eden saw something that caused her to tense in panic. She yanked on the cables, slowing her progress, and allowing her time to read the situation.

Two men stepped from the access door and onto the roof. Both wore dark fatigues, which screamed military or private security. Currently looking the other way, the men had yet to see Eden's approach. But it certainly wouldn't be long.

Brother Pyne tugged at the collar of his shirt. Compared to the loose-fitting robes he had spent half his life wearing, the civilian outfit was stiff and constrictive. Not only did the outfit feel unusual, but Pyne was certain that he stuck out to everyone as a fraud. Surely people noticed him here, sitting in the park in the middle of the night, dressed up like this. Pyne watched as a man strode down the sidewalk a few feet away. Focused on walking in a straight line after a night in the pub, the man paid him no attention at all.

Pyne focused his mind on the matter at hand. Despite his reluctance to integrate with society, he had a mission to complete. While he didn't totally agree with the Grand Master's intentions, a personal assignment was an honor.

Pyne once again adjusted his shirt collar and settled

back on the bench. From the gloom of Hyde Park, Pyne fixed his gaze on the entrance of the Dorchester Hotel across the road. By the time Pyne had tracked down the van to a parking lot in Hounslow and made it back to central London to surveil the hotel, night had fallen. He was certain that Eden would attempt to hear firsthand what the council was planning, but hoped he wasn't already too late.

As the minutes ticked by, Pyne's anticipation grew. A chilly breeze swept beneath his jacket, but Pyne felt no chill. After years of dedication, he ignored all worldly sensations, focusing his mind on what was truly important.

On the other side of the road, a small group of people approached the hotel. Pyne dipped his head to conceal his face and watched. The group passed the hotel without even glancing up at the building. Pyne watched them go and then leaned back on the bench once again.

His gaze drifted away from the hotel, and something caught his attention. An object moved through the night sky, high above the hotel. Even though the object was nearly indistinguishable, blending with the night, it shimmered in the lights of a passing car.

Pyne leaped to his feet and gazed upwards. He jumped over the bench and ran deeper into the park, away from the cover of the trees. Reaching an area where the sky was clear, he squinted upwards. A dark shape slipped through the air high above him.

Pyne swung off his bag and dug out a pair of binoculars. His initial concerns about the binoculars drawing attention to him disappeared as he realized that whatever was up there must be important. As the lenses focused on the shape high above, a surge of exhilaration gripped his chest. He watched aghast as Eden Black piloted a paraglider through the night sky toward the Dorchester Hotel.

21

EDEN THOUGHT THROUGH HER OPTIONS. She could abort the landing, take the paraglider up, and circle again, but the coming dawn limited her time. Or she could land and take her chances with the guards. Having already come so far, Eden quickly chose the second option.

"Gently, gently," she whispered, letting some slack into the cables. The paraglider billowed, hauling her up and away from the roof. Eden angled the front edge of the paraglider down, reducing her speed as much as possible. She drifted closer, her eyes locked on the two men. Fortunately, the hum of the city and the wind were enough to disguise the sound of Eden's approach.

One man lit a cigarette and passed the lighter to the second.

"That nasty habit will kill you one day," Eden whispered, drifting ever closer to her prey like an eagle closing in on a mouse.

When she was ten feet away, she yanked down hard on the cables. The paraglider dropped, sending Eden falling toward the roof. She swung on the cables, sending her straight into the first guard's back. She raised her right arm, smashing her elbow into the big man's neck.

With a grunt of surprise, the guard toppled. His arms flew out in an attempt to arrest his fall, but the strike was too heavy. His face collided with a metal rail, part of the maintenance system, with a dull thump. As Eden had hoped, the strike knocked the man out cold.

Eden landed on her feet beside the prone guard and unclipped herself from the paraglider.

The other guard spun around, his cigarette hanging forgotten from his mouth. He stared in disbelief at Eden looming over his partner's prone form, completely taken aback. The guard spat his cigarette to the floor and reached for the handgun at his hip.

Eden didn't give the guy a chance to reach the weapon. She clipped the glider to the man's belt, then yanked hard on the control lines. The paraglider reared into the air, catching the wind, and pulling the man off his feet.

The guard bellowed as the glider dragged him to the rooftop's edge. Regaining his composure, the guard clumsily reached for his gun.

When the guard was a few feet from the roof's edge, Eden lunged and grabbed one of the paraglider's trailing cables. She pulled at the cable, anchoring herself with a backward lean to counteract the tension. The paraglider jerked to a stop, holding the guard in position two feet from the precipice.

The guard struggled to right himself, his hands lashing one way and then the next.

"Never skip leg day," Eden said, noticing that the guard had bulky muscles in his arms and shoulders, but his balance was awful. All that bulk was purely for show.

Finally, the guard's feet made a solid connection with

the roof. He glanced at his sidearm, clearly deciding whether to go for his weapon or try to unclip the glider.

Eden let another six inches of cable out, just to get the guy's attention. The guard shouted as the glider dragged him ever closer to the edge.

"Throw the gun, or I send you off the edge," Eden said.

The guard whirled around, assessing his situation. To quicken his decision, Eden let out another two inches of line.

"Let's make this simple. You have two options. Do what I tell you, or you'll be sleeping on the sidewalk." She nodded at the street below.

Eden let another inch of the line go, causing the glider to drift into the updraft. The glider jerked upwards, once again yanking the guard off his feet and across the precipice. He gazed down at the street below, his eyes bulging from his skull.

His feet kicked out, striking the rooftop as he tried, and failed, to get control of his movement. The guard's hands whipped frantically through the air, although with nothing to grip, the gesture was useless.

The updraft increased, whipping the paraglider into a frenzy.

"I don't know how much longer I can hold this," Eden said. Although she still held the line, it was honestly becoming a struggle. She feigned a look over the edge, her eyes never actually leaving the guard.

The guard eyed the drop behind him and visibly paled. "Okay, okay! You're crazy!" He plucked his weapon from the holster and threw it across the rooftop.

Eden picked up an accent but couldn't immediately place it.

"I've done what you asked. Let me go!" The guard shouted.

"You want me to let you go?" Eden joked, shaking the cable to give the illusion that she was letting it loose.

The guard kicked out at the rooftop, trying to get his balance.

"Here's the deal," Eden said. "Tell me what floor and room the council meets in, and I'll pull you in."

"No way. You're crazy, lady," the guard snarled.

"Do you know what happens to a human body when it hits a hard surface from this height?" Eden pointed at the street below. "Initially, you'll have the free fall. If you're into that sort of thing, you might even enjoy it. The next bit you won't like so much..."

"I can't tell you anything. I don't know anything!" the guard howled.

"When you hit the pavement, you'll break several bones, that's a given. But it's rupturing internal organs that's the nasty bit. At least it'll be over quickly."

The guard's muscles tensed, although Eden could see that his confidence was ebbing away.

"I'm sorry to hurry you, but time is of the essence here."

Eden jostled the cable. The paraglider moved erratically, pulling the guard closer to the brink.

"Okay, fine," the guy growled. "The meetings take place in the grand ballroom. It's on the ground floor."

"Thanks," Eden said, smiling sweetly. "That wasn't too hard, was it?"

True to her word, Eden heaved the man away from the edge. When he was safely standing on the roof and away from the edge, she turned him around and lashed his hands and legs together with the paraglider's cords. With a solid shove, the guy fell, groaning, to the rooftop. The guard immobilized, she pulled the glider down, taking all the air out of it.

"You won't get away with this," the guy moaned, struggling against his bindings.

"Don't you worry about that," Eden said, dragging the guy across to one of the air-conditioning units and tying him in place. She pulled at the knotted cables to test the strength. They didn't even move.

"I know who you are. I'll tell everyone what you've done!" the guard shouted, his tone becoming desperate again.

Eden stalked across the rooftop and tied the other guy in position. She checked his vitals. Although out cold, his pulse was steady.

"Tell whoever you want," Eden said, glancing around the rooftop. "But no one will hear you from up here. Now hold still." Eden thoroughly searched the men, removing their radios, cell phones, and weapons. She took one radio herself, although decided against the weapons. There would be no fighting her way out of this situation. If she got caught here, she'd already lost.

"Thanks again," Eden said, trotting to the stairs. "Enjoy the view."

22

EDEN PULLED open the door and descended into the hotel. She took the stairs slowly, listening for the sounds of approaching guards. On the first landing, she paused and fitted the radio into her ear. She was pleased to have access to the guard's communications, as now she'd have advanced warning if the two men she'd left on the roof were missed.

She retrieved the night vision goggles from her pack and secured them over her eyes. Knowing the goggles were to be an essential asset for the mission, Eden had collected them from her contact along with the paraglider. She activated the goggles, and the stairwell was instantly bathed in a luminescent green hue.

She set off, picking her way slowly down the first flight of stairs, listening carefully all the way. Reaching the hotel's top floor, Eden pushed through a door and into a luxuriously carpeted hallway. Doors flanked both sides of the corridor, although, with the hotel currently out of use, the floor was as silent as a graveyard.

Eden moved into the corridor, picking her way forward. She paused for a second and assessed the scene ahead.

Although the lights were currently off, Eden could see a motion detector set into the ceiling. Once she started moving down the corridor, the lights would come on. Taking a second to consider her options, she decided it wasn't worth trying to get past this system. Hopefully, the lights would have switched off again before anyone else passed through this part of the building.

Eden lifted the night vision goggles and set off down the corridor. After three steps, the lights blazed, momentarily dazzling her. Eden found the door to the emergency stairwell and pushed through. Once inside the stairwell, she paused again. As with most buildings, the emergency stairwell was not designed for everyday use and, as such, had not been furnished in the same style as the rest of the building. Emergency lights on the ceiling emitted a dull glow. Satisfied no one was approaching, Eden placed the night vision goggles back over her eyes and took the stairs quickly.

She arrived on the ground floor, hustled to the door, and listened closely. Now that she was near the place where the meeting would happen, Eden figured that security patrols would be more frequent. She listened for a full three minutes but heard nothing. Judging by sound alone, Eden would have assumed that the building was empty. However, she knew that not to be the case.

"Strange," she whispered to herself, an unsettled feeling rising within her.

Using both hands to avoid making any noise, Eden swung open the door and shuffled through. She let the door close behind her and assessed the grand corridor. Almost two stories in height, and wide enough to drive a car down, the corridor was decorated with an opulent array of classical paintings. Twenty feet down the hallway, Eden saw the double doors that led into the grand ballroom.

She shuffled onward, her feet sinking into the carpet. She froze and berated herself. It all made sense now. The silent corridor should have been a dead giveaway. The guards didn't need to patrol this part of the building, as it was all secured by a laser intrusion system. Green beams of light swept through the air in a calculated pattern, creating an invisible, ever-shifting barrier.

Eden pulled off the night vision goggles and realized that the lasers were invisible to the naked eye. Had she not been wearing the goggles, she would have triggered the alarm without even realizing she'd done so.

She breathed an inaudible sigh of relief and then backed against the wall. She resecured the goggles and stood motionless, watching the shifting beams for almost two minutes until a laser swiping her way forced her into action. She ducked, allowing the beam to sweep across the wall above her.

Eden had seen such security systems before, except they were usually mounted within the walls. This one emanated from a black cube sitting in the middle of the corridor. The device had obviously been trained to recognize its surroundings and would alert the guards if anything changed. Two similar devices were positioned further down, securing the entire length of the corridor.

Focused intently on the sweeping beams, Eden timed her movements with the precision of a dancer. As a laser swept by, Eden ducked and scurried across the floor. As another beam zoomed two inches above the floor, she stepped across it.

Eden's heart pounded as she inched closer to the door. She took two steps toward the door which led into the grand ball-room. A pair of laser beams swept nearer; one a foot from the floor, the other three feet above. Eden prepared herself to step through the gap. Sweat beaded on her brow as she watched the lasers draw near; the green beams seeming to taunt her.

She leaned, preparing to step over the lower beam and duck under the second. The beams swept another foot in her direction and then changed. One beam zipped high and the other low. Eden twisted into a roll, stepping over the low beam with less than an inch to spare.

She proceeded again before the beams converged into a grid. The beams rotated and swept outwards again, breaking into a set of horizontally tightly spaced bars. Eden watched; her body tensed like a sprinter at the start line. As the beams spun outwards, she dropped and rolled, her timing impeccable, passing beneath the lowest beam with a fraction of an inch to spare. She came up in a crouch, barely fitting in the narrow space between the laser patterns.

The door loomed ahead, tantalizingly close, yet still so far away. The final stretch would be the most difficult with the laser grid at its most dense and unpredictable. She took a deep breath, centering herself, drawing on every ounce of training and experience she could.

The lasers doubled back on themselves, spiraling into a helix. Eden took a chance and shifted three feet toward the door, before dropping to her belly and sliding across the carpet. Milliseconds later, she rose in a fluid motion, twisting her torso and slipping through a narrow vertical gap that appeared for a heartbeat.

With a burst of speed, she launched forward, her body a blur of motion as she navigated the last few feet. Lasers whipped past her, just a hair's breadth from her skin.

Reaching the door, Eden dropped into a crouch, her hand already reaching for the lock. The lasers converged around her. She peered right and left. Every angle was blocked by the incoming beams. The lasers shifted closer, offering her no escape.

Eden reached for the door handle. If the door was locked, she would have no time to pick it before the lasers arrived. Holding her breath, she pushed down on the handle. She barely heard the soft click of the lock disengaging over the pounding of her heart. The door swung open, and Eden slipped through and shut the door a moment before the laser grid swept past.

Eden pressed her back against the door and allowed herself a brief moment of triumph. Assessing the room, she saw no laser intrusion device in here. She counted out five minutes to see if any guards came her way, using the time to assess the room before her.

Opulent crystal chandeliers hung from the ceiling, looking strangely spectral in the green glow of the night vision goggles. Every inch of the giant room's walls was covered with paintings, each in a gilded frame, and each, no doubt, priceless. Luxurious drapes hung closed across the windows and at the far end, an ornate stage was framed by intricate plaster moldings.

Desks and chairs were arranged around the vast space, each with a small lamp and a microphone attached. A pair of headphones sat on each desk, too.

Eden walked between the desks, taking a moment to assess the setup, but being careful not to move anything. It appeared as though eight council members would be in attendance for the meeting.

She strode from desk to desk, looking to see if she could work out where her father might be positioned. She stepped carefully over various electrical cables that ran across the room. Looking like audio cables, Eden suspected this was the system Athena had mentioned that would disguise the members' voices from each other.

She completed a full circuit of the room but was unable to work out where her father might later be positioned. Each of the desks was identical.

Having learned all she could about the place, and satisfied that her presence had remained undiscovered, Eden set about her next vital task—finding somewhere to hide.

23

London, England. Present day.

End of Days Countdown: 5 days remaining

Alexander Winslow stared listlessly out of the window as Baxter drove him to the Dorchester Hotel for today's council meeting. The early morning sun, which normally would have been a welcome sight, seemed to cast a sickly, pallid light over the streets of London. The city, beginning to awaken, felt strangely lifeless and empty to Winslow.

Winslow glanced at his notes, which remained closed on the seat beside him. He should use the journey, albeit just a few minutes, to prepare for the meeting. With the date for the End of Days nearing, the session would be long and intense. However, with no word from Eden, he was struggling to think straight.

By now, Eden could be anywhere. But not even Eden's formidable strength and resilience, which he often regarded with pride, could alleviate his concern.

The problem was, there was one person responsible for her disappearance: himself. If only he hadn't kept things from her. If he'd been transparent, as Eden had repeatedly urged, none of this chaos would have ensued. But, like a fool, thinking he knew best, he had fallen into the habit of a lifetime and kept his cards close to his chest.

Winslow clenched his fists and pushed them deep into the upholstery. When Eden came back, he would change that, once and for all.

But what if it was too late? What if she chose never to come back? Right now, she was out there, alone, facing an unknown threat. And despite his faith in her, Winslow couldn't shake the feeling that this time, the danger was far greater than anything she had encountered before.

Winslow reached for his phone and checked once again for a message or sign of contact. Athena and Baxter had been up all night searching for leads but had found nothing. Still, the screen of his phone remained stubbornly blank.

He closed his eyes and inhaled a deep, shuddering breath. Right now, he had to compartmentalize his emotions, and concentrate on the task at hand. The Council needed him; the world needed him. He couldn't afford to let his personal turmoil cloud his judgment.

"We're here, right on time. Are you ready?" Baxter said, pulling up to the Dorchester's rear entrance.

"Of course," Winslow said, unclipping his seatbelt and gathering his things. "You'll let me know if there's..."

"Of course," Baxter said, turning in the driver's seat and eyeing Winslow. Winslow saw the same concern he had for Eden mirrored in the other man's eyes. Winslow had long suspected the pair harbored affection for each other, and now, with the concern in the younger man's eyes, it was plain to see.

"She's going to be fine," Baxter said, placing his hand on Winslow's shoulder. "I wouldn't want to be the person who gets in her way."

"You're right," Winslow said, swinging open the door. "But that doesn't mean we can't worry."

Baxter nodded knowingly as Winslow climbed out of the car. Winslow brushed down his suit and gazed up at the building. He froze as a sudden, inexplicable sensation washed over him. It was the same uncanny feeling he had experienced the night before—the unmistakable sense that Eden was nearby.

His heart raced, a mixture of hope and trepidation coursing through his veins. He spun around, searching for any sign of his daughter.

But the street behind him was empty. The only movement came from a few scattered leaves, dancing in the gentle morning breeze.

Shaking the thoughts from his mind, Winslow hurried up the stairs.

EDEN LAY in a crawl space beneath the stage. She had found the removable panel quickly, shuffled it across, scampered in, and replaced it. For now, she had the panel completely closed, although planned to shift it aside once the council members were in position. She switched off the night vision goggles to save the battery and made herself as comfortable as possible.

The total darkness combined with silence momentarily lulled Eden into a strange relaxation. She had almost passed out from exhaustion when the resounding stomp of heavy boots on the ballroom's parquet floor jolted her back to the moment. It was clear from the noise that several people moved around the ballroom.

Eden slowed her breathing and concentrated on the sound. The acoustics in the large room made it difficult to tell exactly how many people there were. Eden suspected there were at least five, maybe more. She checked her watch. It was shortly after ten a.m. She had been in the building several hours already. Eden thought about the city, which would now teem with people on their way to work, or tourists enjoying the sights and sounds. The thought of people going about their normal lives was incongruous to her, lying there, potentially on the brink of discovering that her father was involved in something heinous.

Using the sound of shuffling feet to cover the noise of her movement, Eden shifted the panel a quarter of an inch to the side. She peered through the gap with her naked eye. As she'd expected, the ballroom was completely dark, only punctuated by the tiny lamps she'd seen on each of the desks. It was clear the lamps were arranged in such a way that the user could see what was on the desk in front of them, but not anything else around the room. In the glow, she saw people settling themselves at the desks, but little else.

Careful not to make a sound, Eden placed the night vision goggles over her eyes and powered them up. The ballroom appeared, washed in a ghostly green hue. The councilor nearest to Eden was a woman in her early forties. The woman donned the headphones and scribbled a note on the paper in front of her.

Eden moved to the side, allowing her to see the next councilor. He was an Asian man in his late middle age. He, too, was focused on a document on the desk before him.

Eden shifted her attention again and then froze. Her father sat at one of the desks on the other side of the room, giving Eden a view of him in profile. Even in the strange green glow of the night vision goggles, he appeared exhausted, his shoulders sagging, and face lined. Eden felt a sudden welling emotion. Over the last few months, her father had become her confidant above anyone else. Any issues she had, she would go to him first. The part of her wanting to disregard Wolff's words and talk to her father screamed louder than ever.

Eden took a deep breath, steadied her nerve, and waited to see how events would unfold. She suspected that, whatever the outcome, the truth was coming soon.

Winslow turned over the page on the desk before him, clearly studying whatever was there with care.

"Thank you again for attending," Winslow said. He moved from side to side, clearly addressing the other council members, although he wouldn't be able to see where they were.

Eden remained still, spellbound by the proceedings. Her mind spun at the speed of light as it occurred to her that the people in front of her were some of the most powerful humans on the planet.

"We have one item on the agenda today," Winslow continued, looking down at the page in front of him. Although to Eden, this was the voice of the father she knew and loved, the headphones the other council members wore must have distorted the sound as Athena had described.

"As with anything we discuss here, it is of utmost importance. All members will get their chance to share their thoughts and reflections on the issue."

Eden considered all she knew about The Council of

Selene, all the things they controlled, and what Wolff had told her.

"Aries has a report to share with us first on the challenges we will have regarding energy generation."

Movement on the opposite side of the space drew Eden's attention. A figure shuffled some papers and then spoke. "What we're talking about here is a new era where traditional energy means are no longer reliable. This is no small task." His deep and resonant voice boomed through the ballroom. Hanging on the man's every word, Eden wondered what his voice sounded like through the distortion system.

"I have teams refining alternative, autonomous, and adaptive systems in preparation. To give you some examples, our solar arrays now incorporate nanomaterials for higher efficiency and self-repair mechanisms. We've also invested in geothermal systems that tap into the Earth's natural heat, designed to operate independently of any grid. Kinetic energy developments are promising too, capturing energy from natural forces."

Several council members mumbled in agreement.

"Creating energy is just half the battle, however. Storage is the other issue. We're investing heavily in energy storage solutions—batteries that charge faster, last longer, and are made from more readily available materials. We need to create a network that's both decentralized and interconnected. It must be a network that can support itself and adapt without the need for continuous human oversight."

"Without the need for continuous human oversight," Eden mouthed to herself. A chill moved through her at the ominous words.

"This is reassuring," Winslow said. "What is your assessment of the timescale for these systems to come online?"

"The transition is already underway. Almost twenty percent of our solar and geothermal systems are online. The rest are months away from completion."

Several members groaned, causing Aries to stop speaking.

"You will get your chance to ask questions," Winslow said. "For now, please let Aries speak without interruption."

Eden enjoyed hearing her father put the other members in their place.

"Kinetic energy harvesting is more complex, but we've made significant strides," Aries continued. "Pilot programs are exceeding our expectations. Conservatively, we're projecting a complete integration within three years."

"Three years is too long! We have just five days!" A council member interrupted. "How is something in three years' time going to help?"

Eden's heart beat faster, thudding at a volume she feared could give her away.

"That is true," Aries said, this time fielding the interruption himself. "But what we're dealing with is working into the future, not just the event itself."

Murmurs came from around the room.

Winslow cleared his throat, and the other members were silenced. "Thank you, Aries. Please continue your research and keep us informed. That brings us to the crux of our assembly today. Our projections are not merely theoretical constructs but are grounded in the analysis of several thousand years."

Beneath the stage, Eden edged forward, completely tuned in to her father's words.

"Our hourglass, I'm afraid, is nearly empty." Each of his words was measured and slow. "As we all know, the End of Days will happen at 6 a.m. in five days."

Eden peered down at her watch and programmed a countdown timer to the allotted time.

"Of course, we are still unclear exactly what the future holds, but we are prepared for all eventualities."

24

Ely, England. Twelve Hours Later.

"ANOTHER MILE DOWN HERE," Richard Beaumont said, pointing the taxi driver in the direction of the narrow lane where his cottage was situated.

"Please tell me we're nearly there," Vittoria DeLuca moaned from the seat beside him. "What is it with you people, building these lanes so narrow?" DeLuca peered through the window at the pitch-black landscape flashing by.

The pair had landed three hours ago, after several months on the trail of a lost Buddhist stupa in the Maldives. Although they'd worked hard to uncover the place, it had also been a fortifying trip for them both after twenty years apart. DeLuca turned and eyed Beaumont sitting beside her, his face illuminated by the light of a passing car—the first one in twenty minutes. She couldn't help but smile. He had aged well. He was still the same sharp-witted, slightly chaotic person she'd known all those years ago, but now more refined. Like a fine wine, Beaumont joked frequently enough that the comment became a joke in itself.

Beaumont and DeLuca had first known each other twenty years ago when they shared a passion for exploring the more 'out there' theories of the archaeological world. That path had led them to search for a mystical place not even whispered about in the world of mainstream archaeology: Atlantis. When the pair found some compelling evidence that the ancient civilization existed, but had it stolen from them at gunpoint by an unknown and brutal enemy, DeLuca knew they were on to something. Beaumont, however, turned away from the life of danger for a far easier one lecturing at a university. Maybe that was why the years had been so kind to him, DeLuca mused as the taxi rattled around a corner.

The pair had reconnected a few months ago when circumstances had brought them back together. DeLuca still thought they should be out there looking for the lost civilization, which she was certain existed, but was happy to work on that slowly. After all, if the place had been lost for over ten thousand years, what difference would a few more months make? Beaumont would succumb to her ways eventually; of that, she was certain.

"Just here," Beaumont said, pointing to the side of the road.

DeLuca peered through the taxi's windows and saw nothing but darkness on all sides. "What do you mean, just here? Richard, we're in the middle of nowhere."

"You'll see," he said, placing his hand across Vittoria's. "Just because it hasn't got a little white fence and a post box at the end of the drive, doesn't mean we're in the wrong place. Follow me."

Beaumont paid the taxi driver and scrambled out to

fetch their bags. He pulled their cases from the trunk and set off. He dragged their cases through a gap in an over-grown bush and down a narrow path. The cases rattled and bumped across the cobbles. Vittoria hurried after him.

Behind them, the taxi wasted no time in accelerating away, plunging the lane into deeper darkness than before.

Somewhere overhead an owl hooted, and an unidenti-fied creature scurried through the undergrowth.

"These people don't even have wolves," DeLuca said, glancing around. She found the English countryside reas-suring—there were no dangerous animals here.

"This way," Beaumont said, his outline now lost in the shadows.

"I like adventure as much as the next girl, but you better not be taking me to sleep in a bush," DeLuca grumbled, striding as quickly as she dared. "I work far too hard to lie on the ground."

"I think you'll like it. This way."

DeLuca walked toward Beaumont's voice and the sound of the wheeled cases bumping down the path.

"Eww, what's that?" DeLuca moaned as a wet and over-grown bush slapped her across the face.

"Sorry about the hydrangea," Beaumont said, his voice a little closer now. "This garden is a law unto itself. Push through. It won't scratch."

DeLuca shoved the bush to one side. Beaumont was correct that it didn't scratch but splashed a load more rain-water all over her. She stepped through the leaves and saw the outline of a cottage materialize against the star-studded sky.

DeLuca advanced again and collided with something solid. She stumbled, almost crashing to the ground. Recov-ering her balance, she realized the object was Beaumont.

The man had stopped moving and stood, his eyes locked on the house.

"Don't just stand there, it's freezing," DeLuca hissed. "Let's get inside."

Beaumont pointed wordlessly at the front of the house. More specifically, Beaumont pointed at one of the front windows. DeLuca stared closely at the glass and then saw what Beaumont was actually pointing at. A soft glow resonated out through the glass.

"I'm certain I didn't leave that light on," Beaumont said, his voice low. "I'm very particular about things like that."

DeLuca tensed and flashed him a glance. "You've not been here for a long time. Could you have forgotten?"

As the pair watched, the beam of light swung from one side of the room to the other.

"Totally sure," Beaumont said, his voice almost lost in the wind hissing through a nearby tree. "There's someone inside."

Neither the type to shy away from danger, Beaumont and DeLuca abandoned their suitcases and stalked to the front door. Beaumont placed an ear against the oak and listened closely.

DeLuca crept to the front window and peered through. She realized that from halfway down the path, the light could have been a strange reflection, or their eyes playing tricks. Now, with her face inches from the window, there was no doubt in her mind. A beam of light swept through the house.

"There's someone inside, alright," DeLuca whispered, pacing back to the front door. "They're looking for something using a flashlight."

Beaumont nodded, leaned into the flower bed at the front of the house, and pulled out an iron stake.

DeLuca raised an eyebrow at Beaumont's makeshift weapon. For one of the gentlest men she had ever met, he'd produced the hefty-looking pole with impressive speed.

"What?" Beaumont said, somehow seeing the gesture. "I grow roses, and they require sturdy support. This pole, believe it or not, is ideal for training climbing varieties."

"Give me that," DeLuca said, seizing the stake.

Beaumont shrugged and picked up a rock.

DeLuca placed her hand against the door and pushed. The door swung open, fortunately making no sound. DeLuca and Beaumont shared a glance, both raising their makeshift weapons a little higher.

DeLuca ran her fingers across the lock. No signs of damage indicated it had been picked, rather than opened with brute force. She peered over her shoulder to check Beaumont was in position and then stepped across the threshold.

Beaumont placed a hand on her shoulder, and the pair tiptoed into the hallway. Once inside, DeLuca recognized the smell of books and the subtle, musty scent of ancient relics. She knew Beaumont had lived here since shortly after their separation and imagined the cottage to be more of a museum than a dwelling. She expected the place to be full of artifacts, pictures, and books from all of Beaumont's various expeditions and research interests. The pair stopped and listened for twenty seconds. A scraping, padding movement reverberated from somewhere at the back of the cottage.

"Straight ahead, that's the kitchen," Beaumont whispered, an inch from DeLuca's ear. She nodded, and the pair pressed on.

Pacing carefully down the hallway, DeLuca was reassured to feel nothing beneath her feet. Whoever was currently inside was looking for something carefully and methodically, rather than ransacking everything in sight.

DeLuca reached the door at the end of the hallway and paused. She leaned in close and listened. No sound came from inside. The intruder had either let themselves out the back of the property or was keeping still and quiet.

"We go in on my count," DeLuca whispered. "You hit the lights."

Beaumont nodded in agreement, and the pair shared a silent moment. Their time in the balmy heat of the Indian Ocean now felt like a different lifetime entirely.

"Go!" DeLuca hissed, throwing the door open. The pair surged into the kitchen; their makeshift weapons held high.

"Whoever you are, you better have a damn good reason for being in here!" DeLuca bellowed, swiveling from left to right and searching for movement.

Beaumont reached over and hit the switch. The overhead bulbs blazed, filling the room with bright white light. DeLuca and Beaumont gasped in unison. DeLuca dropped the metal bar, which clanged against the flagstones.

They both stood frozen, eyes wide and not understanding the unexpected sight before them.

25

"WHOEVER YOU ARE, you better have a damn good reason for being in here!" someone shouted.

Eden jumped to her feet and sprinted to the window, which she'd left open on purpose. She reached the window in two strides and was about to leap through when she heard a voice above the pounding in her ears.

"What's going on?" the voice said. It wasn't a gruff, menacing voice, but a kind voice that Eden recognized.

Eden swung around and saw Vittoria DeLuca and Richard Beaumont standing in the doorway. Her eyes passed between the two, her lips still unable to form the words.

"I can't tell you. I'll have to go!" Eden said, turning back to the window.

"Wait a second," DeLuca said, her palms held outwards in the universal gesture of patience. DeLuca's gaze met Eden's. Clearly reading Eden's expression, DeLuca appeared suddenly concerned. "You're in some kind of trouble. We can help."

"You can't! You'll be loyal to him." Eden crossed back to

the table and shuffled the papers together. In her haste, she only managed to scatter them around the room. Several fell to the floor.

"Darlin', I've no idea what you're talking about," DeLuca said, flashing Beaumont a look.

"Whatever's going on, we can help," Beaumont said, taking a small step.

Eden stopped moving and eyed the pair of them again. Although she didn't know who to trust, she was painfully aware she needed help to figure out Wolff's riddle.

"Remember that time you rescued me from Lulu King?" Beaumont continued. "You took down five people and saved me from certain death. Let's say I owe you one."

Eden fixed her gaze on Beaumont. She narrowed her eyes, sighed, and slumped back into the seat.

"Whatever it is you're looking for, it looks like you came to the right place." DeLuca casually picked up one of the books and leafed through it. It was an academic text focusing on the reign of Pharaoh Hatshepsut, detailing her monumental building projects and the ways she navigated her path to power in a male-dominated era. Beaumont had penned one of the chapters himself.

Eden's head hung toward the table.

DeLuca placed the book on the table, took another step, and placed a hand on Eden's forearm. "Does your father know you're here?"

"No," Eden said, jolting upright as though a shock had moved through her. "And he mustn't." Eden eyed her hands in silence for a few seconds. "I'll tell you, but you must promise not to tell my father." Eden eyed Beaumont and then DeLuca.

"Of course," DeLuca said. "But first, I think we need a drink."

Five minutes later, they sat around the table, each clutching cups of steaming coffee. Eden explained everything, starting with her abduction, her mysterious meeting with Wolff, and then what she'd overheard in the council meeting.

DeLuca shook her head, her mouth hanging open. She tried to speak but clearly couldn't make sense of anything.

"I can't believe you got in and out of the council meeting without being caught," Beaumont said. "Those things are supposed to be so secure they're almost airtight."

Eden shrugged as though it was nothing. "It wasn't that difficult. I waited a few hours until they were done, then snuck out of the ballroom and found my way to one of the suites at the back of the building. I used a lightweight rope to scale down the back wall."

DeLuca exhaled, releasing a whole lungful of air in one go. "That's quite a series of events, love." She pointed at one of the books. "Why did you come here, though? And what do you need from these books?"

"Wolff said that there is only one way to stop the End of Days prophecy from coming true..."

"The Seal of Solomon," Beaumont said.

"You know about that?" Eden's gaze whipped toward Beaumont. A hint of her usual optimism laced her voice.

"Yes. It's an age-old legend. Whoever wields the Seal of Solomon has the power to make great change. You're telling me that this Wolff character knows where it is?"

"Not exactly," Eden said, hefting her bag from the floor. "They are the keepers of the seal, although its location has been lost for centuries."

"They've not done a great job of looking after it," DeLuca quipped.

"Wolff said that the seal is carefully hidden and will only reveal itself to the right person at the right time."

Eden removed a small leather pouch from her bag and placed it on the table. A silence descended over the room as the two archaeologists eyed the pouch in the way a hungry dog looks at its dinner. Eden opened the pouch and pulled out the parchment.

"Careful with that!" Beaumont said, clearly unable to stop himself when he saw an artifact being handled incorrectly. "You'll need—"

"There's no time for that," Eden said, flattening out the parchment. The Order of the All-Seeing Eye has kept this riddle for hundreds of years, hidden beneath some guy's tomb in London."

DeLuca rounded the table and read the writing on the parchment. "Where the oracle's shadow in the desert lies deep, turn your gaze where the horizon's secrets keep, follow the falcon when the sky is split in twain. There, a sentinel of stone marks the hidden domain."

"This is supposed to lead us to the seal," Eden said, "but I can't figure it out. It could be anywhere."

Beaumont, finally finding his spectacles, paced around the table, and gazed at the parchment. He gazed up at Eden and turned to DeLuca, the muscles in his face twisting with thought.

"It's a tricky one for sure," DeLuca said, rubbing a hand across her face. "We need to break it down, I think. What have you got so far?"

Eden shrugged. "I don't even know where to start. We've figured things like this out before, but I just can't seem to—"

"Wait a second!" Beaumont interrupted, peering hard at the parchment. He tapped gently at the parchment, then, clearly realizing he was now in danger of damaging the artifact, froze. "The oracle in the desert! It's got to be." His eyes blazed with a spark of realization. He leaped to his feet, his chair skidding across the floor, and dashed out of the kitchen.

Eden and DeLuca shared a look of intrigue.

"He gets like this a lot," DeLuca said, pointing a thumb into the other room. "I thought he might have grown out of it, but honestly, I'm glad he hasn't."

Beaumont returned two minutes later cradling a giant leather-bound tome in the way a priest might hold a child for baptism. He placed the book down on the table and took a seat beside Eden. He flicked through the pages with a speed that suggested he knew this book inside and out. "This must be in reference to the Temple of the Oracle. Now where is it..."

Eden and DeLuca exchanged another excited glance. Eden tried to make sense of the pages as Beaumont flicked through. She saw maps of star alignments, texts in forgotten languages, and drawings of archaeological wonders.

Beaumont's finger finally came to rest on a page featuring an elaborate illustration of a temple, its architecture unlike any modern structure.

"Siwa, an oasis in Egypt, is isolated deep in the Sahara Desert. It's a place out of time," Beaumont read the text and then eyed Eden and DeLuca, as though checking they were following his every word. "Alexander the Great visited the Oracle of Amun there, seeking confirmation of his divine right to rule. It's said that the knowledge and blessings he received bolstered his conquests." He paused, then added, "The Templars, ever seekers of ancient wisdom, were rumored to have taken an interest in Siwa, too. Perhaps they were drawn by the same allure that captivated Alexander— the promise of divine insight and power."

"That makes sense," DeLuca said, suddenly contracting Beaumont's excitement. "It's hundreds of miles from anywhere. It would be the perfect place to hide a relic. These temples were famously built in line with the stars and sun." She turned back to the riddle and poked at the parchment herself. "When the sky is split in twain, this could mean—"

"The Equinox," Eden interrupted. "When the night and the day are of exactly equal length. I've got to be at the Temple of the Oracle at sunrise of the equinox."

"What do you think will happen?" DeLuca said.

"It's hard to say, exactly," Beaumont said, leafing through another few pages. "Temples like this were often constructed in harmony with celestial events, like the equinox. The ancients believed that the veil between the worlds grew thin when the day and night were equal, and power—both seen and unseen—was amplified. If the Temple of the Oracle in Siwa follows this tradition, at sunrise on the equinox, you might witness something ... extraordinary."

"Like what?" Eden said.

Beaumont shrugged. "There's no knowing exactly, but if I were to guess, I'd say that the first beam of sunlight will reveal a hidden aspect of the temple."

"When is the equinox?" Eden asked. "I would check, but Wolff took my phone."

DeLuca pulled out her phone and checked the calendar. "It's two days from now."

A heavy knock at the door echoed through the cottage. The three eyed each other suspiciously. Eden visibly paled and gathered up the notes which surrounded her.

"It's late for visitors," DeLuca said, glancing at the clock on the wall.

The noise sounded again, even more impatiently this time.

Beaumont rose nervously to his feet and strode back into the hallway, with DeLuca a step behind.

"I'm coming," Beaumont shouted. The knock sounded once again, vibrating the heavy oak door against the jamb.

Beaumont opened the door to reveal two uniformed police officers, badges gleaming under the porch light.

"Good evening," the taller officer said. "We've had a report of someone lurking around in the gardens. Have you noticed anything out of the ordinary?" The officer's eyes flicked from Beaumont to the hallway behind. Maybe the gesture was a habit, but to Beaumont, it looked as though he was looking for something specific.

Suddenly feeling exposed, Beaumont forced a smile. He hoped the blood flushing his cheeks wasn't visible. "Nothing... nothing to report here, officer."

The officer's eyes bored into him. "I see, thank you," the officer said after what felt like a long time.

The second officer, notebook in hand, nodded. "May we ask if you've had any visitors this evening, or if you've seen anyone on your property who shouldn't be there?"

Beaumont shook his head. "Just me and my partner." Beaumont nodded at DeLuca, who stood behind him in the hallway. "We've been here all night and haven't stepped a foot outside."

The officers exchanged a glance. "Well, if you see anything, please don't hesitate to call us." The first officer handed Beaumont a card. "By the way, you know there are two suitcases in your front garden?"

The officer stepped aside, drawing Beaumont's attention to the suitcases which sat halfway down the path. With a courteous nod, the officers turned and disappeared into the night. Beaumont rushed out to collect the suitcases and then closed the door slowly, his heart pounding.

"Don't worry," Beaumont said, striding back into the kitchen. "It was the police; someone must have seen you coming in and not recognized you. We don't get many visitors around here, so when the neighbors see someone they don't recognize, they can often..." Beaumont's voice caught in his throat as he looked around the kitchen. The room was empty, the chair in which Eden had been sitting two minutes before tucked neatly beneath the table. The back door stood open, through which Eden had evidently disappeared into the night.

26

The Sahara Desert, Egypt. Thirty-six hours later.

End of Days Countdown: 3 days remaining

Eden peered out through the window of the Piper Super Cub light aircraft. The Sahara unfolded below like a vast canvas of endless dunes, its golden hues shifting with the rising sun. As the plane soared over the desert, Eden marveled at the intricate patterns etched into the dunes by the relentless wind. The shadows cast by the ripples and ridges created an ever-changing tapestry of light and shade. In the distance, she spotted a mirage shimmering in the heat. The illusion of water was a tantalizing reminder of the desert's deceptive nature.

"Siwa has a fascinating history," said the pilot, an affable Egyptian named Mahmoud, whom Eden had met in Alexandria. "The oasis has been inhabited for over ten thousand years. It was a stop on the ancient trade routes across the Sahara."

Eden glanced at Mahmoud as he gently eased back on the controls. He raised one hand and pulled the white cotton scarf, a keffiyeh to Egyptians, tighter around his neck. The scarf fluttered frantically in the draft from one of the Piper's windows, which didn't seem to close properly.

"You see, Miss Eden, Siwa is a special place," Mahmood explained, his voice cracking through Eden's headset. "It's in a depression, about 60 feet below sea level. This makes it one of the lowest points in Egypt." Mahmoud had taken it upon himself to narrate the entire journey with his life story and the history of the region. Eden had met Mahmoud in Alexandria and had trusted him immediately. With a tremor of sadness, she realized that his warm smile and caring attitude reminded her of another Egyptian, a man named Little Mo, without whom they wouldn't have discovered the Hall of Records beneath the Giza Plateau or got out alive. In the end, Mo sacrificed his life so that the rest of them could survive. This reminded Eden that too many good people had died on her watch, and that was something she needed to stop.

"The nearest town, Marsa Matruh, is about three hundred miles north of here on the Mediterranean coast," Mahmood continued. "There is the road, look." Mahmoud pointed below them. "The road wasn't built until the 1980s. Before, reaching Siwa was very difficult. Many days travel by camel or donkey through the desert."

Eden peered out and saw the road far beneath them. A succession of trucks and buses rumbled in both directions. Although traveling overland would have been more anonymous, she couldn't spare the two days of travel to get to and from the tiny patch of green in the great ocean of sand. She had used one of her off-the-books bank accounts to pay Mahmoud's fee.

"We will get our first sight of the oasis in a minute or so." Mahmoud's voice rose a few semitones in excitement.

Eden craned her neck, peering through the windshield.

"There, look!" Mahmoud shouted. Right on cue, the oasis emerged like a verdant jewel amidst the desolate sands. From the air, it was a tapestry of lush greenery; a stark contrast to the tawny dunes. In the distance the salt lakes glinted, their mirror-like surfaces reflecting the sky's brilliant blue.

With practiced hands, Mahmoud gently eased back on the controls, guiding the Piper Super Cub into a gentle descent that brought them down to a few hundred feet.

"And here is our airstrip," Mahmoud said, pointing out the thin strip of tarmac that lay a few miles north of the oasis. "Very small airport. But good enough for us." He reduced the throttle, slowly easing back on the power. The plane's nose dipped slightly as they started to lose altitude.

Watching Mahmoud's confidence with the machine, Eden thought of Baxter and his ability to drive almost every machine in existence, and probably several that were no longer around. Although she would never tell him as such —she wouldn't want him to get arrogant, after all—having Baxter by her side during their various missions had been invaluable.

Mahmoud banked the Piper Cub, circling the airport.

"I must compensate for crosswind," Mahmoud explained. "The wind blows across the runway, not down it. This can make landing tricky."

Eden assessed the airport's layout from their vantage point. A modest communications tower, capped with red and white paint, stood at one side. A rust-stained radar dish angled toward the heavens. Two large aircraft hangars sat on one side. A few rugged vehicles sat haphazardly near the main building, and Eden could make out the shapes of a couple of small, propeller-driven aircraft beneath simple metal awnings.

Mahmoud pulled back gently on the yoke, slowing the plane's descent, and leveling it out a few feet above the tarmac. The plane's shadow appeared, racing ahead of them on the ground. Mahmoud throttled back, letting the wheels kiss the ground in a landing better than most commercial flights Eden had been on.

"Impressive stuff," Eden said. "You make it look easy."

Mahmoud taxied the Piper Cub toward a cluster of low buildings and brought them gently to a stop. The engine's roar died down to a contented purr before quieting completely.

Mahmoud swung open the door and scrambled out. The dry desert air rushed in, prickling Eden's skin. Eden swung open the passenger door and clambered down to the sand-covered tarmac.

Completing a full turn, Eden realized how remote this place was. Dunes rose and fell all around them, with one black-topped road leading toward the small oasis town. With surprise, Eden noticed the airstrip didn't even have a boundary fence. She realized that out here, miles from anywhere, they probably didn't need one.

"Here is your vehicle," Mahmoud said, pointing at a cloud of dust a mile or so away. Eden had borrowed a vehicle as part of the deal she'd made with Mahmoud. Although she'd stipulated that she wanted something capable of driving across the desert, she didn't give any further requirements.

"What vehicle is it?" Eden asked, squinting at the dust cloud. Heat currents radiating from the desert made the vehicle dance from side to side.

"I get the feeling that you'll like it," Mahmoud said, with a glint in his eye. "It's what you need around here."

The distant rumble grew louder, and a mustard yellow Land Rover Defender burst into view. Eden couldn't help but grin at the sight of the machine, remembering the one she owned back in England.

The Land Rover hurtled toward them, quickly covering the distance. The canvas that typically covered the back had been rolled down. The Land Rover rumbled to a stop beside Eden and Mahmoud. The driver jumped out and embraced Mahmoud, the engine still running.

"Miss Eden, your vehicle," Mahmoud said, pointing at the car.

Eden transferred her pack from the Piper Cub to the Land Rover and scrambled into the driver's seat. She set the phone she'd bought back in Alexandria up on the dashboard and loaded the map. With a wave at Mahmoud, Eden punched the gas and sent the Land Rover into a wide arc around the airfield.

Ten minutes later, Eden rumbled down the desert road and into the oasis. Small mud brick and boxy concrete buildings crowded around the crisscrossing narrow lanes. She slowed to get a good look at the buildings, some set around tree-shaded internal courtyards.

Following the navigation, Eden turned from the main road and down a dirt track. A group of children, kicking a ball around in the dust, scurried off the road as Eden passed. A sleeping dog raised its head at the sound of the engine, then, sensing no threat, returned to his previous position. To Eden, the place felt as though she'd stepped back in time. As the Land Rover rumbled over the uneven road, she wondered how much the town had changed since the Templars were here over seven hundred years ago.

Eden reached the town center and stopped the Land Rover at the side of the road. Parking spaces didn't seem to exist here, with vehicles left wherever their owners wanted.

She grabbed her phone, jumped out, and walked into the town's small central square. Although the afternoon was wearing on, she had several hours until darkness fell across the oasis. If Beaumont's predictions were correct, she would need to wait for the sun to rise again before the secret was revealed.

First, Eden planned to rest and refuel. Experience had taught her that opportunities to catch some rest didn't come often and, as such, should be valued.

Walking through the central square, she paused to look up at the mud-brick Fortress of Shali, which was by far the oasis' tallest structure. The ruined structure, although still standing after centuries, now appeared as though it were melting into the earth.

Eden ducked into a side street and wove her way through stalls selling everything from the crystalized salt that made Siwa famous, to fabrics and food. After a few minutes, she found what she was looking for, a restaurant whose tables lined the street, allowing her to eat whilst keeping an eye on anyone coming her way.

27

BROTHER PYNE SAT in a small restaurant, partly obscured by the shade of an awning. For most people, the heat was blistering, but Pyne didn't notice things like that.

Pyne peered down at another new outfit. He now wore a traditional Egyptian jellabiya and a white cotton skullcap. Pyne preferred this outfit to the pants and jacket he'd been forced to wear in London. He reflected this outfit didn't feel much different from the robes of the order, which he wore with pride.

Pyne, appearing to be engrossed in the display of a fabric stall across the street, shifted his gaze to a restaurant thirty feet away. His eyes picked out the familiar figure seated at one of the outdoor tables—Eden Black.

Following Eden had been easier than Pyne had expected. After she'd left the Dorchester in London, she had caught a train to Cambridge, less than an hour north of London. Pyne had boarded the same train and sat at the end of the carriage.

From there, fortunately, Eden had gone to ground for a few hours, giving Pyne the chance to organize a car. Come nightfall, Eden had taken a taxi to an address in the nearby town of Ely. Pyne followed and watched from a distance as two people arrived at the house, then spent some time inside before Eden left in a hurry. From there it had been the simple matter of following her to the airport and piecing together her onward plans. Once Pyne learned she was coming to Egypt, he figured that Siwa, with its links to the Templars, was a likely destination.

As Eden ordered food and drinks from the server, Pyne once again considered Eden's impressive abilities. Where Grand Master Wolff had failed, she had figured out the riddle. To have made it this far on her own was a testament to her resolve. She possessed a spark; an innate ability to unravel the secrets that had eluded so many before her.

The phone stashed deep within Pyne's tunic buzzed. He pulled it out and answered.

"Brother Pyne, report." Grand Master Wolff's voice came down the line.

"She arrived in Siwa an hour ago, right on time."

"Very good, very good indeed," Wolff said. "What's she doing?"

Pyne eyed Eden again, this time not bothering to mask his gaze. With Eden facing the other way, he didn't need to worry about her noticing him. Also, in his disguise, there was nothing about him to raise suspicions.

"She's sitting in a restaurant. She's been there about five minutes. I got here a few hours earlier and followed her, driving in from the airstrip."

"Did she see you?" Wolff snapped.

"No, of course not," Pyne said. "She's walking around here like a tourist."

"That's good, that's good," Wolff said. "That means she doesn't even suspect anyone is looking for her."

"Yes, that's what I just..."

"Stay on her tail," Wolff snapped, interrupting Pyne. "Do not engage with her in any way. She is more dangerous than you can imagine. I will arrange transport now and be there tomorrow." The line went dead.

EDEN LEANED back in the chair and felt the warm afternoon sun on her face. As it had been since this whole sorry affair had begun, Eden's mind was a tempest of worry. Having spent several years living on her own and relying on no one, it had taken Eden a long time to feel as though she were part of the crew on board the *Balonia*. Now, with everything that had happened, she felt betrayed and alone.

In her mind's eye, she pictured the people she had recently grown to rely on. She thought of Baxter, Athena, and her father. Of course, they would certainly all say they loved her, but Eden couldn't stand by while they worked toward the End of Days.

To distract herself from the painful memories, Eden pulled the notes she'd made from her pocket. She thumbed through the various pieces of paper, reminding herself what she'd learned from DeLuca and Beaumont, her father, and finally from Wolff himself.

She thought again about what Wolff had told her about the End of Days being the end of life as we know it. Nothing would be the same again. She remembered hearing the same words spoken by her father during the council meeting.

A pair of local children weaved through the streets. The boy wore a light cotton jellabiya, while the girl's dress fluttered behind her. They moved with the carefree agility of youth, darting between stalls and around the legs of shoppers and tourists.

Watching the children, a wave of emotion broke across Eden. People throughout the world deserved to live in peace. They certainly didn't deserve to be dragged into something like this.

The children ducked under a stall selling watermelons and then darted into a backstreet, giggling all the way. Although the children had disappeared from sight, the sound of their laughter continued to ring in Eden's ears.

"Your tea, miss."

The server placed a large metal teapot on the table in front of her. The pot was tall with a long curving spout and polished to a shine.

"Thank you," Eden said, swallowing the emotion and wiping at her eyes.

The server, a boy who couldn't have been older than fifteen, poured the tea into a small cup. The liquid came out in a thin, steaming stream. He replaced the pot on the table and padded back into the restaurant. He returned a minute later carrying a tray laden with local delicacies: fresh aish baladi bread still warm from the oven, a bowl of aromatic ta'meya, the Egyptian take on falafel, and a plate of dates stuffed with almonds. To complement the meal, there was a refreshing salad of cucumbers and tomatoes, dressed with olive oil and lemon. Eden inhaled the comforting scents; her appetite awakened by the feast. She ate quickly, dipping everything in the tahini dip and frequently sipping the sweet, citrus tea.

Eden finished the tea and poured herself another. As she placed the teapot back in the center of the table, a flicker of movement caught her eye. In the highly polished metal, a distorted reflection sent a sudden chill down her spine. It was the unmistakable image of a person, watching her from the café next door.

Eden froze, a chunk of bread already halfway to her mouth. She stared closely at the reflection in the teapot, trying to work out whether it was what she'd first thought. Keeping her movements deliberate and unhurried, Eden continued to eat. She casually took a sip of tea and poured some more into the cup, replacing the pot to give her a better view of what was going on behind her.

A cold, prickling sensation crept over her skin. A man behind her, his eyes locked on her back. With Eden facing the opposite direction, the figure made no attempt to hide that he was watching her. To Eden's heightened senses, he might as well have carried a neon sign above his head which read, *I am watching you.*

Eden fought the urge to turn around and confront her mysterious observer directly, knowing that any sudden movement would betray her awareness of his presence. She focused on the reflection, trying to discern any identifying features. The distorted image made it difficult to make out clear details, but she could see that the figure was male, and wearing traditional Egyptian clothing.

"Damn you, Wolff," she whispered, suspecting that the man was one of Wolff's knights who had somehow followed her here. "Your guided tour ends now."

With a nonchalant flick of her wrist, Eden slid a few Egyptian pounds under the edge of her plate. She stole a look at the teapot. Clearly realizing she was about to make a move, her observer rose his seat.

Eden feigned a casual stretch and stood. She folded her notes, all of which she'd memorized anyway, and slipped them into a pocket. Then, in a sudden burst of energy, she grabbed the teapot from the table, spun around, and charged at the man.

Clearly realizing Eden was coming his way, the man froze. His gaze darted around the street as he assessed his options, weighing the risks of confrontation against the potential benefits of escape. Although his movements were subtle, they removed any doubt in Eden's mind that this was not just a casual observer.

In that moment of hesitation, Eden closed the distance between them, her eyes locked on her target.

When she was ten feet away, the man came to a decision. He stepped back, wheeled around, and bolted down the street.

Prepared for him to run, Eden threw the pot at the man's legs. The heavy metal object sailed through the air, sending a thin stream of tea spiraling out. The man took two more steps, his feet sinking into the sand, before the pot caught up with him. The heavy pot thwacked him on the back of his legs, causing him to stumble. His hands flew up, and he missed a step. The man took another stride, regaining his footing, but this momentary falter gave Eden enough time to close the gap.

Eden leaped, closing the distance between them in a heartbeat. She shoved the man hard, her palms striking his back with a force great enough to crack ribs. The man missed another step and stumbled, his feet scrambling for purchase on the uneven ground. Despite the force of her blow, he managed to maintain his balance, his body twisting and contorting to stay upright.

A heartbeat later, the man found his footing. He rotated on his heel and sent a fist careening toward Eden's face. She ducked, his knuckles grazing her cheek. Eden countered with a rapid jab to his midsection, her fists connecting with a crack. The man grunted, but he didn't go down.

The man dropped on to his back foot and, in a blur of speed, launched into a kick.

Eden blocked it. Her forearm absorbed the impact with a white-hot pain. She responded with an elbow strike, aiming for his jaw. The man deflected it with a sweep of his hand.

Eden bounced into a powerful roundhouse kick. The man moved to block, but Eden's kick was a ruse. As he raised his arms to defend, she dropped low, sweeping her leg across the ground in a lightning-fast strike. Her foot connected with his ankles, the impact sending a shockwave up her leg.

The man's eyes flared in surprise as his legs flew out from beneath him. He toppled backward. His arms flailed in a futile attempt to regain his balance. With a heavy thud, he crashed to the ground, his back sinking into the soft sand.

Eden pounced on the fallen man, her knee pressing into his chest to keep him pinned. She reached for the teapot, grasping its handle tightly.

"You're one of Wolff's men," Eden shouted, holding the teapot high and ready to strike.

The man swung and knocked the teapot from Eden's hands; it thudded to the sand some distance away. He tried to struggle up, but Eden knocked him back again, this time face down. She forced his arm up behind his back. The man struggled against the hold; Eden pushed harder on the twisted arm. When he was still, she yanked his head out of the sand. The man gasped for breath and spat sand from his mouth.

Eden took a second to check her surroundings. People

had stopped to watch the conflict, but none seemed to want to get involved.

"Is Wolff here?" Eden said, getting in close behind the man's head. "Tell me now or I'll push your face into the sand until you go limp." Before the man could answer, Eden shoved his face down into the imprint already left from the last impact. The soft sand and dust almost came up to his ears.

The man gurgled and struggled. After five seconds, Eden pulled his head out again.

"Don't even pretend you don't understand me," Eden snarled. "Where is Wolff?"

"Miss, miss!" Another voice cut through the noise.

Eden cast a look over her shoulder and saw the boy who'd served her food running her way.

"People are coming!" the boy shouted, pointed frantically down the lane. "Two of them, running this way!"

Eden spun in the direction the boy had indicated. Although she couldn't see anyone, she heard the telltale sound of running feet and cries as people jumped out of the way.

Eden leaped to her feet, rewarded the man with a kick to the ribs, and set off in the other direction.

28

EDEN WEAVED amid the stalls and cafés, kicking up dust. The clamor of bartering voices and the clatter of merchants' wares became a distant rumble as she focused on putting distance between her and her pursuers.

Eden ducked in behind a stall selling spices. Countless sacks of brightly colored powders sat open, tempting passersby with their rich, aromatic fragrance. The merchant was too busy dealing with a customer to notice Eden drop behind a large sack.

Eden scanned the crowd for her pursuers. She still couldn't see who was on her tail but, like watching the ripple without seeing the stone, people parted in waves, clearly getting out of the way of someone barging through.

Eden took a moment to assess her options. The tip-off from the boy in the café, and her quick dash away, had bought her some time. She didn't plan on wasting her lead just to get a clear view of whatever thugs were on her tail this time, though.

A greater, more serious question occupied her mind

now—had Wolff figured that she was going to the Temple of the Oracle or was he following blind? Eden hoped it was the latter.

Eden spun around and, keeping low, darted toward a narrow alleyway between mud-brick buildings. Although she planned to find the Seal of Solomon and stop the End of Days, she wasn't giving the relic to Wolff or his cronies.

Inside the alleyway and out of sight, Eden straightened up and sprinted away. A lattice of washing lines cast the space into a kaleidoscope of shadows. As Eden ran, the market's cacophony dissipated beneath sounds from the surrounding homes. Laughter mingled with the clatter of dishes, and children's cries blended with the rhythmic thumping of a carpet being cleaned.

Eden reached a crossroads and barreled right. Picturing the town, she figured that this passage would take her back to her parked Land Rover. From there, she could get out of the town center, lie low for a few hours, and plan her next move. She berated herself for her carelessness. Having not picked up on a tail, Eden had assumed she'd made it here undetected. At least now that her tail had been revealed, she would work on losing them.

The alley became narrower still, now a few inches on either side of Eden's pumping elbows. She slowed her pace to slip beside a stack of clay pots. Glancing through an open door, Eden saw a man sculpting wet clay, transforming it into a pot. His hands moved deftly through the clay and his foot pumped the pedal, which powered the wheel.

Eden ran around a corner, causing a pair of chickens pecking in the dust, to leap noisily into flight. She took a small flight of stairs in two giant bounds and burst out into the dazzling sunshine. She ran across an open patch of hardened earth, surrounded by mud-brick buildings.

Several rusting vehicles sat in one corner, and in another a pair of camels chewed at a bale of straw. A group of children stood around a soccer goal painted on the far wall. Right at that moment, a weathered ball rolled across the dusty ground and landed at Eden's feet. Realizing she'd inadvertently stumbled into the center of a soccer game, Eden spun around and struck the ball, sending it high over the children and into the makeshift goal. The children erupted into a round of impromptu applause. Eden flicked the kids a salute and sprinted on.

Five minutes later, out of breath and covered in sweat, Eden sprinted down the main street and leaped into the Land Rover's driver's seat. She turned the key, and the engine roared obediently to life. Sending a silent thanks to Mahmoud for keeping the machine in good condition, Eden swung the heavy wheel into a full turn and hit the gas.

Pulling out her phone, Eden loaded and checked the map. Although Siwa was smaller than a single borough of a city, and surrounded by the desert on all sides, there were hundreds or even thousands of tracks which radiated like veins out from the center. She figured that her best bet was to head into those tracks and lie low until dark.

Checking the map, Eden saw one such lane ahead. She buried the pedal and wound the Land Rover around a slow-moving truck, its piled crates wobbling. As she pulled in front of the truck, the sharp roar of another engine cut through the air. The noise jolted Eden to attention.

She eyed the dust covered mirror as another vehicle swung out around the truck. Eden recognized the vehicle instantly—a military issue desert patrol vehicle. While similar to the buggies that ferried tourists around, these vehicles had super-charged engines, chunky off-road tires, and a top speed of around eighty miles per hour. As the buggy sped up beyond the truck, Eden saw two black-clad figures sitting in the front seat.

"Damn it." Eden thumped a balled fist against the dash. She dropped the Land Rover into a lower gear and floored the accelerator. The engine roared, shaking through the chassis like an earthquake. The old machine lurched, picking up speed and kicking dust into the air. As the speedometer needle climbed higher, the suspension jostled Eden in her seat. She stole a look at the mirror and saw the desert patrol vehicle drawing near.

She peered down at the map on the phone and tried to formulate a route. Whilst the buggy could outmaneuver the Land Rover through the lanes, and beat it in a flat-out chase, her pursuers were still reliant on seeing where Eden had gone. In a place like Siwa, with networks of tiny lanes and passages, losing sight of a vehicle would be easy.

Eden eyed her phone and picked out a snaking route of sharp and seemingly random turns between the buildings. If she could get out of sight for a few seconds, the drivers of the buggy would have no idea where she'd gone.

Ten feet ahead, she saw the opening to one such track and jerked sharply to the right. Tires wailed against the track, gouging furrows in the dust. Eden teetered on the edge of losing control of the careening four-by-four, but then, traction caught. With a deft twist of the steering wheel and a forceful push on the accelerator, she regained command.

The Land Rover picked up speed. Eden checked the mirror and saw the buggy take the corner with ease, now less than one hundred feet behind.

"Come on," she muttered, tapping the dash.

Eden worked the gears and the Land Rover rumbled on, flinging a cloud of dust high into the air behind it.

As the first turn approached, Eden continued to speed up. She planned to barrel into the curve and straight into another which lay twenty feet beyond. To do that, though, Eden needed a decent lead. In the mirror, the buggy ate up the distance with each passing second.

Eden squeezed some more revs out of the Land Rover as they neared the turning. She eyed the needles, flicking up into the red. The structures on both sides of the road were little more than a blur now—a smudge of the brown mud brick and the green of the trees and undergrowth.

Eden gripped the wheel, the tendons in her fingers standing out like pistons. She checked the mirror, and saw the buggy bounce closer, a cloud of dust fanning high behind it like the tail of a peacock.

Eden gritted her teeth and readied her foot over the brake pedal. She needed to brake at the last minute and send the Land Rover into a skid. Then accelerate hard and turn again. If she could repeat the maneuver several times, that would give her the break she needed. Eden locked her eyes on the corner and pictured the move she was about to make.

Ten feet from the turning, with the high-pitched whine of the buggy now sounding in her ears, Eden hit the brake. She heaved the wheel around, swinging the Land Rover into a spin.

As the road was revealed, a sharp surge of adrenaline coursed through Eden's veins. Three people walked down the track—a woman and two children. On the narrow track, the family stood right in the way of the speeding Land Rover.

Eden cursed herself—in her desperation to put some distance between herself and the buggy, she hadn't considered the idea that there might be people around the corner.

For what felt like several seconds, but in reality was probably less than a heartbeat, Eden just stared.

Still totally unaware of the vehicle heading for them, the woman strode down the lane as she probably did every day. She carried a basket of fresh vegetables, clearly returning home after a visit to the market. Her children darted from side to side; one hitting the ground with a stick, the other chasing a dog.

The Land Rover screeched around the bend and the woman spun around. Her expression blanched and she shouted at her children.

For Eden, the decision was an immediate one. She would hurt herself before any innocent people got caught in the crossfire. Forgetting all about the buggy that was still on her tail, Eden swung the Land Rover off the road. Two rusting trucks with bits missing sat nose to tail on one side and a dog stalked between high grass on the other. Eden leaned on the horn, sending a deep note of warning to anyone nearby.

The woman dropped her vegetables and darted for her children, putting herself further in the path of the speeding Land Rover. The basket smashed to the floor, sending peppers and onions skittering across the dust, crushed beneath the Land Rover's wheels.

Eden stamped on the brake, locking the wheels. The Land Rover whipped to the side, almost throwing Eden from the seat. The steering wheel vibrated frantically, transferring every bump in the road directly to Eden's fingers. The vehicle spun, blurring everything around her into a streak of green and yellow.

The Land Rover bounced across the road, tilting onto one wheel. Eden worked hard to control the skid, but her efforts were futile. The Land Rover's balance faltered, and it toppled over, crashing onto its side in the dust. With the gut-wrenching screech of metal against stone, the Land Rover slid, dragging dust and rocks with it.

For Eden, the world spun from left to right, and then jarred painfully, finally, and silently, to a stop.

29

EDEN WASN'T sure how long the collision knocked her senseless, but it couldn't have been more than a second or two.

When she opened her eyes, the view through the cracked windscreen looked all wrong. She blinked hard. It took a second to realize that the Land Rover was lying on its side. Dust swirled beyond the glass, obscuring the view of the dilapidated trucks and the bushes beyond.

Eden turned and looked through the open roof. A wave of relief crashed over her when she saw the woman and children standing beside the road, scared but unharmed. She'd landed herself in trouble, but no one innocent had been injured or worse. Flexing her shoulders, Eden sprang into action.

She reached for the ignition and killed the engine. The fact that the thing was still running was proof that these Land Rovers may not be the quickest but would run to the apocalypse and beyond. The engine coughed and died, dropping a ten-ton silence over the scene. Her ears finally picked up other sounds from outside the vehicle, and Eden froze. Another engine idled not far away, and footsteps beat across hard earth.

Eden tensed. Whoever had been driving the buggy was closing in. Thinking quickly, she searched for something to use as a weapon. Her muscles throbbing as though she'd just finished a gym session with Arnold Schwarzenegger, Eden searched the door pockets but found nothing. She flipped open the glove box and yanked out the contents. Several documents and a packet of sweets fell out, but nothing she could use as a weapon. She would have to take on whoever was running her way with her hands alone.

Eden scrambled out through the vehicle's open back and stood, her feet shaking. She took a second to find her balance and listen in to the approaching footsteps.

Whoever her pursuers were, they were mere feet away on the other side of the Land Rover. Eden assessed the scene for potential ways to escape. She decided that the rusting trucks, propped up on bricks with looms of wiring hanging out like splayed guts, were her best bet. Eden shuffled away from the Land Rover's cab and tucked in by the rear bumper. The footsteps reached the front of the Land Rover and stopped.

Eden dropped into a crouch like a sprinter on the blocks. In less than a second, the pursuers would realize she wasn't there and round the Land Rover, guns blazing.

She sprinted for the space beneath the lead truck. Under there she would be out of sight and could scramble out through the bushes. She covered the first ten feet with ease; her hands pumping like pistons. Closing in on the truck, Eden leaned, ready to barrel-roll beneath the vehicle. She jumped as something slammed into her from the side. For a second, Eden thought she'd tripped and then felt a weight pushing down on top of her. For the second time in mere minutes, Eden's surroundings whirled around her, disorientating her to where up and down became indistinguishable.

Realizing she was going down, Eden forced the breath from her lungs to prevent herself from being winded. She reflexively moved her arms into a position that would allow her to protect her fall and be back on her feet again in seconds. Strangely, as the ground rushed up to meet her, Eden thought of Athena, who had trained her how to fall in the most effective way some months ago. She remembered Athena's voice as though it were yesterday—*at some point you're going down, that's a certainty, how you fall will make all the difference.*

Despite catching herself on an extended forearm, Eden landed hard. A shockwave bolted up her arm and through her shoulder. The weight of the other person slammed down on top of her, threatening to topple her flat on the ground.

Eden got her other arm in position, pushed back, and rolled to the side, sending the other person into the dust. Eden completed a full roll and landed on her feet. She sprung directly into her fighting stance, whirled around, and pulled back her arm, ready to strike.

Her assailant climbed slowly to her feet. Seeing the person from behind, Eden got her first shock—her attacker was a woman. Dressed in dark fatigues similar to Eden's, the woman moved as though she had all the time in the world.

Eden side-stepped to the right. Whether her opponent was male, female or a cybertronic from Planet Zog, Eden wasn't going down without a fight.

Delivering Eden with the second ground-shaking shock of the conflict, the woman turned around.

"You're pretty difficult to catch up with," Athena said, casually brushing dust from her forearm. "If it wasn't for your love of vintage vehicles, I don't think we'd have caught up with you." Athena pointed at the Land Rover.

Eden remained in her fighting stance, her mind racing to tie together the strands.

"Punch me if you want," Athena said, sighing. "But it won't get you anywhere. Plus, we're here to help you." Athena turned around and pointed over at the Land Rover.

Baxter, leaning against the rear of the vehicle, flicked a casual salute.

GRAND MASTER WOLFF reclined into one of the plush leather seats of the Embraer Legacy 500 private jet. The spacious cabin, with its high ceilings and luxurious furnishings, provided ample comfort as they powered across the Mediterranean on their way to Siwa, Egypt. The jet, borrowed from a member of the order who owned a private aviation company, was the perfect aircraft to make the journey quickly and in style.

As Wolff eyed the ten knights sitting behind him, each occupying their comfortable seat, he considered how their fore-brothers would have made a similar journey many centuries ago. Instead of the luxurious comfort of the Embraer, however, those men would have relied on horse-back and boats to traverse the vast distances between England and Egypt. Wolff considered the Templar's bravery, discipline, and unwavering dedication to their cause even while enduring the scorching sun, biting cold and treacherous terrain.

Wolff took a roll of skin on his left arm with his right hand and pinched hard. He squeezed until tears prickled the corners of his eyes. He certainly would not weaken, not now when there was so much at stake. He once again regarded the men behind him, all silent. He hoped they wouldn't become accustomed to such comforts. He reminded himself that their mission today required the speed of the Embraer.

Departing from an old military airfield in the south of England, they had bypassed the usual security checks and restrictions. The Embraer's cargo hold was loaded with an arsenal of weapons and equipment, ensuring that the men were armed and ready for whatever challenges the mission might present. Both time and these resources were of the essence in their race to catch up with Eden Black and seize the Seal of Solomon for themselves.

Wolff's phone buzzed on the table in front of him, dragging him from his thoughts. He snatched up the phone and answered the call.

"Grand Master, it's Brother Pyne," came a crystal-clear baritone voice, thanks to the Embraer's satellite connectivity.

"Pyne, report," Wolff said.

"It's Black. She knows we're on to her," Pyne said.

"What?" Wolff roared, the information hitting him like a slap in the face. "How could she know we're on to her?"

"I—" Pyne began, but Wolff cut him off in mid-sentence.

"You were supposed to follow and observe, not make contact!" Wolff screamed so loud that his voice could be heard throughout the plane. None of the brothers, however, paid heed to their master's screeching.

"I'm sorry Grand Master. I was observing her and she saw me. I tried to get away, but she attacked."

"She what?"

"She attacked me, Grand Master. But fear not, I'm not injured."

"I don't care whether you're injured!" Wolff howled, moving the phone away from his face. "Where is she now?"

"I'm sorry Grand Master. I don't know, but I know this—"

"You don't know where she is now?" Wolff said. With the crystal-clear line, he didn't need Pyne to repeat the words, but wanted him to repeat his failing one more time.

"No, I'm sorry, I don't. But—"

"If you don't know where she is now, then you have failed." Wolff's grip tightened on the phone, his knuckles turning white. A cold fury raged within him. "We land in one hour. Be at the airport with transport, and we will discuss the cost of your failure. And Pyne..."

"Yes, Grand Master?"

"Don't even consider not being there when I land, or I will track you down and feed you to crocodiles!" Wolff stabbed at the phone and ended the call. Silence returned to the Embraer as the twin turbofan engines propelled them on toward Egypt, Eden Black, and the Seal of Solomon.

30

"You can't be here," Eden shouted. She snapped her mouth shut and glanced from Baxter to Athena. The scene was like something out of a dream. She shook her head, forcing herself to focus.

"You're working with him!" Eden said, pointing a finger at Athena's chest. "I won't let him do it. Humanity deserves better. It deserves another chance."

Athena turned around and threw a glance at Baxter. The pair shared a grin.

"I can't believe you're all in this together!" Eden howled, the rage and fear she'd had bottled up for the last few days finally spilling over. "I trusted you, all of you, and this is what you were planning all along."

Athena let a breath go slowly and spread her hands out in front of her in a gesture of appeasement. "Okay, I understand this is a lot to take in—"

"You understand?" Eden shouted. "Don't make me laugh. You've both been keeping stuff from me from the very beginning. I should have known not to trust you. Any of you!" Eden's balled fists dropped to her sides. She turned on her heel and paced away.

A man and a woman appeared at the window of one of houses across the street to watch the unusual scene unfold. One of them shouted further into the building, clearly telling others they were missing something interesting.

"Whoa there, hold on a second!" Athena said, scurrying after Eden. "Just listen... Eden please..."

"Why should I?" Eden said, whipping around and flashing Athena a look that could burn through steel. "You'll lie to me again. It's obvious that I'm the only one who cares about this, all of this." Eden spread her arms, indicating the world around them. "You're playing with people's lives. That makes you as bad as the rest of them."

"Please, listen for a second," Athena said, exhaling again.

Eden raised her eyebrows and looked hard at the other woman.

"Is it possible that you've misunderstood this?" Athena said softly. "Surely you agree that you can't have all the facts."

Two children charged from a house further down the street as though they were missing the show of the century. They moved closer to get a good view of the action.

"What more facts?" Eden said. "I heard it all, directly from my father in the council meeting—"

"I know. Beaumont said you snuck into the council meeting. That's impressive stuff."

"Really impressive," Baxter muttered, still leaning against the Land Rover. "Those meetings are supposed to be airtight—"

"Beaumont, the snake," Eden growled, her fists tightening further still. "I knew I shouldn't have trusted him."

"How did you get in there without being seen?" Athena said.

Eden opened her mouth to say something and then snapped it shut. "Don't change the subject," she barked. "I can't believe Beaumont would come to you about this. I was only there because I had nowhere—"

"Don't blame him." Athena's tone grew defensive. "He did this to protect you."

"To protect me!" Eden shoved a finger against her chest. "I don't need protecting. It's the world that needs protecting from people like you." Eden swung the finger around and pointed at Athena.

"Eden," Athena sighed. "You can't seriously think that me, or Baxter, or your father mean to cause so much harm. You've got it all wrong."

"I know what I heard," Eden grumbled.

Two young boys walking down the street, their arms draped across each other's shoulders in a sign of friendship that's common in Arabic and Asian countries, paused to watch the action. The Land Rover lying on its side and the ensuing argument was clearly more excitement than the people of Siwa were used to.

"That's clear, but there are also things you don't know," Athena said. "I'll make you a deal. Let's clean up the mess you've made here and head somewhere to talk this through without the audience." Athena pointed at the Land Rover and then nodded at the various people watching the ruckus.

"Yeah, I don't feel like we're making a good impression on the locals," Baxter said, waving at a grey-haired man who had dragged a chair out of his home and settled down to watch. The man fished a pipe from the folds of his tunic and stuffed it with tobacco in the way he might settle in for a sporting event.

Eden's gaze swiftly moved from Athena to Baxter and across their impromptu audience. In the moment of silence, her anger receded an iota, and she thought clearly.

"Sure," she said, pointing a warning finger at Athena as though it were a shotgun. "But if my spidey senses say that you're lying to me about anything, I'm out of here."

"It's a deal," Athena said, her arms folded. She whirled around to Baxter. "When you're ready, Captain."

As Eden stood brooding, her arms tightly folded and her face set into an expression that would give a medieval gargoyle a run for its money, Baxter jogged back to the desert buggy. He spun the buggy around and reversed it in close to the Land Rover's exposed underside.

The buggy and Baxter were now obscured by the Land Rover. Eden heard the engine idling, and Baxter climbing out of the driver's seat. For a second she stood motionless, but when Baxter clunked around with something, curiosity got the better of her. She strode around the Land Rover and saw Baxter pulling a length of tow line from one of the buggy's kit boxes.

"Impressive machine, right?" Athena said, noting Eden's interest and nodding at the buggy. "You want to see it in the open desert. We got eighty out of it earlier."

"It's not all about speed," Baxter said, patting the buggy. "This one's got a reinforced chassis and a custom cooling system. It's designed for brutal places like this, without even breaking a sweat."

Eden grunted, still working hard to keep her icy exterior, although doing so less convincingly than before.

"We're talking a high-torque V8. It's not just the raw power, though that's impressive—it's tuned precisely for this sort of terrain," Baxter said, talking as he ran a towline from the rear of the buggy to the underside of the Land Rover's chassis. He slipped back into the driver's seat and inched the buggy forward. The line pulled taut. The *patter-patter* of the V8 increased to a growl. Baxter applied more pressure, and the buggy's thick tires tore into the road, pinging grit and stones into the Land Rover. The Land Rover wobbled, looking as though it was thinking about toppling over, then slid across the track on its side.

"Whoever you've rented this from isn't going to be happy," Athena said.

Yet again, Eden didn't reply. Silently she cringed at the grinding sound of metal scratching against the road. She hoped Mahmoud was more chilled about his vehicle than she would be. If someone treated her Land Rover like this, it would probably be their last act on earth.

When the Land Rover had slid six feet and still remained on its side, Baxter hit the brake. "We need to give it a shove," he said, glancing at Eden and Athena. He pointed at the Land Rover. "Push it on the top there. That'll topple it over."

"I've got a better idea," Athena said, striding over to the buggy. "I'll drive this. You shove it over. You being the super strong Captain Baxter and all."

"Fine," Baxter said, conceding the driver's seat to Athena.

Athena beckoned Eden across to the buggy and climbed in. She pumped the gas, and the engine howled, sounding more like a racing car than a military vehicle.

Baxter paced behind the Land Rover. "In position," he said, his voice muffled by the two tons of steel, glass, and rubber between them.

"Waiting on you," Athena replied.

"Go!" Baxter shouted, pounding the Land Rover on the hood.

Athena stamped on the pedal, sending a hail of grit into the air. The Land Rover groaned and tilted. The vehicle's body crunched as it rolled across the road. Athena inched forward again, pulling the Land Rover to almost forty-five degrees.

"More!" Baxter shouted, stepping away from the vehicle.

Athena did what she was told. For a few seconds the Land Rover teetered, as though deciding which way to fall, then crashed back down onto its wheels.

"Disconnect that cable," Athena whispered to Eden. "Then get in as quick as you can."

The conspiratorial tone of Athena's voice cut through Eden's worry. Eden unclipped the cable from the rear of the buggy and sunk into the super low passenger seat.

Athena turned around and threw a glance at Baxter, who rounded the Land Rover, brushing his hands together.

"You bring the Land Rover," Athena shouted, raising a hand in a wave. "We'll meet you back at base."

Before Baxter could reply, Athena buried the pedal and the buggy tore away.

31

"GREAT MACHINE, RIGHT?" Athena said, swinging around a corner at a speed which flung half the road's surface amid the trees.

Although Eden agreed that the desert buggy was an impressive vehicle, she simply nodded in reply. She wasn't yet ready to get back on conversational terms, not before she'd heard what Athena and Baxter had to say.

The scenic route Athena had taken involved speeding down several winding roads, across a rocky escarpment, and through a grove of palm trees, whizzing frantically as they passed. Although the journey had been picturesque and riding in the buggy should have made it fun, Eden's thoughts were still focused on the conversation they were about to have.

Athena slowed as they reached a mud brick building. Beyond the lone structure, the undulating desert sands stretched as far as Eden could see. The structure, crafted in the traditional style of the oasis, blended seamlessly with its surroundings, as if it had sprouted from the sands upon which it stood. The sun was making its daily plummet toward the horizon, spreading its colors across the sky, and igniting dunes into a tapestry of light and shadow. The view of the great sand sea, Eden had to admit, was strangely captivating.

As they swung around the building, Eden noticed the Land Rover already in position. The machine was now even more scratched and missing one of its front windows. She eyed the vehicle with pride—even making the journey was a testament to its rugged nature. And, the fact the Baxter had made it here first, Eden thought, proved what a circuitous route Athena had taken them on. Eden eyeballed the other woman. Athena was either trying to soften Eden up or Baxter had to prepare something before they arrived. Either way, Eden didn't like it.

Athena pulled the buggy in beside the Land Rover and cut the engine. They climbed from their seats and Athena led them to the building.

"What is this place?" Eden said, looking at the simple mud brick structure.

"Our private accommodation," Athena said. "It's ideal, I think. We can see anyone approaching for miles from out here. Of course, we've swept it for bugs too, just to be safe. Well, Baxter did."

"He does that before even taking his shoes off," Eden quipped. Teasing Baxter for his habits and routines was one of Eden and Athena's joint passions. Eden remembered she was supposed to be frosty and turned to face the vast expanse of the desert on one side, and then the winding dirt track which led back into the heart of the oasis. She had to agree with Athena's assessment—the location was perfect.

"You're keen to talk," Athena said, gesturing at the door. "Let's get inside."

The women strode to the entrance, pausing briefly to

slip off their shoes, then padding inside. Athena led them through an archway and pulled aside a heavy curtain, revealing the building's dimly lit interior.

Eden gazed around the softly illuminated space, her eyes struggling for a moment with the gloom. Thick, hand-woven rugs in vibrant colors covered the floor. Plush cushions scattered throughout the room invited her to relax in comfort. Tendrils of smoke curled lazily from countless incense sticks, lacing the air with fragrance.

Baxter sat beside a low table, already sipping a cup of Egyptian tea, its steam rising in gentle wisps. As the women entered, Baxter rose and poured two more cups.

Eden looked around at the various doorways which led from the space, each shrouded by drapes. She assumed these led to the building's other rooms. The only wall which wasn't lined by drapes housed a narrow window offering a tantalizing glimpse of the desert.

"I'm here. Now start talking," Eden said, sitting on a cushion. She ignored the tea and poked the table-top with her finger.

Athena and Baxter shared a glance. Baxter nodded almost imperceptibly.

"Okay," Athena said, sitting gracefully with her legs crossed. "What you heard in the council meeting is..." Athena stopped in the middle of the sentence.

"Exactly what I wanted you to hear," a voice boomed through the space.

It took Eden a beat to realize that the voice wasn't Athena's. Once she understood that, she recognized it instantly. She turned around to face the sound.

Alexander Winslow stood in a doorway, holding the heavy drape aside. Winslow stepped through. He let the fabric swing back into position.

"What are you doing here?" Eden sprung to her feet. "Don't you have a lot going on, you know, with planning the end of the world?" Eden's muscles tensed as she fought her warring desires to hug or slap some sense into her father.

Alexander Winslow rounded the table and locked eyes with his daughter.

"I imagine you're feeling somewhat conflicted," Winslow said, settling onto a cushion. "Once again, I am truly sorry to keep you in the dark about this."

"So, it's true?" Eden said. "You are going to cause the End of Days?"

Winslow sighed. His hands rested in his lap. "The End of Days is not caused by one person, or even a group of people. It's an event that's been foretold for thousands of years. I'm afraid that it cannot be stopped entirely."

"Now you sound like Wolff," Eden said, folding her arms. "Once I find the Seal of Solomon, I can stop it."

Athena, Baxter, and Winslow shared a glance.

"I'm afraid things aren't as simple as Wolff has told you," Athena said.

"Wolff is right about the seal having extraordinary power, but I'm afraid his intentions aren't good," Winslow said, his voice calm and even.

"And yours are?" Eden snapped.

"Wolff wants to create the End of Days in his own vision," Winslow said. "He wants to use this prophesied event so that people believe they are powerless, and as such, turn to him as a source of solace. Why do you think he needs you to find the seal for him?"

"Why?"

"He knows the seal can only be discovered by a seeker with good intentions," Athena said.

"He knows your intentions are honest, whereas his are not," Baxter said, pouring more tea.

Eden eyed everyone in turn, her thoughts raging.

"The End of Days has been foretold for thousands of years," Winslow continued. "As long as the Council of Selene has existed, we've been working on this. It is, in a way, the next stage of our organization here on Earth, although what exactly it will involve is still unclear."

"That's rubbish," Eden said, shooting her father an icy look. She turned to face the door, rubbing her face with her hands. "I don't believe this. I can't believe there is nothing we can do."

"I'm afraid it's true," Baxter said, his tone level.

"Remember some time ago I told you that the council's days are numbered, and that soon humanity will be free to choose its own path?" Winslow said.

Eden whirled around to face her father. "Yes, that's why I'm here!" she shouted. "I wouldn't have gone along with anything you'd said if you hadn't told me that. Now I know that was a lie!"

"Oh no, that wasn't a lie," Winslow said. "It has always been my intention to use the End of Days as an opportunity. Change is inevitable, but it's our job to make sure it's a good one."

"What's stopping you? Aren't you supposed to oversee this thing?"

"Whilst I am the chairman of the council, unfortunately, I am not completely in charge. The council members need to decide what to do by majority rule—that's the way it works. There are some council members who will stop at nothing to make sure the council retains its powerful position."

"What can we do about that?" Eden said.

"The person who holds the seal can shape the council in their own image," Winslow said. "They can make whatever changes they see fit."

"I don't understand, how?"

"What the Templars discovered beneath Jerusalem was so much more than a few religious relics. They discovered objects of true power," Athena explained.

"Yeah, Wolff told me all of this," Eden said. "But conveniently, these objects have since been lost, blah blah blah."

"The person who holds the seal on the day of reckoning can decide what happens next," Winslow said. "The End of Days could be an event of destruction like Wolff suggests, or it could be something much, much, more powerful."

"You're telling me this could be a good thing?" Eden said, taking a step back so that she could look at everyone all at once.

"It could be a wonderful thing," Winslow said. "Imagine a world of abundance, where people are free to live, love and worship in any way they see fit. This is what the End of Days could lead to."

Eden thought back to the Ark of the Covenant, which they'd discovered beneath the Pyramids of Giza some months before. The technological advances made from studying the ark and its ability to produce power from the Earth's atmosphere were already showing great promise.

"Put it this way," Baxter said. "We find the seal and we can create the End of Days however we see it."

Winslow silenced his daughter with a stare. "*You* find the seal before Wolff, and *you* can create the End of Days however you see fit."

32

THE EMBRAER DIPPED toward Siwa's airstrip, catching the remnants of daylight. From his window seat, Grand Master Wolff's eyes remained transfixed on the sand unfolding beneath them. The sun, a fiery orb hanging low on the horizon, painted the sky in a mesmerizing array of deep oranges and vibrant reds, casting an otherworldly glow across the desert.

As the jet lined up for its final approach, Wolff thought again about their mission. The significance of this tiny green dot in the sea of sand could not be overstated. It was exactly the sort of place, with its ties to Alexander the Great and the Oracle of Amun, that their fore-brothers would have chosen to hide one of their most precious relics.

The Embraer touched down on the airstrip with a shudder. The aircraft slowed and taxied to one of the hangars, jolting and bumping across the uneven tarmac. They rolled to the far end of the airport and the engines whined to a stop. The pilot emerged from the flight deck and swung open the door, which doubled as a set of stairs. Wolff rose from his seat and led the knights down onto the tarmac.

Two hundred feet away, a pair of headlights cut through the dusk. Wolff turned to face the incomer and heard the grumble of a heavy diesel engine. A military transport truck rumbled into view; a cloud of dust billowed in its wake. The truck grumbled to a stop beside the plane and Pyne scrambled down from the cab.

"As you requested, Grand Master," Pyne said, raising his voice against the gentle patter of the truck's engine. He pointed up at the vehicle.

Wolff stared hard at the taller man, his eyes piercing. In a swift, fluid motion, he reached beneath his cloak and removed a gun, leveling it at Pyne's chest.

"You have failed our order," Wolff said, his voice nothing more than a whisper, "and now you must pay the price."

"But wait, I have something for you. This could—"

"Shut up!" The gun shook as Wolff struggled to contain his rage at Pyne's failure. "I gave you a chance to atone for your transgressions, and you repay me by failing again!"

A flicker of panic crossed Pyne's face. The knight raised his hands in a placating gesture. "Grand Master, please, I have something for you. This could change everything. It could lead us to—"

"Shut up!" Wolff snapped, his voice cracking like a whip. The Grand Master's eyes blazed with a fury. "I have heard enough of your empty promises and failed attempts. Your incompetence has jeopardized our entire mission. Our order will not succeed with this weakness amongst us."

"For the eye and the earth!" the surrounding knights murmured.

"You have proven yourself unworthy of the trust placed in you, and now you will face the consequences of your actions." Wolff raised the gun higher, his finger curling around the trigger.

"Grand Master Please," Pyne said, his voice harder than anyone had ever used to address the Grand Master. "I have something that could change the course of this entire mission. Let me show you, and if you want to kill me, so be it. But this is important."

"Grand Master, I think you should listen to him."

"Shut up, Jenkins," Wolff said, throwing Jenkins a look so icy that it really could have frozen Hell. "You have twenty seconds."

"There is something you need to see." Pyne reached beneath his cloak and pulled out a crumped sheet of paper. "When Eden attacked me, she dropped this. I believe it holds the key to our mission." Pyne held the paper out in front of him.

Wolff's gaze shifted from Pyne to the paper, eyeing both as though they may be poisonous.

"Take this," Wolff said, passing the gun to Brother Jenkins. "Keep it pointed at him. Shoot him on my command."

"On your what?" Jenkins said, accepting the weapon and leveling it at Pyne.

"On my command, shoot him!" Wolff howled.

"What, you mean now?" Jenkins said. "Don't you want to see what's inside the paper first?"

"No!" Wolff shook with rage, his eyes burning with the reflection of the setting sun. "Don't shoot him now. Shoot him if I tell you to."

Wolff reached out and snatched the paper from Pyne's outstretched hand. He unfolded the paper and scrutinized it for ten seconds. The paper contained a series of hand-written sentences in a language Wolff didn't recognize. There were strange drawings, too, linked with arrows and circles.

"What is this?" Wolff snapped, looking up at Pyne. "Are you wasting my time?"

"No Grand Master, look!" Pyne took the paper and turned it around in Wolff's hands. "You see this?"

Wolff looked again, the words suddenly making sense.

"You see what it says there?" Pyne pointed to a line right in the middle of the page.

"It all leads to the Temple of the Oracle at dawn, then we will see the way," Wolff read aloud, his jowls wobbling with excitement. "The Temple of the Oracle at dawn," Wolff repeated.

"Grand Master, I believe that is Eden Black's next move," Pyne said, wiping the cold sweat of a near death experience from his brow.

"Yes. I believe it is. Excellent." Wolff thought for a moment and then spun around to address the assembled knights. "Brothers, unload the plane and get in the truck. We've got a job to do."

"Was that the command?" Jenkins said, his head whipping from Wolff to Pyne and back again. "Shall I shoot him now?"

"No," Wolff said, taking the gun. "For now, Brother Pyne has earned his life."

EDEN PACED AWAY from the mud brick building and onto the cooling sand. The fresh and dry air of the desert revitalized her lungs after the intense discussion inside. She climbed a dune, her feet sinking into the sand and sending a torrent falling behind her. She reached the top and dropped to the sand with her legs crossed. On the horizon, the upper curve of the sun slipped beneath the horizon, casting its long shadows across the desert. Eden looked up at the sky, patterned with stripes of color.

"Some people believe that sunset is a sad time of day," Winslow said, pacing up the dune and sitting beside his daughter. "I see it more as a time of reflection. The day's work is done, and hopefully tomorrow we will get another chance."

"I see where you're going with this," Eden said, eyeing her father. "You're going to tell me that the End of Days is the same, right? An opportunity for humankind to have another chance."

"That's my vision for it," Winslow said. "A world without control, without the greedy people in the middle taking a cut. A corruption-less society without scarcity."

A stray dog ran out across the sands, its eyes fixed on something ahead. Eden followed the creature's gaze but couldn't see a single thing. The dog paused and turned its bedraggled head, gazing at Eden and Winslow.

"I understand that" Eden said, looking at the dog. The creature forgot wherever it was heading and trotted up beside Eden. He slumped to the sand, stretched, and spread out as though Eden and he spent every evening just like this.

"I suppose it's all about perception," Winslow continued. "Consider those who set out to crucify Jesus. In their minds, the solution was simple: extinguish the man, and the movement dies with him. They believed that by silencing the singular voice, the chorus of dissent would falter, and they would maintain their grip on power. They thought, logically, that his end would be the end of a threat."

"They were clearly wrong about that," Eden said, reaching over and scratching the dog on the stomach.

"Quite right. In fact, by trying to quell his influence, they only amplified it."

"That was the start of it, right? If Jesus had never been crucified, who's to know how things would have ended up?" Eden said.

"It's only under pressure that the full strength of a person, or a group of people, becomes visible," Winslow paused. "Some members of the council think we can keep humankind in a bottle and never let it out. It's an age-old mistake amongst those who cling to power—they often misunderstand the true nature of the forces they attempt to control."

"I bet they say things like 'it's been that way for thousands of years, why does it have to change?'" Eden said.

"The remit of the council has always been to do what is right for the continuation of humankind—not necessarily for the interests of the council. Sometimes the two are the same, other times they are very different."

"How would it work?" Eden said, squinting into the last orange glimmer of the sun, dancing lazily in the currents of heat.

"I can't tell you exactly," Winslow said. "We honestly don't know. But my vision is of a world in which people have everything they need—"

"I get all of that," Eden said, her voice sharp. "I'm with you on the vision. But I think there's something you're not telling me." Eden turned to face her father. "There's more to this, isn't there?"

Winslow ran a hand through his hair and folded his arms. Either the heat of the day was already draining, or the topic of conversation had sent a chill through him.

"It's never as simple as solving a puzzle, finding a relic

and saving the world," Winslow said, his voice softer than before.

"I'll say," Eden said. "It was only a few weeks ago that I had to take on a genetically modified cyborg who turned people to stone by looking at them."

Winslow threw his daughter a glance.

"Okay, the turning people to stone bit was made up. That guy was unstoppable," Eden said, remembering that night on the River Thames. For a moment she wondered if Thorne's body would ever be discovered, or if his super strong bone structure had sent him straight into the silt at the bottom of the river.

"Grand Master Wolff and the Order of the All-Seeing Eye are a powerful force," Winslow said. "He will not give up easily. I'm not totally sure what he's planning, but I suspect it'll be an event which forces people under his control."

"Classic false flag," Eden said.

"Exactly that. I suspect Wolff wants a society where every aspect of individual liberty is limited. Imagine a world where people are confined to a set of prescribed actions— work, raising children, and other civil duties. Everyone would be monitored and their movements severely restricted. Technology restricted to government and military use only."

"That sounds awful," Eden said, chilled by her father's words. "You think people would accept that?"

"In the right, or wrong conditions, everything is possible. Particularly when you factor in several generations. People quickly forget what things were like and accept what they are now. We've seen it during times of international conflict."

"We can't let that happen," Eden said, her voice as sharp as flint.

Clearly sensing the tension in the air, the dog lifted its head and gazed at Eden. Then it replaced its grizzled muzzle across her leg.

"Wolff played me," Eden muttered angrily. "And I led him right here. You should have told me all this, and then maybe it would have worked out differently."

"I know, and for that I'm sorry," Winslow said, sounding genuinely dejected. "I've done so much to deserve your mistrust."

"I understand why you've done some of those things," Eden said, leaning against her father's shoulder. "Old habits die hard and all that."

"Old habits need to change," Winslow said, placing his arm around Eden. "It's time for this old dog to learn some new tricks."

The dog lifted his head and eyed Winslow suspiciously.

"Not you," Eden said, rubbing the mutt on the chin. "You're perfect, just as you are."

Running feet pounded across the sand from behind them. Eden whipped around to see Baxter running up the dune towards them.

"A small jet on a private charter just landed at Siwa's airstrip," Baxter said, glancing down at a tablet computer.

"That's no tourist service," Winslow said, sharing a look with Baxter. "That's got to be Wolff."

"What do you think we should do?" Baxter said.

"We proceed as I'd planned," Eden said. "We need to be at the Temple of the Oracle at dawn."

33

EDEN CHECKED HER WATCH. It was just after 5 a.m. She stretched and yawned, trying to force the tiredness from her limbs and eyes. After the group had spent several hours making plans, Eden had attempted to get some sleep. She'd climbed into one of the beds, pulled the covers over her, and clamped her eyes closed. Lying there in the darkness, however, listening to the desert wind, her mind was far too busy to relax properly. Even so, the down time had no doubt done her good.

"Where the oracle's shadow in the desert lies deep, turn your gaze where the horizon's secrets keep," Eden whispered, muttering the words of the riddle out loud. Realizing what was now at stake, a sense of unease simmered in her stomach.

"What did you say?" Athena shouted over the grumble of the buggy's engine.

"How far are we?" Eden shouted back.

Athena checked the dials mounted on the side of the roll cage, which made up the buggy's dashboard. "We're close. The Temple of the Oracle is about half a mile that way."

"Put the buggy in there," Eden said, pointing at a clump of bushes at the side of the road. "Let's do that last bit on foot."

Athena slowed the buggy and bounced from the track. She spun the vehicle around and reversed in behind a thick clump of undergrowth. She killed the engine. Silence surrounded them on all sides. Smaller subtler sounds emerged, insects zinged from the trees, and a creature scuttled in the bushes nearby.

"Do you think someone will be watching?" Athena turned to face Eden.

"I'm not sure. I don't think they know that we're here, but my father seemed worried about Wolff," Eden said.

Athena nodded. "He's a nasty piece of work, for sure."

"We've got a head start," Eden said, climbing out of the buggy, "but for how long, I don't know."

Eden swung her bag on her back and glanced up at the sky. To the west, the glittering brilliance of a thousand stars punctuated the inky night sky. To the east, the first colors of dawn assembled on the horizon, like an army ready to conquer.

Eden turned her attention to the road, just visible in the half-light, curving between the trees. Athena swung a bag onto her back and the pair set off to the temple.

They walked in silence for a few minutes until they saw the temple off to the side of the track.

"This way," Eden said, leading them away from the road and across an area of light undergrowth. "In case Wolff is watching the entrance."

As they pushed through the leaves, the ancient structure appeared ahead of them. They reached a chain link boundary fence and paused to check for anyone inside.

"Looks clear," Athena said.

"Agreed, let's go," Eden replied. She scrambled over the fence and dropped into a crouch on the other side.

"Let's get in there and wait for the sun to rise," Eden said, pointing at one of the crumbling walls.

They slipped between the walls and paused. Eden raised a finger, indicating that they should wait to see if anyone approached. The pair remained stationary for an entire minute, listening for sounds of an approach. Hearing nothing but the buzz of insects and the flutter of wind through palm leaves, they pressed on.

"Imagine this place a thousand years ago," Athena said, as they passed through a doorway and into the temple's central section.

Eden stopped to look up at the once grand edifice, now little more than crumbling chunks of sandstone.

"It's an impressive place," Eden said, her eyes now accustomed to the darkness. She ran a finger across the stone, almost hearing the hushed tones of ancient priests and the shuffling feet of seekers.

"This way, I think." Eden led them to the temple's inner sanctum. They passed through another set of waist high walls and wound toward the center of the chamber where the oracle would have once sat to divine the fates of emperors and warriors. Eden reached out, her fingers brushing against the pocked surface of an archway which remained in surprisingly good condition.

Eden stepped out into a space in the center of the temple. Walls towered above them on all sides. She turned to face the highest wall, standing at several times her height. High above, she saw a small round opening, through which she could see the sky transforming from purple to orange.

"This has got to be it," Athena said. "The first rays of sun will shine through that small window and show us the way."

"Turn your gaze where the horizon's secrets keep," Eden said. "That's the horizon, alright."

"Does the riddle tell us what we need to do?" Athena asked, pacing up to the wall and peering up at the high window.

"We've got to wait until sunrise," Eden said. "These ancient people were big into sunrises."

"Waiting half a year to find this secret room would be really annoying, right?" Athena said.

Eden snorted a humorless laugh. "They were definitely more patient than we are today." Eden paced to the rear of the chamber and sat on a large rectangular rock. Athena wandered across and sat beside her. Both sat in silence for thirty seconds.

"Don't be too angry with him," Athena said, glancing at her friend. "Your father, I mean."

"All these secrets make things so complicated." Eden exhaled, her breath sounding loud in the silence. "Why couldn't he have told me what was going on in the first place? Instead, he kept it all quiet and only told the truth when I was kidnapped by modern-day knights, and then broke into the council meeting to find out for myself."

"Men are complex creatures," Athena said.

"People are complex creatures," Eden said.

They both nodded in silent agreement.

"You're right, though," Athena said, trying to hide a smile. "It would have been a lot easier if he'd told you what was going on first."

"Hey Eden, I've got this going on with work," Eden said, mimicking her father's accent. "There's a group of knights after a relic, and I think they'll probably kidnap you and drag you away to their lair."

"Woah, that was uncanny," Athena said. "What was the knight's lair like, anyway?"

"Exactly what you'd expect," Eden said, shrugging. "It was a crypt with loads of tombs."

"So stereotypical," Athena groaned. "These bad guys have no creativity or flare."

"Taking over the world is a full-time thing," Eden said. "I don't imagine it leaves a lot of time for lair design." She turned to look at her friend. "Am I being unreasonable to expect that my father communicates with me?" Eden said, her tone hard.

"Everything to do with the Council of Selene is not normal," Athena said, glancing down at her hands. "To begin with, I attempted to understand it but gave up after a while. It's a thousand-year-old secret society and bound to have a few idiosyncrasies."

"That's true," Eden said, her voice lightening. "We better hurry up and find the Seal of Solomon, then we can get back to normal."

"You wouldn't want to be..." Athena stopped talking mid-sentence as the first rays of the rising sun painted the sky. While they'd been talking, the new day had arrived.

"Look!" Athena shouted, jumping to her feet.

The ancient stones of the temple now blazed with the sun's rays. Light patterned across the remnants of archways and collapsed columns. Eden shot to her feet and paced across the chamber. Her gaze shifted from the uneven ground to the vivid tapestry of light painting the temple walls.

The sun rose another fraction and sent a bolt of light through the window, which Eden had indicated a few minutes before. The finger of light stretched through the temple. Dust particles sailed through the golden light as though they were shooting stars.

"We've got to find the point that beam of light touches first," Eden rushed to the beam, waiting for it to hit something that might indicate their path.

"There, look!" Athena said, her voice barely above a whisper. She pointed at the chamber's far end. The beam of light from the window now cast a precise golden circle upon the gravel covered floor.

Athena and Eden raced across the chamber toward the patch of light. Eden swept the gravel to the side, revealing a single slab of stone.

"Without that light there is no way of knowing where to look," Eden said, scanning the floor which extended twenty feet in every direction, all covered in sand-colored gravel.

Athena crouched down, took off her bag and continued sweeping the dust from the slab's edges.

"Judging by the seals around the edge here, this slab hasn't been moved in a long time," Athena said.

"Until now," Eden said. "We need to get it out."

"Before we go to all that trouble, let's make sure." Athena slipped a hand-held scanner wand from her bag.

"What good is a metal detector going to do?"

"This is one of Baxter's new toys," Athena said, spinning the device around and showing Eden a color screen set on one side. "It's the latest in subsurface imaging tech, apparently."

"Which means?"

"It's a portable ground-penetrating radar. It sends a pulse that maps what's below us in three dimensions. If there's a cavity under this slab, we'll see it on the display here." Athena held the device lengthways and swept it across the stone. The device's screen came to life with a swirl of colors representing the different densities of materials beneath them.

"I was just going to pull the stone out and have a look," Eden said, rummaging through her bag. "I don't need anything high tech for that." She produced a pair of pry bars.

"We've got something," Athena said, her eyes locked on the pulsating screen. The device in her hand emitted a series of rapid beeps, each one growing in intensity. "There's a void beneath this slab, a hollow space. It could be a chamber or a passage—hidden right under our feet."

Eden shuffled around and eyed the device. Greens and blues swished across the screen, although she couldn't work out what they meant.

"There's an opening directly below us," Athena said, answering Eden's unasked question. "Beneath that, it opens into a wider space."

"How big are we talking?" Eden said, her eyes wide with excitement.

"Big," Athena replied, glancing at her friend. "Fifty feet across, at least."

A noise pounded across the oasis. Eden's face tensed as wonder turned to worry. A powerful diesel engine growled up the access road toward them.

"I think it's time to use my tools," Eden hissed, pointing at the pry bars. "Let's get this thing open and get out of sight."

34

———

Wolff leaned forward in the passenger seat as the truck growled and groaned toward the Temple of the Oracle. He swept the sleeve of his cloak across his face. Despite the early hour, it was still far too hot.

"Can't this thing go any faster?" Wolff growled, banging a fist against the dashboard.

"Yes, Grand Master," Pyne muttered from the driver's seat. He shoved the pedal to the floor and the truck's old engine howled. Pyne wrestled the wheel as they navigated a corner, bumping violently across the gravel track. The truck's lights swept through the undergrowth. Ahead, the road straightened out, offering them the first glimpse of the temple silhouetted against the lightening sky.

"There it is!" Wolff shouted, transfixed by the temple walls.

Pyne swung the wheel, and they bumped up a small incline. The temple grew larger and more imposing as they neared. They emerged into an open patch of dusty ground. Pyne turned the truck toward the temple, washing two massive walls flanking the entrance in the glow from the truck's headlights. He applied the brake, and the truck squealed to a stop, kicking up a cloud of swirling dust.

Wolff wasted no time in flinging open the passenger door and scrambling down. He placed his hands on his hips and surveyed the ruin.

The men filed from the back of the truck and surrounded their leader. Each man was armed with an automatic rifle, plus a sidearm. The way they held the weapons proved that, although these were men of the order, they were warriors too. Wolff nodded to himself, pleased by how imposing his men appeared. Perhaps when Eden Black saw them approaching, she would just hand over the Seal of Solomon without question.

"Brothers," Wolff said, addressing the men with his arms outstretched. "Today, we are on the cusp of greatness. But there is still much work to do. We must stop at nothing to get what we deserve!"

"For the eye and the earth!" The brothers muttered in unison.

"You start from the east wall," Wolff said, pointing to one group of men. "And you start from the west. Brother Pyne and I will search the central chamber. We will trap Miss Black inside so that there is no escape." He clamped his hands together as though he were trapping a fly. "Search every inch of the site. Eden Black is here. You are to find her and bring her to me."

The knights split into teams and strode toward the temple. They paused for a moment as one man cut the padlock from the gate and then they all disappeared inside.

Wolff followed, striding toward the jagged walls within which some of history's most powerful people came to seek sanctuary and solace. His cloak billowed out behind him in the gentle breeze. He paused at the temple's threshold and scanned the walls which jutted upwards like the cracked teeth of a dormant monster.

"Eden Black is here," he said in a whisper, his hands balling. "She is here, and she will find me what is mine."

EDEN THREW one of the pry bars to Athena and together they rammed them beneath the edge of the slab. Eden put her weight behind the bar and gritted her teeth. The ancient slab remained stubbornly in place, refusing to budge. The bar slipped out of place and clanged noisily against the stone.

"It's not working," Eden groaned, wiping the sweat from her brow with the back of her hand.

The truck's engine, which had been getting closer and closer, dropped into an idle patter and then stopped altogether.

Eden and Athena eyed each other, unblinking.

"They're here," Athena said, glancing over Eden's shoulder toward the noise. Her voice was tight, barely above a whisper.

"We're not beaten yet," Eden said, turning her attention back to the slab. "We need to get a better grip on this." With renewed vigor, she scraped away some of the dirt that had compacted around the slab over several hundred years. When she had cleared a trough of an inch or so, she jammed the pry bar inside.

A voice drifted from the direction of the truck now. Although it was too far away to hear the words, Eden recognized the nasal tones. The sound sent a chill down her spine, and for a moment, she froze.

"That's Wolff," she said, glancing over her shoulder. "Come and help me with this." She rammed the pry bar into the gap again. This time, the bar held its position.

Athena scurried around the slab. Crouching shoulder to shoulder, Eden and Athena heaved back on the pry bar. Sweat mottled Eden's brow and forearms.

The slab cracked away from its position and lifted a fraction of an inch. The small victory was quickly overshadowed by the sound of footsteps pounding over the ground from behind them.

"Hold on," Athena said, releasing the pry bar. She shoved the bar in further, making use of their hard-won progress to get some extra purchase.

"Again," Eden said, directing them to heave together. They pulled back, knuckles turning white, muscles straining and skin scraping against the bar.

The stone raised another fraction. A crack was now visible all around the slab. Athena grabbed the second pry bar and forced that into the gap they'd made.

The footsteps approached the front of the temple now. Instead of running straight into the central chamber, the men split into two and branched off to both sides.

"They're splitting up," Athena whispered. "They'll start with the outside and circle into the center."

"That's bought us some time," Eden said.

"It also means we've got no escape," Athena replied.

"We'd better get this up." Eden nodded at the slab. They yanked on the bars with all their might, faces contorted with the effort. The gap widened, now big enough to accommodate a finger.

"Hold it still," Athena said. "I'll lift it by hand."

Eden nodded; her jaw tensed in a determined line.

Athena let go of the pry bar and moved to get her hand beneath the slab.

Eden took the weight, her hands shaking. Her palms, already sweating, became slick. The pry bar wobbled and slipped completely from her grasp. The bar swung out of its groove as the slab thudded back into place, the sound fortunately lost amid the running footsteps.

With lightning-fast reactions, Athena reached out and caught the bar before it clanged to the floor.

Eden and Athena stared at each other in horror. The sound of Wolff's men, their boots thundering across the compacted earth from both sides, grew nearer by the moment.

"We're not giving up," Eden whispered, working the bar back into position. "Try again."

WOLFF EXPERIENCED a sense of satisfaction as he strode into the temple. Alexander the Great had come here to seek divinity from the Oracle. His fore-brothers had thought it important enough to hide one of their most important relics here. Now Grand Master Wolff would become one of the world's most powerful men amid these hallowed walls.

As they passed into a wide corridor, Wolff glanced at Pyne. The other man carried his rifle as though they were on a hunt, which Wolff supposed they were. Having checked the layout of the temple, he strode for the central chamber which lay fifty feet ahead. If he was right, that's where Eden would be. Wolff's heart pounded with anticipation as they neared.

They crossed an open section, which may have been a

small courtyard or maybe intersecting passages. Wolff checked both ways, glimpsing his men as they moved through the complex, weapons at the ready. As instructed, they were doing a thorough job—checking every nook, cranny, and shadowy alcove where a person might hide.

Wolff's mind raced with the intoxicating excitement that their destiny was almost upon them. After years of planning and searching, soon he would have what was rightfully his.

He wiped the sweat from his face and quickened his pace.

"There it is!" Wolff said, pointing at a pair of columns standing on either side of an opening ahead. He imagined how grand the columns must have looked when Alexander the Great came here. This was the largest room in the temple, and where the Oracle would sit and make her proclamations. It was, he supposed, a fitting place to enter the next chapter for the order.

"Come on," he said to Pyne, rushing to the central chamber. From this position he couldn't see what was inside the central room, but he and Pyne would be the first to find out. Pyne raised his weapon; his finger ready to go beside the trigger.

Wolff strode between the columns and into the temple's heart. He paused and surveyed the scene. Dawn's first light streamed in through various openings and bathed the ancient stones in a soft, golden hue. Light patterned across the stone floor, worn smooth by the feet of countless seekers.

Wolff took another step into the chamber, affording him a view of the entire space. The chamber was empty. Wolff spun around, checking that Eden had not merely slipped out of sight.

Wolff's fists clenched at his sides; his knuckles blanched with rage.

The sound of footsteps behind him made him spin around. Pyne raised his gun. A group of his men ran into the chamber.

"Report," Wolff barked.

"Nothing, Grand Master. We've searched every inch of the temple."

Wolff's face contorted with rage, his eyes blazing with a fury that made his men take an involuntary step back. "She must be here!" Wolff strode into the center of the chamber, kicking up clouds of dust. His mind raced with possibilities, trying to make sense of the situation.

"Look again!" Wolff screamed with a force that made the knights flinch. "Search every corner, every crack in the walls. Eden Black is here somewhere!"

35

Eden and Athena crouched in the space beneath the slab. As the men moved around overhead, they stood motionless, listening.

Eden held her breath as a pair of heavy footsteps passed directly overhead. Her stomach crawled its way up into her throat with the fear that whoever was up there would notice scuff marks around the slab. One voice called and another answered.

Eden and Athena eyed each other, both pale in the beams from their flashlights.

"Let's move," Eden mouthed, pointing into a tunnel that led deeper beneath the ground. "It won't take them long to notice the slab has been moved recently."

"Agreed. Let's hope there's another way out," Athena replied.

Hunched over, they navigated their way through the tunnel. The size of the passage would play to their advantage, Eden thought. If Wolff and his thugs found the tunnel, their size would make moving around in here more difficult.

After ten feet of scrambling through the narrow space, the floor dropped away, and the walls widened.

"Look at that," Athena said, her voice no louder than an exhale. The beam of her flashlight illuminated rows of hieroglyphics on the wall ahead.

Eden stepped alongside the wall and recognized animals, gods, and pharaohs. The colors looked as bright and sharp as the day they were etched.

"I haven't seen anything this remarkably preserved since..."

"The Hall of Records," Eden said, finishing her friend's sentence. "We're probably the first people to see these since the Templars."

"Check out this one." Athena's light paused on a particular set of glyphs—a procession of figures led by Anubis, the jackal-headed god, into the afterlife.

"I think that means we're in the right place," Eden said. "Whatever is down here, it goes back far beyond the Templars."

"Agreed. Remember, though, what the Templars found here was ancient, even for them. We're talking thousands and thousands of years old," Athena said.

Eden drew out her phone and snapped a few pictures of the hieroglyphs before striding on. Ten feet further, the passageway descended sharply to the left like a corkscrew. Eden moved carefully, securing each foot into holds carved into the floor. The air grew cooler as they descended.

After twenty feet, the sharp descent leveled off, and they emerged into a chamber. After the confines of the passageway, the wide-open space felt like a cathedral.

"I think we're right beneath that central area in the temple," Eden said, sweeping her light around the chamber.

She noticed lines of holes on the walls, which she assumed would once have held flaming torches.

"What's this guy's story?" Athena said, the beam of her light focusing on a macabre sight. A skeleton sat slumped against the chamber's far wall.

"I've no idea," Eden said, pacing across the space to get a better view of the grisly sight. "I don't want to end up like him, though."

The bones were splayed out as though he'd stumbled backward; the skull frozen in a silent scream. Traces of tattered fabric clung to the skeleton, the remnants of his clothes now reduced to little more than dust and threads.

Athena turned her attention back to the chamber. "I expect the dimensions line up exactly with the temple up there," Athena said, pacing across to a sarcophagus on a raised dais at the end of the room. "I hate to ask, but do you have any idea what we're actually looking for?"

"Legend says that the Seal of Solomon is a ring," Eden said, sweeping her flashlight around the chamber. "It's not just any ring, though, it's more like a master key which Solomon used to command the spirits and demons."

"It sounds a bit far-fetched to me," Athena said, pacing away and looking at the hieroglyphs on the chamber's far wall.

"I'm with you on that," Eden said. "If you asked me about this stuff a few years ago, I'd have said it was all nonsense. Now, after what we've already seen, I'm not so sure."

Athena turned away from the wall and scrambled up onto the dais. Elevated four feet above the chamber's floor, the position offered her a commanding view of the room.

"I'm reserving judgement until you start talking to animals," Athena said.

"The seal is said to be inscribed with a symbol," Eden continued.

"A star?" Athena responded, her tone sharp. Her flashlight, which swung in broad arcs around the room, was now fixed on a point in the center of the floor.

"Correct," Eden said, not noticing her friend's change in demeanor. "In the modern era, the symbol has been used as the Star of David. Its origins, though, are far older, stretching back thousands of—"

"Eden," Athena interrupted. "You need to look at this."

"Sure, I was just saying that..." Eden turned around and saw the focus point of Athena's flashlight.

Right in the center of the chamber, one slab differed from the rest. The shape of a pentagon, it was about six feet across, with a five-pointed star in the center.

"Is that the sort of star you're looking for?" Athena said.

"Just like that," Eden said, her eyes wide. She took a few steps, focusing on the symbols.

"This must mean we're in the right place," Athena said.

Eden crouched down and explored the sides of the slab with her fingers. "It's fixed in position, and I think it would be too big for us to move, anyway."

"Hold on, there's more." Athena swung her light in a circle, illuminating the slabs which surrounded the pentagon.

Eden turned from the five pointed-star and followed her friend's gaze.

"They look like the signs of the zodiac," Athena said, recognizing the symbols.

"They're the decans, actually," Eden said, focusing on one symbol. "The ancient Egyptians divided the night sky into thirty-six segments. Each segment, or decan, represents ten days of the year, functioning as a kind of star clock. They

were used primarily for timing rituals and for the organization of their calendar."

"That's impressive stuff," Athena said. "Which one is
that?" She pointed at one symbol which looked like a lion.

"That's Menkhet," Eden said, sweeping the beam of her
light toward the symbol. "Menkhet is a lion which symbolizes both the fierce heat of the sun and the royal authority."

"How do you know all this stuff?" Athena muttered.

"You try growing up with Alexander Winslow as a dad,"
Eden quipped. "I pretty much learned to walk at archeolog-
ical digs."

"Good point," Athena conceded. "What about this one?"
The beam of her light rounded on another symbol.

"That's Osiris. He's one of my favorites." Eden strode
toward the symbol, which was three feet beneath Athena's
position on the dais. "The symbol is a man with a staff. He's
often thought of as the shepherd of the heavens guiding the
souls of the deceased."

Eden took a step, her feet now pressing on the edge of
Osiris' slab. A grinding noise tore through the silence like a
thunderclap. The slab beneath Eden's feet shuddered, then
dropped to the ground. The boom that followed was not just
loud—it was bone-shaking. The noise juddered through the
stone floor and walls, filling the chamber with the rever-
berations.

Athena's head whipped to the side as a draft thrashed
across her face. From countless holes carved into the walls, a
hailstorm of arrows burst forth.

"Eden, get down!" Athena shouted, her voice lost against
the motion of ancient gears and stones grinding together.

Without hesitation, Athena leaped. Making her body a
shield, she threw herself toward Eden.

36

ATHENA SLAMMED into Eden and they sprawled against the floor. She glanced over her shoulder as a cloud of arrows streaked overhead. Athena pushed down against Eden's back, making sure they both remained out of the firing line. The arrows clattered against the walls and fell to the floor.

Silence returned to the chamber, broken only by Eden and Athena's panicked breathing. They remained motionless for almost a minute. Finally confident that no further projectiles would come their way, Athena rolled aside.

Eden sat up, her body trembling. She looked around the chamber. Dust hung in the air and arrows scattered the floor.

"At least we know what we're up against," Athena said, struggling to her feet. Athena helped Eden up. For a few seconds, the women stood together, allowing the adrenaline to recede.

Finally calming down, Eden picked her way carefully across the chamber and scooped up one of the arrows. She calculated that at least fifty arrows now lay across the floor.

Eden examined the arrow. The shaft was a sturdy reed, the kind she'd seen growing on the banks of the Nile. The arrow's business end was not merely sharpened wood, but a meticulously crafted piece of obsidian.

"That explains this guy's story," Eden said, pointing at the body they'd discovered on entering the chamber. Eden now noticed how sand had settled against the walls at the sides of the chamber in drifts that were at least six inches thick. She kicked aside one of the drifts and found countless more arrows hidden within.

"These people knew what they were doing," Eden said, rubbing her finger across the arrow's tip. "That's sharp enough to hurt in the morning."

"Agreed," Athena said, eyes locked on the skeleton. "Try to stay out of the way of them in the future, okay?"

"I'll do my best." Eden turned her attention back to the five-pointed star in the middle of the room. "My guess is that one of these symbols opens whatever is beneath that star."

"I think you might be right," Athena said, turning back to the star. "The question is, which one?"

Eden tucked the arrow into her backpack and rubbed a hand across her face. She exhaled, concentrating hard.

"The riddle said that we needed to come here when *the sky is split in twain*. During the equinox, when the day and night are equal," Eden said.

"Yep, we've got that far already," Athena quipped.

"Well, the equinox marks the astrological beginning of the new year, and the rising of Aries, which is the first sign of the zodiac." Eden's gaze shifted from one symbol to the next.

"Okay, what does that mean?"

"We should select the first decan of Aries." Eden paced gingerly around the signs, careful not to step on any of them and unleash another hail of arrows. She found what she was looking for and stopped beside a symbol that looked like a bird and three oval-shaped objects.

"What is that?" Athena said, glancing nervously from Eden to the slab and back again.

"This is Khent-kheru," Eden said. "It's often interpreted as a leader, or someone whose voice is meant to be heard." She dropped into a crouch and examined the image closely. "It also symbolizes the purest expression of Aries' energy. They're kind of similar in meaning, as Aries is a sign of initiative and leadership. As the first sign of the zodiac, it's also associated with the burst of life that comes with spring."

"New beginnings," Athena said thoughtfully. "That sort of makes sense, right?"

Eden paused, looking hard at the decan below.

"Go for it, I say," Athena said, boldly. "What's the worst that can happen?"

"Fifty arrows to the chest?" Eden said. "That's not how I planned for today to end."

"Get ready to hit the deck," Athena retorted.

"Here goes nothing," Eden said. She straightened up and raised her foot above the slab. She looked hard at the image on the slab and then lowered her foot.

"Stop!" Athena screamed, halting Eden in her tracks. Eden looked up at Athena, still frozen in position.

"Just a thought, but doesn't the alignment of stars and constellations gradually shift over time?" Athena said. "If we're talking about the time of Solomon, about three thousand years ago, wouldn't they be different?"

Eden's mind whirred, processing the significance of Athena's interruption. "You're right," she admitted. "I think the celestial sphere shifts one full cycle every twenty-six-thousand years, or one degree every seventy-two years."

"Winslow would figure this in a second," Athena quipped.

"Agreed," Eden said, pacing carefully around the symbols again.

"So, what sign would the equinox be in three thousand years ago?" Athena said.

"That is the million-dollar question," Eden replied.

Neither spoke for a few minutes, both trying to solve the problem.

"I've got it, I think," Eden said, stopping and looking down at one of the symbols. "Three thousand years ago, the equinox would have been positioned in the constellation of Taurus, not Aries, because of the backward movement of the cycle. It would have been right at the start of Taurus, so we are looking at this guy." Eden pointed at a symbol, the predominant feature of which was a pair of stars.

"Are you sure this time?" Athena said, flashing Eden an intense stare.

"How sure do I need to be?" Eden said, shrugging.

"I'd say, at least almost certain," Athena replied.

"I'm almost certain." Eden raised her foot above the image.

Standing on the other side of the chamber, Athena dropped into a crouch. Both women prepared themselves, ready to jump to the floor if necessary.

Pulling a deep breath, Eden lowered her foot and pressed down on the slab.

A boom reverberated through the chamber, followed by

a guttural growl. The sound of stone grinding against stone came next.

Eden and Athena dropped to the ground; their muscles coiled tight, ready to spring into action. Both watched the holes which lined the chamber's walls, waiting to see if any arrows shot forth.

The noise swelled into a cacophony. The chamber trembled and dust cascaded from the ceiling. But, this time, no arrows came.

Eden remained low for thirty seconds, before standing up straight and finally turning away from the arrow holes.

"Look!" Eden said, swinging her flashlight at the central slab. The block of stone with the five-pointed star was sinking slowly beneath the chamber's floor.

Eden and Athena picked their way across the chamber, taking great care not to step on any of the other decans. They reached the hole as the stone came to rest four feet below, exposing a six-foot-wide pentagonal recess in the floor.

"It could be a trap," Athena said, looking closely at the sides of the hole. "Anything could slide or shoot out of there."

"It's a risk worth taking," Eden said, dropping nimbly into the hollow. The stone beneath her feet felt solid. Nothing shot or fell in response to her movement. "It looks alright."

"Just get the seal and we can get out of here," Athena said tersely.

"I'm afraid it's not that simple," Eden said, examining each of the five walls which now surrounded her.

Four were completely devoid of anything, but there was a hollow in the fifth.

"Hold on, there's something here," Eden said, shuffling up beside the hollow. She paused, closely eyeing the object.

"What is it?" Athena said, pacing around the hollow to get a better look. "Is it the seal? Please be the seal..."

"It's not the seal," Eden said with a hint of dejection. She reached inside the hollow. Her fingers brushed against something cold and metallic. Disappointment giving way to curiosity, she grasped the object carefully and pulled it out.

"What is it?" Athena said, crouching down to get a better look.

"If I'm right," Eden said, holding the object up. "It's an astrolabe."

They both studied the object in silence for ten seconds. Made from bronze, the astrolabe was an intricate web of concentric circles and other markings.

"How does it work?" Athena said.

"No idea," Eden said, examining a network of lines. "But I expect these marking represent stars, and—"

"Hold on a second," Athena said. "That doesn't make any sense."

"Why not?" Eden asked, meeting her friend's gaze.

"I didn't think these were supposed to have been invented until the Middle Ages, yet this place is at least three-thousand years old."

"Yep," Eden said, smiling. "We've found ourselves another mystery. But I think this will guide us to—"

A thump echoed through the chamber, cutting Eden off in mid-sentence. A thunderous rumbling followed. The sound shook Eden and Athena to the core.

They whipped around, expecting to see a cloud of arrows zipping in their direction. What they saw, however, was far worse. The beams of multiple flashlights whipped down the passage.

In one swift move, Eden tucked the astrolabe into her backpack. She shared a worried glance with Athena.

Ten men, wearing the robes of the Order of the All-Seeing Eye, hurried into the chamber. Unlike when Eden had seen them in the crypt back in London, though, now they were armed. The men fanned out, pointing rifles at Eden and Athena.

37

AFTER SURROUNDING Eden and Athena with their guns raised, the knights waited for instructions.

Eden and Athena stood, frozen in place, waiting for something to happen.

Finally, huffing and wheezing like a steam train going for a speed record, Wolff hustled into the chamber. Sweat prickled his reddened skin, giving his whole appearance the look of a pig midway through being roasted.

"I really hoped I wouldn't see you again," Eden said, scowling at the man.

Wolff marched into the center of the knights and placed his hands on his hips. The gesture and position gave him the appearance of a lackluster superhero. His tiny eyes darted from Athena and then on to Eden.

"Get out of there," Wolff snarled, pointing at Eden, who was still standing in the recess.

Two knights shuffled closer; their guns aimed at Eden.

Athena leaned down, extending a hand to help Eden climb out of the hollow.

"Don't move!" Wolff screamed, his high-pitched voice

reverberating from the walls with the same violent timbre as smashing glass.

Eden froze mid climb and turned to face the little man. "Get out of there, or don't move. Which is it going to be?"

Wolff looked hard at Eden. He squinted, making his eyes appear as little more than folds in his face.

"Get out of there, then don't move," Wolff ordered.

"Absolutely. Thanks for clarifying," Eden said, taking Athena's hand and scrambling out. Eden met Athena's gaze and stepped in front, showing her the obsidian tipped arrow wedged in the side of her backpack.

Clearly understanding her friend's intention, Athena used Eden's movement to swipe the arrow and slip it behind her back.

"You had me fooled back there," Eden said, meeting Wolff's stare. "All that talk of the bad things my father had planned, when all along it was you and the crazy army behind it."

"I spoke the truth. Your father is orchestrating the End of Days."

"I'm really not sure why you trusted this guy," Athena said, pointing at Wolff. "He looks like a weasel."

"Ooooh, low blow," Eden quipped. "You tried to use me to find the Seal of Solomon for you, just for you to create something far worse."

"Actually, I think he's more like a weird crossbreed between a human and a chicken," Athena said, still looking at Wolff's expression.

"I'm afraid to tell you, Mr. Grand Master, that your plan has failed," Eden said, taking another step. "Your hair-brained scheme is over."

Three of the knights took another step closer to Eden and Athena.

Athena used the movement to work the arrowhead away from the shaft. The head came loose but remained attached to the stem.

Wolff clenched and unclenched his jaw. He shifted from foot to foot, his robes dancing. "My plans are far from over," he said, as though delivering the punchline of a joke. "I'll admit, I was hoping you would simply agree to collect the Seal of Solomon for me, but that's no matter." Wolff shrugged and his robes swished. "You have brought me here and now I can collect it from you."

"You're going to be really annoyed about what happens next," Eden said.

"Pass me the seal, now!" Wolff spat, his scant patience already ebbing away.

"I'd hate to be you, having come all this way for—"

"Stop talking and pass me the seal," Wolff howled.

"Before we get to that, I have a question," Eden said. "You're clearly a resourceful man. Why did you need me in the first place? Why couldn't you come and find the Seal of Solomon yourself?"

"Pure laziness," Athena quipped.

Sensing he once again had the upper hand, Wolff grinned. "Legend has it that the Seal of Solomon can only be found by someone who is a true seeker of knowledge. Unfortunately, in this case, it's not enough to be clever or cunning. The seal only reveals itself to those who are worthy, whose intentions are pure."

"Hold on a moment, so you admit your intentions aren't pure?"

Wolff leaned closer, his gaze unsettling. "It must be wonderful to have such a simple view of the world. I'm sorry to be the bearer of bad news, but such pure intention is a luxury we can't all afford. Our fore-brothers, the Knights

Templar, did unspeakable things in the defense of their mission, and now we will do what is necessary."

"For the eye and the earth!" the knights chanted in reply.

"That's a neat trick," Athena said. "Do they always chant like that?"

Eden laughed out loud.

"What? What's so funny?" Wolff snarled, anger flashing across his face.

"It's funny because we've dealt with a lot of evil people," Eden said. "Sick people really—psychopaths, sociopaths, basically all the paths."

"Osteopaths, they're the worst," Athena added.

"All of them, every single one of them, claimed that the awful things they did were for the greater good," Eden said, folding her arms. "Let me give you a hint here, it's never for the greater good if loads of people die as a result."

Wolff's snarl softened into a cold, mirthless smile. "I wouldn't expect you to understand. Since you are not long for this world, I'll make it clear—"

"If I had a dollar each time someone said that to me," Eden said, groaning.

Athena counted sarcastically on her fingers. "You'd at least have enough to buy us both lunch."

"Joke all you like," Wolff said. "People have joked at my expense my entire life, but that will soon end. It's true that some will suffer as our new world is forged, but our vision is worth the pain."

"Eradicate suffering by killing everyone who doesn't agree with you?" Eden said, her anger flaring. "You want a world full of people just like you."

"Now that is a sickening thought," Athena said, shuddering.

"Our vision is one of order and harmony. We will create

a world where chaos and disorder are relegated to the history books. Yes, the path is treacherous, and the cost may be high, but the results are worth it." Wolff spread his arms wide, as if to embrace the grandeur of his own vision. "This is the 'greater good' we aspire to. A world not mended, but reborn, through the guiding hand of the Order of the All-Seeing Eye."

"The Order of the All-Seeing Eye!" the brothers repeated.

"When you put it like that, it makes a lot of sense," Eden said, nodding. "Except for the part about killing everyone who doesn't agree with you."

"That's the bit I'm struggling with, too," Athena said.

"Enough messing around," Wolff roared, shuffling closer.

Athena shuffled to the side and yanked on the arrow-head at the same time. This time it came loose in her hand. She slipped the stem of the arrow into her belt and closed her fist around the separated arrowhead.

Eden glanced down. Wolff was now two feet from the engraved line of decans which circled the chamber.

"Pass me the Seal of Solomon and I will make your end far less painful than you deserve." Wolff flicked a finger and the knights approached. "I'll even leave you down here, which I think is a fitting end for someone of your passions."

"Isn't that kind?" Eden said, glancing at Athena. "I think I've been wrong about this guy all along. Maybe he really does have a heart of—"

Wolff made a signal and a strafe of bullets ripped through the air. They pinged a few times around the chamber before burying themselves into the soft stone walls.

"I'm getting impatient," Wolff said, shuffling forward again. "Pass me the seal, and we will get this over with."

"You know, I think for once we should do what he wants," Athena said. "This time we've been beaten."

"Very sensible decision." Wolff nodded, sending his jowls and cloak into a synchronized dance. "It will be over quickly, that I promise you."

"Just give him the seal," Athena said. She passed the arrowhead to Eden. "It's over. There's no point delaying the inevitable."

"Yes, yes, very good!" Wolff hissed, vibrating with excitement. "Pass it to me now." He extended a hand, which appeared from the sleeve of his cloak like a puppet's.

Eden glanced down at the arrowhead and worked hard to keep her face locked in a disappointed scowl. Approximately two inches across, the arrowhead was around the same size as she imagined the seal to be. The way it glinted in the light would hopefully fool Wolff until he was close enough, too.

"Fine," Eden said. "You promise to make it quick?" She fixed Wolff with her gaze.

"Yes, yes, of course," Wolff said. The little man was sweating profusely now, oily slicks running down his face like rain on a window. He shuddered with excitement.

"Okay, here you go," Eden dropped her hand in preparation for an underarm throw.

"No, no, don't throw it!" Wolff howled.

Eden's arm swung through the air. The arrowhead sailed from her hand, glittering in the beams of the gun-mounted flashlights.

Wolff sucked in a large gasp. The arrowhead spun, sparkling as it sailed across the chamber.

The knights moved closer, each waiting for their leader's

next command. Wolff was too focused on the object to even think about his men. He charged on, his hand outstretched, totally focused on what he believed to be the Seal of Solomon.

Eden looked at Wolff's feet, inches from the booby-trapped decans.

The arrowhead sailed through the air and then, as though pulled by an invisible hand, dipped toward the floor.

Wolff moved again, his cloak now flowing across the decan.

Eden glanced at Athena and noticed that she too was watching Wolff's movements.

The arrowhead dropped lower, entering a vertical fall.

Wolff groaned in desperation. He took another step, sending his cloak into a flurry of vibrations. He leaned, placing his bodyweight behind the foot that was over the decan.

The slab took the weight for a moment, then all hell broke loose.

38

EDEN AND ATHENA sprang into motion, diving into the hollow where the astrolabe had been hidden. They squeezed into the space, ducking out of harm's way.

Eden watched over the lip of the hollow as the arrowhead tumbled past Wolff's outstretched grasp, glinting on its descent. Wolff staggered with unsteady feet. He swung an open hand at the object, clearly attempting to catch it before it collided with the floor. He struck the arrowhead but failed to catch it. The arrowhead spun wildly off to the side.

For almost two seconds, nothing happened. Eden wondered whether the slab Wolff had stepped on wasn't rigged to fire. Then, deep within the walls of the chamber, the ancient machinery roared to life. Dust cascaded from the roof. A volley of arrows zipped from the sconces lining the wall and shot across the chamber.

Eden ducked further into the hollow. She didn't want to witness the onslaught, but also couldn't look away.

The knights who were closest to the walls howled as arrows sliced through their cloaks and embedded into muscle and bone. Some knights fell, wailing in pain, blood gushing from wounds. Others reacted on instinct, ducking beneath the barrage.

Flashlight beams swished from side to side as the stricken knights rolled across the floor, and others spun around, anxiously searching for their mysterious assailant. Believing their unit under attack, the men who remained standing fired on the shadows. Gunfire roared through the chamber and muzzle flashes flared in the gloom. Bullets ricocheted from the ancient walls, striking some men who had initially fired them. Chunks of millennium-old hieroglyphs rained down; their age-old stories sent into oblivion.

Eden and Athena flattened themselves against the bottom of the hollow. Eden's ears rang as another bout of gunfire hammered across the opening above them. The final arrows clattered to the ground, and the gunfire subsided. Raised voices mixed with groans and shouts of pain remained.

Eden tentatively raised her head above the edge of the hollow and assessed the scene.

Four men lay on the chamber floor, two gripping at their wounds trying to stop the bleeding, two rolling around in agony. Six more men climbed slowly to their feet. They looked around with a mixture of shock and confusion.

Eden recognized one of the surviving knights as Wolff's righthand man. In the absence of their leader, he issued instructions to their uninjured knights to help their fallen brothers. The knights leaped into action, crouching beside their comrades, and applying pressure to the wounds.

Not seeing Wolff at first, Eden wondered whether he had been hit. She looked closely and saw him wriggling across the floor toward the arrowhead. By keeping low, the Grand Master had dodged the flurry of arrows, and miraculously avoided a stray bullet too.

A knight, an arrow protruding from his side, reached out to Wolff, pleading for help. The Grand Master brushed him aside, solely focused on the object in the sand.

Although the scene was horrifying, Eden figured that their window of escape was small.

"Let's get out of here," she said, scrambling out of the hollow and helping Athena out after her. They leaped carefully over the row of decans—not wanting to set off another stream of arrows—and sprinted toward the exit.

GRAND MASTER WOLFF'S eyes remained fixed on the Seal of Solomon lying on the sand a few feet away. As pandemonium reigned, he squirmed his way across the floor, remaining as close to the ground as possible.

A knight fell in Wolff's path, screaming and clutching an arrow in his side. Wolff eyed the man and saw that it was Brother Jenkins.

"Grand Master, help me!" Jenkins shouted, clawing at Wolff with blood-soaked hands.

"Get out of my way," Wolff snarled, crawling out of the man's reach. Whatever casualties occurred today were unimportant, so long as the order achieved their objective.

"But Grand Master, don't let me die!" Jenkins howled, clutching his side. "I'm too young to die."

Wolff returned his gaze to the Seal of Solomon, glittering in the flashlight beams. Although from this distance he couldn't see the seal clearly, soon he would be able to study it to his heart's content.

"I thought I was your favorite!" Jenkins cried.

Wolff blocked Jenkins' moaning from his mind and

edged closer to the seal. Now just feet away, he recounted the betrayals, the maneuvers, and the schemes which had got him to this position. He had played the game with the precision of a chess master, and now was mere inches from his prize.

Bullets zipped across the chamber, and another man howled in pain. Totally focused, Wolff didn't even notice. The Seal of Solomon, the fabled relic which could impart divine power into human hands, would soon be his.

Closing the distance, Wolff sensed the weight of history mounted on his shoulders. He was about to make a lasting impact on the world, in the present and for years to come. His heart rate increased with the anticipation of triumph.

The hammering gunfire finally subsided, and Wolff forced himself up on his elbows. He took a second to glance around. Something moved in the shadows. This close to the ground, Wolff couldn't tell what it was. As long as it didn't stop him reaching his prize, he didn't care. Men lay slumped around the chamber; others began staggering toward the passage. Whatever had attacked them a few moments ago, had done a deadly job. The loss of lives was a cost the order could easily bear when the prize was this great. There were many more men he could call upon if needed. Countless men. Although now, he thought, his fingers inches from the Seal of Solomon, he wouldn't need them. With this one small object, Wolff would claim victory over the biggest armies on the planet.

With the reverence it deserved, Wolff plucked the seal from the sand.

Grasping the seal for the first time, a bolt of excitement moved through him. Wolff lifted the object close to his face to get a better look. Gazing at the surface, Wolff felt as though he were staring into the eye of a snake.

Wolff forced himself to his feet and paced across to the nearest knight. It was Jenkins who lay his side with an arrow sticking out of his leg. Wolff bent down and snatched up the man's flashlight.

"Help me," Jenkins hissed again, grabbing Wolff around the wrist.

Wolff pushed him away and swung the flashlight around to get a proper look at his prize. The object glittered in the beam of light. As Wolff turned the object from side to side, he felt as though the air was ripped from his lungs. He searched frantically for the five-pointed star which adorned the Seal of Solomon. It wasn't there. Nothing was engraved on the object, and now that Wolff saw it properly, he noticed it was sharp at one end.

"It's a damned arrowhead," Wolff bellowed, his face contorted with rage. Veins bulged at his temples as if threatening to burst. His eyes blazed with a fire that was almost palpable.

"Eden Black," Wolff roared, his hand closing around the sharp arrowhead so tightly that blood dripped from his fist. "You will pay for this."

39

Siwa, Egypt.

End of Days Countdown: Thirty-six hours remaining

"There's one thing I'm disappointed about," Eden said, holding a flashlight so that her father could examine the astrolabe in the back seat of the Land Rover. After returning to their base in the mud brick building on the edge of the desert, Eden and Athena had told of their near miss with Wolff in the hidden chamber, and their recovery of the astrolabe.

"Yeah, it would have been nice to find the Seal of Solomon right there," Athena said from the front passenger seat, keeping a close eye on the road for signs of Wolff and his men. Mahmoud, Eden's pilot, had informed them that Wolff's men had blocked the desert road a few miles away and were watching the airport.

While Eden and Athena tried to get some rest, Baxter

and Winslow had concocted a plan, which Eden was now eager to learn.

In the backseat beside Eden, Winslow pulled the jeweler's loupe from his eye and glanced at his daughter. "It's never that simple," he said, returning his attention to the astrolabe.

"Oh, I get that," Eden said. "I'm just disappointed we didn't get to see Wolff when he realized he'd done all of that for an arrowhead."

Athena gurgled an impromptu laugh, almost choking on her drink. "I can imagine it now," she said, scowling in a way that was surprisingly reminiscent of the Grand Master. "Damn you, Eden Black!" she said, making her voice unrecognizably nasal. "I'll get you next time!"

"That's exactly what he would say, too," Eden added.

"You were lucky to get out of there," Baxter said, turning the Land Rover onto the main road and accelerating away from the town. "It could have gone a whole lot worse."

"Oh, how I've missed you, Mr. Positive," Eden quipped, catching Baxter's gaze in the mirror. She held his gaze for a moment and then looked away, feeling uncomfortable at the sincerity she saw there.

"This really is an incredible thing," Winslow said. "Move the light up a little."

Eden adjusted the flashlight to give Winslow a better view.

"Solid gold too. Even the value of the metal here would be worth tens of thousands. Add in the archaeological interest, there is no knowing how much—"

"It's not for sale," Eden snapped. "We need to work out what it means."

"Yes, that's very interesting too," Winslow said, glancing at his daughter. The loupe made his right eye look comically large. "The configuration of this astrolabe differs from the designs I've seen in the past." He turned the astrolabe over, studying the object's unique features. The intricate engravings sparkled in the light.

"What does it do?" Eden said, looking closely.

"Patience, Eden," Winslow said, flashing his daughter a grin. He examined the rotating disc, which looked to be etched with a map of the stars. "Just as I thought," he said. "This isn't a navigational device. It's tailored for a specific region, perhaps even one specific place."

"What do you mean?" Eden said, leaning in to get a better look. The markings meant nothing to her, so she straightened up and concentrated on holding the light steady as the Land Rover rocked from side to side.

The houses of the oasis rolled past on both sides, becoming more widely spaced as they reached the edge of the town.

Winslow ran his fingers across the topmost part of the astrolabe. "This part is called the throne, although I've never seen one look quite like this before." He pointed at another part of the device. "This is the tympan and is usually marked with a projection of the sky for a given latitude. This one has an unexpected pattern, which I think suggests it's for a different purpose entirely."

Eden sighed impatiently as the Land Rover rounded a curve. "Thanks for the tutorial, but what is it for?" she said.

"Whoever crafted this was a master," Winslow said, ignoring Eden's question either purposefully, or because he was too involved in his analysis to even hear it. "I believe this piece is not designed to tell us *our* location, like a classic astrolabe." Winslow leaned forward and tapped Baxter on the shoulder. "Pull over when we get to the desert. The sky there should be dark enough for me to read this."

"Mahmoud's meeting us on the desert road to take his Land Rover back," Baxter said, navigating the Land Rover around a series of switchback curves, rising onto the desert plateau. "It should be dark enough there."

"How are you going to explain what you've done to his Land Rover?" Athena threw Eden a smile.

"I think the truth is probably best," Eden eyed her father, then Athena and Baxter.

"Ouch!" Athena said.

"Fair comment, really," Baxter said.

"The truth is you guys ran me off the road and are happy to pay him back," Eden added.

Rounding the last bend, the road straightened out and led directly out across the sand. Within a minute, obsidian darkness filled the Land Rover's windows. From here, the road continued in a straight line for almost three hundred miles, with nothing more than a couple of truck stops.

"There he is," Baxter said, after they'd rumbled on for a few minutes.

Eden looked up through the windshield and saw the man who had lent her the Land Rover the day before. He held a flashlight in his hands, waving it gently to attract their attention. Without the light, Eden realized, he would have been almost invisible in the darkness.

Baxter pulled off the road and everyone scrambled out. He cut the engine and silence enveloped them.

Eden handed Mahmoud a few hundred dollars to pay for the damage. They unloaded the entire contents of the Land Rover onto the sand beside the road.

Mahmoud slung the bag from his back and gave it to Baxter.

"If we're not driving out of here, what's the plan?" Eden said, eyeing the pile of luggage by the side of the road. She

strolled a few paces and gazed along the length of the road.
The asphalt was faintly visible in the light from the moon
and stars. In the distance, she could see the taillights of a
truck shimmering in the heatwaves.

"You'll find out," Baxter said, turning to Mahmoud. "You
know what to do, yes?"

"Absolutely," Mahmoud said. "Drive the Land Rover to
the airport. Easy."

Baxter nodded and handed Mahmoud another few
hundred bucks. "That's for the supplies," he said.

"That is far too much," the Egyptian said, looking at the
notes.

"No, you've done more than enough for us," Athena said.

Mahmoud nodded and tucked the notes away. He
climbed into the Land Rover, started the engine, and
headed off into the night.

"We'll just wait by the side of the road, shall we? Brilliant
plan, guys!" Eden said sarcastically, clapping slowly.

"We've got to work out where we're going first," Winslow
said, raising the astrolabe toward the sky. He shifted his
stance, orienting himself first to the north, then to the south,
aligning his body with the invisible lines of the Earth's axis.

"Fine, but how are we getting there?" Eden asked.
Everyone ignored Eden's question, now focused on
Winslow.

"There it is." Winslow pointed at a particular cluster of
stars. "Light please."

Eden strode across and angled her flashlight down at the
astrolabe.

"The first thing I need to do is set this to match the position of the stars in the sky," Winslow said, aligning one of
the rings. "This movable rule allows me to work out the
angle and, as such, our position. Or at least that's how it

should work, but this one is different." Winslow played with the rule for a few seconds, then placed the loupe against his eye and consulted the engraved rings on the astrolabe's baseplate.

Eden tapped her foot in the sand as her patience ebbed away.

Winslow paused for a few seconds and looked back up at the sky.

"Remember to account for the shift of the stars over the last three-thousand years," Athena said, looking skyward. "That almost tricked us yesterday."

"Naturally," Winslow said, flashing Athena a glance which communicated that he was already several steps ahead of that. He returned his fingers to the astrolabe, tracing the lines of the symbols. With a jerky movement he stopped and looked at Eden. "I think I've got it. Fetch that map, please."

Grateful to move, Eden paced to their bags and dug out a rolled-up map. She unfurled the map on the sand and cast the flashlight beam across it. The map was marked with various lines which she didn't recognize.

"This astrolabe," Winslow murmured, almost to himself, "it's not simply mapping the stars. It's far more precise, more deliberate."

He raised his head, locking eyes with his daughter, a gleam of excitement in his gaze. "This astrolabe is not designed to tell us our location but to direct us to a specific point beneath the stars." With a furrow of his brow, Winslow looked from the instrument to the map.

"What?" Eden said, peering over her father's shoulder to try to see where he was looking. What she saw made no sense to her at all.

Winslow turned around and ran his finger across the

map as though charting a course. "If I'm not mistaken," he said, grinning in a way that suggested he was rarely mistaken, "considering the celestial precession over the past three millennia, in conjunction with the Earth's axial rotation," Winslow stabbed at the map, "it's telling us to go there."

"And where exactly is that?" Eden said, studying the map. Looking more closely now, she realized what had seemed strange about the map when she'd laid it out. Although the various land masses were all in their familiar positions, none had names, and no internal borders were marked.

"That," Winslow said, tapping the map several times to illustrate his point. "Is modern day Portugal."

40

"THERE ARE two ways out of this town," Wolff said, a pair of binoculars clamped to his eyes. He assessed the airport, then groaned when he realized nothing had changed in the last six hours. "They will either come here or try to get out along the desert road. We have both covered."

Crawling out of the chamber several hours before, Wolff had split the uninjured men into two teams. One of them, led by Wolff himself, came to the airport. The other set up camp on the main road, which connected Siwa to civilization.

"See anything?" Wolff barked into the radio.

"Nothing, Grand Master," came the reply from the knights stationed on the road. "The road is empty. A few trucks have passed. We've searched them but found nothing."

"Eden will know we're waiting for her and will have a plan to get away," Pyne said.

"You think that Eden Black and her crew can outsmart me, the Grand Master of the Order of the All-Seeing Eye?"

"No, Grand Master," Pyne said. "I'm simply saying that to underestimate them would be a mistake."

"We will not underestimate them," Wolff said, swinging the binoculars toward the main terminal. "It's a simple fact that unless they attempt a multi-day trek across the desert, they will either have to take the road or come here."

"Yes, of course, that is correct, Grand Master." Pyne dipped his head.

Wolff turned his attention back to the tarmac. He moved his binoculars in a steady, horizontal arc, shifting from one lighted patch to another, but saw nothing. Beyond the illumination, the runway stretched into the gloom.

"I have a message from our men in the hospital," Pyne said, reading a message on his phone. "They are recovering well. In fact, Brother Jenkins says he will join us again soon. Such bravery, don't you think Grand Master?" Without any command from Wolff, Pyne had arranged for the wounded men to be taken to Siwa's small medical center and paid the doctors enough to treat them and keep their presence secret from the authorities.

"Fallen men are no longer our concern," Wolff said, focused on the scene before them. "Why should we care about them? They have failed." He turned his attention to the small cluster of aircraft.

The nearest plane was the Embraer, which had flown them to Siwa the day before. Beyond that sat two light aircraft operated by a local charter company, and beyond that a vintage Dakota Skytrain. The only plane which interested Wolff, though, sat in the hangar behind them. That was the Piper Cub, which he knew Eden had chartered from Alexandria, and as she such would probably use as her means of escape.

A sudden movement caught Wolff's eye. He swung his

binoculars toward it and saw an old, yellow Land Rover rumble up the access road heading to the airport. A few seconds later, the sound of its growling engine drifted through the still night air.

"That's it!" Wolff shouted, pointing at the vehicle. "They're coming. Prepare to surround them!"

Wolff struggled with the binocular's focus wheel, trying to make out the Land Rover's occupants. With no light inside the vehicle, he could only see shadowy figures through the glass.

The Land Rover turned across the runway, driving straight for the hangar in which the Piper Cub airplane waited.

"I was right! I knew I was right!" Wolff hissed to his men. "As soon as they're inside, we go. Don't give them a chance to get on the plane."

"Yes, Grand Master," the assembled knights whispered, preparing themselves to run.

The Land Rover slowed; the sound of the engine dropping to a purr. Thirty feet from Wolff's position, the vehicle turned sharply and disappeared into the hangar.

"Grand Master, I don't think we should rush in there," Pyne said. "It's too simple. Too easy."

"Nonsense. It's them, I'm sure of it!" Wolff replied, his voice pitched even higher than usual. He pointed wildly into the shadows of the hangar. "Eden Black and her crew are right there!"

Wolff raced from their hiding place, the knights fanning out behind him. At the side of the hangar door, he paused, peering inside. The Land Rover's lights had been extinguished. The only evidence anyone was in there was the sound of the idling engine.

"On my signal, we take them by surprise," Wolff whispered. "No mercy, no hesitation."

The knights nodded.

Wolff raised his hand and pointed at the target. The knights snapped on their flashlights and surged into the hangar. They fanned out across the space, weapons raised and ready.

Wolff followed a step behind his men, using his flashlight to illuminate the scene. The Land Rover sat beside the Piper Cub, the occupants clearly still inside. The knights surrounded the Land Rover within a few seconds.

Wolff rounded the Land Rover and positioned himself beside the hood. "Miss Black, we know you are here. Come out now!" He aimed his flashlight in through the windshield but saw nothing but the reflections of his light.

The engine died and a figure moved about inside.

"Stop wasting time, or we will shoot!" Wolff shouted.

The driver's door swung open. A figure stood and then rounded the door. A thin Egyptian man stepped into the converging flashlight beams.

"What! Who are you? Where is Eden?" Wolff shouted, clenching his fists, his rage finally boiling over.

"I am Mahmoud," the man said, smiling as though meeting a group of angry looking knights was a big joke. "I collect my Land Rover. Look at the mess it's been left in. Two windows are broken. Scratches everywhere! Luckily, they pay for the repairs."

"Search it!" Wolff snarled, his voice echoing. "I know they're here. They can't have gone far!"

The knights lunged, pulling open the Land Rover's doors and searching the interior. As flashlight beams swished through the vehicle, the situation became apparent to Wolff.

"Search the plane!" he said, gesticulating to the aircraft.

A pair of knights ran up to the aircraft and pulled on the doors.

"Well, if you insist," Mahmoud said, stepping from the shadows. "But I can assure you there is no one inside." He dug out a set of keys and unlocked the cabin, followed by the various storage compartments. The knights searched the plane and quickly returned with the answer Wolff had feared.

"Nothing, Grand Master," one of the men reported.

An image of calm, Mahmoud took a few steps into the shadows at the rear of the hangar.

"I don't... they must be..." Wolff stuttered.

A loud, metallic clang reverberated through the hangar, causing Wolff and his men to spin toward the door. The heavy hangar doors swung shut, followed by the unmistakable sound of a lock clicking into place.

"What!" Wolff roared, charging to the doors. He yanked on the giant handle, but the doors remained in position. Wolff slammed his fists against the metal, but the doors remained steadfast. He pulled out his handgun and fired an entire magazine of rounds through the door, hitting nothing.

"Find another way out!" Wolff snarled, his eyes wild with fury. "Check the walls, the roof, anywhere. There must be a way!"

THE WOMAN TURNED AWAY from the locked hangar doors and jogged to the waiting airplanes.

Commotion thundered inside the hangar as someone

pounded on the door, followed by a burst of gunfire. Bullets tore through the metal but hit nothing on the other side.

Pyne shrank back into the shadows as the woman passed. As the Grand Master had led the charge into the hangar a few moments before, Pyne had remained outside. Although they knew Eden had arrived on the Piper Cub and hired a yellow Land Rover, to Pyne it all seemed too simple. Eden Black and her team were cunning, clever, and wouldn't do something that obvious.

Pyne's mind raced as he watched the woman approach the planes. She was older than Eden, possibly in her early middle age. She wore a flight suit, and her black hair was tied high on her head like a beehive. She approached the vintage Dakota Skytrain, then paused at the bottom of the aircraft's stairs and did a three-sixty, as though sensing she was not alone.

After assessing the scene, the woman shook her head and climbed into the airplane. Light flooded the flight deck and machinery whirred.

Seizing his chance, Pyne darted from his hiding place and used the other aircraft as cover to reach the Skytrain undetected. He reached the plane and crouched in close to the fuselage.

The port side engine coughed out a cloud of white smoke and purred into life.

Pyne figured he had moments before the other engine started and the plane was ready to move. He stalked toward the nose of the craft, keeping his back pressed to the fuselage in case the pilot should glance out of the window.

He reached the door and heard the second engine growl to life.

Pyne swung around, pulled open the door, and slipped inside. He ducked in behind a crate and assessed the situation. The aircraft's cabin was dimly lit, with various boxes and crates strapped in position. He peeked toward the flight deck and saw that nothing separated him from the pilot. She moved around, preparing the aircraft for take-off.

A radio buzzed and the pilot responded. Over the sound of the engines, Pyne couldn't hear the words. The pilot settled into one of the seats and donned a headset. The engine's sound increased, causing the whole craft to shudder.

Pyne peered through one of the small windows, catching a glimpse of the hangar in which Wolff and his brothers remained trapped. Wherever this plane was going, Pyne was going there too.

He looked around the cabin again and saw a large wooden crate strapped in the center. He stalked up to the crate and lifted the lid. Without hesitation, Pyne climbed into the crate, his body folding into the confined space like a contortionist. He pulled the lid back into place, plunging himself into complete darkness.

The Skytrain accelerated. The vibrations of the powerful engines thrummed through the crate. Pyne braced himself as the acceleration increased.

The crate jostled and shook. Whatever else was in here with him clattered and shifted with each bump and jolt.

With a sudden lurch, the aircraft lifted off; the wheels leaving the ground as it soared into the night sky.

41

"PORTUGAL?" Eden said, turning on her father. "Why would the Seal of Solomon end up in Portugal?"

"That's another story entirely," Winslow said, grinning knowingly at his daughter. He slipped the astrolabe into a bag.

"History lesson incoming," Athena said from the corner of her mouth.

Winslow cleared his throat as though he were about to start a lecture. "As you know, the Knights Templar—or the Poor Fellow-Soldiers of Christ and of the Temple of Solomon, to give them their full title—were a fascinating order."

"Yep, yep, yep," Eden said. "Portugal?"

"Founded in the early 12th century, the Knights Templar began as a monastic military order dedicated to protecting Christian pilgrims on their way to the Holy Land. But their influence grew rapidly."

"That's still a long way from Portugal," Eden said.

"The knights were sworn to poverty, chastity, and obedience, yet they became one of the most wealthy and powerful institutions of the medieval world. In a bid to safeguard pilgrims, the Knights Templar devised a system of financial security that was revolutionary for its time. A pilgrim could deposit funds at their local Templar Commandery, in exchange for a credit note. Then, because the note itself had no value, the pilgrim could undertake their journey in safety. Upon reaching Jerusalem, or any other Templar Commandery across Christendom, the pilgrim could withdraw the equivalent funds in the local currency."

"Like traveler's checks," Athena said, her arms folded.

"Exactly like that," Winslow said. "Through this, and donations from landowners and their own members when they joined, the order became incredibly wealthy."

"I sense a sticky end," Eden said. "Hopefully it'll involve Portugal."

"Over two hundred years, the knights amassed such a fortune that they became the envy of kings across Europe, and the catholic church. The Templars were so wealthy that they even loaned money to King Philip IV of France, which eventually led to their demise. In 1307, King Philip decided he didn't want to pay back his debt, so disbanded the order. On Friday the 13th of October..."

"Spooky date," Athena said.

"You're quite right, that's where the origins of the unlucky number thirteen and Friday the 13th originate," Winslow said, clearly enjoying holding court. "On that date, Templars all across France and later across the rest of Europe were arrested, charged with heresy and other false crimes, and many were burned at the stake."

"And the link to Portugal is?" Eden said.

"Well, when King Philip raided the Templar houses and castles, what do you think he found?" Winslow asked.

"Ahh," Eden said, realizing the direction of the story.

"The Templars had found out what he was planning and had already moved their riches somewhere else."

"Exactly that," Winslow said, pointing at his daughter. "They were an incredibly well-connected order, so they must have had someone on the inside. You can imagine the King's anger when he found nothing. But there's more—"

"There's always more," Athena said, grinning.

"Legend has it that the Templars' treasury held far more than gold and jewels," Winslow continued, his voice dropping into a conspiratorial whisper. "Their vaults were said to contain items of immeasurable worth, objects that transcended monetary value. Among these were relics of profound historical and spiritual significance, including—"

"The Seal of Solomon!" Athena interjected.

"Exactly," Winslow said, nodding.

"But back to Portugal." Eden pointed at the map.

"When King Philip IV orchestrated the Templars' downfall, with Pope Clement V's help, the Templars faced persecution across Europe. However, their story didn't end there." Winslow clasped his hands behind his back. "In Portugal, the Templars had aided the King in driving the Moors from Portuguese lands. This debt of honor, coupled with their significant contributions to the country's defense and growth, was not easily forgotten." Winslow's gaze swept across his audience, ensuring he had their full attention. "Their stronghold in Tomar became a refuge when elsewhere they were hunted. King Dinis of Portugal told the pope that he'd disbanded the Templars, but this was a deft political maneuver. He immediately established the Order of Christ, which conveniently inherited the Templars' wealth, their lands, and, crucially, their members."

"Genius," Athena said.

"You think the seal has been there all these years?" Eden said, glancing excitedly from her father to the map.

"Based on what we see here, I'm certain of it," Winslow said, nodding at the map. "In fact, I know exactly where it is."

"Tell us about that on the way," Eden said. "Chartering a plane from Alexandria is going to be the best, I think, but that's at least eight hours' drive away. Then there's that road-block to get through."

Eden looked around and noticed the others staring at her. A smile crept across their faces in unison.

"What? Come on, let's get moving!" She clapped her hands.

"We've got a better plan," Baxter said, grinning.

"What? We know Wolff is at the airport. I think taking on the roadblock is the best. It's a long way, though, so let's get moving!"

At that moment, the distinct rumble of an engine cut through the stillness. Eden peered at the road one way, and then the next, but saw no headlights piercing the darkness. Then, tilting her head to the side, Eden recognized that the noise wasn't one engine but two. It was a discordant noise that she had heard many times before.

"You've got to be joking with me," Eden groaned. "How did *she* get all the way out here?"

"How do you think we got out here at such short notice?" Baxter said, still grinning.

"I thought she'd gone back to The States?"

"She decided to stay a little longer after visiting us in London," Athena said. "Apparently, the Skytrain has been booked for air shows all around Europe. She's become a bit of a celebrity, apparently."

"There must be another way," Eden groaned. "We'll drive all night and get on a commercial flight."

"Isn't it wonderful that she's always here to help us?" Winslow said, glancing at Baxter and Athena.

"I'll ride a camel to Cairo and hide on a cargo ship for two weeks," Eden said, her hands balled into fists.

"Some people are so wonderful and selfless," Athena said, as the three broke into giggles.

"I'll walk across the desert, day and night," Eden groaned, eliciting an even louder laugh than before.

"Hold on," Eden said, suddenly alert. "I know she's a great pilot, as people won't stop mentioning, but she can't land out here. It's pitch black." Eden pointed into the desert, which was completely dark.

"I've got that covered." Baxter removed a small device from his pocket. "Or rather, Mahmoud sorted that for us." He turned toward the sound of the engine and saw the Skytrain's landing lights. "She's right on time."

Baxter clicked the device and dozens of flares, their tips buried deep in the sand on either side of the road, burst into life. With a symphony of hisses and crackles, the flares turned the empty strip of asphalt into a shimmering runway.

The deep, throaty drone of the vintage Dakota Skytrain grew nearer.

"She's actually a really nice person," Athena said, padding across to their bags. "Remind me why you don't like her again."

"She's just *there* all the time."

"Yeah, to rescue us when we need it," Athena said. "Remember that time we were stuck in the middle of the Atlantic Ocean?"

"Don't remind me." Eden rolled her eyes, then pointed

at Baxter. "I had to listen to these two discuss their favorite aircraft of all time, for hours and hours."

"It's an important discussion," Baxter said. "Here she comes."

"She's so, argh!" Eden made a noise that was halfway between frustration and surrender. "Captain Baxter, Captain Baxter," Eden said, mimicking Byrd's Southern twang. "That's all she ever talks about."

Athena placed a hand on Eden's arm. "Now you're sounding jealous," Athena said, to a roar of laughter from the others.

Eden blushed and tried to deny it, but her words were drowned out by the Skytrain roaring overhead.

The vintage aircraft sailed forty feet above them; the thrust from its engines whipping sand into great spirals.

Eden cupped a hand above her eyes and watched the brushed aluminum fuselage slide overhead, reflecting the light of the flares like a jewel.

"You've got to admit, that is cool," Baxter said, as the Skytrain dipped toward the road. For a second, the plane swept above the tarmac and then touched down. The plane decelerated; tires screeching against the blacktop. Once stationary, one propeller accelerated, whipping the air into a frenzy, and turning the great silver beast one hundred and eighty degrees. Two minutes later, the Skytrain trundled alongside them, and the engines dropped into an idle drone. Through the cockpit window, Nora Byrd flicked them a salute.

42

Eight Thousand Feet above the Mediterranean Sea.
Present Day.

End of Days Countdown: Twenty-four hours remaining

Eden stood in the Skytrain's small flight deck and peered over Byrd and Baxter's shoulders at the various controls and dials. Although she would never admit it, and scolded herself for even thinking about it, flying the vintage machine was an impressive skill.

"You know, I don't think I've ever met anyone who attracts trouble like you," Byrd said, throwing a glance over her shoulder at Eden. "When was the last time you had a quiet five minutes?"

"Trouble is a state of mind for Eden," Baxter said, a smile playing on his lips.

"You pair are lucky I know how to handle myself," Eden replied, shouting above the drone of the twin propellers.

"You concentrate on the flying, and I'll do everything else. Doesn't this thing go any faster?"

The inky surface of the Mediterranean glimmered under the light of the rising sun beneath them.

"Faster?" Byrd scoffed. "Women of this age don't do speed. And yes, I'm talking about both me and the Skytrain. We've got grace in bucket loads, but speed is something left for the younger generation."

Baxter chuckled, earning himself an icy glance from Byrd. "What's ticklin' you, Captain Funnybone? Don't think because I got my hands full, I can't slap you."

Now it was Eden's turn to laugh, although the cheer didn't last long. She glanced down at her watch to see the countdown timer, which she'd set to the supposed End of Days, pass the twenty-four-hour mark.

"Altitude?" Byrd said.

"Holding steady at eight thousand feet," Baxter replied, peering at one of the many dials. "Shouldn't be a problem to climb higher if needed."

Byrd glanced over at her co-pilot. "You know, Captain, flying through the night like this, it reminds me of my Air Force days."

"Agreed, Captain," Baxter replied.

Eden rolled her eyes and audibly groaned, the sound of which was fortunately covered by the purring of the engines.

"Back in those days, preparation was everythin'. Weather, mechanical issues, enemy fire—you never knew what you might face."

"We won't face anything that dramatic tonight, hopeful-ly," Baxter said.

"You know, flyin' one of those new fangled airplanes is child's play compared to this," Byrd said, examining one of the controls. "Modern flight is all done with computers and electronics. This is real and raw."

"That's all very impressive, but how long do you think it'll take to get to Portugal?" Eden said.

Byrd dragged her attention away from the controls and flashed Eden an icy stare. "Look darlin', when I got the call to say y'all were in trouble, I was sitting pretty in the South of France. When I say sitting pretty, you got no idea quite how pretty. They got wine that people write poetry about, and cheese that's knocking on heaven." Byrd turned her attention back to the controls, a glimmer lighting her gaze. "And I tell ya, that server boy, the one young enough to be callin' me 'Ma'am'... well, I caught him looking a little too long."

Now both Eden and Baxter laughed.

"It's a marathon, not a sprint," Baxter offered.

"Never a truer word spoken, Captain," Byrd replied, throwing Baxter the sort of glance that could melt the arctic. She glanced at another of the dials.

"If you wanna fly charter, honey, I'll drop you off at the next airport. This old dame demands patience," Byrd said, clearly clocking Eden's frustration.

"I'm enjoying it," Baxter added.

"Now that's the nicest thing I've heard all day. You can stay." Byrd threw Baxter the sort of smile that knocked men far stronger than him to their knees.

"Creep," Eden said. "While we are running this marathon, we should make a plan for when we finally arrive in Lisbon."

"You go, Captain," Byrd said, nodding towards the cabin. "I'm good up here for now. I'll holler if I need anything."

Baxter removed the headset, climbed from the seat, and followed Eden back into the cabin.

The inside of the Skytrain had none of the exterior's vintage glamor. Metal ribs lined the walls with cables and ductwork snaking from end to end. Two rows of utilitarian seats mounted at the sides showed their lining where the fabric had worn through.

Baxter placed his laptop on a wooden crate, strapped in position at the rear of the plane. Athena, Winslow, and Eden stood around the crate. Winslow unfurled the map across the top and used a flashlight to illuminate it.

"There's a funny smell down here," Eden said, crinkling her nose.

"Smells like Wolff and his men," Athena replied. "I, for one, don't look at body odor as a badge of honor."

"We best make sure he doesn't catch up with us, or he'll bring back Eau de Dark Ages," Eden quipped.

"I suppose a coffee is out of the question," Winslow said, rubbing a hand over his face. The lines of exhaustion had made a home around his eyes.

"Afraid so," Baxter said, fingers drumming on the keyboard. A mosaic of images filled the screen showing a Gothic manor house set amid a tropical garden.

"Nice place," Eden said, leaning over the crate to get a better look. "Where is it?"

"This is Quinta De Regaleira, near the town of Sintra in Portugal," Winslow said. "It's the exact location that the astrolabe directed us."

"What's special about it?" Eden said, flicking to the next photograph. "This place doesn't look old enough to contain anything left by the Templars."

"Technically, you're right," Winslow said, his voice raised as though he were addressing a hundred people. "It was built in the early twentieth century by the eccentric millionaire, António Augusto Carvalho Monteiro."

"I've had enough of eccentric millionaires since meeting Mr. Van Wick," Eden said, the memory of their recent encounter still fresh in her mind.

"Don't remind me," Athena said, shuddering dramatically.

"Monteiro was very different," Winslow said, flicking through the photographs. "And this is likely to capture your imagination."

Eden and Athena leaned in; their faces illuminated by the screen's soft glow.

"Recognize that?" Winslow said, stopping on a photograph of a grand archway.

"That's the cross of the Knights Templar," Eden said, pointing at a line of crosses carved directly into the stone.

"Yes, it is," Winslow said.

"Was this Monteiro some kind of Templar fan boy?" Eden said.

"Much more than that." Winslow scrolled through the photographs which showed crosses within intricate mosaic floors, ornate ironwork gates, and even on top of fountains.

"Super fan," Athena said. "He loved the Templars."

"Monteiro worked on the estate's design with the illustrious architect Luigi Manini. It's a fusion of Gothic, Egyptian, Moorish, and Renaissance symbols," Winslow said. "Now, although Manini and Monteiro never disclosed the official meaning of their designs, experts believe that every sculpture, every tower, and every carving throughout the estate has a symbolic meaning."

"It's a code," Eden said, her interest piqued. A shudder moved through the Skytrain as they hit a pocket of turbulence. "It's all pointing toward something. But what?"

"You're getting ahead of yourself," Winslow said, glancing at his daughter. "Don't ask what..."

"Why?" Baxter said. "Why did Monteiro choose to build his palace in that particular place?"

"He liked the view?" Eden said, steadying herself as the plane leveled out.

"I believe Monteiro was part of one of the modern descendants of the Knights Templar, of which there are many," Winslow said. "While there is no record of anything notable being on the site beforehand, I suspect he knew differently."

"You think there was some kind of Templar building there?" Eden asked.

"Exactly," Winslow replied, flicking to the next photograph. "It's what's below ground here that makes it really interesting."

Eden, Baxter, and Athena examined the picture. Eden gasped, not quite understanding at first what she saw. The image showed what appeared to be an inverted tower, descending deep into the earth.

"This is the larger of the two Initiation Wells on the property," Winslow explained. "People believe Monteiro had them built for ceremonial purposes. The well contains nine flights of stairs, which supposedly symbolize the nine knights who started the order, and the base of the well is inlaid with the Templar Cross."

"We've seen this before," Eden said, turning to Baxter and Athena. "This looks exactly the same as..."

"The entrance to the Hall of Records beneath the Giza Plateau," Athena said.

Baxter leaned in and studied the photograph closely. "It definitely looks similar, but that could be a coincidence."

"It could, but it probably isn't," Winslow countered. "We know the Knights Templar were in Egypt." He pointed at the astrolabe. "They certainly visited the Pyramids of Giza. I think there's a good chance they figured out how to access the Hall of Records."

"I thought we were the first ones," Eden said.

"It was impressive, I'll give you that. If you could work it out, though, I expect the Knights Templar could too."

"Charming," Eden muttered, her mind racing with the implications. "But what's at the bottom of the well? It's got to lead somewhere, right?"

Now Winslow grinned. "A network of tunnels and passages stretch beneath the entire estate. Some are naturally occurring, and others are dug from the rock."

"But they've been explored already?" Eden said, looking at a photo which showed tourists taking pictures.

"Yes, but as with everything, there is more than meets the eye," Winslow said. "I believe that there is a certain path through the tunnels which a seeker must take. Remember, the Templars were experts at hiding in plain sight."

"And let me guess, that route is somehow hidden in the gardens above," Athena said.

"Exactly that," Winslow agreed.

"So, we've got to solve a riddle that's been hidden in plain sight for over one hundred years," Eden said. "And that will show us the way through the secret passage."

"That's right." Winslow folded his arms.

"Where do we even start?" Athena said, scowling.

"Oh, that bit's easy," Baxter said, locking eyes with Winslow.

Eden's gaze narrowed. She looked from one man to the other.

"When we show you this, promise not to get freaked out," Winslow said, looking directly at his daughter.

Eden folded her arms tightly. "I'll make no such promise."

Winslow flicked to another photograph.

Eden and Athena gazed at the picture, their expressions morphing into ones of astonishment.

"This doesn't make any sense," Eden said. "How is that even possible?"

"That is a question I can't answer," Winslow said, looking over his daughter's shoulder at the photograph.

The picture was of a statue; one of the many within the grounds of Quinta da Regaleira. That statue was constructed in marble and, although discolored from the last hundred years, still very detailed.

"It looks exactly like you," Athena said, gazing from the computer screen to Eden and back again.

Baxter rounded the crate to get a better look, and the three stared from the statue to Eden and back again.

"The likeness is astonishing," Winslow said. "And before you ask, no, I can't explain it."

"Wait a second," Athena said. "Do you remember that sculpture we found in the Hall of Records that looked like you, too?"

"How could I forget?"

"Do you want to know what I think?" Winslow said, eyeing his daughter. "It's the prophecy. The Seal of Solomon will only reveal itself to certain people, so maybe this is a sign that…"

"That person is me," Eden said, leaning in close to the screen. She shook her head slowly, not quite making sense of it all. No one spoke for several seconds.

"Okay, so it does look a bit like me," Eden admitted, straightening up. "How soon can we be there?"

43

Sintra Air Base, Portugal.

BROTHER PYNE LISTENED from the crate as Eden and her team discussed their next move. Although cramped in the tight space, he couldn't believe how lucky he had been. He strained his ears above the rumbling of the Skytrain's engines and listened closely as the illustrious Alexander Winslow told of Quinta da Regaleira and what may lie in the tunnels beneath it.

Pyne's mind raced with the possibilities. The legendary Seal of Solomon, hidden away for centuries, could be within their grasp.

As Winslow spoke of ancient maps and cryptic clues, Pyne committed as much as he could to memory. This was the score of a lifetime, and he was determined to be a part of it.

Hours later, Pyne now straining against the needs of his bladder, the plane began its descent and eventually landed. He tried not to groan and grunt as the Skytrain bounced down onto the runway, each vibration moving straight into his spine. The plane taxied for some time and then ground to a halt.

Pyne held his breath, listening intently as Eden and her team gathered their gear and prepared to disembark. Footsteps echoed through the cabin, followed by the clunk of the door opening.

Silence fell as the group exited the plane. An engine groaned to life and rumbled away, suggesting to Pyne that they'd driven away in a vehicle. He counted to a hundred, then counted again, ensuring they were truly gone. Slowly, cautiously, he pushed against the crate's lid. The wood creaked as he applied more force.

With a final, desperate shove, the panel gave way. Pyne climbed out and his legs nearly gave out beneath him. He held on to the crate and stretched his legs to get the blood flowing again. He allowed time to let his eyes adjust, too. As his body prepared itself for motion, he took stock of his surroundings.

The inside of the Skytrain was as he had seen it a few hours before, except now thick beams of daylight piled in through the small windows. The air smelled of fuel and dust.

Moving as carefully as he could, Pyne paced towards the flight deck. He concealed himself behind a stack of crates and leaned out, peering into the flight deck. Seeing both pilots' seats sitting empty, he breathed a sigh of relief.

Through the windshield, several aircraft were lined up on the tarmac as though ready for their next maneuver. It took Pyne a second to realize that they were military aircraft. He swallowed, understanding the additional challenge this presented. To stop Eden from obtaining the Seal of Solomon, he would first have to escape from a military airport without being seen.

Pyne reached inside his cloak and removed a cell phone. With no usual need to communicate with anyone outside the order, he rarely carried such a device. On this occasion though, thankfully, the Grand Master had given him one to send updates from Siwa. He jabbed at the unfamiliar buttons and called the Grand Master.

"Pyne! You'd better have a good explanation as to why you left us trapped in the hangar," Wolff hissed down the line.

"Grand Master, I have news," Pyne said.

"We had to break our way out," the Grand Master continued without giving his subordinate a chance to speak. "Fortunately, it takes much to keep me confined. I had one of the brothers driver the Land Rover through..."

"Grand Master, it's important," Pyne interjected. "I know where the Seal of Solomon is, but you don't have long." Pyne explained where he was and what he had learned.

"Portugal," Wolff said, clearly thinking it through. He shouted to someone, probably their pilot. Fortunately, the jet that the Grand Master had at his disposal was far faster than the vintage Skytrain. "We're on our way. We will be there in five hours."

"How shall I proceed, Grand Master?" Pyne said.

"Follow them," Wolff said. "And if they find the seal, you are to take it from them." The line went dead.

Pyne stashed the phone away and crossed to the door. He peered out through the window. Fortunately, there didn't appear to be any people nearby. He pulled the door open and slipped out onto the tarmac. The sun was high in the sky, and the heat was already oppressive. Staying close to the fuselage to remain unseen, Pyne assessed his situation. An aircraft hangar sat at the edge of the tarmac; its large yawning mouth exposing a gloomy interior. A line of fighter

jets sat in front of the hangar, with a large transport helicopter beyond. He saw several military vehicles inside the
hangar. He figured that getting use of one of those would be
his best chance of escape.

Pyne spun the other way and saw the control tower.
Fortunately, though, the area surrounding the Skytrain was
free of people to get in his way.

Using the Skytrain's fuselage as cover, he paced toward
the hangar. He reached the back of the plane and slipped in
behind the tail, which would obscure him from anyone
watching from the control tower. He had a one-hundred-
yard dash to the safety of the hangar. He turned back
towards the control tower and decided that moving casually
would be best. That way, if anyone did see him, they might
think he was an engineer heading to the hangar for parts.
He straightened up, loosened his limbs once again, and
strode away from the Skytrain.

"And who in the name of all things holy might you be?"
came a voice from behind him. Hearing the voice, Pyne
froze.

He spun around and saw Nora Byrd: the pilot who had
flown the Skytrain from Siwa. Her hands were now smeared
with grease, and she gripped a large wrench. The starboard
engine cover hung open beside her. She stepped toward
him, wielding the wrench like a weapon.

"No one's approached this plane since we landed, so you
better start explaining where you came from."

Pyne stepped backward and glanced over his shoulder.
Then, bolting like a sprinter, he spun around and ran. His
legs, still stiff and uncooperative after hours in the crate,
took a few strides to get the message. Once they did, he sped
up fast.

Fifty yards from the hangar, Pyne risked a glance over

his shoulder. Byrd was some distance behind him, although catching up fast. Having not just spent countless hours trapped in a box, she was faster than him.

Pyne changed plans, whirled around and charged for one of the fighter jets. He ducked beneath the wings and then weaved around the landing gear, hoping the obstacle would slow Byrd down.

As he emerged from the other side of the plane, a bolt of pain shot through his leg. His knees bent as Byrd's wrench thwacked him in the legs, sending him sprawling to the tarmac.

"Oh man, not this again!" Pyne yelled, falling face first. He landed hard, but immediately leaped up again. He'd only just climbed to his feet when another, greater force, smashed him in the back.

Pyne hit the ground; the impact jarring his body. A knee pressed hard into his back and strong hands locked his arms in position. He bucked and twisted, trying to shake his assailant off, but Byrd held on.

"I told ya," Byrd said. "You gotta explain to me what you're doing messing around back there. Start talking."

Pyne worked one of his hands free and shoved himself to the side. He scrambled along the tarmac a foot before Byrd yanked him back into position.

"No, you don't," she said, not even sounding out of breath. "These muscles were built from decades of work on those airplanes," Byrd said, wedging her hands around Pyne's throat and squeezing hard.

Spots of color danced in Pyne's vision as he struggled for air. Desperately, he reached out, his fingers snaking across the tarmac, searching frantically for something he could use as a weapon. His hand closed across something. He swung around and noticed he held the cable which ran between a pair of chocks. With a desperate yank, he pulled the chocks toward him. The heavy blocks clattered across the tarmac.

Byrd looked up at the incoming weapon. Her grip around his throat loosened for a moment. The reprieve was enough. Pyne sucked in a desperate breath and swung the cable, the chunky metal wedge whistling through the air. One corner of the wedge caught Byrd across the side of the head with a sickening crack. She reeled back, letting go of Pyne's neck completely.

Pyne sucked in a grateful breath and surged upward, throwing her to the ground. He stood, his legs wobbling beneath him, gasping for air.

Byrd's unfocused eyes panned from right to left and then she suddenly snapped into focus.

"Say, that's not very nice," Byrd said, anger now lacing her voice. "Now you're going to pay for that." She wiped away the blood which trickled from her forehead with the nonchalance of cleaning up spilled oil. Then she charged at Pyne.

Pyne spun, searching for something he could use to his advantage. Thirty feet away sat a fuel truck.

Pyne whirled to the side, missing Byrd's outstretched fingers by an inch, and sprinted towards the truck. If he could get in the cab and start the truck, then he figured he could get out of here before Byrd had the chance to raise the alarm.

Although he could hear Byrd's footsteps coming up behind him fast, this time he didn't turn. He rounded the truck, scurried up to the cab, and flung open the door as quickly as he could. He felt the door hit something but didn't realize what it was until he looked down and saw Byrd's comatose figure lying on the floor. Sprinting just a foot behind him, the door had smashed into the side of her head.

"I didn't mean to kill her," Pyne said out loud, jumping down to the ground. Whilst Grand Master Wolff's plans often involved killing, the act had been something which Pyne never agreed with. In his opinion, violence had no place in their modern order, which was probably why Wolff had sent him on his mission to begin with.

Pyne checked the pilot's vitals and was pleased to see that she was still breathing, her pulse steady.

"I can't just leave her here," Pyne said, looking down at her prone figure. He hefted her up from the tarmac and bundled her inside the cab of the fuel truck. He climbed out of the cab and secured the locks on the outside of the cab doors. The primitive system was only designed to open from the outside. It would take her a while to get out once she came around. He jumped back down onto the tarmac and listened again for any sound that would indicate their brawl had been noticed. When none came, he set off again, now limping from the strike with the wrench, into the hangar.

He entered the hangar's cool shade. He knew where Eden and the team were going, but without a vehicle, he was useless. He scanned the shadow of the hangar and saw a Humvee standing at the far side.

"That'll do," he said, charging toward the vehicle.

He reached the Humvee and tried the door handle. To his surprise, it opened easily. Pyne peered inside and saw the keys dangling from the ignition. Not second-guessing his good luck, he climbed into the driver's seat and started the engine.

44

Quinta da Regaleira, Portugal. Present Day.

End of Days Countdown: Twelve hours remaining

"Nice ride this," Eden said, glancing around the cab of the Renault Trafic van that Baxter had procured for the job. The fine dust which lay throughout the vehicle suggested that whoever he'd got it from clearly worked in some form of construction.

"It'll get us there unnoticed," Baxter said from the driver's seat. "What more do you need?"

"Something that isn't going to make me sneeze the whole time," Athena said, holding a hand over her nose.

"You can tell a lot about someone by the state of their vehicle," Eden said.

"Maybe this person is allergic to cleaning products," Athena said.

"It's alright for you two, you're getting out in two minutes," Baxter said, winding up the narrow road which led toward Quinta da Regaleira. "I've got to spend the next few hours back there."

"A big strong guy like you, I'm sure you'll manage," Eden said, placing her hand on his upper arm.

"Your dad's got the best deal," Athena said, eyeing Eden. "Volunteering to stay back in the apartment all night. It's alright for some."

"Agreed, but I'm glad he's staying out of trouble this time," Eden said, remembering how their last mission involved having to rescue her father from a maniac.

"There it is," Baxter said, slowing the Renault. "Remember, if you have any trouble…"

"We'll let you know straight away," Eden said. "With Wolff so far away, it'll be fine. If the Seal of Solomon is here, we will be back out with it soon."

Baxter pulled the Renault to a position where he could see the street in both directions.

Eden swung open the door.

"Be careful," Baxter said, locking eyes with Eden. "There's always danger in places like this."

"Cheers, Mr. Positive!" Athena said, swinging open the door and sliding out.

"We'll be back before you know it," Eden said, following her friend.

Baxter grinned weakly as the women grabbed their packs from the back of the van and disappeared into the gloom.

Eden and Athena crossed the road and stared up at the estate, which was positioned on the steep hillside above them.

"I'm not sure why we couldn't do this during daylight," Athena said, swinging her pack off her shoulders and fetching a rope with a grappling hook.

"It's not like we're here to make some brass rubbings. It's pretty important that we have the place to ourselves." Eden took a deep breath, inhaling the faint scent of moss and earth.

"Here goes," Athena whispered, swinging the hook in an underarm motion. She let go, and the rope sailed high, clanging against the bars. When the rope didn't fall back down again, Athena pulled on it to test its strength. Satisfied it would hold, she scaled upwards and disappeared over the wall.

Eden followed, climbing the rope with ease. Given the lay of the land, the wall's opposite side was considerably lower than the one Eden had climbed. She pulled in the rope and jumped down the other side with ease. She landed in a crouch and joined Athena, standing behind a large tropical plant.

"No security patrols by the look of it," Athena said, a pair of night vision goggles clamped to her eyes.

"It'll pay to stick to the shadows, though." Eden pointed at the statues which lined a broad avenue at the lowest point of the estate. They stalked across the grounds, scurrying from the shelter of one bush to the next. All around them, the estate was alive with small creatures stirring in the undergrowth and, every so often, the solemn hoot of an owl.

"There she is," Athena said, pointing up at the statue. The pair crossed an open paved area to get a better look. "They do say everyone has a doppelgänger." She used her flashlight on its lowest setting to examine the statue. "It's pretty weird that yours is a statue." Athena cast a look at Eden. "Actually, knowing you, it's quiet fitting."

"I've no idea what you're talking about," Eden said, stepping in close to the statue. "I don't think it even looks like me."

"I can tell you, you're wrong about that. It's the spitting image."

"It's a passing resemblance at best."

"I bet it was embarrassing to be naked in front of Baxter and your father," Athena said, lowering the beam of her flashlight across the statue's bare form.

Eden threw her friend a glance. "Two things, it's not actually of me. Second, it didn't feel weird, until you started going on about it. Now it feels really weird, thanks." Eden subconsciously wrapped her arms around her body as though she had been caught in a state of undress. Shaking the uncomfortable thoughts from her mind, she stepped up to the statue and pushed aside the numerous plants which grew around the pedestal.

"Look at this," Eden said, pointing her flashlight at an inscription in the marble. Eden read the instruction out loud. "When the warrior's gaze pierces the veil of night, twins gurgle before the scales of light."

She slid out her phone and took a picture.

"I hate riddles," Athena groaned. "Why can't people write things in simple ways?"

"You know how this works," Eden replied, throwing her friend a look. "It's never that easy. Look at the things the riddle mentions." Eden's light played across the inscription.

"Warrior, twins, and scales," Athena said. "It's the zodiac signs again."

"Exactly. Except this time, we're only talking one hundred years old, so I think our modern-day zodiac will do."

"Orion is the warrior," Athena said, scowling as she raked her memory. "Gemini are the twins, I think."

"Castor and Pollux. The names of the Gemini twins, I mean."

"Now you're showing off," Athena said, raising an eyebrow. "And Libra is the scales of justice which are held by Themis, the Greek personification of divine law."

"Now who's showing off?" Eden quipped. "But where does that lead us?"

The women stood, scowling up at the statue in silence for almost a minute.

"It could be the position of the signs in the sky above us," Athena said, eyeing the night sky.

"You're right." Eden tapped her chin. "Although it could be something much simpler than that, look at how she's standing." Although the statue held both arms at her sides, one wrist was bent with a finger extended.

"She's pointing into the garden," Athena said. "Could it really be that simple?"

"This is hiding in plain sight, remember?" Eden said. "It's supposed to be simple."

Eden and Athena exchanged a glance and set off at a jog. They followed a path which wound its way through jungle foliage until they came to a small crossroads. One path rose toward the manor house; its spires and balconies silhouetted against the night sky like a fantastical dreamscape. The other path dipped down and curved further into the gardens.

"Look!" Eden said, pointing at a statue standing over the fork in the path.

Athena focused her flashlight on the statue, revealing not a man but an owl perched regally atop a pedestal. Its eyes, crafted from opalescent stones, glinted in the light.

"Could this be our warrior?" Eden said.

"I thought Orion was supposed to be a warrior or a hunter?" Athena worked her light across the bird's wings,

which were subtly embossed with patterns of the constellations.

"That would be too easy," Eden said, studying the owl's
talons, which gripped a sphere she thought probably repre-
sented the globe. "I think Monteiro was cleverer than that."

"What makes you think this is Orion?" Athena asked,
still searching the statue for whatever it was Eden had
found.

"How many owls have you ever seen wearing a belt?"
Eden pointed at the belt strapped around the bird's midriff.
Three large jewels glittered from the belt.

"Orion's belt, of course," Athena said, grinning.

"Owls are closely associated with the Greek goddess of
wisdom and strategy. You might know her. She's called Athena."

Athena pouted, folding her arms.

"I can't believe you didn't notice, as it's basically of you,"
Eden said.

"And it looks as though she's pointing us that way."
Athena pointed at the owl's wings, one of which was
extended to the left.

"At least one Athena knows what she's taking about,"
Eden said, setting off down the path indicated.

The path curved through the garden, with a steep mossy
bank on the right and a lake on the left. Eden peered up at
the trees on the right, clinging precariously to the hillside.
They reached a small plaza and slowed to a walk.

"Where now?" Eden said, spinning around. "We're
looking for twins."

Water trickled from a fountain built into the wall at the
side. In the silent garden, the sounds, which would
normally be gentle, sounded like a train.

"We're looking for gurgling twins. This must be the

spot." Athena directed the beam of her flashlight at the fountain, which featured two lizards, their bodies coiled around a giant shell. Water spurted from their open mouths, falling into a clamshell.

"I'd say these lizards are a nod to the Gemini twins," Athena said, tracing the flow of water with her light. "Lizards are creatures of rebirth, shedding and regrowing their tails. I think the way these two intertwine represents the interconnectedness of the twins, as well as the dynamic cycle of life."

"You're good at this," Eden said, throwing Athena a grin. "Either that or you've been spending too much time with my father."

"I am Athena the wise one after all, and you're a lady in the park who forgot to put her clothes on."

"Enough of that," Eden said, spinning around. "Where do you think these lizards are leading us?"

"I'm beginning to like this Monteiro guy. I think he's got taste," Athena said. "I'd say they're both pointing at that place." Athena pointed at the estate's small chapel.

Eden and Athena paced up to the chapel. The pristine white stone glowed in the beams of their flashlights.

"I think we're in the right place," Eden said, focusing her beam on a series of reliefs showing biblical scenes, esoteric symbols, and above all, the Templar Cross.

"There're loads of them, look." Athena's light followed a row of Templar crosses around the roof. "This guy really loved the Templars."

They approached the door and found that, unsurprisingly, it was locked.

Eden drew out her lock picks and set to work on the padlock. Within two minutes, the lock clicked open.

"I'm glad you brought those," Athena said, "as I would have suggested bashing it open."

Eden pushed open the chapel door and stepped inside. Athena followed, both their flashlights sweeping through the space. What they found was a shrine to the Templar legacy. A celestial fresco adorned the vaulted ceiling, glimmering faintly with traces of gold leaf. The stained-glass windows, unlit by the night but still visible in the torchlight, were vibrant mosaics of sacred symbols and narratives. Most obvious of all, was the chapel's floor, simply a giant mosaic of a Templar Cross.

"I think we've found the place," Eden whispered, her voice loud in the small space. "Now look for the scales."

Eden and Athena split up and searched one side of the chapel each. It didn't take Eden long to find what she was looking for.

"There, look," Eden said, pointing at one of the windows. Set within the stained glass was the image of a scale; its trays slightly out of balance. Athena shuffled across, being careful not to move any of the pews out of position and gazed up at the symbol.

"It looks like one tray is pointing downwards, don't you think?" Athena said.

Eden moved her light down across the wall, which was devoid of any carvings. She dropped to her knees and studied the pew sitting directly beneath the window.

"It's got to mean this pew," Eden said, running her light across the carved wood.

"Look there," Athena said. Carved into the chunky arm rest, was another, smaller version of the scale.

Eden traced the carvings with her fingertips, searching for anomalies in the woodwork. As she applied pressure, a subtle indentation gave way beneath her fingers. With a faint click, a section of the pew's flank shifted, uncovering a concealed nook.

"What's in there?" Athena hissed, excitement lacing her tone.

Eden coaxed the secret panel wider and slid her fingers inside. She drew out a scroll concealed in a leather pouch.

"It's exactly like the one I got from Wolff," Eden said, placing the package on the pew. An embossed Templar Cross glittered from the leather. She carefully drew the parchment out of the leather pouch and opened it out.

"It's going to be another riddle, isn't it?" Athena said.

"I'm afraid so." She shone her light on the parchment and read the words. "In the holy nine's silent tread, initiates must seek what lies unsaid. Therein lie the streams of arcane lore, coursing unseen through the earth's ancient floor."

"Monteiro, what are you doing to us?" Athena huffed. "Just as I was starting to like you."

"Shhh!" Eden replied, her expression hardening.

"What? I'm saying that these riddles are hard to understand."

"No, not that," Eden hissed. "Someone's coming, listen."

45

Nora Byrd groaned. Her head pounded as though a herd of elephants were tap dancing on her skull. She opened her eyes and blinked several times. At first, her surroundings spun and whirled around her. After a few seconds, they came into focus.

"What's going on 'round here, huh?" she said, her voice little more than a hoarse whisper. She pulled herself upright to get a better view. She was in the cab of a truck, looking out at the airfield. The Skytrain sat one hundred feet away, now cloaked in darkness.

"I must have been out a while," she said, finally recalling the sequence of events which had led her to ending up here. "The snake got the jump on me. That hasn't happened in years. Losing your touch, Byrd."

She raised a hand to her head and noticed that her wounds had already started to heal.

"He really did get the jump on me. No time to worry about that," she said, steadying herself on the dashboard. "If he was in the Skytrain that whole time, the chances are he heard where they're going." She patted down her pockets, looking for her phone but found nothing.

"Damn, it'll still be on the flight deck."

Byrd shoved against the door, but it didn't move. She tried again, pushing her total body weight against the thing. Still, it didn't move.

"No time for this," she groaned, reaching beneath the passenger seat, and pulling out a fire extinguisher. She threw the thing through the glass and then kicked the remaining shards out with her boots.

She half-scrambled, half-fell onto the tarmac. She held on to the truck for a few seconds to let the world stop spinning. Once her dizziness had passed, she staggered back to the Skytrain. She reached the plane and hauled herself up the steps. Inside, she found her phone exactly where she had left it, sitting on the console.

With shaking hands, she called Baxter. It rang once, twice, three times. She paced through the plane, her heart pounding, until finally, Baxter picked up.

EDEN AND ATHENA switched off their flashlights and sat in silence for almost half a minute. The faint gurgling of the lizard fountain and the distant hooting of an owl drifted in through the door, which remained slightly ajar.

"I'm certain I heard something," Eden said. "It was a clang, like someone shutting a gate, or even climbing over the fence."

"Let's take a look." Athena scurried back over to the door of the chapel, Eden a foot behind. Athena dug into her bag and drew out a set of infrared goggles, slipping them over her eyes. She nudged the door ajar and gazed into the shadowy gardens. She scanned the gardens in both directions and then froze.

"What is it?" Eden hissed, noticing the muscles in her friend's back and arms stiffen.

"Someone's coming this way," Athena said, the hard edge returning to her voice. "They're passing the house now, about fifty feet away."

"Could it be a routine security patrol?" Eden said, gazing into the darkness herself, but seeing nothing without the aid of night vision.

"It's not likely," Athena said. "They're not using a flash-light. That means they're either finding their way by the light of the sky, or they're using some kind of night vision themselves."

"But no one knows we're here." Eden's watch vibrated, indicating an incoming call. "It's Baxter." She thumped the answer button and turned the volume down to its lowest setting.

"One of Wolff's men is here," Baxter said, his voice a distant hiss from the watch. Not expecting to face human threats this evening, they had come without their usual comms set up. "Byrd called. Somehow the man got on board the Skytrain back in Siwa."

The news sent a shiver through Eden's body.

"This guy is dangerous," Baxter said. "He knocked Nora unconscious and somehow got out of the airport without raising the alarm. If he shows up, get out of there."

"It's a bit late for that," Eden whispered. "He's here."

The noise of Baxter's sharp inhale came through the phone.

"He hasn't spotted us yet," Eden said. "And I plan to keep it that way."

"Get out," Baxter said, tension lacing his voice.

"Negative," Eden replied, glancing at the countdown on her watch. "We have no time for that. We're too close. We get what we came for and then we get out of here." Not wanting to hear Baxter's attempts to get them back to safety, Eden ended the call. She turned her attention back to Athena. "At least now we know who he is. What's he doing?"

"He's stopped at the junction with Athena the owl, I think. He's just standing there."

"Good, that means he doesn't know where we are." Eden turned her attention back to the parchment. "Hold on a second. I think I know where this is leading us." She read from the parchment. "In the holy nine's silent tread, initiates must seek what lies unsaid."

"It's got to be the Initiation Well," Athena said, climbing slowly to her feet. "Let's go."

Eden rolled the parchment and slid it back inside the leather pouch and then placed it inside her bag. She checked the chapel was as they'd left it, and then followed Athena out into the garden.

With the goggles still in place, Athena led them across the plaza and ducked in behind the gurgling lizard statues.

"I can't see him," Athena said, peering out from around the statue. "He must be up there somewhere."

"There's a track this way. It will lead us all the way there," Eden said, remembering the detailed map of the estate they'd studied during the flight.

"I'll lead," Athena said, turning toward the path.

Eden clamped her hand across Athena's shoulder and together they scrambled up the narrow path, which weaved its way through the tropical plants. They reached an open patch of ground where their narrow track joined a wider one.

Athena froze and dropped into a crouch. Although Eden couldn't see what had caused the movement, she knew it wasn't good.

"Forty feet, three o'clock," Athena hissed, pulling Eden's ear close to her mouth. "Stay low."

Eden checked her watch. "We haven't got time. You got zip ties?"

"Wouldn't leave the house without them," Athena replied. Even in the total darkness, Eden sensed the other woman was smiling.

"It's time to take this player off the board," Eden said, crouching out of sight.

Athena peered from behind the outcrop as the man advanced in their direction. Eden tuned into the crunch of his boots on the gravel. The duo held still as the knight closed the distance to mere feet.

Athena gave Eden's arm a silent, unseen nudge—their cue to act. In seamless unison, the two women leaped into motion.

"Looking for something?" Athena leaped out in front of the man and delivered a kick which would normally break ribs. Her foot thwacked against the knight's stomach, but the man barely moved. She swung back and struck again, attempting to slam a fist into his jaw. The knight raised his guard, and he weathered both strikes with ease. Once he sensed Athena was off balance, he closed in.

While the man's attention was focused on Athena, Eden took her chance. She rounded the looming figure and went low, sweeping his legs out from beneath him. Still focused on striking Athena, the knight didn't know she was there until his legs gave way and he stumbled. His hands swung through the air, reaching for something to steady his fall. He attempted to take a step backward, but Eden swung again, knocking his other foot out of position.

Athena darted and shoulder-barged him further off balance. For a second, the knight teetered, desperately trying to find his balance. Finally, he slammed down into the gravel. Athena stepped up to the man and pinned him to the floor.

"This is for Byrd," Eden said, aiming a kick at the man's temple. "No one hurts one of our crew."

As Eden's foot swung toward the man's skull, a series of intense lights snapped to life. She staggered back, shielding her eyes with her hand as spots danced across her vision.

"It's a trap!" Athena said, pulling off the night vision goggles.

Figures emerged from the shadows, converging on their position from all sides. The men took another step. The eye within the triangle shone from the chests. Each held a rifle, a flashlight mounted on the barrel, which they now pointed at Eden and Athena.

Eden swung around, frantically looking for a way out. They were surrounded by a wall of gun-toting men.

"Very sweet gesture, not wanting someone to hurt your crew," Wolff said, stepping out from behind a tree and following his knights toward the path.

The man they'd knocked to the ground buckled, throwing Athena off balance, and then he got back on his feet.

"Good work, Brother Pyne," Wolff said, as the encircling men tightened around Eden and Athena.

Eden scowled at Pyne, glad that she'd got a couple of kicks in before the entourage arrived.

Almost two feet shorter than his men, Wolff staggered onto the path. His cloak swaying around his bulky midriff.

"How?" Athena said, checking the night vision goggles. "This place was clear. No heat signatures at all."

"You know, when our brothers first sought sanctuary in this land, they had none of this technology. They had to rely on instinct alone. They say that a warrior monk could tell the direction of his enemy by smell alone," Wolff said, linking his hands together.

"It's true that people did use to stink in those days," Eden said. "Your cloaks must have some kind of thermal insulation designed to confuse infrared."

Wolff's jowls wobbled and his piercing gaze fixed firmly on Eden. "Impressive Miss Black. Indeed, you are correct. Although we may be an ancient order, we can borrow tricks from the modern world when needed."

"All except him," Eden said, pointing at Brother Pyne.

"That's right, Brother Pyne's cloak is made of regular fabric," Wolff said. "We needed something to draw you out into the open, you see."

The knights took another step, further tightening their net.

"Take their bags," Wolff said. "It's time that we enlist the help of these two capable women."

46

Baxter sat in the uncomfortable driver's seat of the Renault van; his hands clenched tightly in his lap. The silence in the vehicle was deafening, broken only by the occasional creak of the old suspension as he shifted his weight.

He stared at the road through the windshield; his mind a whirlwind of worry and frustration.

With limited time, and not expecting trouble, they had gone in without their usual array of technology. Baxter had suggested waiting until they could source the equipment they needed, but their need to find the seal before Wolff and his men caught up had ultimately won out. Now, with no way to monitor Eden and Athena's progress, or communicate with them, Baxter felt the full weight of that decision. Eden and Athena were out there, and he was stuck here, blind, and helpless.

He peered at the digital clock on the dashboard. As the minutes ticked by with agonizing slowness, Baxter's imagination ran wild, conjuring a thousand scenarios, each more dire than the last.

He ran a hand over his face, feeling the rasp of stubble

against his palm. The waiting was the worst part. The not knowing, the inability to help. It made him feel useless, which he wasn't accustomed to and certainly didn't enjoy.

A shadow moved across the driver's side window. Baxter turned around. His heart leaped into his throat, as a figure materialized from the gloom. As the figure neared, Baxter recognized the unmistakable silhouette of a knight, the distinctive eye and triangle etched on his chest.

Baxter lunged for the door handle, swinging it open with all his might. The heavy metal door slammed into the knight, sending him staggering back with a grunt of pain.

Baxter leaped from the driver's seat. He raised his fists raised, ready to fight. He charged toward the knight and landed a strike on the man's jaw. The knight took another step backward. Baxter saw three more knights emerging from the shadows all around him. These men held weapons, which they leveled at Baxter.

The knights advanced; their movements precise and coordinated. Baxter knew he was outmatched, but he wasn't going down without a fight.

He ducked and swung at the nearest knight. His fist connected with a satisfying crunch. The knight staggered back, but before Baxter could press his advantage, another of the men raised his rifle and fired, raking the ground at Baxter's feet with a hail of bullets.

Baxter bobbed down again, narrowly avoiding the deadly spray. He could feel the heat of the bullets whizzing past,. With a quick, desperate move, he kicked out at the nearest knight's legs, sweeping them from under him. The man went down with a heavy thud, rifle clattering to the ground. Baxter lunged for the fallen weapon. He swung around to the rear of the fallen knight, using the man's body as a shield against the incoming fire.

Baxter gritted his teeth and aimed the rifle back at the shooters. He had a clear shot. One squeeze of the trigger and he could even the odds. But before he could fire, a sudden, blinding pain exploded at the back of his skull. Stars danced across his vision as he fell to his knees. The rifle slipped from his grasp.

Rough hands grabbed him, wrenching his arms behind his back with brutal force. He struggled, but his body wouldn't cooperate. The world spun around him, blurring the knights into a menacing kaleidoscope.

He felt the cold, hard press of a gun barrel against his temple. "Don't move," a gruff voice ordered. "Or I'll put a bullet in your head."

Baxter remained still. The pain in his head was over-whelming, a pulsing, sickening throb that made it hard to think.

As they hauled him to his feet, he glimpsed the knight he'd used as a shield. The man was stirring, pushing himself up from the ground with a groan.

"THERE'S one thing I don't understand," Athena said as the knights escorted them toward the grand manor house at the heart of the estate.

"Why anyone listens to an idiot like this?" Eden pointed at Wolff ambling at the front of the group.

They turned a corner and the house emerged like a vision from another age. The spires and turrets reached up into the sky as though plucked directly from the pages of a medieval tale.

"That wasn't what I had in mind, although it is an

important question," Athena said. "I don't understand why you were about to knock that guy out for hurting Nora Byrd, when you've frequently said she's one of the most annoying people you've ever met."

"You're right," Eden said, laughing despite the fraught situation. "It seems like she keeps showing up, whether or not I like it."

"Yeah, mostly to rescue us."

"And to flirt with Baxter, which is honestly the most sickening thing I've ever seen."

"Even more unsettling than Van Wick's secret lab?" Athena asked.

"Okay, agreed," Eden said, eyeing one of the gargoyles perched at the corners of the rooftop. The creature peered back at her, its grotesque face lifelike in the sweeping flashlight beams. "That was the most disgusting, but Byrd and Baxter's flirtations are number two."

"I'm pretty sure it's nothing," Athena said. "I think Baxter only has eyes for—"

"Quiet!" Wolff roared, reaching the house and flinging open one of the doors. The fact that the place was already unlocked proved how organized these men had been. Eden and Athena had walked straight into their trap.

Wolff led the group into the house; their footsteps pounding heavily across wooden floors.

In the swishing flashlight beams, Eden eyed the intricate plaster moldings and finely patterned wallpaper.

Wolff turned left, leading the group into a room. Windows lined two walls, offering views of the gardens and the paved area beside the house. A knight flicked a switch and lights blazed.

The knights shuffled on, pushing Eden and Athena into the center of the room. One knight dumped their bags on a heavy wooden table and retreated to guard the door.

Eden took a few moments to assess their surroundings. The crazy dream like style of the house and gardens continued in the interior. The main feature of the room was a giant fireplace, carved with hunting scenes. The vaulted ceiling was studded with ornamental roses, and the floor was a mosaic of various signs and symbols. Although Eden took in the details of the design, she was really assessing their options. Two armed monks blocked the door and the windows. Right now, she decided, their options were non-existent.

Wolff paced into the center of the room and peered dramatically up at the ornate ceiling. He inhaled and wiped the sleeve of his cloak across his face.

"I don't know why I didn't think of this place before." Wolff spun around as though seeing the place for the first time.

"Because you're an idiot," Eden replied.

"I don't think he intended for us to answer that," Athena said.

"This is the perfect place to hide a relic as important as the Seal of Solomon," Wolff said, eyeing the room's carvings. "Monteiro was one of our brothers and knew the history. What an amazing man he was, creating this estate, and this wonderful house."

"Maybe we should show him some respect and get out of here," Eden said.

"This is the hunting room," Wolff pointed at the floor. "You see, the animals and wildlife in the mosaic? Of course, it's the fireplace that's the true star of the show here." Wolff stared up at the giant fireplace. As though he'd only just remembered why they were there, Wolff turned to face

Eden and Athena. "I expect you're wondering how we got two steps ahead of you."

"It hadn't even crossed my mind," Eden said, her arms folded. She might be this guy's prisoner, but there was no way she'd admit that they'd been outsmarted.

"That's all down to Brother Pyne here," Wolff said, pointing at Pyne, whose imposing figure now filled the doorway. "He slipped aboard your plane back in Siwa."

"Yeah, I figured that much," Eden said. "Funny, at the time, I thought a rat had died in one of the air vents."

"As soon as you and your crew disembarked, Pyne called and told me everything. With our modern jet on standby, we were able to make the journey in a few hours, during which we had already figured that you would come here. Thus, we set the stage and lay in wait." Wolff paced across to Eden and Athena's bags and tipped the contents out onto the table. "Now that wait is over. It is finally time to fulfill our destiny."

Wolff rifled through the objects, poking them as though they might somehow contaminate him.

"What is this?" Wolff said, picking up the leather pouch which held the parchment they'd discovered inside the chapel. Noticing an embroidered cross on the pouch's side, Wolff lips parted in a grin.

"It's my shopping list," Eden quipped. "I like to write on parchment, as it makes everything feel more important."

"I know exactly what you mean," Athena said. "I write mine in ancient Sanskrit."

Continuing to ignore Eden and Athena's interruptions with irritating success, Wolff slid out the parchment and flattened it on the table. He read the antique text.

"This has got to be it," Wolff said, pausing to wipe his face with the sleeve of his cloak. "It has to be. There is no other option." He straightened up and his gaze rose to the ceiling. "This is the piece we've been looking for all these years. This will show us the path to the Seal of Solomon and unite us with our destiny as leaders of this sinful planet!" Wolff raised his hands, as though speaking directly with the almighty. His hands dropped to his side, and his gaze locked on Eden's. "And *you* are going to get it for me."

47

SILENCE HUNG in the room for several moments. Eden met Wolff's gaze head-on, and she noticed something wild, almost demonic, lurking in his eyes. There was a glimmer of madness, obsession, and dangerous intent there, which Eden had seen too many times before. An unsettling chill trailed down her spine.

"I'm not the hired help," Eden said, her voice hard and her arms crossed. "The only thing I'm going to do for you is feed your body to vultures."

"Ha! I love it!" Wolff said, clapping his hands. "But I'm afraid you are wrong. You will do exactly what I need you to do."

Eden raised an eyebrow. "You know, for as long as I can remember, people have tried to get me to do what they want." Eden spat the words as though they were venomous. "First, it was at school, doing those boring tests and learning pointless things. Then, it was my father, wanting me to toe the line for his corrupt archaeological sponsors. Since, there have been many abhorrent people who have threatened me. I'll tell you this... it's never worked."

Wolff's stare intensified. His eyes narrowed into slits. Despite the chill, Eden met his gaze unflinchingly.

"I do appreciate your candor," Wolff said, interlocking his fingers. "But as you'll soon realize, this situation is somewhat different."

"Different because you're less scary, less intelligent, and frankly, deranged," Athena said.

"She's right, I don't think you'll even make my top ten villains list," Eden said.

"Let me give you some advice..." Wolff said.

"Oooh, life advice from a psychopath. My favorite!" Athena said.

"Just because you haven't done something in the past, doesn't mean you won't do it now. Change should be welcomed," Wolff said, his voice carrying a note of conviction. "To fear change is human, but to grasp its importance as a catalyst for betterment is to possess true wisdom."

"Did you read that inside a fortune cookie?" Athena said. "If not, you should send it in."

"Change is the architect of evolution," Wolff continued, his arms spread wide. "Across history, it is those who have adapted to change whose names are remembered. Let me tell you about one man who did just that."

"Boring lecture incoming." Eden fake yawned.

"Jacques de Molay was the true essence of that truth. Even in the face of unspeakable adversity, he stood by his convictions, refusing to renounce us even at the peril of his own life. He has become an inspiration."

"Hold on a second, you just told me change is important..."

"Not just important, it is the currency on which the human race will survive!" Wolff bellowed, a fire now burning in his eyes.

"Alright, yes, I get that," Eden retorted. "You tell me this Molay dude stood steadfast in his convictions..."

"Exactly!" Wolff said, wielding his chubby finger as though it were a magic wand.

"He doesn't get it," Athena sighed.

"They're opposites," Eden said, sighing. "Change and standing steadfast are opposites. You're talking nonsense."

Wolff snapped his mouth shut. His eyebrows rose on the outsides and fell in the center, giving him an owlish look.

"She's got a point," came a voice from the other side of the room.

Eden swung around to notice one of the knights eyeing the Grand Master. He was slimmer than the others, with a pronounced overbite on his lower jaw.

"I have suggested that we plan these speeches in advance, to prevent this sort of thing from happening," the knight continued.

"Shut up, Jenkins," Wolff snapped with a venom that made the other man drop his gaze back to the floor.

"To summarize the conversation we were having before you went all History Channel on us," Eden said, her hands planted on her hips. "You and the Brothers Grimm here can go for a hike."

Wolff's visible frustration ebbed away, and a grin lit his face. "I thought you might say that, so I have prepared a little incentive to help you see the light." Wolff stepped aside like a showman presenting an act. He pointed at one of the large windows, offering a view of the grounds.

Eden's instincts sent a silent alarm ringing through her body. Yet again, she had the sense of pieces moving in a dark game they had only begun to comprehend. Her eyes flicked from Wolff to Athena. The levity that so often played upon

Athena's features had drained away, showing that she felt the same.

Eden shot Wolff a gaze of pure fire and paced across the room. Approaching the window, she realized that from her previous position she hadn't been able to see the large terrace area at the side of the house which lay directly beneath them. Noticing movement down there, she felt a visceral dread coiled within her gut.

Reaching the window, the sickening whisper in Eden's stomach became an all-out roar. Before she could fully comprehend what lay below, Wolff spoke again.

"On the 18th of March 1344, Jacques de Molay, the last official Grand Master of the Knights Templar, was burned at the stake. Whilst his execution ended his life, it fortified his legend."

Illuminated by a set of pole mounted floodlights, Eden noticed that Wolff's men had constructed a pyre on the paved area beside the house. As Eden watched, several men dragged a large cabinet from the house and set about smashing it up with axes and hammers. While they did this, another man poured fuel across the shards of smashed up furniture which were already arranged around a pole in the center of the pyre.

"As the flames consumed Molay's mortal form, he became a martyr," Wolff continued. "Whilst his death offered us a beacon which has guided us through the ages, it was surely an incredibly painful way to die."

As Wolff continued talking, his tone taking on the cadence of a lunatic, Eden noticed that the wood was arranged with a statue in the center. Eden realized it was the statue that had started this whole escapade almost an hour ago; the one that everyone thought looked like her.

Two figures emerged from the gloom at the edges of the

garden. Eden noticed they moved unnaturally, as though they were dragging something heavy. They stepped into the light and Eden's heart did a full rotation. Two knights dragged Baxter to the statue. Baxter fought and kicked, but the knights held him firm. The knights dragged him in through the pyre and up to the statue. As the men tried to secure him in place, Baxter worked one of his hands free and slammed a fist into the knight's jaw. He spun around and turned his attention to the other knight, elbowing the man in the throat.

Hearing the scuffle, the knights who were smashing apart the cabinet rushed over to help. The four men subdued Baxter, and within a few seconds, he was locked in place.

"I think you'll agree that in this situation, change is the best option."

Eden whipped around and charged for Wolff, ready to smash his head into the wall and not stop until he let Baxter go. She had only got three feet across the room when a powerful arm gripped her from behind. Eden lashed out, still managing to send a fist into Wolff's jaw.

Wolff yelped in pain, staggering backward.

Another knight closed in on Eden, grabbing her wrists in a steel-like grip. Eden struggled for a few seconds, and then, realizing it was futile, stopped.

Wolff grimaced. His eyes glistened with madness and shock from the attack. He touched his lip and eyed his bloodstained fingers.

"Seize her as well," commanded Wolff. His voice carried a malevolent edge unlike any he had displayed before. He pointed at Athena. "Let's give young Eden two reasons to do what she's told."

Two more knights approached Athena.

"Touch me and you'll regret it," Athena snarled, dropping into her fighting stance, and taking a step backward.

Unaffected by her threats, the monks approached. Athena struck out, landing three solid punches on the leading man. The men pushed on and within a few moments, had her arms locked in position. Athena kicked out but got nowhere. The monks, positioned on either side, dragged her out of the room.

Wolff turned to face Eden with a mocking angelic look on his face. "This time you'll do want I want."

48

Eden watched at the window as the men appeared below. They dragged Athena to the pyre and secured her in position beside Baxter. The rest of the knights finished breaking up the cabinet and added the wood to the pyre. In a move which sent a sickening feeling through Eden's guts, one knight appeared with a container of fuel. The man flipped off the top and splashed fuel across the pyre.

"Of course they wouldn't have used gasoline in De Molay's day," Wolff said casually. "But unfortunately, we are short of time."

Eden turned around and eyed the Grand Master. For a second, she stood coiled, ready to attack. The knights stationed by the door straightened up, clearly preparing themselves to intervene. Realizing how truly outnumbered she was, Eden took a step back and relaxed her posture.

"You are an intelligent woman," Wolff said, placing the palms of his hands together. "You will have assessed your options and hopefully decided that your best choice, the route offering the greatest chance of survival for you and your friends, is to do what I want." Wolff's flabby lips formed into a grin. He flicked a wrist toward the window, through which Eden could see Athena and Baxter struggling against their restraints. "We will get this over with, and you and your friends can go."

A long moment of silence passed. Eden's gaze burned into Wolff's as she searched for a flicker of humanity in the man. She found none.

"How can I trust you?" Eden said, unblinking. "How do I know you'll let us go when you have the Seal of Solomon?"

Wolff bared his teeth and cackled. "You know how to make the Almighty laugh?" he said, none of the humor making it to his voice.

Eden didn't reply.

"Tell him your plans." Wolff cackled again. "Thank you for perfectly illustrating one of the problems with humanity in the modern world," Wolff said, waving his finger at Eden. "To progress, you must accept that you are not in control. You never were and you never will be. Control is an illusion. What you need is faith in something more powerful than yourself... which, in this case, is me." Wolff scooped Eden and Athena's possessions into one backpack and passed it to one of the knights. He left the parchment and a flashlight on the table beside the other backpack. He removed two objects from the folds of his cloak.

At first, Eden thought Wolff was drawing a weapon, then realized he held a pair of stop watches. Wolff pressed a few buttons on one watch and then the other.

"Both these watches are synced to a thirty-minute timer." Wolff turned the watches around, allowing Eden to see the displays. He pressed a button on the top of each watch and the countdown began. "You will take one, Pyne will take the other. When the timer gets to zero, I will either have the Seal of Solomon in my possession, or Pyne will start the fire." Wolff passed the watch to Pyne and placed the other on the table beside the flashlight. "You can stay in here as long as you want, to study the parchment," Wolff said, pacing to the door. "But be aware, time is ticking."

Eden let Wolff reach the door before speaking. "I know where to go," she said.

Wolff swung around, his grin wider than before. "Excellent," he said, his hands pressed together as though in prayer. "Now hurry up and fetch me my seal."

"GET OVER HERE and untie us right now!" Athena yelled, tugging against the ropes which bound them both to the statue. All the movement achieved was digging the rough rope into her skin.

"Stop pulling at the ropes," Baxter said. "You're making it tighter. Wait a moment."

Standing back-to-back with the statue between them, Athena and Baxter were positioned either side of the statue which they thought looked like Eden.

"What kind of knot is this, anyway?" Athena asked, feeling Baxter's fingers working deftly at the ropes that bound them.

"Looks like a bowline," Baxter replied, his brow furrowed in concentration. "It's a good knot but has its weakness."

Baxter's nimble fingers probed the intricate twists and loops of the rope. It was delicate work, made all the more challenging by the rough fibers digging into his skin and the awkward angle of his bound hands.

"This is a right mess," Baxter quipped, working at the ropes, but clearly getting nowhere.

"You're right again, Mr. Obvious. I was really trying to avoid crazed maniacs for a while. Clearly, that didn't go well," Athena said.

Around them, the knights dragged more wood to the pyre. One knight stacked each piece carefully, clearly planning to speed up the combustion.

"They're not messing around, are they?" Athena muttered, eyeing the growing pyre which surrounded them.

"No, they're not," Baxter agreed grimly. "Which means we need to get out of here, fast."

He redoubled his efforts, his fingers flying over the knots with a desperate speed. A moment of heavy silence passed between them as the gravity of their situation sunk in.

"Remember Lebanon?" Athena asked, a hint of a smile in her voice despite their dire circumstances. "You weren't that keen on your role to start with. What was it you said, something about babysitting Winslow's pride and joy?"

Baxter gazed off into the darkness, nostalgia lining his face. "I didn't know Eden was going to turn out to be..." Baxter said, his voice trailing off.

"Almost ... almost ..." Baxter said, his fingers still working at the knot.

"Be what?"

But Baxter wasn't listening. His focus was entirely on the knot. With a final, desperate tug, he felt the rope slacken.

"Got it," Baxter said, glancing at Athena. "Now we're getting somewhere."

EDEN ROUNDED the corner and sprinted to the rocky outcrop which concealed the opening to the Initiation Well. Not caring who saw her this time, she covered the distance in less than five minutes. Her heart pounded fiercely from the ascent up the incline. She inhaled the crisp night air in gulping breaths, beads of sweat forming on her forehead.

Eden reached the small opening, little more than a fissure in the rock, and paused. Reverting to instinct, she swept the flashlight through the trees. Although she couldn't see any of Wolff's warrior monks nearby, she was certain the Grand Master had instructed them to stay close.

She turned her attention to the fissure and shone the beam of her flashlight inside. The passage continued for a few feet, before abruptly veering to the right.

Eden lifted the watch hanging from her neck. The digits clicked away, nonchalantly passing the twenty-three-minute mark. She sucked in two deep breaths, taking a moment to calm her nerves. Although the pressure of the situation lay heavily on her shoulders, she had to think clearly.

Eden removed the parchment and read the riddle out loud one more time.

"In the holy nine's silent tread, initiates must seek what lies unsaid. Therein lie the streams of arcane lore, coursing unseen through the earth's ancient floor."

She turned her attention back to the rocks towering overhead.

"The first line I understand," Eden said, muttering the cryptic verse under her breath. "But what's the stream of arcane lore?"

There was no time to think. Eden peered over her shoulder and then slipped into the fissure.

She paced along the passage as it twisted through the rock. After a few feet, a stone balustrade appeared, ornately carved in contrast to the rugged stone walls. Eden stepped up to the balustrade and stared into the void beyond.

"This place," Eden muttered, taking in the spiral staircase which wound its way down into the ground. Resembling an inverted tower, the well descended deep beneath the earth.

"It really is uncanny," Eden said, remembering the passage they'd descended on the way into the Hall of Records beneath the Giza Plateau. The winding staircases were almost identical, except the one in Giza ended in primeval waters.

Conscious of the ticking clock, Eden set off down the first flight of stairs. She paused at the first landing and peered across the parapet. There were nine such landings, symbolic of the nine circles of Hell in Dante's inferno, or perhaps the nine knights who originally started the Templar movement.

Eden took the second set of stairs as quickly as she dared on the damp stone. The air became more saturated with the smell of wet earth with each step she took. Halfway down, she paused and tuned in to the sounds around her for a moment. The silence was so profound that Eden felt as though she could hear the whispers of those who had walked the path before. Supernatural murmurings aside, it also meant that if someone was following her, they were doing a great job of remaining deadly quiet.

Eden descended the last stretch of stairs, a familiar shiver creeping its way up her spine. This unexplained yet unmistakable sensation was one she had encountered on numerous occasions. Though the source of the sensation remained a mystery, the implication was clear: something important had happened here.

She took the final stair and crossed to the base of the

well. The concentric circles of stairs wound their way upwards, disappearing into a small circle of night sky. She swept the beam of her flashlight over the mosaic floor, once again depicting the Templar Cross.

"Follow the streams of arcane lore, coursing unseen through the earth's ancient floor." Having committed the second line of the poem to memory, Eden repeated it out loud. "Now, I've got to figure this out." She spun around and strode into the passage, leading deep into the hillside.

49

HEARING BAXTER'S WORDS, Athena felt a surge of hope. If he'd managed to loosen the knots, then maybe they had a chance.

She twisted and wriggled, testing the ropes that bound her hands and feet. Although her hands were still tied tightly, there was slack in the rope that bound her to the statue. She flexed and strained, trying to work the rope looser and looser.

"I think I can get my foot free," she hissed to Baxter.

"Do it," Baxter urged, still working feverishly at the knots binding his hands. "Any slack you can create, any leverage, it all helps."

Athena gritted her teeth and pulled, ignoring the burning pain as the rough fibers scraped against her skin. Inch by hard-fought inch, she worked her foot out of its confines, until finally, with a last, desperate tug, it came free.

"I got it!" she exclaimed, a hint of triumph in her voice. "My foot, it's free!"

But the elation was short-lived. Even as she spoke, a flicker of movement caught her eye. One of the knights, a burly man with a scar on his cheek, approached, holding a flaming torch.

"Time's running out," Athena urged, a new note of desperation entering her voice. "They're coming."

Baxter redoubled his efforts, his fingers flying over the knots, but getting nowhere.

The knight reached the edge of the pyre, his eyes glinting with a cruel, fanatical light. With a deliberate, almost ceremonial movement, he lowered the torch toward the pyre.

"Wait!" a voice rang out across the courtyard.

Athena turned to face the sound and recognized the knight they'd knocked to the ground—Brother Pyne.

The knight with the torch hesitated. The flickering light cast eerie shadows across his scarred face.

Pyne stepped forward. His gaze moved from Athena to Baxter and back again.

"The Grand Master's orders were clear," Pyne said, his voice steady despite the tension in his frame. "We wait until thirty minutes have passed. They still have time."

The scarred knight frowned, clearly unhappy with this turn of events. "They are heretics," he growled, his hand tightening on the torch. "They deserve to burn."

Pyne shook his head. "It is not for us to decide their fate. That is the Grand Master's privilege."

Pyne took the torch and eyed Athena and Baxter. Athena caught the man's gaze for a second and saw something there. There was a flicker of uncertainty, of conflict, deep within him. It was a look Athena recognized as a man torn between duty and conscience.

EDEN STRODE DOWN THE TUNNEL, her flashlight beam swinging from one wall to the next. The tunnel was narrow, the air cool and heavy with the musty scent of earth and stone.

Eden reached a fork in the tunnel and considered her next move. One passage stretched to her right, another to the left. Both tunnels twisted out of sight some distance ahead. She turned from one option to the next, her ears straining for the faintest of sounds that might hint at the correct path.

"Therein lie the streams of arcane lore," Eden murmured, the words sounding like a mantra. Seeking some sign, some whisper of the past to guide her, she finally surrendered to intuition. She turned to the left and walked on. The passage curved and narrowed and the floor grew rougher, causing Eden to pick her way carefully. With each twist and turn, the passage delved deeper and became narrower. The walls of the tunnel bore the marks of age and elements—crags and grooves caused by millennia of water's slow sculpting. Mineral deposits glittered like crystals set into the walls.

Eden moved with care, sweeping the flashlight from side to side. The passage narrowed further, forcing her to edge sideways between a pair of stalactites. The temperature dropped another notch.

"Forget Dante's inferno," Eden whispered. "This is more like Dante's freezer."

Eden heard a noise. She'd become so used to the silence that even the gentlest noise roared in her ears. She spun around, looking for the source of the sound. She stumbled backward. Her shoulder struck a towering stalagmite. The impact sent a jolt of shock through her body, and she dropped the flashlight. The light crashed to the floor and went out, plunging Eden into a darkness so deep it was blinding.

"Dammit," Eden muttered, turning one way and then the next, looking for any spark of light. In the pure blackness, every direction appeared the same. Eden reached out and found the stalactite which she'd bumped into. She took a moment to steady herself on the rough stone and then rubbed her shoulder.

Her pulse roared in her ears and each breath sounded like a train letting off steam. As the shock dissipated and the noise of her breathing returned to normal, Eden again heard the sound which had startled her. In any normal situation, it was a sound that would go unnoticed. But here, in the warren of passages, it growled like a hungry animal. Eventually, Eden recognized the noise. Somewhere in the tunnel ahead, water trickled and splashed across rocks.

"Wait a second," Eden said. "Follow the streams of arcane lore, coursing unseen through the earth's ancient floor. That's got to be it."

With renewed excitement, Eden dropped into a crouch and felt around for the flashlight. She shuffled around the passage until she found it, the batteries lying beside. Eden fumbled with the batteries, pushing them back into the flashlight and snapping it closed. She pressed the button and a beam of light once again shot from the bulb. Eden breathed a sigh of relief and pointed the flashlight at the sound. She paced carefully, pushing herself down the ever-narrowing passage.

Twenty feet further on, the tunnel once again split into

two. This time Eden followed her ears. She stopped and listened, turning her attention from one opening to the other. Listening closely, she decided the sound of the water came from the passage on the left. She set off, her shoulders rubbing against the walls. The ceiling of the tunnel dipped down now, forcing Eden to move hunched over and then crawl on her hands and knees. Scrabbling forward, Eden considered the lay of the land above her. Quinta da Regaleira was set on a steep hillside, dotted with several grand estates including the frequently visited Pena Palace and the Moorish Castle. There was no way, this far beneath the ground, of knowing which direction the tunnel led.

The tunnel opened up again, allowing Eden to climb to her feet. She stood listening for a moment. Not only could she now hear the sound of water, but moisture laced the air. She staggered on, her muscles aching. The passage turned sharply to the left and Eden saw what she was looking for. At the end of the passage, a stream of water thundered into a pool.

"This must be the stream of arcane lore," Eden said, pacing up to the waterfall. She angled her flashlight at the source of the waterfall. Water spurted from a crack in the rock, before cascading down the wall and into a pool which took up most of the tunnel. Eden shuffled around the pool as far as she could without falling in.

"This has got to be the stream of lore," Eden said. "But what now?"

Eden swept her light across the waterfall again, looking for anything that suggested what she should do next. Through the trickling water, she saw something carved into the rock.

"Oh, it had to be," Eden said. Etched on the wall behind

the cascading water was the faint outline of two wiggy lines, one on top of the other. "Aquarius, obviously."

Eden splashed through the knee-high water. She held a hand in front of the cascade to get a better look at the symbol. Although worn by the centuries of falling water, the twin lines were still clearly visible.

She traced a finger across the symbol. To her surprise, the surface wasn't rough like the rock walls of the tunnel, it was smooth to the touch, like glass. Eden stepped back in confusion. She noticed that the surface dully reflected the beam of her flashlight like an old mirror whose reflective surface had been worn away.

Whatever Eden was looking at, it was not naturally occurring. She ran her fingers across the surface again, not caring that the falling water now drenched her clothes. On one side, the mirror had been carefully fitted into the rock wall. Eden retraced her steps and saw that the other side stuck out away from the wall, and behind the mirror there was an opening. Eden stepped around, splashing through the water, and peered into the opening. There, a passage led on behind the waterfall.

Eden swung off her backpack and slipped into the opening. Even though water thundered into the pool, the rear of the glass panel was completely dry. For the first few feet the passage was only two feet wide, then it widened and descended into a set of steps hewn into the rock to make the steep descent easier. The steps were another clear indication that the chamber was of human construction.

At the bottom of the staircase, Eden paused. Her heart raced with anticipation. With trembling hands, she focused the flashlight on the wall ahead. Slowly, realizing that what she was about to see might alter the course of history, Eden turned the corner and stepped into an underground chamber.

50

GRAND MASTER WOLFF paced out of the house and toward the pyre. His eyes swept over the scene before him, taking in every detail—the grim-faced knights, the pyre ready for destruction, and the two prisoners bound to the statue in the center.

As he drew closer, Wolff's gaze lingered on Athena and Baxter. Even in their dire circumstances, they remained defiant, struggling against their bindings. It was a spirit Wolff had seen before, in the eyes of countless heretics and unbelievers. It was his mission to extinguish such defiance.

He crossed to Brother Pyne, who stood holding a flaming torch. The firelight danced across Pyne's face, casting his features into sharp relief. Watching the flames dance, Wolff felt a welling excitement. Soon, those flames would yet again cleanse his problems from the world.

"How long?" Wolff snapped.

Pyne checked the stopwatch. "Ten minutes, Grand Master."

Wolff nodded, a slow smile spreading across his face.

"You hear that?" Wolff spun around, his robes swirling about him, and fixed his gaze on the prisoners.

"You have ten minutes remaining. Is there anything you would like to say? Repent for your sins, perhaps."

"Yes," Athena said, her back arched as she struggled against the ropes. "I would like to tell you to—"

Wolff cut her off with a harsh, barking laugh. "Such spirit! Such passion!" he howled; his fists clenched at his sides. "Death really does bring out the best in people."

He stepped closer to the pyre. "Fear not." His voice dropped to a low, almost hypnotic cadence. "We will pray for your souls."

"Pray for their souls!" the assembled knights chanted.

Wolff let the chant wash over him, feeling the power of it, the rightness of it. This was his destiny, his sacred charge. He turned back to Pyne, his eyes alight with a fanatical gleam. "Add more gasoline," he ordered. "This fire will burn with fury."

MINDFUL of the dangers she had encountered in the trap-laden chamber beneath Siwa, Eden lingered in the doorway and assessed the scene. Although the chamber was small, every inch had been sculpted with care and precision. Carved reliefs adorned the walls, depicting scenes of battles, symbols of faith, and knights in various heroic positions. The floor mosaic was a tableau of Templar icons interlaced with geometric patterns of various colors.

Eden focused on the only object inside the chamber: a stone altar sitting right in the center. She leaned closer and saw an inscription carved into the altar's face. Eden focused on the inscription but couldn't read the words from the door.

She eyed the stopwatch. Nine minutes remaining. Desperation overtaking caution, she placed a foot onto the mosaic floor. She tuned every sense into the surrounding chamber, listening for the creak of ancient machinery or hidden trap doors. Nothing happened.

With growing confidence, Eden took a step into the chamber, and then another. Step by measured step, she advanced until she came to stand before the altar.

"They who seek with guileless core shall find the seal of yore. Where the judge's silent vigil lies, 'neath the scales that weigh the skies." Eden read the altar's inscription out loud, then read it twice more.

The meaning hit her like a physical blow. Suddenly, it all made sense. Wolff knew that whatever forces were at work here, they would not reveal the seal to him. He needed someone with pure intentions to do his dirty work. Eden turned her attention to the riddle's second line.

"Judge's silent vigil. Scales that weigh the skies," Eden said, echoing the cryptic words. The concept of Libra, symbolized by scales, appeared in her mind's eye. "There has to be a depiction of Libra here," she thought aloud, sweeping her flashlight's beam across the chamber's interior.

Her light moved across the floor, following the intricate mosaic. Amongst the mosaic's patterns and symbols, she noticed the constellation symbols. There was the lion, the bull, the twins, and then, partially obscured by the ages, the delicate balance of the scales.

Eden crossed to the symbol, crouched down, and brushed away the dust. She traced the outline of the symbol with her fingers, feeling for anything that might betray a mechanism or a hidden catch. Finding nothing, she stood and swept her light through the room. Without realizing it, she took a step, now standing directly on the Libra symbol embedded within the floor.

A grinding noise reverberated through the chamber. Dust fell from the ceiling, filling the air. Eden dropped into a crouch, ready to flatten herself against the floor, should anything shoot her way.

Movement caught her eye, but it wasn't a hail of arrows coming her way, nor was the floor of the chamber disappearing beneath her. Instead, the altar, which had previously seemed like a solid slab of rock, parted in two. The two halves pivoted outward, parting like the petals of a flower in the sun. A low rumble accompanied the movement.

As the world stilled once more, Eden took a hesitant step. The dust swirled and settled, revealing a secret kept hidden through millennia. Nestled within the opened altar, much like a precious pearl cradled within an oyster, lay an ancient ring. The box that housed it, swathed in velvet, seemed untouched by time.

Eden leaned in close, her heart in her throat.

The ring itself was forged from gold that emanated an almost divine glow. It was intricately patterned in what Eden thought was Ancient Hebrew.

She gasped, focusing on the centerpiece: a sizable obsidian stone. In the center of the large dark stone, leaving no doubt in Eden's mind that this was the relic she had sought, was the hexagram.

"The Seal of Solomon," Eden said, her breath coming in short, sharp gasps. With an unsteady hand, she plucked the ring from its cradle. She held it up and turned it side to side in the light, sending sparkles across the chamber. The gold glimmered, and the hexagram glinted darkly. For a moment, Eden thought about the hands that were supposed to have held this object, and the power it was rumored to yield.

The walls of the chamber shook with the violence of an earthquake. Eden whipped around; the beam of light cutting frantically through a new cloud of dust falling from the ceiling. The mosaic floor at the room's far side dropped away into the void. A slab of rock fell from the roof, smashing through the floor just a few feet away.

Eden slid the seal into her pocket, spun on her heel, and bolted for the door. When she was still a few feet away, one of the giant slabs which made up the passage wobbled. The slab toppled inwards, destined to seal the opening. A low, grinding groan, the sound of stone scraping against stone, reverberated through the chamber.

Eden dug her toes into the ground and leapt toward the falling slab. She jumped under the rock, pulling herself through as quickly as possible. The rock tumbled closer as she pulled herself through in a blur of desperation and adrenaline. Without looking back, she scrambled through the passage, her fingers scratching at the floor. When five seconds had passed and she hadn't experienced the crushing blow of the falling slab, she paused and turned around. The opening to the chamber was now a wall of solid rock. Her ears ringing, Eden turned and rushed toward the well.

51

Wolff watched closely as the knights doused the pyre with more gasoline. He lifted the stopwatch and eyed the countdown. Each disappearing second brought him closer to his destiny.

"Two minutes," Wolff announced, his voice cutting through the tense silence. "Two minutes until the flames of righteousness consume the unworthy."

Athena and Baxter struggled at their bonds.

The knight with the scarred face finished emptying the can of fuel across the pyre and dropped the canister to one side.

Wolff paced around the pyre, his eyes never leaving the prisoners. "Do you feel it?" he asked, his tone almost conversational. "The weight of your sins, the burden of your heresy? In just two minutes, all of that will be burned away. Your souls will be cleansed by the flames."

Athena glared at him. Defiance blazed in her eyes. "You're insane," she spat. "You're nothing but a murderer, a fanatic."

Wolff smiled. "I am a servant of something greater than

myself, and you, my dear, are nothing but kindling for the flames."

A sudden gust of wind swept through the area, pulling at the knights' gowns, and carrying with it the scent of rain and the crackle of electricity. Wolff peered up at the sky. Dark clouds swirled overhead. Lightning flickered within their depths, illuminating the suddenly darkened sky. The first drops of rain fell, slamming against the ground like tiny cannonballs.

"We must light the fire before the rain washes away the fuel." Wolff roared, his hands held high.

"Grand Master, Eden will be here soon," Brother Pyne said, still holding the flaming torch. Wind whipped through the gardens and the light danced frantically. "You gave Eden your word that you would wait for thirty minutes."

"I don't care what I said," Wolff spat in reply. His face contorted into a mask of fury. "Are you questioning my authority, Brother Pyne?" Wolff raised his voice over the beating rain. "Do you dare to challenge me?"

"Dare to challenge me!" the brothers repeated. Their voices instantly lost in another boom of thunder.

Wolff stepped beside Pyne, his voice low and dangerous. "Need I remind you of your oath, of your sacred duty?"

Pyne stood his ground; the torch still gripped in his hand. "I swore an oath to the order, to our sacred mission. But what you're doing here ... this is madness. This is not the way. We should show mercy."

Wolff shook his head, a mirthless smile playing across his lips. "No, Brother Pyne. There can be no mercy. No restraint. The flames of righteousness must consume the heretics, must purge their sin and their corruption from this earth. Pass me the torch."

For a long, tense moment, Pyne didn't move. The wind

howled around them. The flames of the torch danced and swayed.

Wolff removed his revolver and pointed it at Pyne. "Pass me the torch now, or your body will burn with them."

Pyne shook his head, a sad smile playing across his lips. "If this is your will, I want no part of it. I will not stand by and watch you murder the innocent in the name of faith."

Wolff's face contorted with rage. "You will die with them, heretic." He raised the gun and slid his finger across the trigger and squeezed. As the shot rang out, a blunt force jolted his shoulder.

Wolff whipped around to see Athena glaring at him. A chunk of firewood lay on the floor beside him. Athena had worked one of her feet free and kicked the chunk at him.

"Who are you calling a heretic?" Athena shouted, pulling at the bindings, her back arching.

Wolff scowled and turned back to face Pyne. The knight was bent double, gripping his stomach. He wheezed and coughed, each breath a rasp, confirming that the bullet had indeed found its mark.

Pyne staggered back, his hands desperately clutching his abdomen. His legs faltered beneath him, a strangled groan escaping his lips as he crumpled to the floor. Blood seeped between his fingers, coloring his skin. His eyes met Wolff's, as he struggled to speak.

"We will pray for your soul," Wolff said, sliding his gun away and turning his attention back to the pyre.

As dust continued to hang in the air, Eden shuffled the stopwatch from her pocket and checked the time. She had three minutes to get the seal to Wolff before the maniac started the fire.

For a second Eden froze, considering her options. If Wolff had the Seal of Solomon and could harness the power that was supposed to be contained within the ring, there was no knowing what damage he would do. But, by the same token, Eden knew the awful fate Athena and Baxter would face if she didn't comply. She slid the ring out and gazed hard at the glimmering hexagram etched into the surface of the stone. Right now, she had no choice. She had to get the seal to Wolff, and then they would decide what to do. She closed her hand around the object, anger building inside her.

Eden raced back through the passages, taking care to use the same route as she had on the way in. Getting lost amid the labyrinthine passages down here right now would be disastrous. Within two minutes, she was back at the base of the Initiation Well. Large raindrops thundered down the shaft, thumping against the Templar Cross set into the floor.

Eden paused for a heartbeat, glancing up at the mouth of the Initiation Well. When she had descended the stairs fifteen minutes before, there hadn't been a single cloud in the sky. She pulled the Seal of Solomon from her pocket and eyed the obsidian hexagram. A thought flashed through her mind, before she rejected it as plain crazy.

Eden sprinted up the spiral staircase, taking the stairs three at a time. She reached ground level and checked the time. One minute remaining. With the pyre positioned beside the house, it would be almost impossible to get there on time. Nevertheless, she set off at a sprint.

Now lightning forked across the sky, followed by thunder which pounded up and down the hillside. Wind howled through the trees, driving the rain in horizontal sheets.

Eden tilted her head and slid around a corner, the path quickly turning into a sodden torrent of water. As the house came into view, lightning once again flashed down from the sky, striking and scorching one of the trees. An almighty crash boomed through the garden as bark and branches were flung in all directions.

Eden rounded the last corner and saw what appeared to be a vision from a nightmare. Wolff stood beside the pyre, oblivious to the rain. In one hand he held a flaming torch; the flame whipping from side to side in the wind but still refusing to be doused by the falling water. Wolff's knights stood shoulder to shoulder surrounding the pyre, their hoods pulled down over their faces. Eden saw Baxter and Athena, pulling frantically against their bindings.

Eden pushed with increased fervor, her strides rapidly eating up the ground between her and her goal. She neared and heard a deep, resonant chorus of voices fill the air. The knights chanted, giving the whole scene the air of a depraved ritual.

"Stop!" Eden shouted, racing on. "I have it! I have it!"

A clap of thunder drowned out her voice. She charged on, covering the distance in a few strides.

Wolff approached, holding the flaming torch in both hands. He raised the torch high above his head and tilted his head to the sky as though he were in some kind of trance.

Athena and Baxter tugged against the ropes, but still couldn't get free.

"I have it!" Eden shouted again. She shoved through the knights and ran into the circle. The knights continued chanting; their voices getting louder and more crazed.

"I have it! I've done what you asked!" Eden said, rushing up to Wolff.

Wolff turned slowly, the rain running down his face in thick rivulets. He cast a steely gaze at Eden. For a long moment, nothing happened. Then Wolff's face split into a grin.

"You have it, yet you are late," Wolff said. He held up the stopwatch, its screen showing a row of flashing zeros.

"Well, I'm here," she said. "Do you want the Seal of Solomon or not?"

"Show me." Wolff extended a hand.

A crack of thunder rolled across the landscape. Lightning lit up the sky and the rain smashed down like angry fists. If Eden hadn't seen Wolff's men pour gallons of gasoline over the pyre, she would have been reassured that the rain would sufficiently douse the flames. Eden reached into her pocket and grasped the seal. Once again, it felt startlingly warm to the touch.

"Don't do it!" Athena's voice cut through the chaos. "Don't give it to him. Get out of here!"

Eden whipped around to see her friend straining against the ropes.

"Athena's right," Baxter shouted. "It's not worth it. Two lives mean nothing."

"Well..." Wolff said, gesturing Eden toward him. "Do you have it or not?"

"Untie them and it's yours," Eden said, taking two steps.

Wolff tilted his head back and roared a deep laugh. "You are in no position to negotiate," he said, making a gesture with his hand. The knights took a step forward, tightening the circling around Eden and the pyre.

"You have no escape. Give me the Seal of Solomon now, before I change my mind about letting you live."

Another crack of thunder bellowed from overhead.

Eden glanced from Athena to Baxter and then to Wolff. Finally, reluctantly, she took the Seal of Solomon from her pocket and held it out to Wolff.

Wolff peered at the ring and froze. His jaw locked; his lips formed a circle. For almost five seconds Wolff stood statue-still, staring at the seal. Then, as though trying to catch up on lost time, he dropped the flaming torch to the ground and snatched the ring from Eden's hands.

"My whole life I have waited for this moment! My whole life!" he shouted, rain and spittle flying from his lips. "My brothers, we have done it!" Wolff gazed at the knights, who were still chanting in a trance-like state. "The world will soon be ours! Gone will be this time of sin. A new day is dawning!" Wolff spread his hands wide as a bolt of lightning split the heavens in two, silhouetting the house against the sky.

"Now you have what you want," Eden shouted. "You need to let my friends go!" She pointed frantically at Baxter and Athena.

Wolff stared up at Eden as though he had forgotten she was there. For a long moment, he said nothing at all. When he spoke, his voice was a hiss through the pounding rain.

"Oh, I can't do that," Wolff said, his voice soft. "I'm afraid you, like Jacques de Molay, will become martyrs. Except, no one will remember who you are. Tie her up with the others."

52

PYNE LAY motionless on the ground for some time. He opened his eyes to slits and checked his position. When he was sure the Grand Master's attention was focused on the fire, he crawled into the shadows. Once out of sight, he moved slowly, carefully, every breath sending a fresh wave of agony through his body.

He reached the edge of the courtyard and staggered to the house. Once at the door, he leaned on the doorjamb, his breath coming in short, painful gasps. The adrenaline that had carried him this far was starting to fade, replaced by a bone-deep exhaustion and a throbbing pain in his side.

He eyed Athena and Baxter, still tied in the center of the pyre. He sent a prayer of thanks that Athena had distracted Wolff at the key moment. If she hadn't, Wolff's bullet would certainly have done more damage.

He glanced back into the courtyard as Eden Black rushed into the circle. She had clearly achieved Wolff's task, but two minutes late.

Watching the young woman barge through the knights, Pyne felt a wave of relief. For now, he would watch what happened and if he was not required, he would melt into the shadows and find a way to repay Athena's kindness later.

With shaking hands, Pyne unfastened his cloak, wincing as the fabric pulled away from the wound. He probed at the injury, gritting his teeth against the fresh wave of pain. To his relief, the bullet had only grazed the skin, leaving a deep, ugly furrow but not penetrating the muscle beneath.

It was a small mercy, but one he was grateful for. A more serious wound would have been the end.

Pyne tore a strip of cloth from his cloak and bound it tightly around his waist. He hissed in pain as he pulled the knot tight. The crude bandage would have to do for now.

BEFORE EDEN COULD REACT, a pair of knights appeared at her sides and pinned her arms in position. Eden yanked an elbow loose and swept it to the left, catching one knight in the chest. The knight grabbed Eden, even more tightly this time.

The knights lifted Eden from the ground and carried her to the pyre. They picked their way through the smashed-up wood; the reek of gasoline still evident over the pounding rain.

"Why couldn't you just listen to us?" Athena shouted as Eden was manhandled into position between Baxter and Athena.

Eden glanced over at her friend but wasn't met with the angry expression she had expected. Athena nodded down, directing Eden's gaze at her feet. Eden followed her friend's gaze and immediately noticed what Athena was indicating. Although Athena's hands and arms were lashed tightly against the statue, she had managed to work her legs free. Until now, with the men so far away, such freedom had been useless. But now, with two of the knights attempting to lash Eden to the statue, their luck might be about to change.

A bolt of lightning flashed across the sky, followed by a ground shaking thunderclap. The lightning must have hit something nearby, as the electric lights which had been illuminating the courtyard died. The only light now was the flickering flame of the torch, which Wolff still held.

Eden struggled as the knights positioned her against the statue. When she was in position, one man held her still, while the other stepped closer to Athena to get the rope.

"Now!" Athena shouted, heaving her legs up high and smashing the knight in the nose. With a bone-shattering crunch, the guy's nose became a mess of blood and bone. Before the man fell to the floor, Athena struck him on the side of the head again. The knight's body went limp, and he fell into the pyre, scattering wood in all directions.

As Eden predicted, the knight holding her turned to see what misfortune had befallen his brother. As soon as his attention was elsewhere, Eden head-butted him on the side of the skull. The impact loosened his grip enough for her to free one of her arms. She sent two wild and heavy fists into the man's ribs, cracking at least one. The man wheezed, staggering backward, and bending over. Eden swung an elbow into the thug's neck, sending him stumbling toward Baxter.

Although still bound to the statue, Baxter swung his head forward and cracked the knight on the temple, sending him crumpling to the floor.

"Nice to see you using your head for once," Eden said, glancing at Baxter.

"My pleasure," Baxter said groggily. "Although I'd be lying if I said that didn't hurt."

"I really think we need to get out of here," Athena said.

The rest of the knights, having watched the scuffle, advanced on the pyre. Wolff stood to one side, gazing entranced at the seal.

"Sure thing," Eden said, ducking down and taking a knife from one of the fallen knights. She sliced the ropes binding Baxter's hands and handed him the knife to free Athena.

The circle of knights approached again; their eyes locked on the pyre.

"We need the Seal of Solomon!" Eden said.

As Baxter turned to free Athena, Eden charged for Wolff. She reached the Grand Master in three steps and sent a powerful right hook into the man's jaw. An expression of confusion flashed across Wolff's face, before twisting into anger.

Before he could react, Eden snatched the ring from Wolff's hands. "Thanks for looking after it!" she yelled, momentarily glancing down at the glimmering object. The hexagram caught her eye as it reflected a flash of lightning.

"Eden, move!" Baxter shouted.

Eden ducked as a fist the size of a cannon ball flew past her head. She gazed around to see that the knights had surrounded her now. In the near complete darkness, the men were a wall of flowing gowns and fists.

"I think this is going to hurt," Eden muttered.

To stop the Seal of Solomon from dropping to the floor, Eden slipped it on the index finger of her right hand. The ring fit as though it had been designed especially for her.

Eden straightened up and eyed the monk who had attempted to knock her head from her shoulders. She rocked back and swung a kick, striking the knight in the ribs. Having kicked out at these battle-hardened brutes a few moments ago, Eden expected the strike to feel as though she was kicking a brick wall and elicit little more than a grunt from the knight. The man shot backward as though jet powered. He collided with two other men, and all three sprawled to the ground.

Eden noticed another man approaching in her peripheral vision. She swung around as the man's fist flew toward her face. She saw the strike coming as though in slow motion. She tried to parry but a moment too late. As the giant fist neared her jaw, Eden prepared herself for the pain about to explode in her cheek. The fist struck. A moment passed. Eden felt no searing pain and wasn't smashed to the ground. The knight withdrew his fist and examined it, as though he too was confused about what had happened.

With a sense of disinterest, Eden sent a low blow into the man's ribs. Seven feet of muscle and bone cartwheeled across the garden and collided with a tree.

A thick arm closed around Eden's neck and yanked her back into a foul-smelling cloak. She grabbed the arm and heaved it upwards, flipping the man over her head and smashing him into the floor.

"Eden, I've no idea what you're doing, but we really should get out of here!" Athena's voice cut through the din, finally pulling Eden back into focus.

She whirled around, easily weathering another punch from one of the knights. Although she was taking them on with ease, they kept coming back.

"Sure thing," Eden said, an idea coming across her mind. Eden charged back around the pyre, snatching the flaming torch from Wolff. She leaped back into the pyre, the torch held high.

"What are you doing with that?" Athena said, rubbing her wrists where the ropes had secured her in place.

"Come close and watch!" Eden said, shuffling in between Baxter and Athena.

The knights inched their way closer, watching Eden with a growing sense of unease. The boldest of the knights reached the edge of the pyre and took a step into scattered wood.

"But we're surrounded," Baxter said, completing a three-sixty-degree turn. "There is no way out!"

The knights, clearly aware of this too, marched further into the pyre. She kicked the wood aside and climbed through the remains of the smashed-up furniture.

"I really hope you've got a plan," Athena said, glancing at the knights.

"Of course I've got a plan," Eden shouted. "I've always got a plan! Take this!" Eden thrust the flaming torch in Baxter's direction and picked up one of the fuel containers.

"Eden!" Athena said, urgently. "Making it up as you go along does not constitute a plan!"

Eden threw the container high in the air, sending spirals of fuel in all directions. She grabbed the torch back from Baxter and held it out like a weapon.

"Touch me!" Eden shouted to her friends.

"This is really not the time for public displays of affection!" Athena shouted.

"Just do it! Now!" Eden shouted in reply. When she felt Athena and Baxter move in close behind her, their hands on her shoulders, Eden jabbed the flaming torch into the falling streams of gasoline.

The pyre instantly became a blaze; its flames leaping into the sky. Fire shot through the wood with dancing tongues, consuming everything in its wake. The flames danced out across the courtyard where the fuel had spread. The knights leaped backward, scattering in disarray. One knight's cloak, caught by a burning stream of fuel, ignited with a roar. Panicked gasps and cries broke out as the men tore off his burning cloak.

From the center of the blaze, Eden watched the chaos as though it were a movie on a screen. For some inexplicable reason, she didn't feel a single tinge of heat.

A pair of knights dropped to the ground and rolled in a frantic attempt to smother the flames tearing at their cloaks. Other men ran, desperately trying to get away from the fire.

"What is going on?" Athena shouted, looking around in confusion. The wood beneath their feet was burning and yet they felt no pain.

"It must be the Seal of Solomon," Eden replied, glancing at the ring on her right hand. "Don't ask me how. But it's giving us some kind of protection."

"How long will it last?" Baxter said, his voice mid-way between confusion and fear.

"I don't think we should hang around and find out," Eden said, watching the chaos. The knights scrambled and pushed against each other.

Eden, Athena, and Baxter backed away through the fire. The flames flickered around them, but still had no effect. Once they were through the fire, they ran across the courtyard and scaled the fence, leaving cries of chaos in their wake.

53

BROTHER PYNE STAGGERED out of the house and picked his way toward the Humvee. He slung his hood up against the rain, which continued to hammer around him. He glanced over his shoulder as another shout boomed from the courtyard. Pyne felt a growing shame that the order of which he was once a proud member, had descended into merciless chaos. He bemoaned the fact he was injured and unable to help, but right now he needed to get away and seek refuge.

"Brother, help me brother!" came a voice from behind him.

Pyne turned around to see Grand Master Wolff rush from the building. "They are getting away with the Seal of Solomon. We must stop them!"

Pyne cast a glance over his shoulder, confused for a moment as to why the Grand Master hadn't recognized him. He realized that the Grand Master had mistaken him for another of the brothers.

"Of course, Grand Master," Pyne said, making his voice sound deeper than usual. "In here." He marched toward the

Humvee and climbed into the driver's seat. He thumped the cabin light, turning it off, to retain his anonymity.

"How has she done this?" Wolff groaned, scrambling into the passenger seat.

A clap of thunder resounded from the sky, adding its own percussion to the mixed sounds of chaos and pain.

"Shouldn't we stay and help our fallen brothers?" Pyne said, glancing in the rear-view mirror.

Wolff pressed his lips together. The muscles in his face tensed as though he were mimicking the nearby gargoyles.

"No. They have chosen their destiny," Wolff hissed. "The order is more important than any man. The order must be saved so that we can rise again."

Pyne checked the rearview mirror. Flames washed the walls of the manor house in a surreal light. The stone gargoyles now seemed to snarl and writhe in the firelight; their grotesque features animated by the dancing shadows.

"Wait, look!" Wolff shouted, his fist smashing against the dashboard. Only just visible in the light of the raging fire, three figures crossed the road fifty feet ahead. Keeping to the shadows, the figures reached a dust covered Renault Trafic van and climbed in.

"It isn't over," Wolff snarled. He pulled his gun from beneath his cloak. "Let's see if they can outrun this."

"I CAN'T BELIEVE you let them get a drop on you," Eden said, as they all scrambled into the front seats of the Renault Trafic.

"You're not in a position to be critical," Baxter replied, starting the engine. "You were out there playing fetch for that maniac." He yanked a lever and the windscreen wipers screeched into action, barely clearing a patch of glass before the rain filled it again. He hit the gas and swung the wheel, sending the Renault chugging up the hill and away from Quinta da Regaleira.

"All in an effort to stop you getting barbequed," Eden said. The thought of her friends in danger yet again raced through her mind.

"Yeah, thanks for that," Athena said, placing a hand on her friend's arm. "That thing is seriously powerful." She pointed at the Seal of Solomon on Eden's finger.

"I know. The sooner we get it somewhere safe, the better. In the wrong hands, this could be deadly," Eden said, eyeing the obsidian stone.

The three sat in silence as Baxter swung the van around a sharp corner, tires howling on the asphalt. The road snaked its way up the hillside, affording Eden a view of Sintra's town center several hundred feet below. As they drove around the corner, a sudden glare from a pursuing vehicle caught Eden's eye. She sat bolt upright and leaned in close to the rain smeared window, straining to see what was behind them.

"What is it?" Athena asked, clearly sensing the change in her friend's demeanor.

"It could be nothing," Eden said, staring back into the gloom. "But I think we've got company."

Eden glanced at her friends as they all paled. The headlights appeared again, this time sweeping through the cab as their pursuers rounded the corner.

"You're right," Baxter said, his eyes on the mirror. "Something's coming this way, and fast. Hang on." Baxter downshifted and punched the accelerator. The engine responded, roaring with a groan of exertion, rather than a groan of power. Even so, the van jolted.

Eden wound down the window. The howling storm tumbled in, filling the cab with rain. The growl of a robust engine shifting through its gears cut through the clamor of the storm.

"Does the protective force of that thing work in high-speed collisions?" Athena asked, pointing at the Seal of Solomon on Eden's finger.

"I have no idea, and I don't want to find out," Eden said, leaning out of the window. "Fifty feet behind, and closing fast," she shouted.

The following headlights swept through the rain like searchlights.

The Renault's engine whined and howled as Baxter urged every bit of power from it. The chassis shuddered under the strain, tires biting against the wet asphalt as it rumbled up the next incline.

"I don't suppose we've got any weapons in here?" Eden said, glancing around the van. "What's in the back?"

"A load of observation gear," Baxter shouted over the roaring engine. "This was a treasure hunt, remember? We weren't expecting hostiles."

"We should always expect hostiles," Eden said, her gaze fixed on the winding road ahead.

A sharp crack erupted behind them. Eden's first thought was thunder from a lightning strike nearby, until a hail of bullets slammed into the back of the Renault.

"Get down," Eden yelled, pulling her head back inside the van and ducking into the footwell.

Baxter maneuvered the van with renewed urgency.

Another pop erupted from behind them, followed by a thud as another bullet sliced through the van's skin, and straight out the other side. Two further rounds ricocheted off the chassis, shaking the van violently.

"Let's hope the magical powers of this ring come through," Athena said.

"I really don't think it'll stop bullets," Eden groaned, laying a hand over the ring.

"We'll find out soon enough," Athena muttered.

"Hold on!" Eden said, pointing out through the windshield. Ahead, the road twisted up and out of sight. A short stone barrier on the right offered only scant protection from the drop. A flash of lightning split the sky, illuminating the sharp rain-lashed rocks over one-hundred feet below the road.

Baxter gripped the wheel as he forced the groaning Renault up the steep gradient. The old vehicle struggled to maintain its grip, spraying grit and mud as the tires spun. Rain hammered against the windscreen, antagonizing the flailing wipers.

Another volley of gunfire rattled from behind them. Bullets hammered through the van's rear doors, jolting like the beat of a drum.

The bend reared up fifty feet ahead. The menacing sharp left skirted around a precipice.

"We've got to slow!" Eden shouted. "We'll never make the corner at this speed."

As though showing agreement, the Renault hydroplaned across a large puddle. The vehicle swung to the side, threatening to send them spiraling out of control. Baxter fought with the wheel, keeping them as straight and level as possible.

Another bolt of lightning seared the sky, briefly illuminating the twisted path ahead.

"Hit the brakes!" Eden shouted.

Baxter did what he was told. He feathered the pedal to prevent the van from sliding.

The corner was on them now. Twenty feet away, the small stone barricade loomed close. Beyond it, relentless torrents of rain fell into the void. The Renault plowed on, heading directly for the drop. The vehicle swung to the left. Tires squealed, finally finding a grip on the road. The Renault shuddered, rattling, as it spun sideways toward the precipice.

Miraculously, when they were two feet from the wall, the tires found grip and the Renault barreled forward.

Baxter slammed down on the accelerator, dragging them out of the corner. Eden and Athena inhaled sharply; their faces washed with the pallor of close calls. For a few seconds, no one said a word.

"Maybe the ring is still protecting us," Athena said, glancing down at Eden's hands.

Then, as though answering Athena's comment, the vehicle behind rammed them hard.

54

"YES, THAT'S IT!" Wolff shouted as the Humvee smashed into the Renault. The impact was bone-jarring, coupled with the sound of metal crumpling and glass shattering. The Renault shuddered and bounced along the rain-slicked road.

Pyne sat with the hood still up, focused on the road ahead. He had delayed and slowed their progress up the hill, allowing the Renault to get around the corner safely. His mind ranged through possibilities. The ideal, he decided, would be for Eden and her team to get away with the seal.

Wolff leaned from the window again and squeezed off a few more shots. The muzzle flashes illuminated his face in a strobe-like effect, casting his maniacal grin in a hellish light. The first two bullets tore through the van's thin metal skin, then Pyne swung the wheel, sending the rest of Wolff's barrage off amid the trees.

The wind howled through the open window, driving sheets of rain inside the Humvee. Wolff seemed oblivious to the deluge, his eyes wide and wild, fixated on the prey ahead.

"Hit them again!" he commanded, slipping back through the window, and dropping into the passenger seat. He swept a hand back through his sodden hair and licked his lips in anticipation.

Pyne hit the gas and the Humvee's V8 engine roared, propelling four tons of armored metal toward the Renault van.

Wolff leaned forward, his face nearly pressing against the windshield. He pounded his fist against the dashboard, desperation creasing his forehead.

In a matter of seconds, the gap between the two vehicles vanished. With a sickening crunch, the Humvee's bumper crashed into the Renault. The van lurched to the right, fighting for purchase on the treacherous road. The smaller vehicle shuddered under the impact, bouncing from right to left.

"Go around!" Wolff screamed; his voice almost lost in the din. "Drive them off the road!" He gestured wildly, pointing to the narrow gap between the Renault and the hillside.

Brother Pyne assessed the gap between the Renault and the hillside. Not able to blow his cover while Wolff had a weapon, he hit the gas.

EDEN, Athena, and Baxter watched in horror as the armored behemoth drew alongside them. When the Humvee filled the passenger window, it slowed to match their speed.

"They're going to ram us off the road!" Athena yelled;

her eyes locked on Wolff's pale figure illuminated by the dashboard lights.

Baxter glanced out the driver's window and saw how close the sheer drop was. He gripped the wheel with renewed vigor.

"There's no way we can outrun them," Eden said, getting her first proper look at the vehicle. "I'm no expert, but my guess is that thing has a V8 under the hood."

"I reckon we can outmaneuver them, though." Baxter turned his head to face the Humvee, ignoring the road ahead for a few seconds.

"You should definitely look at the road!" Eden said, her eyes locked on the thin band of asphalt down which they were speeding.

"Wait for it," Baxter said, every muscle tensed. A second stretched itself to four times its normal length, then Baxter saw what he was looking for. The driver of the Humvee swung the wheel.

Baxter slammed the brake pedal to the floor. The Renault's wheels locked, and the tires screeched. The force of deceleration threw them all forward, seatbelts straining.

The sudden reduction in speed caught the Humvee off guard. Committed to its attack, it swerved into the middle of the road where a moment ago the Renault had been. As the Humvee bounced toward the precipice, the driver acted in panic and countered too hard, sending the vehicle into a spin. The headlight beams sliced through the night as the wheels tore at the sodden road, hurling arcs of mud and water into the sky.

Finally, the Humvee came to rest facing across the precipice. The front wheels sat just inches from going over the edge.

"Go, go, go!" Eden shouted, shaking a finger at the open road behind the Humvee.

Baxter floored the accelerator and the Renault rumbled on.

Eden glanced into the Humvee as they passed and got an icy look from Wolff in return.

"That was too close," Eden whispered, trying to hide the tremble in her voice.

Athena nodded, pointing ahead. "We're not out of this yet."

Baxter accelerated up an incline and around another tight corner. The storm continued to rage. The wind howled through the trees and rain pounded against the roof.

Eden kept her eyes locked on the wing mirror, knowing deep down what she would soon see. Less than one minute later, the Humvee's headlights reappeared.

"Some people just won't give up," Eden groaned, trying to assess the distance.

The sound of the powerful engine once again increased as Wolff closed the distance. The Humvee swung around the corner; its tires barely gripping the road.

"Can we go any faster?" Athena said, glancing at the dials.

"Negative, we're already red lining," Baxter replied. "Plus, we really don't want to come off the road."

"Next time I'm choosing the vehicle," Eden groaned.

A burst of gunfire split the air. The muzzle flashes illuminated Wolff hanging from the passenger window.

Eden flinched instinctively, her body tensing as she anticipated the impact of bullets against metal. Fortunately, the shots went wide.

"We can't outrun them," Baxter said, eyes fixed on the road ahead. "We need to find another way."

Eden spotted a small dirt track on the right, barely visible through the rain and foliage. "There!" she shouted, pointing at the track. "We might not outrun them, but we'll lose them on foot in the forest."

"It's not a great plan, but it's the best we've got," Baxter said through clenched teeth.

"You're welcome to make suggestions yourself," Eden quipped.

The Humvee's speed increased further, the headlights becoming brighter and brighter with each passing second.

"I'm all out of ideas," Baxter said. He yanked the steering wheel. The Renault's tires screeched as the vehicle skidded across the rain-slicked road. The momentum sent Eden and Athena lurching against their seatbelts. For a heart-stopping moment, the van teetered on the edge of control, its rear end swinging out in a wide arc. The tires gripped, and the van barreled up the track, instantly cloaked by the trees on both sides. Branches whipped and scratched at the vehicle and the old suspension creaked and groaned, struggling to absorb the impact of the uneven ground.

Eden held on tight, the movement throwing her against the door on one side and Athena on the other. Baxter fought to reduce their speed and get control of the vehicle.

Up ahead the Renault's headlights illuminated a twisting, narrow track. Overhanging branches and dense foliage reached out from either side, making the path more suitable to walkers than motor vehicles.

Eden risked a glance behind them. For now, the Humvee was still out of sight. Although the large 4x4 would manage the terrain more easily than their van, it appeared as though the narrow path had bought their smaller vehicle some time.

"Stop here," Eden said when they'd rattled one hundred

feet from the road. Ahead, the track twisted into a steep ascent. "Swing the van around and block the path."

Baxter nodded, bringing the Renault to a halt. He spun the steering wheel and maneuvered the van until it sat across the track, blocking the way.

Eden swung open the door and piled out at the same moment the van stopped moving. Her feet sinking into the muddy ground, she rushed for the cover of the trees. Athena followed just moments behind. Baxter stopped to retrieve a flashlight from beneath his seat and followed.

Once they were together, Eden led the way up the slope and away from the track. They pushed through the dense forest, branches clawing at their clothes and rain-soaked leaves slapping against their faces.

After a minute's reprieve, the menacing growl of the Humvee drifted through the forest. A few seconds later, the vehicle's headlights swept up the track like searchlights.

Eden paused and glanced over her shoulder.

The Humvee rumbled easily up the slope, not skidding and bouncing like the Renault had. The Humvee stopped twenty feet down the slope from the Renault. For a few seconds, nothing happened, and then the doors swung open.

"Come on," Baxter hissed, his hand on Eden's shoulder. "We're wasting our head start."

Eden nodded and the trio trudged up the hillside.

55

"I KNEW they wouldn't get far," Wolff said, scrambling out of the Humvee and stalking up to the Renault. His feet sank into the sodden earth but he paid no attention. He stopped ten feet away and inspected the van, which sat perpendicular to the road, its frame battered and scratched.

Brother Pyne killed the Humvee's engine and turned off the lights. Amid the chaos of the wild drive and the whipping storm, Wolff remained unaware of Pyne's true identity.

"Come out with your hands up!" Wolff shouted; his gun leveled at the vehicle. He paused, clearly listening for any movement inside. When there was none, he signaled for Pyne to go around the back as he approached the driver's door.

The wind howled through the trees, branches creaking and groaning under the onslaught of the storm.

Wolff reached the driver's door and wrenched it open.

"Nothing," he shouted over the sound of the hammering rain. "They're gone."

"Same, the back is empty too," Pyne said, rounding the vehicle, his hood pulled down low.

Wolff scowled and slammed the door closed. He stepped away from the van and gazed up the track.

"They're on foot in a place they don't know. They can't have gone far."

Pyne, nodded, his expression grim. He leaned inside the Renault and disengaged the handbrake. Then he rounded the front of the vehicle and pushed against the grill. For a second, the Renault remained wedged but then it started to move. It rolled slowly across the rutted track until gravity did the work, dragging the van down the embankment and smashing it into a tree.

With the way cleared, Wolff and Pyne turned their attention to the track. The narrow trail wound its way up the hillside, disappearing into the storm-lashed forest. The wind whipped through the trees, sending leaves and branches swirling through the air.

"This is not over," Wolff said. "We will find them, kill them, and the seal will be mine."

"But Grand Master, we don't have flashlights and the forest is pitch black," Pyne said, making sure his face remained obscured by the hood.

"I have something even better," Wolff said, removing an object from beneath his cloak.

Pyne turned and regarded the object for a long moment before he recognized what it was.

"The night vision goggles," Wolff said, fitting the device over his eyes. "With these, they won't even know we're coming."

BAXTER TOOK the lead as they climbed the hillside. For the first few hundred feet they had picked their way between the trees, feeling their way with outstretched arms. When Baxter was sure Wolff was far enough away not to be attracted by the light, he switched on his flashlight, which made their progress a lot quicker.

Although Eden had countless sarcastic things to say, the raging storm made all non-essential communication impossible. The rain fell incessantly, soaking through their clothes and chilling them to the bone.

Branches clawed at their clothes and hair. Wet leaves slapped against their faces as they climbed.

Eden glanced up as lightning split the sky, flashing somewhere beyond the canopy of the trees. The thunder followed a beat later; its deep, resonant booms shaking the forest floor.

Ten minutes later, the terrain grew even more challenging. Rocky outcrops jutted from the hillside; their surfaces slick with rain and moss. Baxter scrambled up first and turned the flashlight around to illuminate the outcrop for Eden and Athena.

Eden gritted her teeth, trying to ignore the pain in her muscles, the biting cold, and the fear that somewhere, cloaked by the darkness were Wolff and his thugs. They reached the top of the hill and emerged from the cover of the trees. Countless rocky outcrops dotted the summit. Without the protection offered by the undergrowth, the wind and rain tore past, threatening to tear them from the hillside. The lightning flashed and thunder boomed. The lights and sound were now even closer together. Baxter led them past rocks, and they emerged into a small clearing.

"Which direction from here?" Eden said, following the beam of Baxter's light.

"That's the High Cross," Baxter said, pointing his flashlight at a cross-shaped monument that crowned the highest outcrop, and as such, the hill's summit. "If we head down that way, we'll pick up the main road again. It'll be downhill from here."

"That's good news, I suppose," Eden muttered, suppressing a shiver. "Come on Athena, keep up!" Eden spun around, expecting to see Athena dragging herself up the slope behind them. Eden blinked the rain from her eyes as she tried to focus. Athena wasn't there.

"I'm sure she was right behind us," Baxter said, swinging the light down the slope.

"If you think this is funny, you're wrong!" Eden shouted, pacing back to the top of the slope. As she reached the path, Eden heard a voice that sent a shiver through her spine.

"I'd like to see you use the seal to protect your friend now!"

Eden swung around, but at first saw nothing. Rain and wind forced her eyes to slits.

Baxter swung the flashlight toward the noise.

"Up here!" the voice came again.

Baxter raised the flashlight and there, standing on the top of the rocks, directly in front of the High Cross, stood Wolff and one of his knights. Wolff had an arm clamped around Athena's neck and a gun pointing at her head. As far as Eden could tell, the other man was unarmed.

Lightning slashed the sky and thunder rolled. The rain pummeled the earth with the relentless force of a thousand drummers.

Eden took a step forward.

"Stay right where you are!" Wolff bellowed. "If you move, I'll put a bullet in your friend's head. You have already worked out that the seal has some special protective powers, but they only apply to the wearer or those nearby." Wolff pointed at Athena. "I'm afraid this young lady, right now, is as mortal as the rest of us."

Athena struggled, but Wolff held her with surprising strength.

Eden and Baxter shared a glance. Baxter nodded almost imperceptibly.

"Don't do it!" Athena shouted, her voice hoarse. "You can't let him have it! My life is not worth that!"

"What a brave young lady!" Wolff shouted. "Such self-lessness, but I'm afraid also foolishness."

Eden's muscles tensed, ready to deliver an explosive movement. She scowled up at Wolff, wishing she could go up there personally and throw him from the rocks. A bolt of lightning slashed the sky, followed almost immediately by an explosion of thunder, bigger than before.

"Fine," Eden shouted, when the thunder rumbled away. She grabbed her right index finger in preparation to remove the seal. "How shall I get this to you?"

"Come to the base of the rock and throw it up," Wolff said, excitement lacing his voice.

"No, Eden! Don't do it!" Athena shouted.

Eden stepped up to the base of the rocks and met Wolff's stare. Looking at the little man, she realized how much she detested people who thought they were above the law. Her stomach broiled with rage at the thought of him having something so powerful, but with Athena's life on the line, there was no choice.

The wind howled, whipping around her, tugging at her hair and clothing. Another bolt of lightning split the sky, followed by a deafening crack of thunder. Eden flinched, her heart pounding. A crazy thought flashed into her mind.

The thought was so outrageous that Eden dismissed it as pure fantasy.

"Quickly or your friend will die!" Wolff shouted, his rain-soaked face turning beetroot red.

Eden glanced down at the Seal of Solomon, took a deep breath, and calmed herself. The obsidian carved hexagram seemed to pulse with a faint, otherworldly light. Eden frowned, trying to make sense of the strange sensation that washed over her. As though answering, the wind slowed and changed direction.

With the wind now buffeting him from behind, Wolff stepped closer to the precipice. "You have ten seconds to comply!" he roared. His arm tightened around Athena's neck.

In the middle of the clearing, Eden stood transfixed. She thought back through the last couple of hours. Before she'd gone down the Initiation Well and retrieved the Seal of Solomon, the sky had been clear and cloudless, the air still.

"The seal," she whispered, her voice almost lost in the howling of the wind. "It's controlling the storm. I'm controlling the storm."

Baxter glanced at her; his brow furrowed in confusion. "What are you talking about?" he shouted over the roar.

Eden held up the seal; her eyes blazing with a newfound determination. She whispered to Baxter, her voice almost lost in the wind. "Don't you see? The storm, the lightning, the thunder ... it's all connected to the seal, to my emotions. This is far more powerful than protecting the wearer. This could change the world. Force countries into famine, and flood cities. That's why Wolff wants it."

Eden shook her head, trying to dismiss the idea as absurd, but the more she thought about it, the more sense it seemed to make.

"Five seconds!" Wolff shouted. "Don't think I won't do this."

"It's not a great plan, but it's the best we've got," Eden muttered the phrase, which had become something of a slogan for her. Acting on instinct, she raised the Seal of Solomon.

"What are you doing?" Wolff bellowed. "Stop messing about! I am not joking!"

Eden focused all her thought energy on the little man standing high above her. She locked her eyes on him and concentrated as hard as she could.

"You have three seconds," Wolff said, pushing the gun harder against Athena's head.

For another second nothing happened. The clouds directly above Wolff churned with renewed ferocity. The wind picked up too, and rain fell harder than ever before.

"Stop it!" Wolff shouted, pointing at Eden. He turned around to eye the knight standing beside him. "Get down there and kill her!"

"No Grand Master, I won't do that," Pyne said, pulling down his hood for the first time. Wolff's eyes bulged and his jaw hung loose.

"You!" Wolff said, his eyes locked on Pyne. "I shot you." Clearly unsure what to do, Wolff moved the gun from Athena's head and leveled it at Pyne.

Athena took her chance. She swung an elbow, striking the Grand Master in the face, and charged away.

Wolff lunged for Athena, but she was already several feet away, scrambling down the rock face.

"Pyne, stop her! Stop her!" Wolff shouted, frantically pointing at Eden.

"No, Grand Master," Pyne said, his baritone voice cutting through the wind like a foghorn. "For too long I have listened to your crazy plans and done nothing because of my oath, but I can no longer stand by. Our order was established to protect, not harm."

Wolff swung from Pyne to Eden, his gun wavering between his new foes.

Eden continued to focus on Wolff. The seal throbbed on her finger. She reached out with her mind, somehow becoming aware of the storm's energy. It felt as though the raw, untamed force of the wind and the rain, was passing directly through her.

With a surge of will, she unleashed that power.

The storm intensified, the wind howling like a banshee, the rain lashing down.

Eden closed her eyes to slits against the rain, which pounded with the power of a sandstorm. The wind boomed and bashed like a thousand cannons, whipping her hair across her face.

"Impossible," Wolff roared, his face pale. "You cannot disobey my rule! I will be powerful. I will return the world to..."

Lightning split the sky, not once, but in a dazzling display of raw, elemental power. Bolts of electricity, each one brighter and more intense than the last, split the heavens with a frequency that was both mesmerizing and terrifying. The lightning danced across the sky, leaping from cloud to cloud in a frenzied, chaotic ballet. The lightning shot down from the swirling clouds and struck the High Cross, which towered above Wolff and Pyne.

Eden's voice rose above the clamor, shouting the words the Templar Grand Master had used all those centuries ago. "You have used the word of faith for your own greed, and for that you will pay. You will be summoned to the tribunal of Heaven!"

The lightning zipped down the cross, bolted out, and struck Wolff in the chest. The Grand Master's face contorted in an expression of shock and pain.

Pyne backed away, his feet scrabbling across the rocks, the glow of the flare on his face.

Wolff convulsed as the electricity coursed through him. Unable to control his movements, Wolff rolled toward the precipice. As quickly as it came, the lightning receded.

56

"WHAT JUST HAPPENED?" Eden said, stepping forward. She blinked several times, willing her eyes to adjust to the darkness.

Baxter joined her. Above them, the High Cross stood tall against the sky. Despite the lightning strike, the stone remained unmarked.

"Where's Athena?" Eden said. A bolt of worry surged through her when she noticed there were no people on top of the rock.

"Right here," Athena said, scrambling down the rock face and running across to Eden and Baxter. "What exactly just happened?"

"Honestly, I've no idea," Eden said. "Where's Wolff?"

Baxter swept his flashlight downwards to reveal the answer to Eden's question. Wolff lay at the foot of the rock. They ran toward the fallen figure, but it was clear he wouldn't be getting up again. His cloak was torn and tattered, and his skin was scorched by the incredible force of the lightning. His head sat at a funny angle and his limbs splayed out beneath him.

"And Pyne?" Eden said.

The trio spun around but saw no sign of the knight.

"I don't think he'll bother us," Athena said. "Not after refusing to follow the Grand Master's orders."

Eden released a breath, tension finally drifting from her body. Exhaustion rose through her and she swayed on her feet. Her surroundings seemed to tilt and spin, and for a moment, she feared she might collapse. Strong arms encircled her, holding her steady. She locked eyes with Baxter.

Slowly at first, the storm abated. The lightning and thunder receded out across the ocean. The wind died down and the rain slackened to a gentle patter.

Within ten minutes, the storm had completely disappeared; the clouds moving on to wreak their aggravation elsewhere. As the final tendrils drifted away, a tapestry of stars emerged, twinkling softly. The coming dawn colored the sky in a deep purple. Moonlight cast a silvery sheen across the clearing and turned the lingering droplets of water into sparkles.

Eden cast a glance at the Seal of Solomon, still on her finger. In the moonlight, the ancient relic pulsed with a faint, otherworldly light.

"That's a seriously powerful thing you've got there," Athena said, wringing the rain from her hair.

Eden nodded, taking a deep breath, and straightening up under her own weight. The exhaustion which had threatened to overwhelm her faded, and some strength returned to her limbs.

"That must have been the End of Days we've all been waiting for," Athena said, turning to gaze up at the High Cross. "I mean, what could possibly top that?"

Eden glanced down at her watch and checked the countdown timer she had set while she lay beneath the stage eavesdropping on the Council of Selene's meeting. "That wasn't it," she said. "We've still got twenty-eight minutes."

"Oh, come on!" Athena groaned, dropping her arms like a petulant teenager. "What could be more impressive than using a lightning bolt to stop the deranged leader of an ancient order?"

Eden shrugged, her expression grim. "Honestly, I've no idea, and I'm not sure I want to find out."

"I've got to agree, that is the sort of stuff I expected from the End of Days," Baxter said, nodding at the High Cross. "It's an old prophecy, so it could be a few minutes out?"

"Not according to my father," Eden said. "He's certain that the prophecy will be correct, and that the End of Days will take place at six o'clock this morning."

Athena, clearly sensing her friend's weariness, walked Eden over to a nearby rock and helped her sit down. For several minutes they sat in silence, the weight of what they had experienced hanging heavy in the air.

An engine, pounding like a drumbeat, pierced the tranquil dawn. The roar reverberated up the hillside, pounding and churning the still morning air.

Without realizing they were doing it, Eden and Athena turned to look at Baxter.

"What?" Baxter said, returning their gaze. When no one replied, he conceded with a resigned shrug. "Fine, that's a Bell UH-1 Iroquois—a 'Huey'. It's a Vietnam-era chopper."

The chopper drew closer.

"And why might it be coming this way?" Athena asked. "I'm not sure I can face any more running and fighting."

"Private military is my guess," Baxter said. "They're the only ones who'd fly something that old for operations. Craft like that are collectors' items now."

"I know exactly who that is," Eden said, closing her eyes

as another wave of exhaustion washed over her. "Of all the people I don't have the energy for right now."

"It's got to be your friend, Captain Byrd," Athena said, throwing Baxter a glance.

"It is exactly the sort of chopper Byrd would pilot, yes," Baxter said, his excited tone eliciting a laugh from Athena. "And she does have a passion for vintage aircraft."

The helicopter rose above the tree line and moved out across the clearing. The downdraft from its rotors sent leaves and debris swirling through the air.

"Just as I thought," Baxter said. "A Bell UH-1, in its classic livery, too. Beautiful machine."

"Alright Captain," Athena said.

The chopper descended toward a small, level patch of ground between the rocky peaks. The landing skids touched down with a gentle thud and the engine powered down.

The cockpit door swung open and a familiar figure emerged. Nora Byrd, her dark beehive of hair high on her head, offered a wave. She was dressed in her trademark black flight suit. She hopped out of the chopper and opened the rear door.

Alexander Winslow stepped out of the chopper and crossed toward Eden, Baxter, and Athena.

"We've had a watch on your location for the last hour, but couldn't fly in the storm," Winslow said, hugging his daughter. "I had a feeling the conditions would improve as soon as you figured out what you were doing." Winslow picked up Eden's right hand and examined the seal.

"Hold on a minute," Eden said, annoyance rising in her voice. "You knew what would happen when I put it on?"

"Yes, of course," Winslow said. "That's what makes it such a powerful relic. That's why we had to make sure Wolff didn't get it. Where is he, by the way?"

Athena pointed over at Wolff's prone figure at the foot of the rocky escarpment.

"I see," Winslow said. "Baxter, Athena, please load his mortal remains in the chopper. I need to have a word with my daughter." Winslow took Eden by the arm and led her across the clearing. "We don't have much time, I'm afraid. Less than five minutes, to be exact."

They reached an area which offered views out over the landscape, with the Atlantic Ocean in the distance. The water was already patterned in the coming light of the new day.

Winslow strode across to a railing and leaned across it, taking in the view. Eden joined him and the pair stood in silence for half a minute.

"Come on," Eden said. "You said that we didn't have much time."

"Yes, of course," Winslow said, clearing his throat.

"Like, soon," Eden said.

"You are going to be great at this," Winslow said, smiling at his daughter.

"I've no idea what you're talking about."

"Let me start at the beginning." Winslow held up a finger to silence his daughter's interruptions. "The End of Days has been prophesied within the Council of Selene for millennia." Winslow turned away from the rising sun and faced his daughter. "We all knew this was coming and have been preparing for it for a very long time."

"I know. I heard you talking about it in the meeting. But you still don't know what's going to happen, right?" Eden said, sounding exhausted.

"We didn't know what was going to happen. Nobody did. Many people thought of it as the end of something, but I have always thought of it as the beginning."

"I'm really not in the mood for optimism," Eden said. "Nor talking in riddles."

"Eden, I have always believed that the End of Days is a change rather than an end," Winslow said. "And now, finally, I know what that change is."

"Do you feel like telling me?" Eden replied.

"My time leading the Council of Selene is at an end. The world is changing fast. Too fast for me to keep up with. We need someone new to take the role."

Eden raised one eyebrow, listening to her father's words.

"The council has its challenges within a changing world. And honestly, it has never been more important."

"Why are you telling me this?" Eden said, meeting her father's gaze.

"You really must be tired," Winslow said.

For two seconds, father and daughter remained silent.

"Oh no," Eden said, her other eyebrow joining the first in full-on astonishment as her father's meaning hit home. "You can't be serious?"

"I have never been more serious," Winslow said, placing a hand on Eden's shoulder. "You are to take over as the leader of the council."

"Woah, hold on a second," Eden said, taking a micro-step backward. She blinked several times, her exhaustion fading. "I've told you many times that if it were up to me, there wouldn't even be a council. You know, I think we should do away with the whole thing and let humanity find its own way."

"Exactly, and I partly agree with you," Winslow said. "The council does need to change the way it operates."

"It needs more than that," Eden said.

"And maybe in the future, it will no longer be required.

But, as you will soon find out, the council has a part to play in navigating the difficult times ahead."

Eden stuttered an answer, her thoughts moving too fast to comprehend.

"There's more," Winslow said. "What Wolff told you wasn't totally wrong. The Seal of Solomon is linked to the End of Days. The prophecy states that the bearer of the seal will help forge a future for humanity."

"Hold on a second. I don't even want this thing. You take it." Eden grabbed the ring and attempted to pull it from her finger. It wouldn't budge, her knuckle seemingly too big for it to fit over.

Her father gave her a knowing look.

"I'll take it off later. A bit of soap and that will slide straight off." Eden scowled.

"For now, at least, you are the bearer of the seal. It will help protect you, give you wisdom, and, in extreme cases, do the sort of thing you just witnessed." Winslow flicked a thumb back at the High Cross.

"Oh no, that's never happening again," Eden said, watching dawn color the eastern sky.

"It also means that the council are obliged, because of the prophecy, to accept you as their leader. You can reshape the organization as you see fit."

"I can make any changes I want?" Eden said, sliding along the railing until their shoulders were touching.

"Yes," Winslow replied, his tone unwavering. "You are the bearer of the seal. The council must honor your wisdom."

For almost a minute, neither spoke. In those silent moments, a sense of calm washed over Eden. Finally, as the sun's uppermost edge slipped into the sky, Eden spoke. "Alright," she said, her voice quiet but resolute. "I'll do it."

The watch on Eden's wrist beeped, signaling the arrival of the prophesied moment. Without thinking, with her eyes still fixed on the rising sun, she tapped the watch to silence the alarm.

Winslow turned to face his daughter and a smile spread across his face. The golden light of the dawn illuminated his features, casting him in a warm glow. "And there we have it," he said, his voice a mix of pride and relief. "The End of Days, and a new beginning."

57

The Dorchester Hotel, London, England. Three days later.

THIS TIME, Eden was told to use the front door. At her allotted time, so as not to make contact with the other members, she cut through the crowds toward the hotel. The sun shone brightly overhead, its warm rays filtering through the leafy green canopy of the trees lining Park Lane. Daredevil that she was, she darted across Park Lane between a red double-decker bus and a taxi, earning a honk from the taxi driver.

Eden paused for a moment and gazed up at the building rising above her. She climbed the stairs, shoved through the door, and paced into the hotel's grand lobby. As was the case last time, security was invisible, although Eden had no doubt they were there, waiting in a room nearby should anyone unauthorized come this way. Fortunately, for them at least, this time Eden was expected.

Eden made her way to the elevators, her boots thudding on the marble floors. An elevator waited for her, programmed to take her to the floor she needed. The doors slid open on the second floor, and Eden found the room in which she had been instructed to wait. This was what the council called her 'Holding Room'. Already, Eden felt a prickle of annoyance at all this secrecy. To her, if you made decisions that affected people, you needed to be accountable.

As she waited, Eden glanced down at her finger, which had held the seal three days ago. For a moment back there, she had feared that it had become stuck on her finger for life, like a superstitious curse. Fortunately, after a bit of persuasion, she had worked it loose. The seal was now under lock and key in a vault somewhere in London, the location of which was only known to Eden and her father.

The light beside the door turned from red to green, signaling to Eden that it was time for her to make her way to the council chamber. She opened the door and padded through the hallway, her feet sinking into the thick carpet. Heading for the door to the grand ballroom, Eden remembered her very different experience here a few days ago.

Eden pulled open the door and shoved her way through the blackout curtain. She found her seat using the plan she'd memorized and sat without speaking for four minutes while the other members found their places.

As Eden's eyes became accustomed to the darkness, she saw the tables at which the other members sat, illuminated by tiny lamps on gooseneck stands. Beside the light was a microphone system, which distorted the speaker's voice enough that it couldn't be identified. Eden grabbed the microphone from her desk and pulled out the cable. The tiny green light on the microphone's stem faded out.

When the council members were all in place, Eden heard her father's voice from the other side of the room.

Although the voice was weirdly disguised, she recognized his tone.

"Once again, members, thank you for your attendance today. This is a very important meeting," Winslow said. "I know you'll all be wondering about the event which was prophesied to take place three days ago."

"What happened?" another member interjected.

"The prophecy must have been wrong," one other said. "I can't believe it. All that planning wasted."

Eden resisted the temptation to go over there and slap the speaker across the face. It appalled her that a council member valued their own time more than stopping a supposed global disaster.

"Council members, please, there will be time for your questions," Winslow said, his voice now authoritative. "An event did take place at the prophesied time."

Mumbles echoed through the chamber and Eden heard several members lean forward, clearly waiting impatiently for their leader's next words.

"A bearer of the Seal of Solomon has come forward with the intention of leading the council into the next generation."

An unsettled noise rose from the members spread around the room.

"What does that mean?" one person said.

"It's written in our scripture that the bearer of the seal will lead the council," another member said.

"Divine wisdom," a third added.

"That is all true," Winslow said, his voice cutting through the interruptions. "Which means that my time as Helios, leader of this council, is over."

"I don't understand. How can this be possible?" someone said. "Where did they get the seal from?"

"Who are they?"

"Council members please," Winslow boomed. "Your questions will be answered in time. For now, you must listen. The bearer of the seal is with us now. With that, I thank you for your support during my tenure, and hand you over to the new Helios."

Another mumble rose from the assembled people as they sat, waiting for what might happen next.

In the darkness, Eden grinned for the first time. She climbed to her feet and listened carefully to the expectant sounds of the council members.

"Council," Eden said, her voice loud, clear and without distortion. The members emitted another gasp of shock. "I am the bearer of the Seal of Solomon, and as such, I will take leadership of this organization. Although the origin is not fully known, I understand this council has operated in much the same way for thousands of years. In fact, I discovered a set of tablets some time ago which we now know mention the Council of Selene before the Great Deluge."

"We have been a guiding light to humanity for millennia," a member said haughtily.

"I'm talking now," Eden snapped, spinning to face the speaker. "Your interruptions are no longer welcome in this chamber. You will have a time to speak, but now is not it. Whilst humanity and the problems we face have changed unrecognizably since those days, this council has not. That is a problem. We are here to serve the needs of this planet, not to have the planet serve us." Eden's hand crashed against the table as she spoke passionately. "Members, I do not know the direction my role as leader of this council will take. But I tell you this, there will be a change. Some of it you may like, some of it you may not, but it is coming."

"But protocol states that all developments must be—" a member argued.

"Protocol states that, as the bearer of the seal, I am able to reform this council as I see fit." Eden's voice rose above the interrupter. "I make that first change today."

The unmistakable sound of movement cut through the ballroom. A series of mechanical clicks sounded as bolts were drawn back. In a great golden torrent, sunlight burst in. A second window was thrown open, bringing even more light with it.

Eden blinked several times as her eyes became accustomed to the light. She stepped out from behind the desk and spun around, eyeing each of the council members in turn. She was pleased to see that the members resembled society itself. There were members from various races, and parts of the world, there was also a mix of ages and genders. What the members shared right now, though, was their look of awe and disbelief.

Eden turned and glanced at Athena and Baxter wrestling open the final window. Beyond the window pane, treetops swayed in the breeze.

"Until now, you have held the reins of power anonymously," Eden said. "That ends today. Anyone who doesn't like that is free to leave."

Eden's gaze swept across the room to see if any of the council members would move. No one did.

"Change is never easy," Eden said, her voice ringing loud. "Under my leadership, we will bring this council into the light. We will work together to create a world that is equitable and sustainable for all. And we will do so with transparency, with accountability, and with the full participation of the people we serve."

"I have a question," a woman said. She pushed the voice cloaking microphone away and stood.

"Go ahead," Eden said, turning to face the woman.

"If we're not anonymous, we don't need to use the code-names anymore, right?"

"That's correct," Eden said.

"What do we call you?"

"Eden," she said. "Eden will be fine."

58

"EDEN WILL BE FINE!" Athena hooted with laughter as the pair wound their way through the narrow streets of Soho. "Could you be any more rockstar if you tried?"

Following the intense council session, Eden had a building sense of stress and fatigue at her temples. She had decided that a stroll through the bustling and anonymous streets of London, followed by a hearty meal at one of the city's renowned pubs, was exactly what she needed. Liking the idea, Athena came too.

"I don't know what you wanted me to say," Eden retorted, elbowing her friend in the ribs. "I can't believe they've been calling each other these crazy names for hundreds of years. Hold on a second," Eden said, whirling around to face Athena. "That means Athena isn't your real name, either."

Athena grinned and raised an eyebrow. "Now that really would be telling."

"As leader of The Council of Selene, I command you to tell me your real name!" Eden aimed her index finger at her friend.

"I couldn't, possibly." Athena sidestepped Eden and paced away down the narrow street.

A bellow of raucous laughter rolled from a pub; its patrons spilling across the pavement. Eden glanced through the patterned glass as she hurried past.

"Hold on, that's not fair." Eden caught up with Athena and shot her a glance. "You know almost everything there is to know about me, and I don't even know your real name."

"Sometimes mystery is good, though, right?" Athena said, weaving around a group of tourists dawdling the other way.

"Not in this instance," Eden replied. "I count you as one of my closest friends and I don't even know what country you grew up in."

Athena led them down a passageway that cut between a funky coffee bar and a noodle shop. Striding into the alley, Eden inhaled the mingled smells of soy sauce and coffee. Whilst unusual, it wasn't totally unpleasant.

"It was a long way from here," Athena said, her voice reverberating from the brick walls on either side. The noise of the bustling people muted, replaced by a whirring extractor fan high above them.

Eden picked up on a sadness in her friend's tone that she hadn't heard before.

"It's funny," Athena continued. "When you use a name for long enough, it becomes real. Does that make sense?"

Eden stepped alongside Athena and threw her a glance. "I understand, I suppose. A rose by any other name would smell just as sweet."

"Exactly," Athena said, her tone lightening. "I've been called Athena for so long now that I feel like that's who I am."

"I get that. But I also think you're trying to wriggle your

way out of this. I'm not saying I'll ever call you it. I just want to know. You clearly had a name before people called you Athena?"

"Yes, of course," Athena said.

"Well, what is it?"

"Fine," Athena said, stopping dead. She turned to face Eden. "You really want to know?"

"Absolutely."

"My birth name was…"

Athena's words died in her throat as the clamor of heavy footsteps reverberated down the passageway.

Eden and Athena whirled around to face the noise, their instincts already kicking in. Two hulking figures filled the lane; their broad shoulders almost touching the brick walls on either side.

The leading man glanced up, his dark eyes locking on Eden, and broke into a run. Despite his size, the man moved at a speed born from a life of disciplined training.

"Let's continue this later," Athena said. "I vote we get out of here."

"Agreed," Eden said, whirling around and setting off at a sprint.

Charging down the lane, legs pumping and feet slapping the uneven cobbles, Eden tried to picture the narrow streets that lined this part of London.

"Turn left, then right. That'll bring us out near Piccadilly Circus," she said, between deep breaths.

"Roger that," Athena said, pulling in front of Eden as they neared the corner.

From Piccadilly Circus, Eden figured, they could disappear in the crowds and slip into the Underground or a passing taxi.

The further they ran, the darker the alley became. Eden

glanced up at the thin strip of sky, only just visible between towering buildings on both sides.

"Why does this always happen to us?" She glanced over her shoulders to see they'd gained a lead on their pursuers. Although the men were fast, Eden and Athena still had the upper hand in terms of speed and agility. If they could stay ahead, Eden figured, they wouldn't have to entertain whatever these two wanted from them.

Eden swung around the corner and prepared to accelerate as fast as she could. The plan, however, didn't go as she expected when they both came to a bone-jarring halt. Eden stumbled backward, feeling as though she'd collided with a wall of solid brick. She scrambled to stay upright on the uneven stones. Her arms swung in search of something to arrest her fall.

Athena stumbled backward and slammed into a wall.

Finally finding her balance, Eden looked up. Her eyes flared with shock and fear. Before them, looming like twin mountains and completely blocking the narrow passage, stood two more men.

Eden and Athena barely had time to register the threat, let alone fight their way past, before rough hands swung at them. Fortunately, instinct kicked in and Eden lashed out with a right hook. Her fist connected with one of the trunk-like arms which was currently heading her way. The man grunted and his arm swung wide, just missing Eden's jaw.

Beside Eden, Athena threw a sharp elbow into the other man's ribs, followed by a swift punch to his jaw. The move was so quick; the assailant didn't see it coming. His head snapped back, but he didn't give an inch of space.

Eden took a half step back and sent a one-two combo at her attacker. The man blocked the first strike, but the second connected with his nose. Cartilage crunched and blood spurted. Growing in confidence, Eden dipped below a blind punch and prepared for her next shot. Before she could move, a pair of solid arms closed around her. She struggled, thrashing and buckling against the hold. She landed a couple of elbows but got nothing but a grunt in return.

Broken Nose slammed a meaty fist into her stomach, driving the air from her lungs. Pain exploded through her midsection, and she tried to double over, but the man from behind held her solid.

Athena made a last-ditch attempt at their freedom and lashed out with a series of rapid kicks and punches. The man in front of her deflected almost all of them, and then finally, grappled her against the wall.

"Not this again," Eden groaned, taking several deep breaths as she finally accepted defeat.

"Alright, fine," Athena said, as the man behind her loosened his grip. "I'll come with you, but I'm making a formal complaint."

"Who are you, and what do you want?" Eden said, allowing the men to maneuver her.

With two men on either side of Eden and two taking care of Athena, the group wound their way through the narrow lane.

"You need to work on your customer service," Athena said. "A please and thank you is all it would take."

As Eden had expected, none of their comments elicited a reply. These men were the strong, silent, and brainwashed type.

"It's likely these fellas aren't used to thinking for themselves," Athena said.

"Yeah, the classic RoboCop type," Eden replied, almost stumbling over the cobbles.

The group turned the corner and onto a slightly wider street. Twenty feet away, three people thumbed through a guidebook. Eden glanced at the people and turned to catch Athena's gaze. Eden subtly shook her head. Whoever these brutes were, and whatever they wanted, Eden wasn't about to risk the lives of innocent people.

The thugs marched Eden and Athena past the tourists, who were still totally absorbed in their guidebook and turned into the next street. They stomped up to a door with paint peeling off in long strands.

Several bolts ground open and the door swung inward. The men shoved Eden and Athena inside. The door swung closed, plunging the room into almost complete darkness. For several seconds, Eden couldn't see a thing. Her sense of smell, however, was working overtime. The combined scents of damp, sweat and chemicals hung in the room like a plague of insects.

The men shoved Eden and Athena into the next room and down a metal staircase. At the bottom of the stairs, they emerged into a cavernous room, walls stained with water damage and mold. Eden's eyes darted from side to side, searching for something she could use as a weapon, or an indication of what the place was used for. She saw nothing that could help their situation right now.

"Lovely place you've got here," Eden retorted, her voice echoing. "I'm really into the whole post-apocalyptic movement myself."

Without response, the men shoved them through the room. Approaching the far wall, Eden noticed a heavy metal door. One of the men reached out and yanked it open, revealing a dimly lit room.

Two firm pushes sent Eden and Athena stumbling into the room before the door slammed shut behind them.

Eden swung around, trying to make sense of where they were. About twenty feet square, the room was more of a cell. Although darkness cloaked most of the space, a flame burned near the far wall. As though under its own control, the flame moved, hovering in midair.

Eden watched, aghast, as the flame swept to the right and divided into two flames. She noticed in the added light that a candle now burned beside the original flame. The flame moved two inches and lit another candle.

Realizing what was happening, Eden stepped backward. A man in a long black cloak and hood was lighting the large candles with a much smaller candle. The man continued to work in silence; his face and body totally obscured from Eden and Athena.

Watching the man work, Eden felt a sickness broil in her stomach. Whatever was about to happen, she didn't think she would like it. The flame moved with meticulous precision from wick to wick. The hands that held it were as steady as that of a brain surgeon.

When a dozen candles flickered, casting an orange glow around the small room, the man turned to face Eden and Athena.

Eden noticed the emblem emblazoned on his chest and the simmering worry within her crystallized into terror. The triangle with the eye in the center—the emblem of the Order of the All-Seeing Eye—glowed eerily in the candlelight.

"Thank you for coming to see me," the figure said, his voice deep and sonorous.

"It's not like we had a choice," Athena said, her teeth clenched.

"Who are you? And what do you want?" Eden replied, more bravely than she felt.

"It's not what I want," the figure said. "It's what I can do for you." With that, the figure flipped down his hood.

Eden reeled backward, not quite believing what she saw. There, before them, lit by the dancing light of the candles, was Brother Pyne.

59

"Do you remember in the good old days when people being dead meant they were actually dead?" Athena said, her sarcasm cutting through the tension.

"I blame these modern film series," Eden said. "If a character's popular, they have to keep coming back."

"This is far more important than being popular," Brother Pyne said, pressing his hands together.

In the dancing light from the candles Eden could see that, although Pyne's face showed the bruises from their conflict in Egypt and Portugal, he appeared to be in good health.

"If it wasn't for you, I would have died at the hands of Grand Master Wolff," Pyne said, staring intensely at Athena.

"It was nothing, really. If I had the chance to kick a log at him again, I would do it gladly," Athena said, shrugging.

"Still, it was an act of bravery," Pyne said. "When you did that, I had no choice but to save you."

"Wait a minute," Eden said, eyeing Pyne. "You pushed Wolff from the rocks. It wasn't the lightning strike at all."

"Well, he still was struck by lightning," Pyne said. "But I must confess, I acted in rage, and pushed him to his death."

"I'd hate to have you on my team," Eden said.

"I had doubts about Wolff as Grand Master from the very beginning. It soon became clear to me that he was a man consumed by his own ego. All he wanted was power and control."

"Not the sort of traits you'd choose in a leader," Eden said, folding her arms.

"I have since learned that Wolff had our previous Grand Master dismissed on false charges—charges of Wolff's own invention. He killed a good man and bribed his way into the leadership. Wolff cared nothing for the true purpose of our order and for the sacred duties we uphold. He saw the Order of the All-Seeing Eye as a tool for his own personal gain."

"I don't remember you caring when you followed me to Siwa," Eden said.

"And almost ran us off that mountain road in your Humvee," Athena said.

"And knocked out Nora Byrd," Eden said.

"For someone you claim not to like, you really do go on about that quite a lot," Athena said, eyeing her friend.

"It is true, I should have acted sooner," Pyne nodded sorrowfully. "Whilst I had my doubts at that time, I was little more than a soldier in the ranks. I swore an oath of allegiance and obedience, and that was something I could not break."

"How did Wolff stay in control if he was so bad?" Eden asked, intrigued.

"Anyone who dared to oppose him, anyone who questioned his methods or his motives, was swiftly and brutally dealt with," Pyne said bitterly. "We lost many good brothers that way."

"It all sounds very sad to me, but why are you telling me this?" Eden said. "By the way, I really think you should work on your public relations."

"This place could do with a spruce up too," Athena said, glancing at the discolored concrete walls. "But I doubt you brought us here for interior design advice."

"She's right," Eden said, pointing a thumb in Athena's direction. "You have ten seconds to get to the point or we're out of here." She glanced at the door and realized there were at least four men stationed outside. Pyne probably had enough muscle to keep them here as long as he wanted.

"Yes, of course," Pyne said, nodding deeply. "I wouldn't unnecessarily take up your valuable time. I know you are busy, especially with your new appointment as leader of the Council of Selene." Pyne's eyes locked on Eden. "Congratulations, Helios."

Eden's gaze tightened on the man. "How do you know about that?" She realized immediately that the question revealed her ignorance about the true power of the Order of the All-Seeing Eye.

"Our order and yours have run in parallel for centuries, right from our humble beginnings, in fact," Pyne said. "Does it really seem feasible that an order of nine knights could spread all across Europe in just a couple of centuries, building up enough wealth to incite jealously from kings?"

"The Council of Selene helped you," Eden said, her train of thought finally catching up.

"Exactly." Pyne pointed at Eden. "The council provided us with the knowledge about the relics we required to spread our power all across Christendom."

"What happened?" Eden said. "Why did you not remain loyal to the council?"

"Power corrupts," Pyne said with a shrug. "I'll admit that the order had become too powerful. But, enough of the past, I brought you here to talk about the future."

"What do you want from us?" Eden snapped.

"This is not about what I want," Pyne said, the palms of his hands pressed together. "This is about what I can do for you."

Eden's gaze suddenly narrowed with distrust. Pyne took a slow step, his cloak flowing.

"This is a new start for both The Council of Selene and our order," Pyne said. The emblem on his cloak glittered in the candlelight.

"Hold on," Athena interrupted. "If Wolff's dead, assuming his re-animated corpse isn't going to come walking through the door, who's the new Grand Master of the order?"

"When we returned here, as protocol dictates, we voted for a leader..."

"It's you," Eden said, pointing at Pyne. "You are the new Grand Master."

"Indeed, it is both my honor and duty to serve the order until the end of my days. I must acknowledge our debt to you."

"How did you figure that one out?" Athena said, clearly as confused as Eden.

Brother Pyne took a deep breath. His eyes filled with a mix of sorrow and anger.

"You have done what no one else could," Pyne said. "You have freed our order from a curse and that is a debt which I must attempt to repay."

"What do you have in mind?" Athena said. "Taking us for dinner isn't going to wash."

"Too right," Eden groaned. "Although I am hungry."

"This is something the order has never done before," Pyne said, reaching into the folds of his cloak. He produced a small, intricately carved wooden box and placed it in his palm.

"Within this box lies a key, a key that will grant you access to our order's library. The library is a store of ancient texts, hidden knowledge, records, and a few artifacts of great power, which I know will interest you."

Eden studied the box, annoyance finally giving way to intrigue.

"We even have, and I know this will interest you, a record of the Council of Selene's membership over the years."

"How did you get that?" Eden asked, more amazed than annoyed.

"We have contacts everywhere. We made it our business to know the name and origin of each member in case they should ever become useful."

Conceding to intrigue, Eden reached out and seized the box. She examined it closely and flipped open the lid. A tiny key rested on a velvet lining. Turning the box from side to side, she noticed words etched into the wood.

"Is that Latin?" Eden said, squinting at the text.

"If that's another riddle, I'm throwing that thing into the Thames," Athena said, looking over Eden's shoulder.

"I'm afraid so," Pyne said. "I'll read it for you, if you'd like."

"Oh please," Athena groaned.

Pyne took the box back and squinted at the text. "Where sacred visions once unfurled, by Nahe's gentle, winding curls," he read, slowly. "Twelve paces north from the ancient well, seek the hand that once did raise. Three stones high and two stones wide, find the mark of the hidden scribe."

"Oh man," Athena said, looked at Eden. "You can't be seriously thinking..."

Eden only smiled in reply.

"And that is your first clue to finding the library," Pyne said, passing the box back to Eden.

"What sort of gift is that?" Athena said, pointing at the box. "You've just given us a load more work."

"Seekers of the library have to find it for themselves," Pyne said, a broad smile stretching his cheeks. "I have no doubt that you are capable."

"And what do you ask in return for this... weird and annoying gift?" Athena said.

Pyne shook his head. "Nothing. Consider it a token of our gratitude. The road ahead will be long and perilous, but you do not walk it alone. The Order of the All-Seeing Eye stands with you."

"Alright," Eden said, tucking the box away. "But I'm not going on another quest right now."

Pyne bowed his head. "Of course, Helios. Our library has already stood for millennia and will be there whenever you are ready to find it."

"And none of this Helios nonsense," Eden said, wiggling a finger. "We're not doing codenames anymore."

"As you wish," Pyne said, nodding again. His eyes locked on Athena, glimmering mischievously. "That means you'll start being known as..."

EPILOGUE

The *Balonia*, the Puerto Rico Trench, Atlantic Ocean. Three weeks later.

"LOOK AT THIS," Eden said, pointing at the large screen on the wall of what she still couldn't believe was her office and living quarters on the ship's top deck.

Athena and Baxter paced across the room and stared at the document Eden had loaded. Her father, Beaumont and DeLuca stopped their conversation and glanced over too. In fact, Eden realized reluctantly, the only one missing from their little entourage was Nora Byrd.

"What exactly am I looking at?" Athena said, her hands planted on her hips.

They had set off from England five days ago, and had made good progress across the Atlantic, heading toward the Caribbean. The *Balonia*, although designed to blend in amongst the yachts in various ports around the world, served as the Council of Selene's mobile command center. Designed to lead the council from anywhere in the world, the ship spent long stretches of time at sea, housing a diverse array of staff and all the necessary facilities to keep their operation running smoothly.

As the newly appointed leader, Eden had taken over the accommodations on the top deck, which her father had previously occupied. The luxurious suite featured an office, a spacious bedroom, and its own private rear deck. Meanwhile, Winslow had moved into Eden's former quarters on the third deck. Despite Eden's initial discomfort with the trade, Winslow had insisted, saying that he would welcome the change of scenery.

"This document is about fire walking," Eden said, pointing at the screen.

"Yes, it's certainly interesting," Beaumont said, placing his glasses on his nose and peering at the screen. "It's a ritual that's been practiced for thousands of years across many cultures. In fact, the earliest known reference to the practice dates back over a thousand years, in India, I believe."

"What's it for?" Athena said, glancing from the screen to Beaumont, who was clearly something of an expert.

"It's a test of strength, courage, and a connection to the divine."

"And total craziness," Athena said, studying the picture. "Why would anyone choose to do that? It looks painful."

"And why might you be showing us this?" DeLuca said, flashing Eden one of her hard stares. "What you did back in Portugal was a modern miracle, don't try to discount it."

"We did walk through burning gasoline and didn't feel a thing," Baxter said.

"Scientifically speaking, the explanation for fire walking is based on the principles of thermal conductivity." Beaumont continued, now talking to himself.

"And it works by concentration, or something like that," Eden said. "We were all focused on other things, right?"

"I'm not buying it," Athena said, swinging around to the others. "What do you think?"

"It seemed pretty magical to me," Winslow said, grinning at his daughter. "And is in line with the reported powers of the seal."

"I'm not saying the seal doesn't have any power," Eden said. "I'm merely exploring the possibility that there is a totally rational explanation."

"Like Pyne pushing Wolff off the cliff," Athena said, tapping her chin thoughtfully.

"I think we must consider the fact that this might be nothing to do with the Seal of Solomon at all. Maybe we were just doing this." Eden pointed at the screen.

"I know you're the boss now and everything," Baxter said, nodding at the screen. "But fire walking is totally different. The stones used there are nowhere near as hot as the flames we walked through. Remember, Wolff poured a load of gasoline on the pyre."

"Yes, but it was also raining hard. That probably reduced the temperature." Eden said.

"I see what you're doing here," Athena said, spinning around to look at her friend. "It makes you uncomfortable to admit that the Seal of Solomon has any special power."

"I will admit it if I need to," Eden said. "But first we should look for a logical explanation, don't you think?"

"Well, I'm not sure," Beaumont said, shrugging.

"And what if there is no logical explanation?" Winslow said.

"He's right," DeLuca said. "Some things just defy logic."

"Plus, what about the lightning?" Athena said. "I know I was quite distracted at the time, but it appeared as though you used the Seal of Solomon to bring on that storm and strike Wolff down with a bolt of lightning."

"You're right, the lightning was intense," Eden acknowledged, "But that area of the Portuguese Coast is known for its storms and unpredictable weather patterns." She tapped on the keyboard and a map appeared. "We were there, right on top of the hill." She paced across the room and pointed at the screen. "We were exposed to the elements. If lightning is going to strike, then that's where it would happen."

"Also, that time of year can be tricky around the ocean," Baxter said. "Prime conditions for thunderstorms."

"Exactly," Eden said. "Thanks, Captain."

"That does make sense," Winslow agreed. "But it's still pretty unlikely that it occurred right at that time, and just happened to strike Wolff."

"It's got to be more likely than that piece of metal and stone actually controlling the weather," Eden said, folding her arms.

"You're now trying to convince yourself that the lightning strike was a coincidence?" Athena said.

"It's a possibility that I don't want to ignore," Eden replied. "All we've got to go on is a lucky escape from a fire and a fortunate lightning strike."

Everyone in the office exchanged a glance.

"What?" Eden said, clocking on to their look.

"There's one way to try it for real," Winslow said, pacing across to the window and staring out at the clear blue sky. "Conjure up a thunderstorm and we've got our proof."

Eden turned to her father. "Are you sure that's a good idea? We don't want to do any damage to the *Balonia*."

"You start the storm, then you stop it again," Athena said, shrugging.

"I'm really not sure it's that simple," Eden said.

"Well, there's only one way to find out," Baxter said, pacing to the door. "I'll get the Seal of Solomon from the vault and let's put it to the test."

Ten minutes later, the group stood on the *Balonia's* rear deck, looking out at the undisturbed ocean on all sides.

Eden held the Seal of Solomon in her hands. She glanced at the obsidian stone, which glimmered in the sunlight.

"Fine," Eden said, exhaling. "Let's see what happens."

Eden slipped the seal onto her index finger and focused her thoughts on the clear blue sky. She tensed, trying to recreate the intensity of their escape back in Portugal. She imagined the rain lashing down and the wind thrashing through her hair. Three minutes later, Eden opened her eyes.

The sky remained cloudless, and the sun continued to shine.

"I told you," she said. "It was all a random series of events. I don't believe any of this magical stuff."

"Maybe you need to say something to get it working," Beaumont suggested.

"Yes," Athena said. "You know, like a spell."

Eden cast her friends a doubtful glance and closed her eyes again. She tried a few words in ancient Hebrew, then switched to Latin. She opened her eyes again, but the weather remained stubbornly clear and calm.

"I don't understand," Athena said, frustration creeping into her tone. "If the Seal of Solomon really has the power to control the weather, why isn't it working now?"

"Because it's a hoax," Eden said, slipping the artifact from her finger. "Wolff was wrong. He was chasing shadows. This is an ancient myth, mixed with good timing and a load of hope."

Eden turned the seal over in her hands, tracing the intricate engravings with her fingertips.

"The problem with objects like this, is that the promise of power is still dangerous," Eden said, her eyes tracing the horizon. Gentle waves lapped against the Balonia's hull. "If people, like Wolff, know there's a chance that this is the answer to their desires, they'll seek it out."

"We've got it in our care now, though," DeLuca said.

"But for how long?" Eden replied. "This ring hadn't been seen for almost a thousand years and look at the trouble it caused. We won't be around forever to make sure it doesn't slip into the wrong hands." Eden moved her gaze from one person to the next.

"What do you think we should do?" Baxter said.

"I know exactly what to do." Eden drew back her hand; the seal clutched tightly between her fingers. She eyed the churning waters of the *Balonia's* wake.

"Wait, what are you doing?" Baxter said, jumping forwards to block Eden's throw.

"I'm doing exactly what the Templars should have nine-centuries ago. Power or not, people believing in this makes it dangerous."

"No... no... wait!" Beaumont cried, his hands covering his mouth.

Everyone stood aghast and rooted to the spot as Eden threw the seal as hard as she could. The relic spiraled through the air, catching the sunlight in a blaze of brilliance.

Baxter reached the railing and swung for the seal, his fingers whipping uselessly through the air.

The entire crew watched in silence as the seal arched across the *Balonia's* lower deck, dropped into the water, and was immediately sucked into the ship's wake. For several seconds, no one spoke.

"You know we're right over the Puerto Rican Trench," Baxter said, pointing at the water. "This is the deepest part of the Atlantic. Nearly thirty thousand feet of water right there."

"Then I'm pretty confident that, even if the thing has some magic power, no one will find it again," Eden said, turning and strolling back inside. "Enough of this magical mumbo jumbo. I've got work to do. See you guys for dinner."

EDEN WAS WORKING at the computer an hour later when a knock sounded at the door. Without waiting for a reply, Alexander Winslow walked in. He closed the door behind him and threw his daughter a grin.

"It looks as though you're settling in," he said, eyeing the room, which was exactly as it had been when he occupied it.

"I'm not changing a thing," Eden said. "It's perfect as it is."

Winslow padded across the office and settled into one of the sofas. Eden stood from the computer and dropped onto the sofa beside her father. For almost a minute, neither spoke. Eden assumed her father had come to see her for some reason, although he clearly wasn't in a rush to get to it. She took a breath and enjoyed the rare moment of peace and quiet.

"It's been a crazy few weeks, right?" Eden said, finally.

"You know," Winslow said, turning to face his daughter. "I don't think I've ever been prouder of you."

"I can't believe everything that's happened," Eden said, not quite knowing how to respond to her father's praise.

"Did you see the look on the faces of those councilors when we opened the windows? That was the last thing they were expecting."

"It certainly was, and you're going to make an excellent leader. But that isn't what I'm talking about," Winslow said.

"Ahh, you're talking about what happened with Wolff. I did what I had to." Eden shrugged. "Honestly, it was nothing. Anyone would have done the same."

"That isn't what I meant either," Winslow said.

Eden turned toward her father; her brow furrowed. His gaze bored straight into her, forcing her to look away. She flushed red, knowing exactly what was coming.

Winslow placed his hand on Eden's shoulder. "That was a neat trick with the Seal of Solomon. I don't think anyone saw the switch."

Eden's red flush turned full on beetroot.

"I don't..."

"I know exactly what you're thinking, Eden. Remember, I know you, and I did this job before you. I know what's at stake."

Eden looked at her hands. Her frown broke into a smile. She flicked her wrist with the flourish of a magician and the Seal of Solomon appeared in her palm.

"What did you throw instead?" Winslow said.

"One of those obsidian arrowheads Beaumont's always collecting. I figured it fooled Wolff back in Siwa, so would probably do the same here."

Winslow chuckled. "Beaumont has thousands. He won't miss one. It was a clever trick. Even as Hel..." Winslow stopped himself. "Even as the leader of the council, you are working within limitations."

Eden turned the Seal of Solomon from side to side. The star sparkled.

"I figured there was no way I could get the seal from the vault without someone asking where it had gone. Once they realized it wasn't where it was supposed to be, another legend would begin," Eden said.

"Exactly, an unanswered question soon turns into a rumor, and before long, you've got buried treasure!" Winslow said. "It's very clever. This way not only are people convinced it's useless, but they saw it disappear beneath the waves. Very clever indeed."

"I feel bad about lying," Eden said, looking through the window at the ocean beyond.

"A lie is only bad if the intention is bad," Winslow said. "You kept the truth from them to protect them."

"But I want to lead the council with transparency," Eden said, eyeing her father. "No more secrets and no more lies."

"I'm afraid that simply isn't possible. Not everyone can, or should, or even wants to know everything. You must draw the line somewhere. Where that line sits, is something you'll have to figure out. For what it's worth, I think you did the right thing here."

Eden shuffled closer to her father, and the pair sank into a comfortable silence.

"You must be quite satisfied with your logical explanation, too?" Winslow said after two minutes had passed. "A random lightning strike and then Wolff was pushed to death by one of his own men because he'd been corrupted by the order's power."

"I thought it worked out quite nicely, yes," Eden said, flashing her father a smile.

"There is one little thing that I think you've forgotten, though," Winslow said, dragging his phone from his pocket. He showed Eden a picture of the statue, which looked just like her. "And remember the other one in the Hall of

Records beneath the Giza Plateau, which also looked like you."

"I think it's time for me to tell you where you really came from," Winslow said, locking eyes with his daughter.

"Wait a minute," Eden said, her voice hard. "Wolff was right about one thing. He told me the prophecy stated the child of the one leading us towards the End of Days would be the sole bearer of redemption. And here I am."

Winslow narrowed his eyes and gazed at his daughter for several seconds. "You're telling me you don't want to know?"

"Of course I want to know, but it won't change anything," Eden said. "I'm your child, even ancient prophecy thinks so."

"Prophecy can be wrong, too. Plus, I think it's important that you know, because not everything can be explained all that easily," Winslow said.

"Now, that I don't believe," Eden said, folding her arms.

"In a way, you chose to come with me, many years ago, while I was exploring the remote jungles of the Amazon."

Eden listened for several minutes as her father told her of a mission to discover a remote, never-before-seen pyramid and the unknown tribe of people he'd stumbled upon while there. It was an adventure which had ended with the loss of one of Winslow's team, for which he felt immense guilt.

"You just came running out and hugged me," Winslow said, his voice more laden with emotion than Eden thought she'd ever heard before. "Then, because of their fear of modern world diseases, the tribe, your family, said that you couldn't return to them. I have no doubt that if it weren't for you, they would have killed us all."

"And you told no one about this?" Eden said.

Winslow shook his head. "When we got back home, I found someone to give you the records you needed, and Eden Winslow was born. Officially speaking. I knew if I said it to anyone, people would try to explain who those people in the jungle are, why they knew about modern diseases, and could communicate with us. To understand those things could lead to their destruction."

Eden gazed out the window as the tectonic plates of her understanding shifted and moved.

"There is no logical explanation for how a tribe living there, totally disconnected from civilization, would speak English, right?" she said, after a minute of silence.

"Only one," Winslow said, meeting Eden's gaze. "They were here first."

"Wait a second. You think I'm part of some race that's older than regular humans?" Eden said.

"I mean, 'regular humans' is definitely not the politically correct term," Winslow said, his tone lightening. "But yes."

"That doesn't explain why those statues look like me," Eden said. "That leads to even more questions."

"Who taught the ancient societies to develop language and writing systems, to build and look to the stars?" Winslow said. "We as 'regular humans' are just beginning to re-discover the power of the natural world, especially those things we can't sense for ourselves." He pointed at the window. A few spots of rain now flecked the glass. "Look at that, for example. Do you know how unusual rain is in this part of the Atlantic?"

Eden closed her palm around the Seal of Solomon. The metal was warm in her grasp.

"Are you telling me that anything's possible?"

"I'm telling you that there will always be things you don't understand."

For several minutes, the pair watched rain run down the windowpane. "What are you going to do with the real Seal of Solomon?" Winslow said.

Eden peered up at her father, her eyes shining with excitement. "When we saw Grand Master Pyne, he told me about the Lost Vault of the Templars. Have you heard about it?"

"Oh yes," Winslow said, rubbing his hands. "Apparently, it contains more treasures than the Hall of Records. They're supposed to have built it when they discovered the remains of the Library of Alexandria. Fascinating stuff."

"Well, I think I might take it there," Eden said, smiling.

Winslow put an arm around his daughter and pulled her in close. "That sounds like an excellent idea."

AUTHOR'S NOTE

Thank you so much for joining me and Eden for another adventure. I'm loving writing these books and sharing them with you totally brings them to life. This book was very international in its construction too—I started writing it in January 2024 in Goa, India, while staying in a tiny hut right on the beach. A few weeks later, Mrs. R and I visited Portugal to research the scenes set there, and I wrote a few scenes on that journey too. The rest was written at home in Nottingham, England, where I'm now composing this author's note to you.

If you've read the author's notes in the previous books in this series, you'll know what to expect. In the next few pages, I will detail the fascinating history behind the events of this book, the parts that are true, and those to which I've added my creative flair.

The legend of the Knights Templar has fascinated me for a while, and I realized it was high time they made it into one of my books. I am no Templar expert, and this book is not in any way a historical record, but there are some interesting events on which it is based.

This book opens with the final Templar Grand Master, Jacques de Molay, burning at the stake in Paris. This is well documented and took place on March 18th, 1314. Interestingly, and totally by chance, the day I sat down to write this scene was March the 18th 2024. Exactly 710 years later—spooky, right?

By the 18th of March 1314, Jacques de Molay had been in the custody of King Philip IV of France for approximately seven years. Many of the horrors which de Molay and the other knights endured during this time are documented, but I didn't go into them here. Whatever your opinions on the Templars themselves, those arrested were treated horrifically by King Philip.

The order to arrest the Templars was given on October 13, 1307. King Philip's men seized Templar properties and arrested many knights across France. The charges brought against the Templars included heresy, blasphemy, and various obscene rituals. It is widely believed that King Philip's true motive for targeting the Templars was to seize their immense wealth and eliminate his debt to the order. However, despite the thorough search of Templar properties and the torture of many knights, none of the fabled Templar gold, relics or treasures were ever found. This has led to countless theories and speculation about the fate of the treasure, with some believing that the Templars were tipped off about their arrests and able to move the treasure in time.

Some experts claim that the treasure was smuggled out of France before the arrests, possibly to Scotland or Portugal, where the Templars had strong connections. Others speculate that the gold was smuggled across the Atlantic, reaching the Americas before they were officially discovered by Europeans in 1492. Could the Templars really have been there almost two hundred years before? That's another book, perhaps. This theory, while highly controversial, is not entirely implausible given the Templars' extensive maritime experience and resources. As skilled sailors and navigators, the Templars had access to advanced ship-building techniques and possessed a deep knowledge of ocean currents and wind patterns.

If the Templars did indeed reach the Americas before Columbus, they may have hidden their treasure in remote locations, such as the alleged Templar sites in New England and the Caribbean. Some even suggest that the Templars left behind clues and symbols, like the Newport Tower in Rhode Island, which bears a striking resemblance to Templar architecture. While these theories remain speculative and lack concrete evidence, they certainly capture the imagination of thriller writers like me!

Although the Templars making it to the Americas may require some imagination, their seeking refuge in Portugal while King Philip arrested their brothers in France is widely accepted. King Dinis I of Portugal, who had been a strong supporter of the Templars and was loosely related to a prominent figure in the order, negotiated with the Pope to create a new order, the Order of Christ. The Order of Christ then absorbed the Templars and their assets in Portugal. Basically, the same order, but with a new name. In the first chapters of this book, when Brother Thomas arrives at the Templar Commandery in Portugal to find his brothers hiding in plain sight, that's exactly as it would have been, as I understand it.

The Order of Christ went on to become a powerful force in Portugal, playing a significant role in the country's maritime explorations and colonial expansion. Many famous explorers, such as Vasco da Gama and Prince Henry the Navigator, were members of the Order of Christ. The order's influence extended beyond Portugal, with some theorizing that Christopher Columbus, who had married into a Portuguese noble family, may have had connections to the Order of Christ and, by extension, the Templars. There we go again with ideas of the Templars related to the discovery of the New World!

To this day there are several fascinating Templar sites throughout Portugal, including the Convento de Cristo in Tomar, Almourol Castle and Castle of Pombal. One slightly more fantastical site which features in this book is Quinta da Regaleira with its incredible Initiation Wells. Located in Sintra, near Lisbon, Quinta da Regaleira is an early 20th-century estate that was built by Antonio Augusto Carvalho Monteiro, a wealthy Portuguese businessman with a deep interest in esotericism, Freemasonry, and the Knights Templar. The estate features a series of underground tunnels, grottoes, and two Initiation Wells that were never used for water collection but rather for symbolic, ritual purposes.

These wells, known as the Unfinished Well and the Initiation Well, are adorned with spiral staircases, carved symbols, and astrological references. The Initiation Well is believed to represent the journey of the soul through the nine circles of Hell, Purgatory, and Paradise, as described in Dante's Divine Comedy. The estate also boasts beautiful gardens, filled with esoteric sculptures and hidden symbols that allude to alchemy, Masonry, and Templar mythology. Whether any of these symbols amount to a secret code or map, I don't know, but they might!

The curse Jacques de Molay issued in his dying breath is, as far as my research stated, true. I made efforts to get the wording right, although different sources claim slightly different things. Eerily, both King Philip and Pope Clement died within the specified timeframe, leading many to believe in the power of the Templar Curse.

In fact, Pope Clement died just one month after de Molay's execution, on April 20, 1314. King Philip, who was only forty-six years old at the time, died six months later, on November 29, 1314. His sudden death, likely from a stroke, shocked the kingdom and fueled the legend of the Templar Curse.

The curse didn't stop there, however. Some believe that it continued to affect future French kings. For example, Louis XVI, who was beheaded during the French Revolution in 1793, was said to have been wearing a medallion with the Templar Cross when he was executed.

Throughout history, many legends have circulated about the Templars and their alleged possession of powerful relics, such as the Holy Grail, the Ark of the Covenant, and the Seal of Solomon. The Seal of Solomon, as described in this adventure, is a legendary magical signet ring which belonged to King Solomon, granting him the power to command demons and spirits.

King Solomon was a biblical figure and the ruler of the united Israel and Judah. He was renowned for his wisdom, wealth, and power, and is credited with building the First Temple in Jerusalem. According to biblical accounts, Solomon was gifted with divine wisdom and had the ability to communicate with animals and command spirits.

During their time in Jerusalem, the Knights Templar established their headquarters on the Temple Mount, the site of Solomon's Temple. Some legends suggest that the Templars conducted extensive excavations beneath the Temple Mount, possibly in search of ancient relics and treasures associated with King Solomon and the Temple. While there is historical evidence of the Templars' presence in

Jerusalem and their interest in the Temple Mount, the extent and nature of their excavations remain a topic of debate.

Legend claims that the Templars used the Seal of Solomon, and other powerful relics, to amass their power and influence. Although there is no evidence to support this, they did become incredibly powerful in a very short space of time—which, of course, ultimately, was part of their downfall.

I loved having Eden and her crew visit the Siwa Oasis in Egypt during this book. Mrs. R and I traveled the three-hundred-mile desert road to Siwa in January 2023. Siwa is located in the Western Desert of Egypt, not far from the Libyan border—which we were constantly reminded of by the police and army checkpoints on the desert road.

I have a saying in my travels, which I often find to be true: *the harder it is to get somewhere, the better it is when you do.* Siwa is a testament to this. Unless you charter a plane, it's an eight-hour bus ride in and out on that one lonely road. Arriving in the small town feels like you could be on another planet. That feeling is amplified when staring out at the desert, and knowing the next civilization is hundreds of miles away.

As described in Eden's adventure, one of the main attractions in Siwa is the ruins of the Temple of the Oracle of Amun, which dates back to the 26th Dynasty (663-525 BCE). The oracle was believed to have been consulted by Alexander the Great during his visit to Siwa in 331 BCE. According to historical accounts, Alexander the Great visited the oracle to seek confirmation of his divine status and legitimacy as a ruler. The oracle allegedly pronounced him as the son of Amun, the supreme god in the Egyptian pantheon, thus cementing his claim to the Egyptian throne.

Many legends also suggest that King Solomon visited the oasis during his reign, seeking wisdom and knowledge from the oracle. Some go as far as speculating that the Seal of Solomon may still be there. That would certainly be an interesting twist!

Siwa's location has made it a strategic point for various groups throughout history, including the Knights Templar. As skilled navigators and desert travelers, the Templars likely used Siwa as a stopping point during their journeys across the Egyptian desert. The oasis would have provided them with a reliable source of water, food, and shelter, making it an essential link in their desert trade and pilgrimage routes.

Given the Templars' interest in ancient knowledge and relics, it is plausible that they would have been drawn to Siwa's mystical reputation and its association with figures like Alexander the Great and King Solomon. The Templars may have sought to uncover secrets or obtain powerful artifacts believed to be hidden in the oasis.

That brings us to the Templars in the modern era and my totally fictional Order of the All-Seeing Eye. During this book, I was playing with the idea of power corrupting those in charge, rather than poking fun at any particular order. I think we can see this in all sorts of organizations, from large corporations, governments, and other bodies around the world. I felt I had to do this sensitively, hence why I made Grand Master Wolff quite such a ridiculous character. I enjoyed playing with the idea of a leader hell bent on returning the world to a sort of medieval state, too.

In reality, there are several modern organizations that claim a connection to the Knights Templar, none of which my fictional order is based on—so please don't come after me with your swords and rituals! Seriously, though, many of these organizations do good work and are nothing like my Order of the All-Seeing Eye—although now Grand Master Pyne is in control, I think they'll turn their efforts to good. Maybe we will see them return in a future Eden Black book!

Now on to the cheery subject of the End of Days. Throughout history, various religions and cultures have put forth prophecies about the End of Days. These prophecies often describe a future period of great upheaval, destruction, and judgment, followed by the emergence of something new. In some faiths, the End of Days is associated with the coming of a figure who will usher in an era of peace. While the specifics of these prophecies vary widely, it's fascinating to me that so many cultures share these ideas. I couldn't resist referencing it in this book, and asking the question about what that might involve. Although a few minutes with modern day news media would make you believe that every day is the End of Days, I wanted to make the point here that, in my story at least, The End of Days is a change that's long overdue.

It's always my intention with the stories, that you come for the action but feel as though you're spending time with characters you know and love along the way. I enjoyed, slightly cruelly, driving a wedge between Eden and her friends and family for the first part of the book.

I'm also enjoying working with Winslow's character during these books, as he comes to terms with how his life has changed and learns that he couldn't and shouldn't do things alone. I think there is a lesson for us all (certainly for me) in there.

I was also pleased to finally develop The Council of Selene in this book. A few readers asked what might become of the council as they'd gone quiet for the last couple of adventures. As you'll now know, it's not the end of the council, but there's a lot of change!

Now here's a question I get a lot: What about the statues that look like Eden? I can't, and don't want to answer all the mysteries in one book. That's one which you, and Eden, will have to discover soon.

Once again, thank you for your company and I can't wait for our next adventure together.

Luke

May, 2024.

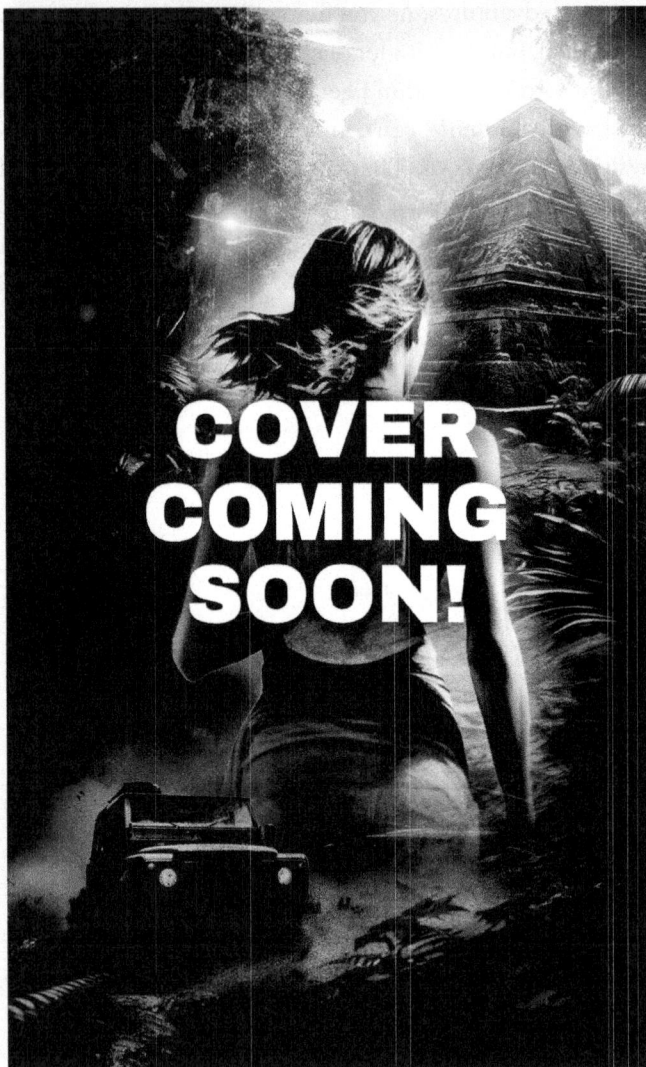

Eden Black will return in The Lotus Code

. . .

The Lotus Code is available for pre-order.

Search online for "The Lotus Code by Luke Richardson" or
visit this website: www.lukerichardsonauthor.com/lotus

THE HEIDELBERG CODEX

BONUS
NOT SOLD
IN STORES
NOVELLA

AN EDEN BLACK THRILLER

LUKE RICHARDSON

Start this not sold in stores Eden Black adventure for FREE right now

www.lukerichardsonauthor.com/codex

WHEN A MYSTERIOUS CODEX is stolen from a secure archive in Heidelberg, Germany, Eden Black must race against a reclusive billionaire to decipher an enigmatic riddle left by the visionary nun Hildegard of Bingen and unlock the secrets of the legendary Templar Vault.

From the winding streets of Bingen to the imposing walls of Schloss Rothenberg, danger lurks around every corner as she endeavors to crack cryptic clues that have remained hidden for eight hundred years.

In this not-sold-in-stores novella, pulse-pounding suspense intertwines with fascinating historical intrigue. Eden races against time to unravel the mysteries of the Templar Vault before the billionaire hell bent on power.

www.lukerichardsonauthor.com/codex

THANK YOU!

Books are difficult to write.

Not a month goes by where I don't think it's "too hard," or "not worth it." Every time this happens — as though by magic — I get an email from a reader like you.

Some are simple messages of encouragement, others are heartfelt, each one shows me that I'm not doing this alone. Those connections have kept me going when all seemed lost, and given me purpose when I didn't see it myself.

A special heartfelt thank you to those who support me on Patreon. These people support me with a few dollars, pounds or euros a month. In exchange it's my pleasure to share my travels with them through postcards and other random gifts from the road.

Some Patreon supporters even get the opportunity to read my books early. If that resonates with you, check out my Patreon here:

https://www.patreon.com/lukerichardson

Don't feel obliged, the fact you are here is more than enough.

Thanks goes to (in alphabetical order):

Allison Valentine and The Haemocromatois Society

Anja Peerdeman

Chris Oldfield author of 'The Less Years' series

David Berens (for the cover)

Fritzi Redgrave

James Colby Slater

Jan Galloway

JazzLauri

Jim Howie

Ken Preston

Kirsty 'Wisey' Wiseman

Mark Fearn from the Bookmark Facebook Group

Martha Richardson (Mrs. R)

Marti Panikkar

Melody Highman

Ray Braun

Rosemary Kenny

Sue Laughton

Tim Birmingham

Toulla Corti (www.toullacreative.com)

Valerie Richardson

HAVE YOU READ MY INTERNATIONAL DETECTIVE SERIES?

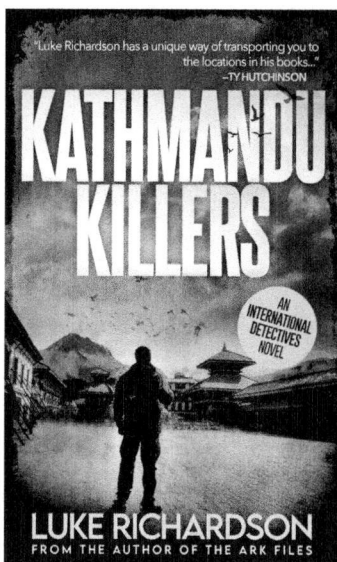

You visit a restaurant in a far-away city, only to find you're on the menu.

Leo Keane is sent abroad to track down Allissa, a politician's daughter who vanished two years ago in Kathmandu. But with a storm on the horizon and intrigue at every turn, Leo's mission may be more dangerous than he bargained for... A propulsive international thriller!

READ TODAY

www.lukerichardsonauthor.com/kathmandu

Printed in Great Britain
by Amazon